More Valuable Than Gold

In a World of Secrets and Betrayal One Man Uncovers Truth.

By: Rodney Ray

R-Squared Productions, LLC

Praise for More Valuable Than Gold

Very few novels have the power to change lives—but "More Valuable Than Gold" by Rodney Ray is one of them. This is more than just an adventure story—it's a soul-stirring journey that gripped me from the first page and never let go. In a literary world where plots often feel predictable and characters forgettable, Ray delivers something rare: a fast-moving, deeply thoughtful narrative that keeps you guessing and leaves you thinking. The characters live and breathe with raw authenticity, especially Asher, whose reflection on time—"the sole entity of genuine value..."—still echoes in my heart. I'll read this book again and again, not just for the thrills, but for the truths tucked between the action. If you read it once, don't be surprised if you find yourself coming back for more. Rodney Ray has crafted a masterwork—equal parts adventure and eternal insight.

Dr. Toby Frost
Senior Pastor
South Main Baptist Church
Greenwood, SC

The characters and events portrayed in this book are fictitious. Any similarity to real persons, living or dead, is coincidental and not intended by the author.

ISBN: 979-8-9988163-1-4

Cover design by: germancreative
Library of Congress Control Number: 2018675309
Printed in the United States of America

Dedication

To those who seek truth in ancient stories,
and to those who carry faith through modern storms.

And to my wife, family & friends—
your love, patience, and belief in me are more valuable
than gold.

Epigraph

"so that the tested genuineness of your faith—more precious than gold that perishes though it is tested by fire—may be found to result in praise and glory and honor at the revelation of Jesus Christ."
— 1 Peter 1:7 (ESV)

Table of Contents

Introduction

I want to invite you to take a journey with me—a journey through history.

Though this novel is a work of fiction, it's woven with truths meant to stir the heart and inspire the spirit.

As we walk through the pages ahead, my hope is that you are both challenged and encouraged.

More than just entertaining, I pray this story becomes something deeper.

Let's begin.

Rodney

Prologue

Jerusalem – 4 BCE

The sound of iron scraping stone echoed through the darkness as the final slab slid into place.

Sweat traced the temple mason's brow, though the air inside the chamber was bitter cold. By torchlight, he double-checked the markings on the wall–symbols few would recognize now, but that meant everything to the one who had commissioned this burial. Not of a body, but of something far more dangerous.

Behind him, the soldier stood motionless, cloaked in silence and shadow. His presence wasn't for protection. It was insurance.

The mason turned. "It's done."

The soldier offered no reply. Instead, he stepped forward and pressed a seal into the soft mortar where the stone met the wall. It was a symbol of Herod's reign–one the mason would be wise to forget. One no man would dare to break.

"You never saw this place," the soldier said.

The mason swallowed hard. "I understand."

"You don't," the soldier replied, drawing his blade with a whisper of steel. "But you will."

Outside, the night was still. No witnesses. No moonlight. Only the hush of history being sealed—deeper than truth, deeper than blood.

And hidden beneath it all... 50 tons of gold.

The Morgue

A body lay on a cold metal table, motionless beneath the harsh glow of fluorescent lights. The quiet, sterile air of the Jerusalem Institute of Forensic Science carried the faint scent of antiseptic—clean, clinical, yet unable to mask the underlying presence of death.

For Dr. Eli Cohen, this case should have been routine. As a forensic pathologist, he had spent years solving the silent stories of the dead, determining causes and times of death with practiced precision.

But this? This was something he had never experienced.

His gloved hands hovered over the lifeless form, his mind working to impose logic onto the impossible. The injuries were grotesque, the kind inflicted not in a moment of rage but with deliberate, methodical intent.

And yet, it wasn't just the brutality that unsettled him. It was the pattern.

A specific arrangement of wounds—ones that should have belonged to a body centuries old, not to a man found in the modern world.

Not here. Not now.

He had read about these wounds. In fact, nearly everyone had. But to write them—to list them as the official cause of death on a death certificate? That was unheard of and, without question, would be a first.

He leaned in, heart pounding.

As he continued the examination, only one word came to mind—*bizarre.*

The Archaeologist

Professor Asher Meyer, Ph.D., towered over his class of 23 students at the University of Jerusalem, standing more than six feet tall. With his athletic build and piercing blue eyes, he looked more like a handsome athlete than the scholarly mind guiding a college lecture. The contrast was not lost on his students, who often misjudged him based on appearances alone.

Although becoming a college professor was never his dream, it now served a practical purpose—managing the financial obligations left in the wake of his pending divorce. At thirty-eight, his life bore little resemblance to the dreams of his youth.

Growing up in Jerusalem, one of the most historically rich regions in the world, he developed a deep fascination with archaeology. This interest began with childhood visits to the Western Wall with his father and school trips to ancient temple ruins. While he excelled academically, consistently ranking at the top of his classes from high school through college, he also had a passion and talent for sports. During his early college years, he actively participated in campus and community sports leagues.

By his sophomore year, he faced a pivotal decision: whether to pursue a professional career in athletics or commit fully to academia. He wrestled with the choice, torn between his love for competition and his hunger for discovery. In the end, he chose scholarship over sports, seeing archaeology as the perfect bridge between his two passions—an ideal blend of intellectual challenge and physical activity.

Yet now, he found himself doing precisely the opposite. He was tied to a position that offered neither mental nor physical challenges.

This class, *First Century Jerusalem*, was a breeze for him. Armed with a bachelor's degree in archaeology, a master's and doctorate in anthropology, and a decade of fieldwork, he could have written the textbook himself. He had explored nearly every site it described, many more than once. In fact, he had noted at least three errors that he fully intended to address with the publisher.

Born and raised in Jerusalem, he knew the city like the back of his hand. Though raised a Reformed Jew, he was not a man of faith. To him, the Bible was not a sacred text but an indispensable guide to ancient ruins—a tool for uncovering history rather than discovering a living god.

He was fluent in Hebrew, English, and Modern Greek; conversant in Arabic; and familiar with the largely extinct languages of Aramaic and Koine Greek—making him at ease practically anywhere in the Middle East. Yet, despite his extensive knowledge and training, the classroom never felt natural.

His heart yearned to be back in the field, unearthing secrets buried for centuries. But for now, he needed stability—something secure while he worked to put his life back on track.

Just three years ago, life had been markedly different. He was happily married, held a promising job, enjoyed a vibrant social circle, had a flourishing career, and was on the verge of securing a book deal that seemed destined for success. Everything felt simpler and more structured. Then, in what seemed like the blink of an eye, it all began to unravel.

Betrayal and disappointment replaced those things.

In truth, he wasn't surprised—life had been teaching him that lesson for years. He found trusting women risky. Actually, he believed people in general couldn't be trusted—too often, they were uninformed and easily misled. And he was determined to prove them all wrong—especially by proving, once and for all, that his claims in *Herod the Great and His Great Treasure* were factual.

The idea for the book came to him while working on his Ph.D. dissertation, which explored the Herodian dynasty, a lineage of five rulers. Of them, Herod the Great stood out as the most renowned and celebrated for his monumental building projects, ambitious political maneuvering, and immense wealth. His fortune, amassed through heavy taxation, extensive land holdings, and strategic Roman alliances, captivated Asher's imagination. Yet, more than Herod's political genius or architectural feats, it was his legendary treasure that intrigued Asher most.

While his dissertation was a success, the book was a different story. Many of the colleagues he had counted on for endorsement and support did the exact opposite. Some dismissed his research as biased, while others, in his view, were too ignorant to even debate the subject. Proving them all wrong became his mission. The bigger question was how. He needed funding—for research and promotion—but money was the one thing he had in short supply.

"Dr. Meyer, do you believe Herod the Great was a genius or a madman?" asked a student in the front row, a hint of challenge in his tone.

Asher recognized the bait instantly. It was common knowledge around campus that he had written a book and the controversies surrounding it. He hesitated, weighing his options. Engaging in the debate would consume the rest of the class period, a tempting prospect given his growing impatience with routine lectures. He enjoyed a good mental challenge—the kind this debate would surely provide. Few topics intrigued him more than the paradox of Herod's rule. But was it worth the time?

Time—more precisely, the use of time—was always on his mind. Not just as a historian but as a man captivated by how it shaped everything: reputations, legacies, and even truth itself. After a brief pause, he decided to spend his wisely. "Only time will tell," he said in jest.

Little did he know how prophetic those words would become.

The Mysterious Benefactor

In a Boston medical office, Winston Saunders sat on the examination table and waited for the doctor. Weak and frail, he didn't need a doctor to tell him he was in extremely poor health. His pale skin clung to his thinning frame, and sores dotted his body, oozing and bleeding intermittently. His condition was worsening rapidly, and without some kind of corrective treatment, he would die, probably within the next six months.

As usual, Winston knew this visit would be a waste of time. It wasn't that Dr. Isaiah Hartell lacked sympathy—he simply wasn't equipped to treat Winston's mysterious illness. No, Winston wasn't here seeking a cure; that, if it existed at all, would have to come from elsewhere. This trip was solely about renewing his prescriptions. Without them, the pain would become unbearable.

Natalie, Winston's personal nurse, sat nearby. She was a natural beauty, appearing to be in her mid-thirties, with flowing sandy-colored hair and a warm demeanor. Single and deeply committed to her work, she had become an indispensable part of Winston's life. She lived with him, ensuring his health and well-being around the clock. Beyond her duties as a nurse—administering medications, monitoring his condition, and managing his treatments—Natalie also took on the roles of cook, occasional chauffeur, and full-time companion. Though the demands of her position could be overwhelming, she approached them with grace and professionalism. Her efforts were well-compensated, and she seemed to genuinely take pride in her work, a fact that Winston silently appreciated, even if he rarely said so aloud.

Dr. Hartell stepped into the room with a practiced smile, breaking the silence with a familiar greeting. "How are you feeling today?"

Winston knew this was not a serious question but rather an icebreaker. *Just get to the point and write the prescription already*, he thought. Instead, he responded, "Never better."

"That's the spirit," Dr. Hartell quickly replied, oblivious to the edge in Winston's tone. "How did your appointment with the specialist go?"

Winston resisted the urge to lash out. *Maybe try reading the file, genius,* he thought before delivering his standard, measured response. "More tests, more questions, and no answers," he said flatly.

The doctor flipped through the hefty stack of paperwork in Winston's file. "Looks like they really put you through it," he observed, his tone casual. "I haven't had time to review everything; frankly, most of this is out of my expertise. But it seems they're leaning towards some kind of mitochondrial disease."

Winston offered a slight nod, masking the growing irritation simmering beneath his composed exterior. *How long must I endure this charade of an 'examination'?* he wondered, his patience ebbing with every passing moment.

"Do you have a follow-up scheduled for more tests?" Dr. Hartell pressed, his tone neutral.

"Yes," Winston replied. It was a lie, of course. He did have tests in the works, but not with the usual specialists. His relentless research had led him to a different doctor—albeit unconventional and risky. It was a Hail Mary, but that was all he had left.

Dr. Hartell continued flipping through the thick stack of papers in the file. "And it looks like we're due to renew your prescriptions."

Brilliant deduction, Winston thought, resisting the urge to roll his eyes.

"How is your pain?" Dr. Hartell asked, glancing up briefly.

On the wall behind him hung the inevitable pain chart. It ranged from zero to ten, with a smiley face perched smugly at zero—a bright, cheery grin that mocked Winston's current state. He once wore that face: confident, in control, triumphant. That was the old Winston. The new Winston found himself trapped at the other end of the spectrum, somewhere beyond the frowning face at ten. Agony and misery had etched themselves into his features.

This chart is a joke, Winston thought bitterly. It didn't come close to capturing the scope of his suffering. He wasn't a ten—he was at least a 13, maybe even a 14. His skin felt alive, crawling and itching with a constant, unbearable sensation. His head pounded, each throb like a hammer striking an anvil. And his body—his entire body—seemed to be transforming into something alien, something unrecognizable.

Yet, sharing these truths wasn't an option. A confession like that would mean tests, hospital stays, endless prodding—and Winston had no time for that. No, he couldn't afford to sit on the sidelines, not now.

"It's about the same," he replied coolly, the words slipping out with practiced ease. It wasn't entirely untrue. After all, today's pain was no worse than yesterday's. But that was hardly a comfort.

"I'll tell you what," Dr. Hartell said, tapping his pen thoughtfully on the desk. "I'll up your dosage to help you stay ahead of the pain. If things worsen, make sure you let me know."

This was what Winston appreciated most about Dr. Hartell. He was quick with the prescription pad. The man didn't ask too many questions or waste time on unnecessary chatter. The good doctor understood that these meds were Winston's lifeline, crucial to enduring until his next appointment—an appointment that required an international flight and far more energy than Winston currently possessed.

Dr. Hartell rose from his chair, signaling the end of their exchange. "I'll have my staff call in your prescriptions. Is there anything else you need?"

It was hard to tell who wanted to get out of the room quicker.

"No, that's all," Winston mumbled. It crossed his mind to say thanks, but Winston Saunders was not known for being gracious.

Home Alone

Asher sat at his kitchen table, his gaze fixed on the envelope that had been lying there for two days. Or was it three? He had moved it once, maybe twice, hoping it would somehow disappear. Now, it rested in the center of the table, demanding his attention.

The envelope was pristine, with sharp edges and clean, unassuming print—starkly contrasting to the chaos it represented.

The return address at the corner was unmistakable, betraying its contents. He didn't need to open it to know what awaited him inside.

He had meant to open it the day it arrived. He had even picked it up, felt its weight, and traced its edge with his thumb. But then he'd put it down again, telling himself there was no rush. A few more hours wouldn't change anything. Those hours had stretched into a day, then another, until days had passed, and now it sat there, an unwelcome guest he couldn't ignore any longer.

His eyes bore into the envelope as if he could read through the paper. He stretched out a hand, his fingers brushing against the smooth surface, but then pulled back. It wasn't the words he feared—it was what they represented. Finality. Failure. Loss.

Asher leaned back in his chair, rubbing his temples. He could feel the envelope watching him, taunting him with its silent patience. *Get it over with*, he told himself, his hand hovering above it again. But instead of picking it up, he let it stay, unmoved, its secrets still safely sealed. Just one more day, he reasoned—just one more day.

His thoughts drifted to a happier time, a memory from what felt like a lifetime ago. He had met Rita during his final year of college when his world was still full of possibility. She was the blonde American tourist, her laughter bright and easy as she explored Israel for the summer. That year, he had been working as a tour guide, leading groups through museums and archaeological sites scattered across the region. It was a job he loved, sharing the history he was so passionate about with visitors from around the world.

From the moment he saw her, he had been captivated. Something about the way she moved through the ruins, curiosity shining in her eyes, drew him in. For him, the attraction was instant and undeniable. Rita, however, was harder to read. She seemed perfectly content to keep her distance, listening politely to his stories but offering little more than a fleeting smile. She played it cool, at least at first, which only intrigued him more.

The flirting began subtly, almost innocently, but it didn't stay that way for long. Technically, the rules forbade tour guides from fraternizing with their guests, but within a week, those rules had become more of a suggestion—one they thoroughly ignored. When it came to women, Asher always moved quickly; it was just his way. He enjoyed the chase, the excitement, but just as quickly as he pursued, he often let go. None of his relationships had lasted more than a few months, and he liked it that way.

Marriage was never on his radar. Why waste time on something that didn't fit into his carefully laid-out future? Asher was certain about what he wanted in life, and it wasn't a wife or kids. Companionship and intimacy had their place, but only as far as they didn't interfere with his ambitions. He had big plans and wasn't about to let anyone—or anything—slow him down.

Asher dreamed of traversing the globe, uncovering archaeological wonders, and savoring the thrill of discovery. He pictured himself seated at elegant tables with a glass of wine, captivating audiences with stories of ancient ruins and forgotten civilizations. A wife—and especially children—didn't fit into that vision. To him, it wasn't just a career but a lifetime adventure, a pursuit that demanded freedom and unrelenting focus.

There was so much to see, so much to experience, and he intended to seize it all. The idea of adding the "baggage" of domestic life felt like an anchor that would drag him away from those ambitions, consuming the time he needed to chase the life he had carefully imagined for himself.

Asher held a philosophy about time—it was the sole entity of genuine value. Everything demanded time. Remove time, and all endeavors become impossible. Unlike money, fame, or relationships, which can be gained and lost repeatedly, time is a one-time opportunity; once it's gone, it's irretrievable. Plus, you never know when your time will end. To him, his time was to be cherished and safeguarded above all other things. Wasting it was the ultimate sin.

But there was something different about Rita that made him reconsider everything. At first, she had been reserved, keeping her distance, but as they spent more time together, that changed. She began to truly listen, gazing into his eyes as he spoke, no longer just a polite observer but an engaged participant. She hung on every word, and the twinkle in her eyes drew more out of him. He truly wanted to go on and on. Time seemed to stand still when he was with her. For him, it was mesmerizing, and it appeared to be the same for her.

Maybe, just maybe, she *could* fit into his dreams. The idea was surprising, but the more he thought about it, the more plausible it seemed. Rita could be more than just a companion; she could be an asset. He envisioned her as a partner in his adventures, handling travel arrangements, organizing his findings, and managing speaking engagements. She had the intellect and charm to navigate those roles effortlessly, and the possibility of sharing his world with her became increasingly appealing.

Best of all, she was willing. Rita showed genuine enthusiasm for his lifestyle. They shared a mutual passion for archaeology, and their connection felt natural and effortless. It was a win-win, a partnership that made perfect sense. Together, they could chart a future that combined his ambitions with her presence—a compromise he never thought he'd consider, let alone desire.

Another advantage of their relationship was their shared indifference toward religion. Asher, raised in a Jewish household, drifted away from the faith in his teens, becoming increasingly skeptical of its teachings and rituals. Rita, on the other hand, grew up in a household entirely disconnected from religion. Their mutual lack of faith provided a sense of alignment, sparing them the potential friction of religious disagreements.

However, the real challenge came when Asher introduced Rita to his parents—David and Leah. Their relationship with Asher could best be described as complicated. As a teenager, Asher's gradual abandonment of Judaism had been a source of profound disappointment to his parents. While their bond had remained intact—cordial, even close at times, especially with his mother—the undercurrent of tension was ever-present.

The more intense strain began during Asher's college years following the death of his beloved paternal grandfather. The loss struck the family hard, sending his father into a deep depression.

In their search for solace, they discovered the Christian faith, which offered them a new understanding of the Messianic prophecies they had grown up with. *The Dead Sea Scrolls*, ancient texts that predated Jesus, significantly influenced their belief, describing him with precise details aligned with Christian teachings about the Messiah. For them, all the puzzle pieces suddenly fit together perfectly. The emptiness they had been trying to fill was now filled with a peace found within the pages of the New Testament. David referred to it affectionately as the Gospel of Peace; Asher just viewed it as the crutch they needed to overcome their loss.

The shift in faith came at a significant cost for Asher's parents. Friends and even some family members began to distance themselves, struggling to comprehend or accept their conversion. Their embracing of Christianity made others feel like they had betrayed their Jewish heritage—a legacy deeply intertwined with identity and history. This judgment weighed heavily on David, who wrestled with the sting of rejection from those he had once trusted and cherished.

Yet, amid the external strain, David's greatest fear was losing his relationship with Asher. The spiritual divide that had emerged between them was a chasm he desperately wanted to bridge. Just as he had once tried to share and explain his Jewish faith to Asher when he was a child, David now hoped to present his new beliefs in a way that would resonate, a way Asher might eventually embrace. David dreamed of the day Asher would find the same peace and purpose in Christianity that he and Leah had discovered.

But for Asher, their conversion only further validated the path he had chosen by walking away from his childhood beliefs. To him, their newfound faith was yet another reason to reject what he saw as stories and rituals that failed to hold any meaning in the modern, rational world he inhabited.

Over the years, David and Leah had several discussions with Asher about their newfound faith, each time hoping to help him understand the convictions that had transformed their lives. Their journey had led them to what they saw as undeniable truths. The prophecies in Isaiah and other scriptures painted a portrait of Jesus they found impossible to ignore. To them, it wasn't about abandoning their Jewish roots but about seeing those roots fulfilled in an unexpected and profoundly meaningful way.

But for Asher, these conversations were anything but enlightening. Each discussion inevitably spiraled into heated arguments and sharp exchanges. The words exchanged often cut deep, leaving wounds that took days—sometimes weeks—to heal. His mother, ever the peacemaker, would gently step in, her calming presence acting as a buffer between Asher's frustration and David's fervor. In her soft yet firm voice, she would remind them of the importance of family and the need to be patient and understanding with one another.

Her influence, so reminiscent of Asher's late grandfather, often diffused the stress of the moment. But the issues themselves were deeply rooted and defied simple resolutions. Despite her efforts to restore their family, the divide remained, and every conversation circled the same unresolved tensions.

Asher struggled to reconcile his parents 'newfound beliefs with the views they attempted to teach him as a child. He also couldn't help but notice the hypocrisy in their transition away from Judaism when compared to his own. He pondered how his grandfather would have reacted to such news; undoubtedly, he would have disapproved. Yet, Asher also remembered his grandfather as a gentle and loving man who, despite his strong convictions, never turned his back on him. Asher believed his grandfather would have extended this same grace to his parents; it was simply his way.

Asher longed to emulate his grandfather's strength and understanding but found it incredibly challenging. He remembered a proverb his grandfather had shared with him as a young boy about iron sharpening iron, suggesting mutual growth and strengthening. However, this situation felt more akin to stone-crushing stone, where he felt crushed down instead of built up. Even though it wasn't his intention, David lacked his father's gentleness. Through the years, the harshness of his words had wounded Asher deeply, and he found it exceedingly difficult to forgive and simply move forward. Instead, Asher felt a mixture of anger and relief. No more would he be judged for making decisions he felt best. They had their truth, and he had his.

And their hypocrisy didn't end there. Early in his life, they had expected him to marry a woman who shared their Jewish faith and traditions. Now, they were disappointed she wasn't Christian. He simply ignored them when they attempted to address the matter with him. He had always been his own man, and that wasn't about to change now. The more they lamented over the subject, the stronger his resolve became. And Rita had a way with people. Her infectious smile and laughter slowly began to win them over. Though they never gave their blessing, they finally stopped being in total opposition.

Everything was falling into place, and Asher took pride in how seamlessly he had orchestrated it all. He relished the feeling of being in control—of his life, his choices, and his future—and this moment was no exception. Control wasn't just an aspiration; it was his reality, and he embraced it with confidence.

He and Rita had waited until he completed his doctorate to tie the knot, and when the day finally came, it was nothing short of spectacular. They held the ceremony at Ein Hemed National Park, a hidden gem nestled in the hills west of Jerusalem. Surrounded by lush greenery, ancient stone ruins, and flowing springs, the park's serene beauty provided a breathtaking backdrop for their union. Rita's parents and a host of friends had flown in from the United States to celebrate with them.

Most importantly, it was the wedding he wanted on his terms. There were no Jewish traditions, no symbols of the faith he had long since left behind. The absence of rituals tied to his heritage wasn't an oversight; it was deliberate, a statement. This was a new chapter, free of the constraints of the past, precisely as Asher had planned it.

Instead of a honeymoon, they spent the days following the ceremony hosting Rita's parents, who stayed with them for the entire week in Jerusalem. Asher, ever the consummate guide, took them on tours of the city's historical sites, showcasing the rich tapestry of its past. To Asher, it felt like a fitting prelude to what their marriage would be: a blend of exploration, history, and companionship.

But looking back, Asher saw it differently. The lack of a honeymoon, the immediate obligations, the subtle compromises—these were the first cracks in the foundation. What had seemed logical and controlled at the time now appeared to be the beginning of a pattern, one that would lead to a series of bad choices in their marriage. Choices he would come to regret.

After her parents departed, Asher threw himself even deeper into his career. With his impressive credentials, he was in high demand, able to pick and choose from a range of prestigious archaeological projects. Together, he and Rita became international travelers, jetting off to remote and challenging sites that offered the promise of groundbreaking discoveries.

But the glamour of the lifestyle quickly faded. These expeditions were far removed from the smooth, hassle-free experiences Rita had enjoyed as a tourist in Jerusalem. The living conditions were harsh, the locations isolated, and the work grueling. At first, Rita was a trooper, throwing herself into the adventure with determination. For the first couple of years, she adapted, even finding moments of enjoyment.

Over time, though, her enthusiasm began to wane. She started arriving later on trips, shortening her stays, and finding excuses to leave early. Eventually, she stopped going altogether. Each missed trip widened the distance between them, the strain on their marriage growing with every new expedition Asher undertook.

Recognizing the toll it was taking, Asher decided to make a change. In an effort to salvage their relationship, he took a job in Jerusalem, joining the team working on the Temple Mount excavation. The work was far more routine than he was used to, lacking the excitement and prestige of his earlier projects. Still, it allowed him to be home every night, something Rita appreciated. For a time, it seemed like a step in the right direction, but Asher couldn't ignore the feeling that something fundamental in their marriage had already shifted.

After several months of being home, Asher began to notice what he saw as radical changes in Rita. She started bringing up the idea of starting a family—a subject that had always been off the table for him. From Asher's perspective, this wasn't just a shift; it was a betrayal of their original agreement. They had been clear about their priorities before getting married, and now, to him, it felt like she was reneging on that understanding. The pressure she put on him to reconsider left him feeling cornered, as though she was asking him to abandon his dreams.

As if that were not enough, Rita had started attending his parents ' Christian church. This development struck a particularly raw nerve with Asher. His rejection of religion—especially his parents 'faith—had been a defining part of his identity for years. To see Rita not only embracing faith but doing so under the influence of his parents was painful. It was as though his parents were finding yet another way to exert control over his life, this time through his wife.

And to make matters worse, Rita would come home after church brimming with enthusiasm, eager to share details about the sermon or the new friends she had met. She wasn't just attending occasionally; she had become a regular. Week after week, her connection to this new community seemed to deepen, and with it came a request that grated on Asher's nerves—she began asking him to join her.

That wasn't going to happen. Ever.

To Asher, this wasn't just a phase or a harmless hobby. It was yet another sign that the woman he married eleven years ago no longer existed. The captivating, adventurous, and faithful partner with whom he had built his life had disappeared, replaced by someone whose priorities and values felt increasingly foreign. The gap between them, once a crack, was now a seemingly unbridgeable divide.

He began to see her as weak and gullible, traits he associated with all religious people, but especially Christians. His disdain reached a new level when, for his last birthday, she gifted him a Bible with his name engraved on the cover. Seriously?! The gesture felt absurd to him, almost insulting. He considered throwing it straight into the trash. But he was still in "save my marriage" mode, so he set it aside, resolving to give it some time before confronting her. He would eventually sit her down and explain the truth—the real truth.

Asher knew little about Christianity, but what he did know struck him as nothing more than made-up stories. As a scientist, he prided himself on dealing with facts, evidence, and rational explanations. To him, disproving the things she had learned wouldn't just be easy—it would be inevitable. He was determined to guide her back to what he considered solid ground. It was, after all, the logical thing to do.

At least one positive aspect of his new job was his renewed interest in Herod the Great. It felt like his life had come full circle, bringing him back to the historical figure who had first captured his imagination as a student. Herod was a fascinating and controversial figure in Jewish history, a man whose legacy was as complex as the era he lived in.

Herod the Great was not Jewish by birth but of Edomite descent. The Edomites had been forcibly converted to Judaism generations before his birth, a fact that gave Herod a tenuous connection to the faith he ruled over. Despite this, many of his subjects viewed him as an outsider, an illegitimate king imposed on them by Rome. Yet, Herod managed to cement his place in history with grand architectural projects, most notably the extensive renovations of the Second Temple in Jerusalem, which elevated it to one of the ancient world's most magnificent structures.

His reign was marked by a delicate balancing act. Israel was under Roman control, and tensions ran high between the Jewish population and their occupiers. Herod's ability to navigate these tensions was remarkable. He kept the peace by playing both sides expertly appeasing the Romans with his loyalty while pacifying the Jewish people with monumental projects and political maneuvering. For all his flaws, Herod was a master of strategy, a man who knew how to play the game and survive in a world rife with conflict and betrayal. For Asher, diving into the layers of Herod's life and reign was a welcome distraction and a reminder of why he had chosen archaeology in the first place.

Herod has remained a figure shrouded in mystery, his life and legacy a source of endless fascination. But for Asher, one mystery stood above the rest: the lost 50 tons of gold, silver, and sacred treasures looted from Herod's Temple following the Roman legionnaires' brutal sack of Jerusalem on Tisha b'Av in the year 70 CE. The mere idea of such immense wealth and history, hidden somewhere for centuries, stirred something deep within him—a spark he hadn't felt in years.

This was the kind of enigma that rekindled his passion for archaeology. It was more than a professional pursuit; it was a quest. Asher immersed himself in studying Herod's life and reign, devouring every detail that might offer a clue to the treasure's fate.

Theories about its location were as varied as they were tantalizing. Some believed it lay hidden in vaults beneath the Vatican, taken there by the Romans who had plundered it. Others speculated it had been discovered and seized by the Nazis during their relentless quest for valuable and historical artifacts in World War II. The possibilities were endless, and each one only fueled Asher's obsession further. It was the pursuit of the unknown, the thrill of unraveling history's secrets, that sustained his passion—the very passion that drove his life.

Asher had his own theory about the location of Herod's lost treasure, a theory he believed could stand apart from the speculation of others. All he needed was support and funding to prove it. But convincing others wasn't easy, especially given the reception of his book on the subject. While it had garnered attention, it had also drawn its fair share of criticism.

According to his critics, the main issue was that his book left too many questions unanswered. While Asher claimed to know the answers, he purposefully withheld them, hoping to craft his narrative in a way that left readers intrigued and yearning for more. Evidently, he had left them wanting too much more. His approach, designed to spark curiosity and intrigue, had backfired for some, who found the lack of resolution frustrating.

Though it wasn't a work of fiction, the book had the pacing and suspense of a novel, weaving historical analysis with speculative intrigue. To Asher, this was its strength; it made history come alive. But to his detractors, it felt incomplete, more like an elaborate teaser than a definitive exploration. Despite the criticism, Asher stood by his approach. The mystery wasn't just something to solve—it was something to experience, and he was confident his theory had the potential to uncover the truth. All he needed now was someone willing to take the journey with him.

It all seemed to happen on the same day, though in hindsight, Asher couldn't be certain. What he did know was that it all unraveled very quickly. First came the devastating blow: he was fired from his job as an archaeologist. His employers accused him of dedicating too much time to his book and not enough to the excavation work they were paying him to do.

Then, as if to hammer the final nail into his ambitions, his publisher called with bad news. Or rather, his so-called publisher—an arrangement built more on promises than substance. Despite their initial enthusiasm, no money had ever exchanged hands, and now even their interest had disappeared. The future he had so carefully planned seemed to collapse in an instant, leaving him grasping for solid ground.

The final blow came when he arrived home to find a note waiting for him. Rita was gone. She had moved out, explaining in carefully chosen words that she needed space to "figure things out." She assured him it was temporary, a short-term separation to give them both time to evaluate their relationship.

But her absence didn't feel temporary to Asher—it felt like betrayal. Anger surged through him, and when he called her later, the conversation turned heated. He said things he couldn't take back, words sharp enough to leave lasting scars. They were harsh, but in his mind, they were also true. Asher believed he had only voiced what needed to be said, but even so, he wished he could take them back.

Communication between them had all but ceased, and he could no longer see a clear way forward. Yet, despite everything, a part of him still clung to the faint hope that something might change, that they might find their way back to each other. But as the days stretched on, the reality became difficult to ignore—moving on might be the only way to heal, even if his heart wasn't ready to let go.

The teaching position at the university was the one stable thing in Asher's unraveling life—a temporary anchor amid the wreckage. It gave him a purpose, a foothold to begin rebuilding. Yet, as he looked back on the last eleven years, the weight of regret was crushing. He had wasted so much time and so many dreams on a life that now felt like a mistake. Time he could never reclaim. Resolving never to repeat those missteps, Asher vowed to regain control of his life—and this time, to never let it slip through his fingers again.

Asher shook himself free from his thoughts, his gaze returning to the envelope on the table. It was still there, beckoning his attention. Taking a deep breath, he reached for it. The envelope opened easily, almost as if the contents were trying to escape their confines.

He slowly unfolded the papers, and the bold title at the top confirmed what he already knew: *Divorce Decree.*

To Russia, With Hope

Winston and Natalie boarded the private jet, every step an exhausting battle for Winston. His body, frail and betraying him, made even the slightest movements feel monumental. He knew his time was running out, and this last-ditch effort had to succeed. The strange illness ravaging his body defied clear diagnosis. Most doctors suspected a mitochondrial disease, a disorder rooted in DNA mutations, but some of his symptoms didn't fit the pattern. The mystery deepened, as did Winston's desperation—this gamble had to pay off.

Additionally, doctors were puzzled about why Winston had developed the disease. Typically, mitochondrial disorders are inherited and passed down from parent to child, but neither of his parents showed any signs of it. The anomaly only added to the puzzle surrounding his condition. But Winston knew why he was afflicted—a truth he guarded fiercely.

This trip held promise. Winston was smart—really smart, almost too smart—so smart that he could practically find the cure himself. And perhaps that's precisely what he had done. Amidst his extensive research, he discovered a Russian doctor renowned for his extensive work with survivors of the Chernobyl nuclear disaster. Actually, it was Natalie who first mentioned the Russian doctor when she saw an article in *Time* magazine about him. Many Chernobyl survivors suffered from a similar condition that affected their DNA.

Dr. Sergey Vinogradov had achieved promising results that appeared to reverse their condition. The notable advantage of Russian medicine was the lack of extensive governmental oversight. Doctors like Vinogradov could provide services that would take years or even decades to get approval in the United States. Furthermore, he was easily accessible. In the States, seeing specialists often required months of waiting. However, one phone call and $10,000 could secure an appointment with Dr. Vinogradov within forty-eight hours. That kind of immediacy was priceless for Winston.

The journey, however, was punishing. The increasing pain pushed Winston to his limit, and he instructed Natalie to triple his usual dose of pain medication. With her reluctant assistance, he found temporary solace in a deep, restless sleep as the jet carried him toward what he hoped would be salvation.

It was evening when they touched down in Moscow, and Winston and Natalie made their way to their hotel. The city felt strange and unfamiliar, a stark contrast to the familiar streets back home. Due to the ongoing war, Dr. Vinogradov's suggested meeting in Moscow rather than his office in Ukraine, near Chernobyl. He deemed Moscow was much safer and more accessible. Under the circumstances, Winston's hotel room was the most practical venue for their meeting.

Still, the arrangement felt unusual to Winston. His experiences with specialists in the United States had always been in clinical settings. The idea of meeting a doctor in a hotel room struck him as unconventional at best. Yet, as unconventional as it was, despair left him little choice but to proceed.

Typically, Winston would have faced a grueling day-long series of tests, followed by at least another day of waiting for a consultation. However, Dr. Vinogradov assured him he could complete an examination in under an hour and begin treatment the same day. Under different circumstances, Winston might have balked at such an expedited process, but these were far from normal circumstances. Desperation had stripped away his reservations—he was willing to take the risk.

The toll of jet lag, combined with Winston's chronic pain, nearly pushed him to his breaking point. The trip would have been unthinkable without Natalie's unwavering support—her quiet strength, her steady presence. She tended to him with care, ensuring he never felt alone in his struggle. When exhaustion weighed too heavily, she would sit beside him, gently stroking his hand, her touch a silent reassurance that he wasn't facing this battle alone.

Because of his tendency to take extra pills when the pain became unbearable, Natalie had to ration his medication carefully to avoid running out mid-journey. Winston had considered buying pills on the street to bridge the gaps, but besides the risk of arrest being too high,—Natalie would never allow it.

And he couldn't do anything that might cause her to quit. Losing her was unthinkable; she was his anchor. Without her touch, without her presence, even the simplest tasks would have been impossible.

For this trip, Natalie had arranged adjoining hotel rooms, providing her with privacy while keeping her close enough to Winston's room if he needed her. Seeing him struggle with mounting pain, she did everything she could to comfort him.

Dr. Vinogradov had scheduled his appointment for the next morning, so Natalie helped him settle into bed. Exhausted, Winston quickly drifted into a restless sleep, his hope resting heavily on what the next day might bring.

A loud knock on his door startled Winston from his slumber. Blinking groggily, he tried to focus on the clock on the nightstand—9:00. *Was it morning or evening?*

Sunlight spilled through the curtains, answering his question. Morning. He had been asleep for ten hours. His appointment with Dr. Vinogradov was at 9:00 AM, and evidently, the doctor was a prompt man.

Winston reached for a small device around his neck, the one he used to beckon Natalie, and pressed it.

Except this time... nothing.

He pressed it again. Still no Natalie.

Another loud knock on the door forced Winston to take a different action.

He glanced toward his wheelchair. Normally, Natalie would help him into it, but struggling to get in would take just as much effort as walking to the door.

Gritting his teeth, he steadied himself before forcing his legs to move, inching toward the peephole.

Peering through it, he recognized the large man on the other side from magazine photos—though today, he was dressed more like a businessman than a doctor.

Opening the door, Winston took in his appearance—an expensive suit tailored to perfection and a black medical bag clutched in his hand.

Winston invited him into the room, and the doctor stepped inside. Although he spoke with a heavy Russian accent, the doctor's English was clear and easy to understand. Dr. Vinogradov extended his hand, and Winston assumed the doctor wanted to shake hands. Instead, he took Winston's hand and began to examine it, noting several dark spots and small blisters.

Dr. Vinogradov pulled a pair of glasses from his coat pocket, slipped them on, and leaned closer. "These abrasions... same as others on body?" he asked in a clipped, heavily accented tone.

"Yes," Winston replied with a sigh.

The doctor nodded and gestured toward a nearby chair. "Please, take off shirt. Sit here," he instructed.

Winston complied, removing his nightshirt to reveal an upper body marred by sores. Some oozed clear liquid, while others had developed thick scabs. Dr. Vinogradov studied them intently, his gaze sharp and methodical. After a moment, he asked, "What other symptoms you... experiencing?"

"Mainly pain," Winston replied, his voice weary. "Lots of pain. It feels like my skin is crawling. Sometimes I get blurry or double vision, and I'm constantly exhausted."

Dr. Vinogradov nodded, his expression unreadable. He opened his medical bag and retrieved a stethoscope, placing it firmly against Winston's chest and then his back. "Breathe deep," he instructed, the command clipped but clear.

Winston complied, each breath labored. The doctor continued his examination, poking and prodding methodically.

Suddenly, the door to the adjoining room creaked open, and Natalie stepped inside. Winston turned toward her. "Where have you been?" he demanded.

"I went downstairs to get something to eat. It was more difficult than I had expected with the language barrier and all," she said apologetically.

Winston gestured toward her, addressing the doctor. "This is my nurse, Natalie."

Dr. Vinogradov nodded, a faint smile breaking through his otherwise stern demeanor. "Yes, her voice—I know from phone talks," he said, his heavy accent evident. They had spoken several times while arranging this meeting.

The doctor returned his attention to Winston and continued his methodical examination. After a few more minutes, he placed his stethoscope back in his bag and straightened up. "I have treated many with symptoms like yours," he said, his tone firm but not unkind. "I am confident I can help you."

The remark stunned Winston. He hadn't been in the room for ten minutes, and the doctor already claimed to have a diagnosis? The declaration was both astonishing and unsettling. Was this man a genius—or a complete quack? He hadn't taken his temperature, performed any blood work, checked his blood pressure, or even done a basic X-ray. No urine sample, no lengthy questionnaire, nothing beyond a stethoscope and some quick prodding. Did he even own an ophthalmoscope or any other standard diagnostic tools? The lack of thoroughness gnawed at Winston, leaving him skeptical.

As Winston's pulse quickened and he struggled to make sense of the situation, the doctor abruptly interrupted. "We start today—your treatment," Dr. Vinogradov announced with quiet certainty.

Winston's mind reeled. *Today?* The word echoed in his head, stirring equal parts hope and apprehension.

The doctor noticed the confusion in Winston's expression and tilted his head slightly. "This... is problem?" he asked, his thick accent giving the question an almost casual weight.

"Problem? Uh, no, no, I guess not," Winston stammered.

The doctor continued, "Alright, stand up, please. You will receive injection in hip."

Winston hesitated briefly before struggling to his feet.

Dr. Vinogradov reached into his medical bag, retrieving a syringe and a vial. He held them out to Natalie. "You are his nurse, yes? You give him injection," he instructed.

Natalie took them without hesitation and filled the syringe before retrieving an alcohol swab from her medical supplies.

Dr. Vinogradov added, "This will bring relief. It is not cure but necessary part of main treatment."

Natalie administered the injection into Winston's right hip. Almost immediately, a wave of warmth coursed through his body, intensifying into a sharp, burning sensation. Winston's face flushed, and his knees buckled slightly as he swayed, dangerously close to collapsing.

Anticipating the reaction, Dr. Vinogradov stepped forward and said calmly, "Sit, please. This is normal."

Winston lowered himself into the chair, his mind racing with fear and confusion. *What did he inject me with?* For a brief, chilling moment, he wondered if it might be poison. But the thought seemed irrational—after all, how would that benefit the doctor?

Noticing the worry etched on Winston's face, Dr. Vinogradov offered reassurance. "Momentarily, you will feel improvement," he said, his tone steady.

Within moments, Asher realized the burning sensation had eased, replaced by a surprising sense of relief. His body, aching with pain moments ago, now felt lighter.

"This is for temporary relief. Continued treatments are needed. Six to nine months—this I expect for complete cure," Dr. Vinogradov nonchalantly continued.

The doctor's words caught Asher's attention—one word standing out above all others, the word he had longed to hear.

Cure.

The Cost

Winston's mind buzzed with a barrage of unanswered questions. Across the room, Dr. Vinogradov had eased into a chair and withdrawn a pack of cigarettes from his jacket. He offered one to Natalie, who shook her head politely, then lit one for himself without so much as a glance at Winston. The casual disregard for etiquette was at the least odd, but when Winston considered the unconventional nature of the entire encounter, he let it slide. If a cigarette-smoking doctor could deliver the cure he desperately needed, Winston figured he could live with a little secondhand smoke.

Unsure how to continue the conversation, Winston waited for Dr. Vinogradov to take the lead. But the doctor simply sat back, puffing on his cigarette, his gaze fixed on Winston.

The silence stretched.

Finally, unable to contain his urgency, Winston broke it. "So, what's next?"

Dr. Vinogradov lowered his cigarette, exhaling a thin stream of smoke. "Assuming continuation of treatments is your wish..."

"Of course, I want to continue," Winston interjected, his voice firm. "Are you certain you can cure my condition?"

The doctor confidently replied, "Yes, I have seen many cases such as yours. From the moment I observed your hand, your condition was clear to me. Your body shows signs of extensive radiation exposure, contaminating your system and mutating your DNA. The path to cure is straightforward, yet the cost..."

Winston saw it coming. He knew what was next—the money. It was always about the money. Russia's chess masters had nothing on this doctor—he had Winston in check with few available moves. Negotiation was futile; Winston was entirely at the man's mercy.

Still, this wasn't the time to appear weak. His body was failing, but his mind remained sharp. He'd worked through impossible situations before, and he'd find a way out of this one, too.

For now, he'd play along. The price would be steep—of that, he had no doubt.

'How much?' Winston asked."

"The price for each injection... is 100,000 American dollars. You need one every month. Like I say, six, nine months max," the doctor explained. "Payment is upfront... Swiss account. To ship these drugs is risky. You come here, to Russia, for injections. Also, daily injections—less expensive—your nurse can give at home."

Though the price was steep, Winston wasn't surprised. It was higher than he had hoped, but he had expected it to be costly. While it would require shifting funds around and tightening his finances, it was doable. And he couldn't blame the good doctor—he was clearly capitalizing on his recent success and popularity.

Capitalism was alive and well in Russia.

Of course, all of this could be a money grab and a complete waste of time. But Winston knew money wouldn't be the issue if his health were restored. Admittedly, money was tight, tighter than usual, but he had a plan to fix that. But his plan required time, and hopefully, this drug would, at the very least, give him the time he needed. Besides, it wouldn't take long to see if the treatments worked. A one-month investment was a gamble Winston was more than willing to take.

"When can we start?" Winston asked.

"Immediately, comrade," the doctor replied, "but first... there is matter of 100,000 American dollars."

Winston, not usually one to haggle, responded, "Minus the 10,000 I've already paid, correct, comrade?"

The doctor hesitated for a moment before chuckling. "Of course," he replied smoothly.

Winston smiled, feeling as though he had momentarily moved his king out of check and regained a sliver of control—something that felt increasingly elusive. “I’ll have the money transferred by tomorrow,” Winston stated confidently.

"Good, we meet here tomorrow. And I start preparations for daily shots. Should I discuss with Natalia?" he inquired.

"It's Natalie, but yes," answered Winston.

Apologetically, the doctor replied, "Of course, Natalie. My apologies." He extinguished his cigarette and moved toward the door. Natalie followed, ensuring he left without issue. After the door clicked shut, Winston allowed himself a small sigh of relief. The meeting had gone better than he had anticipated, and things were falling into place for the first time in a long while.

Now, it was time to set his entire plan into motion.

First Contact

Asher hurried around his apartment, preparing to leave for his 10:00 lecture. Punctuality was one of his hallmarks, and he always allowed an extra 15 minutes to account for traffic delays. Today, that buffer would prove essential. A sharp knock on his door interrupted his routine. Asher opened it and found a courier holding an envelope.

"Asher Meyer?" the courier asked.

"Yes," Asher replied.

The courier extended the letter and an attached card. "Sign here," he instructed. Asher scrawled his signature, and the courier detached the card before handing over the envelope. "Have a good day," the courier said briskly before departing.

Asher stared at the envelope, his mind already turning. *What's she asking for now?* he thought, assuming it was from Rita or her attorney.

However, the return address was not from Jerusalem but Boston, MA. Asher could also tell that it was more personal than business. He tore it open to reveal a handwritten letter, the shaky script at the bottom signed by someone named Winston Saunders—a name entirely unfamiliar to him. The uneven handwriting suggested an older individual. Intrigued, Asher began to read.

> *Dr. Meyer,*
>
> *I hope this letter finds you well. I recently came across information regarding your manuscript, Herod the (Great and His Great Treasure). Your research is extraordinary and aligns closely with my own interests. Together, I believe we may have an opportunity to uncover additional truths that have long remained hidden.*
>
> *I am particularly interested in helping to fund further research on this topic, as it is of historical and cultural significance. I would greatly appreciate the chance to meet and discuss this further. I propose you visit me in Boston as soon as possible. Travel and lodging will be provided*

at no cost to you, along with a payment of $5,000 for your time. Please contact me at the number below so we can arrange the details.

Warm regards,

Winston Saunders

Confused, Asher lowered the letter. How had this person even heard about his book, which had never made it to publication? The only people with access to it were a small circle—his potential publisher, an editor, and several colleagues who had reviewed it. Yet, the letter indicated that Winston might have actually read the manuscript.

The promise of funding for further research immediately grabbed Asher's attention. It was more than he could have hoped for—resources to pursue the book's ideas and the chance to possibly validate his work. Still, it seemed almost too good to be true. Was this a genuine opportunity or some sort of elaborate prank?

Slipping the letter into his pocket, he glanced at the clock. He had used up all his extra travel time and hurried out the door, deciding to let the mystery simmer until after class.

Deciding whether Winston Saunders was eccentric or if his offer was the breakthrough Asher had hoped for would have to wait, at least for now.

Who's Who

Asher struggled to focus during his lecture, his mind preoccupied with the mysterious Winston Saunders. Questions swirled—who was this man? By the time the class concluded, Asher could barely wait to dig deeper.

Hurrying to his office, he firmly closed the door for privacy and sat at his computer. Fingers flying over the keyboard, he conducted a Google search for Winston Saunders. The results were underwhelming—dozens of men with the same name, but none appeared to be connected to Boston or anything remotely relevant to his inquiry.

The return address on the envelope was simply a post office box, which provided no help. Despite Asher's efforts, this Winston character remained elusive—no digital footprint, no property ownership records, nothing. Asher became suspicious that Winston might be using an alias, adding another layer of mystery to the puzzle he was determined to solve. Without a photo or further details, identifying the man behind the letter felt like searching for a needle in a haystack.

Asher turned his attention back to the letter. Though it didn't explicitly state the next steps, he could anticipate what would follow. *He'll obviously ask for personal details—name, date of birth, maybe even bank account information to "transfer" the advance payment,* he thought. The more he considered it, the more skeptical he became. Could this be an elaborate ploy by a con artist? Flattering his academic ego to exploit his finances and personal information?

The idea simmered, growing more absurd and infuriating by the second. *This is as lame as the Nigerian Prince scam,* Asher concluded. Shaking his head, he crumpled the letter in his fist and hurled it into the trash can. There was no way he was falling for that.

Over the next 24 hours, doubt began to creep into Asher's mind. Had he acted too hastily? Perhaps the request was legitimate, and he had thrown $5,000 into the trash. What if this Winston character was genuine? At the very least, Asher reasoned, he could request the money in advance. If Winston was serious, there was a chance he might comply.

The idea felt increasingly plausible, and Asher decided it was worth a shot. He had an online payment account, a secure platform that allowed him to transfer without any risk to his finances. If Winston agreed to send the funds there, it would lend credibility to the offer. With a mix of skepticism and cautious optimism, Asher resolved to explore the possibility further.

Asher returned to his office to retrieve the contact information from the letter. However, upon reaching the trash can, he was met with a disheartening sight—it was empty. The custodian had evidently emptied it. The letter was gone, and with it, the promise of $5,000. His streak of bad luck seemed unbroken.

For the next thirty minutes, Asher sat in quiet frustration, reflecting on the many failures that seemed to define his life. Failed relationships, career setbacks, unfulfilled dreams of becoming a novelist, a strained bond with his parents, and now the possibility of losing this business opportunity—all weighed heavily on him.

Suddenly, a spark of hope crossed his mind—he remembered performing an internet search on the phone number in the letter. Surely, it would still be in his browser history. But before he could check, his attention caught on the flashing light on his desk phone—a detail he had somehow overlooked—indicating a new message. Intrigued, he pressed the button, and a scratchy voice filled the room.

"Asher, this is Winston Saunders," the voice began. "I received confirmation that my letter was delivered, but I haven't heard from you yet. At your convenience, please contact me. My direct number is..."

Asher scrambled for a pen and notepad, quickly jotting down the number as Winston listed the best times to reach him, accounting for the seven-hour time difference.

A wave of relief swept over him. According to the timestamp on his phone, the message had been left just two hours earlier. Glancing at the clock, Asher realized he was well within the window Winston had provided. Faced with a decision, he debated whether to act immediately or wait a day or two to maintain the upper hand.

Leaning back in his chair with a self-assured grin, Asher propped his feet on the desk. For the first time in days, he felt in control. Tomorrow would be the day to make the call. He'd keep it short and to the point, exuding confidence. His priorities were clear: first, secure the transfer of funds; second, learn more about Winston and his motives. Asher felt confident that his plan was solid—foolproof against any potential scam.

That night, Asher struggled to sleep, his mind racing as he repeatedly reviewed his plan, trying to anticipate Winston's questions. The strategy seemed solid, yet a sense of uneasiness lingered. Amid all his focus on securing the money and unraveling Winston's identity, he suddenly returned to the critical question.

How did Winston know about the contents of my unpublished book?

The thought gnawed at him. The manuscript wasn't online, and he doubted anyone with a copy would have shared it without his consent. A chilling idea surfaced—*Had Winston hacked into my personal computer?*

The possibility sent a fresh wave of paranoia coursing through him. If Winston had access to his computer, he'd know everything—every search Asher had made, every document, every note.

Yes, that must be it. I've been hacked!

The Call

Asher woke early, ready to make the call, only to remember the time difference that meant he'd have to wait. The best time would not roll around until after lunch, and a lecture on his schedule meant pushing it back even further. Still, that worked out—it let him keep things casual. He'd use his work phone, the same one Winston's message had come through on. It felt right, keeping things professional and separate from his personal life.

Asher tried to distract himself from the wait, but his mind kept circling through all the who's, what's, and why's about Winston. *What would Winston say? What exactly did he want?* He was so lost in his musings that the buzz of his cell phone startled him. He glanced at the caller ID: Rita. His thumb hovered over the "decline" button, but curiosity—or maybe pride—won out. With a sigh, he answered, "Hello."

"Asher," her voice came through, tender and loving, a tone so foreign to the distance between them. It tugged at something deep inside him, stirring memories he struggled to move past—moments of warmth, of tenderness, and the ache of what was lost. Like the faint whiff of her perfume, it lingered, pulling him into a longing he couldn't escape.

"Rita," he said, her name catching in his throat as a flicker of hope stirred—maybe she had called to take it all back. For a moment, he let himself believe it. But then her voice came, soft and steady.

"Asher, did you get the papers?" Her voice was soft, but there was no hesitation—just quiet resolve.

And just like that, the flicker was gone.

His chest tightened, the fragile hope shattering as reality settled in. Just as quickly as it had appeared, it was replaced by the anger that hovered just beneath the surface. "Yeah," he said quietly. "I got them."

"Okay, well," she said softly. "I just... I wanted to make sure. And to talk and make sure you didn't have any questions."

He let out a bitter laugh. "Questions? What questions could possibly exist, Rita? Besides, It looks to me like your mind is made up."

"Let's not start this again," she said, her tone steady but weary as if she'd prepared for this.

"Why not? It's the truth, isn't it?" he shot back. "You're the one walking away, Rita. You're the one who gave up."

"I'm not doing this, Asher," she said quietly, though there was resolve in her voice. "I'm tired. I just want to move on."

He could hear the exhaustion beneath her calm tone, which only stoked his frustration.

"Blame it all on me," she continued softly. "It's okay. If it helps you, go ahead. Say it's all my fault."

"Because it is," he shot back, his voice sharpening. "You're the one who changed, Rita. I kept my end of the deal. I stayed the same. You're the one who broke it, not me."

She let out a quiet breath, steady but tinged with sadness. "That's fair, you're right, Asher. I did change. But it wasn't without reason. We drifted apart."

"Drifted apart?" he repeated bitterly. "That's one way to put it. Or maybe it's because you started chasing something I'll never understand."

She hesitated, and he could sense her searching for the right words. "Yes," she admitted softly. "I know you don't understand. And honestly, I'm not sure I can explain it in a way that would make sense to you."

"Try me," he pressed, his frustration sharpening his tone. "Because from where I'm standing, it looks like you threw everything we had away for... what? Some new belief? A God you didn't even care about before?"

Her voice trembled, but she didn't raise it. "I didn't throw anything away, Asher. I found something. Something that changed me. Something I couldn't ignore, even if I tried."

"To the point of walking away from everything we built?" he demanded.

"It wasn't a choice between you and this," she said, calm but resolute. "It was... it was something I had to face, something I couldn't unsee once I understood it. And I knew it would hurt you, and I hated that. But I couldn't go back. I can't go back."

He shook his head, the disbelief and anger bubbling over. "You traded me for a fantasy, Rita. For lies, myths, and stories. And now you want me just to accept that?"

"I don't expect you to accept it," she said, her voice steady. "I don't even expect you to understand. I just... I just need you to know it wasn't something I did lightly. I prayed..."

"You prayed?" he interrupted, his voice dripping with sarcasm. "Did you pray for us or just for a way to justify walking away? Besides, your God doesn't want divorce, does He? 'What God has joined together, let no man separate. 'Isn't that how it goes?"

Her silence fueled his argument, so much so that he felt a pang of guilt. But the anger, the hurt, was too raw to hold back. "I didn't think you'd have an answer for that one. Maybe you need to do a little more Bible study instead of pinning this on some god that doesn't exist."

Trying to stay composed, Rita answered, "You don't have to belittle my beliefs, Asher. I don't have it all figured out—it's all so new to me and, in many ways, foreign. But something awakened in me, a yearning I can't ignore. I know it's foolishness to you, but it's not to me."

Her words hung uncomfortably in the air.

"And you chose this foolishness over us?" he said bitterly.

Ignoring his snide comment, she remained calm. "It wasn't about choosing one over the other," she said with a trembling voice. "It was about seeing the truth and knowing I couldn't pretend otherwise."

"Truth?" he repeated, his voice rising. "Here's some truth for you. This God of yours, He takes and destroys. He took my parents." His voice grew harder, the pain spilling into anger. "And now He is taking you. Not just you, but us—our life, our marriage, everything we built together, even our future. Yeah, that's your God, I hope He's happy. He's thorough; I'll give Him that."

Her voice broke then, trembling with emotion. "I don't know what else to say."

"There is nothing else," he replied, his voice hollow.

"You're right, you're always right," she said in defeat. "Goodbye, Asher."

The line went dead. He stared at the phone in his hand, then at the papers on the table. Anger, bitterness, and regret churned inside him. And yet, after it was all said, he couldn't ignore one gnawing truth: it wasn't his fault.

Tears welled up in his eyes, unexpected and unwelcome. He wiped them away hastily, though their warmth lingered on his cheeks. The sudden surge of emotion startled him, and for a fleeting moment, he considered picking up the phone and calling Rita again. Maybe there was still a chance to mend what had been broken, to bridge the chasm between them.

But even as the thought crossed his mind, he knew it was futile. Their differences were too vast, their paths too divergent. He couldn't live in the shadow of her newfound faith, and she couldn't return to the life they'd once shared. It was time to let go and accept that their story had reached its end.

He drew a deep breath and set the phone down beside the papers with deliberate finality. Perhaps the upcoming call with Winston would be the first step toward a new beginning.

The hours leading up to the call passed uneventfully. His lecture provided a much-needed escape, a chance to immerse himself in the one thing that still brought him joy: archaeology. Talking about ancient civilizations and sharing his knowledge with students felt effortless, almost second nature. But he held onto the hope that an opportunity to return to the work he loved was on the horizon. Maybe this call with Winston would be the turning point he needed, the start of a new chapter he could fully embrace.

As he settled back into his office, he went over the conversation he was about to have with Winston in his head once more. Two cups of coffee fueled him with caffeine, giving him a jittery edge. He hoped it would convey a sense of urgency when he made the call. Taking a deep breath, he picked up the phone and dialed the number. It rang several times before the familiar voice from the message answered on the other end.

"Hello, Asher. Thanks for returning my call," Winston said, his voice trembling slightly. "I've been eagerly wanting to talk to you. I see you received my letter as well."

A lump formed in Asher's throat as he replied, "Yes, I did. I've gone over it, but I have a few questions."

"I would expect no less. Please, go ahead," Winston replied.

Asher's mind raced as he thought, *Where should I begin?* All his preplanned conversation slipped entirely from his mind. He quickly realized that he should have written it all down.

Sensing Asher's hesitation, Winston spoke up, "Perhaps I should begin first. I'm sure you have lots of questions about me."

Realizing this was one of the main questions, Asher tried to regain his composure and replied, "Yes, that would be nice."

Winston continued, his voice carrying the weight of his years, "I'm what many call a man of many talents. I'm an MIT graduate with degrees in Physics and Mechanical Engineering. But I consider myself a self-taught man. I'm retired now and like to dabble in different things in my free time."

As Winston spoke, Asher listened intently, feeling a mixture of surprise and admiration for the man's background. His voice, seasoned with the weight of experience, carried a specific authority that Asher found compelling. Despite his initial suspicions, Asher couldn't deny Winston's impressive credentials.

Winston continued, “At the same time, I'm a very private man, trying to keep out of the spotlight of social media and such. I’m sure you struggled to learn much about me on the web. Not to worry, I’m just an ordinary guy, just like you."

"I see," Asher replied, his tone respectful. "Your background is certainly impressive. It's understandable that you prefer to keep a low profile. I must admit, I did struggle to find information about you online."

Deep down, Asher couldn't shake off the feeling that there was more to Winston than he let on. Despite Winston's assurance of being an ordinary man, Asher wondered what lay beneath the surface.

"Mr. Saunders, I..." Asher began, but Winston interjected smoothly, "Please, call me Winston."

"Of course, Winston, before we go further," Asher interjected, "there's something that's been nagging at me. How did you come across my unpublished book in the first place?"

Ah, yes, the book," Winston chuckled lightly, his voice carrying a hint of amusement. "It was during one of my many conversations with individuals at the University of Jerusalem that your work was mentioned. While I have not read it, I was informed that you have performed extensive research concerning the lost treasure of Herod the Great. As I said in my letter, I am greatly interested in the lost treasure and hoped some type of collaboration might be useful to both of us."

Asher listened intently, intrigued by Winston's explanation. "So you're familiar with the treasure," he remarked, his tone curious.

"Probably not as knowledgeable as you, but I find the entire story fascinating," Winston said, his tone smooth and measured. "I think we would both agree that Herod the Great is one of history's most enigmatic figures."

Asher adjusted the phone, leaning back in his chair. Despite his initial reservations about Winston, the man's genuine interest in Herod struck a chord with him. Few things put Asher more at ease than the chance to dive into his favorite subject. "He is, without a doubt. Our best source is Josephus, though his accounts are frustratingly incomplete. His mentions of Herodium's storerooms are intriguing but vague enough to leave plenty of room for speculation."

As Winston expected, Asher knew his history—not just the surface-level facts, but the gaps, the uncertainties, the details that only a true scholar would catch. It was one thing to quote Josephus and another to recognize the flaws in his accounts.

Ah, Josephus," Winston replied, shifting slightly in his wheelchair as he considered Asher's words. He knew the name well—the Jewish historian turned Roman insider whose works were some of the only surviving records of Herod's reign and the fall of Jerusalem. But how much of it was truth, and how much had been carefully crafted to please his Roman benefactors? Josephus had been a master of walking the line between loyalty and survival, and his writings often left more questions than answers.

Herodium, too, was one of those lingering questions—a testament to Herod's paranoia and ambition. The fortified desert palace, built atop an artificial mountain, was both an extravagant retreat and a final resting place, rising above the Judean landscape and located just south of Jerusalem. If any of Herod's legendary wealth had been hidden away, the tunnels, storerooms, and secret chambers beneath Herodium would have been the obvious place.

Winston was intrigued not only by the subject but also by the man discussing it. He was sharp. Passionate.

"What do you make of his references to the treasures?" Winston asked, eager to hear Asher's thoughts.

"More like educated guesses," Asher replied. "Herod's wealth would have been immense. He amassed it through heavy taxation, control of lucrative trade routes, and the favor of Rome, which ensured a steady flow of resources. His construction projects alone—palaces, fortresses, and public works—speak to the scale of his financial power. It's hard to imagine just how much gold and wealth he accumulated during his reign. And honestly, I believe it's even more than what most estimates suggest. Herod was not only a master builder but also a shrewd strategist when it came to amassing resources—wealth on that scale is easy to underestimate."

"Fascinating," Winston said, his voice tinged with intrigue. "And do you think the gold is still hidden, intact, somewhere today? What about the rumors of later plunder—Crusader involvement or possibly Nazi expeditions during World War II?"

Asher let out a short laugh. "The Crusaders might have looted artifacts linked to Herod, but the evidence tying them to his treasure is thin. As for the Nazis, the stories are even flimsier. They were ambitious enough to try, but there's no solid proof they found anything related to Herod."

"Ah," Winston said lightly, "but you strike me as someone who wouldn't dismiss even the thinnest lead."

Asher smirked at the compliment. "Any information can be useful, but when it comes to Herod, it's not just about following the stories—it's about understanding the man. His treasure wasn't just a stockpile of gold. It was his statement of power, designed to outlast his enemies. He didn't just stash it somewhere random—it would have been somewhere deliberate, likely close to home."

"Close to home? Any idea where those locations might have been?" Winston asked with intrigue.

Asher considered his words carefully. "Masada is a strong possibility. Its location and fortifications made it an ideal fallback, but I'm not convinced it held the lion's share of his wealth. The Nabataeans, on the other hand, were Roman allies with vast trade networks and secure storage locations. If Herod needed to move something discreetly, they may have been his first choice."

“What about his other palaces?” Winston asked as he probed deeper.

"Perhaps," Asher said, his tone guarded. “But protecting his gold meant protecting his power. Herod didn’t take chances. He killed his wife and even his sons to secure his throne. You can bet, wherever he hid his wealth, it would have been in a place no one would dare disturb."

"Such as?" Winston prompted, leaving the question hanging in the air.

Asher paused in contemplation. “Herod was unpredictable, and that’s what truly deepens the mystery. Let’s just say there are theories that need a bit more digging—no pun intended.”

Winston chuckled softly on the other end. "I see the archaeologist in you hasn’t lost his sense of humor. But it’s the mystery that makes it so fascinating, isn’t it?" His voice lowered slightly as though he was sharing a secret.

“Agreed,” Asher answered softly.

"To me, Asher,” Winston said suddenly in a serious tone. “The idea that a treasure of this magnitude could still be waiting, untouched, after all these centuries—it’s exhilarating. And I believe someone like you is destined to be the one to finally uncover it."

The words filled Asher with a sense of pride, a rare acknowledgment of his years of hard work and dedication. Still, he tried to remain humble. "Maybe, but if it exists, it’s not just about the gold. Finding where and how he hid it—it’s the kind of discovery archaeologists dream of."

Winston listened intently, his interest piqued by Asher's words. "I couldn't agree more," he said finally. "And together, I believe we can unlock those mysteries—and perhaps even find the gold."

The way Winston said it felt deliberate, like he was dangling a carrot to see if Asher would bite. Despite their shared interests, the phrase tugged at something in Asher, prompting a question he couldn't ignore.

"So, you're more of a treasure hunter?" Asher asked with a hint of intrigue.

Winston laughed softly, his response light but with a hint of calculation. "Yes, of sorts. I believe it might actually be possible to find the treasure, and I'd like you to lead the team in searching for it."

Lead the team? Asher wasn't sure he had heard that correctly.

Before Asher could form his next question, Winston continued, "Let's table the conversation for now. When you visit, I'll outline my plan and you can see if you have any interest. No pressure, just an opportunity. Naturally, I'd prefer to discuss this face-to-face, perhaps at my residence in Boston. Would that be acceptable to you?"

The idea stirred a mix of emotions in Asher—excitement at the prospect of diving deeper into a mystery that had fascinated him for years, but also hesitation. *Why him?* Winston was clearly a man who could hire anyone, yet here he was, extending an invitation like it was a personal favor.

"I suppose I could make that work," Asher said cautiously, though his mind raced ahead to the possibilities.

Winston's chuckle on the other end of the line was warm but faintly knowing. "Tell you what, let me wire the funds to you in advance. Is that acceptable to you?"

How did this happen? Winston had preempted Asher's intentions, offering to wire the money before Asher could mention the topic. It seemed to confirm his suspicions that Winston was a hacker. But Asher had never put his thoughts about getting the money on his computer. It felt as though Winston could read his mind.

Asher realized he needed to respond and said, "Yes, that's fine." Then he asked, "But how do you know I will come?"

Winston confidently replied, "I fully trust you. Besides, as you see, we both have so much to gain from an alliance. Also, I can send you the money for your airfare if you'd rather book it yourself. First Class, of course."

Asher couldn't shake off the feeling of being outmaneuvered. *How did Winston anticipate his every move?* Trying not to sound dumbfounded, Asher replied, "Of course, whichever is fine."

Winston continued, "I assume weekends would suit you best, considering your teaching commitments?"

Once again, Asher was reminded that he was dealing with a highly intelligent and astute individual—someone who always seemed to be a step ahead. "Yes, weekends would be ideal," he concurred.

Winston proceeded, "And, of course, I'll take care of all accommodations here in Boston. But I have plenty of space at my home and would be delighted if you stayed here. It would afford us more time to discuss matters. However, I completely understand if you prefer other lodging."

At first, Asher was hesitant, still leery about Winston's actual plans, but he found himself surprisingly comfortable with Winston's proposition. There was a strange connection to him and a certain sincerity in Winston's tone that struck a chord with Asher, easing his doubts ever so slightly. Besides, Asher reasoned, he had ventured into far riskier situations in the past than visiting a house in Boston.

With a newfound sense of resolve, Asher made up his mind to proceed with caution but also to keep an open mind about what lay ahead. After all, every adventure carried risks, but sometimes the greatest rewards awaited those who dared to take them.

Asher boldly replied, "Your offer is generous, Winston, and I appreciate it. Staying at your home would indeed provide us with more time for discussions. I accept your invitation and look forward to our meeting."

"Very well," Winston replied smoothly. "Natalie, my assistant, will handle the arrangements. She'll contact you on your cell phone. Is that all right with you?"

Asher, trying to remain calm, said, "Yes, that's fine." After Asher shared his cell number, Winston concluded, "Well, I look forward to seeing you soon."

As they hung up, Asher felt a renewed sense of purpose. What had started as a day of frustration and uncertainty had ended with the promise of hope.

For the first time, he felt like the gods were on *his* side.

The Flight

As Asher settled into his plush seat in first class, he couldn't help but revel in the luxurious surroundings. Although Asher had flown first class before, he still felt a sense of accomplishment. While he had utilized his frequent flyer miles to upgrade in the past, this time someone else was covering the entire cost. The flight attendant greeted him with a warm smile, her eyes sparkling with hospitality. "Can I get you something to drink?" she inquired.

Returning her smile, Asher replied, "How about a glass of champagne? I feel like celebrating."

Momentarily, she returned with a glass of bubbly. "Thank you," Asher said, accepting the drink with a nod of appreciation. She had a radiant beauty that caught his eye. As she moved away, Asher found himself lost in thought, his mind wandering to the possibility of finding someone who could captivate him as Rita once had. One thing he knew for sure—if he ever did, he would be more guarded in his choice.

As passengers continued to board the plane, Asher's focus turned to his destination, Boston. He had informed several of his colleagues at the University about his trip; however, he hadn't disclosed the full details of his journey, keeping the more sensitive aspects to himself. On the notepad where he'd previously jotted down Winston's name and phone number, he added the address, creating a breadcrumb trail for safety reasons.

Oddly, memories of his grandfather filled Asher's mind, and he yearned for the calming presence his grandfather once provided. If only he were still around, Asher knew that many of his challenges with his parents would most likely not exist. Perhaps it was time for him to embody more of his grandfather's peacemaking spirit.

Asher felt compelled to call his mother. He remembered how, even during the challenging years, he always called her before departing on a trip. She had always been his biggest fan, listening intently as Asher described his upcoming adventures. He knew they all shared blame for their fragile relationship, but Asher also recognized that much of the fault lay with him.

It was time to change that. It was time to call his mother.

As she answered the phone, Asher's heart raced with anticipation.

"Hello?" came her tender voice.

"Hey, Mom," Asher greeted with a hint of emotion.

There was a moment of silence before his mother's voice, filled with both surprise and concern, responded, "Asher, is everything okay?"

"Yes, Mom, everything's fine," Asher reassured her, his voice faltering slightly. "I just wanted to let you know I'm taking a business trip to Boston. I'll be staying with a colleague."

His mother's voice carried a hint of concern as she responded, "You're going to Boston? What for?"

Asher paused, debating how much to disclose. "Just some work related things," he replied vaguely. "I'll call you when I get back and tell you all about it."

His mother's voice brightened with delight. "Oh, Asher, that would be wonderful," she said warmly. "How long will you be gone?"

"Just for the weekend, Mom," Asher replied reassuringly. "I'll be back Sunday." As they ended their conversation, Asher couldn't shake the weight of guilt that settled over him. He was their only child, and he had brought heartache to the parents he loved deeply. Reflecting on their strained relationship, he realized that repairing his bond with his mom would likely be easier than with his dad. Asher found himself pondering the irony of how a faith meant to unite often ended up dividing.

As the plane made its way to the runway and the engines roared to life, Asher's thoughts were interrupted by the anticipation of the journey ahead. Next stop: Boston and the pursuit of lost treasure.

Raising his glass in a toast to himself, he took a sip of champagne and allowed himself to dream of what awaited him.

The Car Ride

As Asher disembarked from the plane into the terminal, a chauffeur awaited him, holding a sign with the name "Meyer." Since it would be a quick trip, Asher had brought his bag on board. The chauffeur graciously took his bag and led him to a limo waiting just outside the airport.

Stepping out of the airport doors, Asher encountered the chill of a Boston winter. Despite the overcast skies, he could tell the sun was setting, and the temperature lingered in the low 20s with a brisk wind. Though it didn't seem to be snowing, a layer of snow covered the ground. This was quite different from the weather he had left in Jerusalem, where the temps were in the low 60s.

Thankfully, the limo was conveniently parked nearby, and the chauffeur opened the door, allowing Asher to step into the warmth of the back seat. Before closing the door, the chauffeur informed him, "It will be a 45-minute drive, sir. Please relax and enjoy yourself." As the door closed, Asher couldn't help but notice a bottle of champagne chilling in an ice bucket. Retrieving the champagne, he read the label – Dom Pérignon Brut Champagne 2010. *This guy really spares no expense,* Asher mused, as the limo smoothly pulled away.

Behind the tinted windows, it was challenging for Asher to discern their exact destination, especially since he was unfamiliar with the Boston area. Before long, the limo had transported them out of the city and into the countryside. Asher, mindful not to consume the entire bottle of champagne, savored a bit more than half of it. Having slept most of the flight, he was excited about finally meeting Winston face-to-face and learning more about the mysterious man.

Even if the talk of finding treasure was just a bunch of hot air, maybe he could get Winston to help find the right publisher and fund the publicity needed to make his book a success. Winston seemed to possess the two vital elements Asher needed: money and connections.

Asher was still determining where this journey would lead, but he was confident it would be memorable.

Secrets Within

The limo pulled up in front of a home almost precisely 45 minutes after leaving the airport, just as the chauffeur had promised. From the front, the chauffeur said, "We have arrived, sir." It was when the chauffeur opened the door that Asher really could see where he had arrived. This was no ordinary home. At least that is not how Asher would have described it; chateau was a far better fit. The architectural complexity made it challenging to determine if it stood two or three stories high. Snow began to fall again, adding to the two inches of powder already on the ground.

Fortunately, the drive and walkway had been cleared. The chauffeur retrieved Asher's bag and escorted him to the front door. Before they could knock, the door swung open, revealing a woman. Her beauty momentarily took Asher by surprise. Was this the same woman he had spoken to on the phone while making travel arrangements? With her light complexion and sandy hair cascading in waves, high cheekbones, slender nose, piercing blue eyes, and full lips, Natalie possessed an undeniable allure. She wore minimal makeup, her natural beauty requiring no enhancement. Her figure was equally striking, and her attire gracefully accentuated her curves. Standing about five feet seven inches tall with a slender waist, her well-toned shoulders, arms, and legs hinted at a dedication to regular exercise. This trip was turning out to be full of surprises.

"Are you Natalie?" Asher asked.

"Yes, please come in," she replied.

Realizing his job was complete, the chauffeur retreated to the limo and drove away.

Asher walked into the grand foyer and continued to take it all in. The room was massive, even by foyer standards, and contained entrances to three rooms, two hallways, and a grand staircase ascending to the second story.

"You may leave your bag here," she continued, pointing to an area next to the door. "Mr. Saunders is waiting for you in the study. This way, please." Gracefully, she led him into a room off the foyer.

It was a large room with a high ceiling. The floors were wooden, as were the walls. In the center of the ceiling hung a large chandelier that provided light for the room, although it appeared deliberately dimmed. One wall was lined entirely with bookshelves, while the others displayed oversized paintings. The collection appeared to be by the great masters—Rembrandt's *The Abduction of Europa*, Sandro Botticelli's *The Birth of Venus*, and Leonardo da Vinci's *Mona Lisa* were among those that stood out. French doors framed by windows occupied one wall, their heavy curtains drawn back. On a console table near one of the windows rested *The Bust of Nefertiti.*

Other wooden console tables were scattered throughout the room, each showcasing a variety of artifacts spanning nearly every era of history. Asher immediately recognized pieces from the Middle Ages, and some even appeared to date back to prehistoric times. All these items had to be either replicas or reproductions, but it was still an archeologist's dream.

The room's focal point was a large fireplace set into the most prominent wall. A fire crackled inside, its warm glow casting flickering shadows across the space. Seated before it in a wheelchair was a man, his eyes fixed on the flames.

"Sir, your guest has arrived," Natalie announced.

The man turned his gaze toward Asher and slowly rose from his chair. To Asher, he looked frail and delicate. Winston extended a slightly trembling hand. "Welcome, Asher," he said, his voice steady but aged.

Asher accepted the handshake, careful not to apply too much pressure. "A pleasure to finally meet you, sir," he replied with a polite nod.

"Please, sit," Winston said, gesturing towards a lone chair positioned by a small wooden table. On the table sat a wine decanter and two empty glasses. Asher eased into the chair, his eyes briefly glancing at Natalie.

Winston carefully settled back into his wheelchair. Once seated, he adjusted his posture and took hold of the chair's wheels, guiding himself to the table.

Winston signaled for Natalie to pour the wine. She obliged, filling both glasses before returning the decanter to its place on the table.

"That will be all for now," Winston said, glancing at her. "Please have our meal prepared in 15 minutes."

Natalie nodded in acknowledgment and quietly exited the room, leaving Asher and Winston alone.

Asher considered himself a wine connoisseur and began to examine the glass. It was a red wine that pleased the eye, and Asher quickly evaluated it without appearing to be a snob.

Winston picked up his glass and said, "I trust your flight was enjoyable."

"As much as twelve hours of flying can be," Asher responded with a smile.

Winston lifted his glass for a toast, "Well, here's to an enjoyable evening."

Smiling, Asher nodded in agreement and gently touched his glass to Winston's. They both took a small sip. The wine was smooth and full-bodied. Thus far, everything about this visit had been remarkable, and he had little reason to doubt it would continue in the same fashion.

Glancing around the room, Asher remarked, "You have quite a collection."

"Yes," Winston replied, a glint of pride in his eyes. "We probably have more in common than you realize regarding antiquities and such."

"Are you a collector?" Asher asked, his curiosity piqued.

"You might say that," Winston said with a knowing grin. "Actually, I dabble in archaeology myself – strictly as a novice, of course. Nothing like your level of expertise. Please, feel free to have a look around the room."

Asher took Winston up on the offer and decided to start with the paintings. The urge to inspect the artifacts right away tempted him, but he figured it was best to play it cool. Approaching the *Mona Lisa*, he studied it closely before moving on to the other works. While he wasn't an art expert, it was clear these were exceptionally well-made reproductions.

Eventually, his attention shifted to the *Bust of Nefertiti*. He was well acquainted with the original, having seen it in person at the Neues Museum in Berlin.

He also knew this piece was one of the most frequently replicated artifacts in the world. Scholars have even questioned the authenticity of the original.

As if reading his thoughts, Winston's voice cut through the quiet. "Go ahead, Asher. Pick it up. Take a closer look."

With deliberate care, Asher lifted the bust, half-expecting it to feel hollow like most replicas. But it wasn't. Its weight suggested it was solid, far heavier than he anticipated.

"She's one of my favorites, too," Winston remarked, watching him closely.

Asher returned the bust to its spot on the console table, ensuring it was perfectly centered. On a nearby table, his eyes landed on another familiar piece—the *Peking Man*. Since the original had disappeared, he recognized this as another reproduction. But it wasn't alone. Asher's gaze swept the room, his mind racing as he tallied over a dozen of the most iconic artifacts in history, each displayed as if it belonged there.

"Where did you acquire all of these?" Asher asked, unable to mask his curiosity.

"Here and there," Winston replied with a grin.

Asher continued through the room until he arrived at the French doors. Peering through the glass, he found himself looking out onto a snow-covered balcony. Though clearly designed for relaxation in warmer months, the area was now blanketed in white, the outdoor furniture barely visible beneath it.

To his surprise, the snowfall had ceased, and the clouds had lifted, revealing a full moon that cast a silver glow over the landscape. The estate's backyard stretched before him, sloping gently toward what appeared to be a large pond or small lake. Being the adventurous type, Asher would love to explore this area more, but that would have to wait until a future trip and better weather.

As Asher continued gazing through the window, Winston's voice interrupted his thoughts. "Enough about me; let's talk about why you came—your book."

Returning to the table, Asher took another sip of wine.

"As I mentioned before, I think you're onto something," Winston said, his eyes sharp with intent. "I believe the lost treasure can be found and claimed. And, Asher" — he leaned forward slightly — "I believe together we can do exactly that."

Asher thought, *Ah, we're getting to it quickly.*

"I agree, but I have to be honest—this won't be easy or cheap," he replied, probing to see just how much Winston was willing to invest in the project.

"Under most circumstances, I'd agree with you," Winston replied, leaning back slightly in his wheelchair. "But in this case, I believe it is more affordable than you might think."

Asher tilted his head slightly, the comment catching him off guard. "I'm not sure I follow," he admitted, his tone laced with curiosity.

Winston smiled like a Cheshire cat, his voice calm and enigmatic. "Yes, I'm sure you don't. But I'm sure you'd agree that finding the treasure would be easy—if only one could return to that time in history and learn its whereabouts."

The words lingered in the air like a riddle, and Asher's mind churned, trying to grasp what Winston was implying. Was he speaking metaphorically, or did his words hint at something more literal?

"But for now," Winston said, his tone shifting as he took hold of his chair's wheels, "it's time for dinner. Come with me."

Dinner is Served

Asher followed Winston to the nearby dining room, where Natalie finished arranging the table. The polished silverware gleamed under the soft glow of the chandelier, and the crystal glasses sparkled with anticipation. A delicate aroma drifted through the room, hinting at the culinary delights awaiting them.

Natalie stepped back from the table, her expression poised and professional. "Please, have a seat," she said to Asher, gesturing towards the plush chairs. "Dinner will be served shortly."

Taking his cue, Asher settled into his seat, marveling at the exquisite surroundings. The room exuded an air of sophistication and refinement, perfectly complementing the estate's grandeur.

Winston wheeled himself to the head of the table. Asher observed only two place settings, indicating the meal would be for just the two of them.

As they settled into their places, Winston leaned back, his eyes alight with a glint of memory. "This house," he began, his voice tinged with nostalgia, "has a storied history that stretches back well over a century."

Asher leaned forward, eager to hear more. "If only the walls could talk, huh?" he joked.

Winston nodded, a faint smile playing on his lips. "Indeed. It was built in the late 19th century by the illustrious Vanderbilt family," he explained. "They spared no expense in its construction, importing the finest materials from around the world."

"As one of the wealthiest and most influential American dynasties, they were known for their opulent lifestyle, with lavish parties that became hallmarks of the Gilded Age," Winston continued, his tone rich with mystery. "But one of my favorites took place here in 1902. President Theodore Roosevelt was said to have been a guest here. Are you familiar with him?"

Asher, well-versed in history from around the world, gave a slight nod of recognition and replied, "Yes, of course—Teddy Roosevelt, I believe most called him."

Winston's eyes gleamed with amusement. "Ah, yes, yes indeed. But do you know where he got the 'Teddy 'moniker?" he asked, tilting his head slightly.

Asher's eyes darted around as he thought before answering, "No, I don't believe I do."

"Quite the story, actually, and legend has it that this house played a part in it," Winston said with delight as if revealing a well-guarded secret. "Roosevelt was quite the outdoorsman and an avid hunter. While on a guided bear hunt in Mississippi, he refused to shoot a bear that his guide had tied to a tree. Seems he deemed it unsportsmanlike. Shortly afterward, a political cartoon appeared showing the president on the hunt, with a small bear tied to a rope."

Asher raised an eyebrow and said, "I'm sure it's safe to assume that Roosevelt didn't find it funny."

Winston grinned, shook his head and replied, "Actually, quite the opposite. Roosevelt thought it portrayed him as a fair and ethical hunter."

"But I'm not seeing the connection to the house," Asher said, confused.

Winston straightened, his voice continuing with a storyteller's cadence. "Well, it's said that a grand Christmas gala was held that year, and Roosevelt was in attendance. Thinking it would create a good laugh, the host presented the president with a stuffed bear, a Teddy Bear if you would. Supposedly, the bear was handmade by a local artisan and given as a symbolic gesture of respect for his compassion."

Winston's gaze lingered on the ornate ceiling as if conjuring images from the past. "The story goes that Roosevelt laughed heartily and told the guests, 'Perhaps there's something to this!' At the end of the evening, the hosts distributed small bear replicas to the guests as keepsakes. Whether this event truly inspired the Teddy Bear we know today is uncertain. Some say fact, others mere legend."

A slow smile crept across Asher's face as he considered the story. He leaned forward slightly. "And you? Are you in the fact or legend camp?"

Winston returned his gaze to Asher, his eyes glinting with amusement. "Mainly, I just enjoy the story. And never let the truth get in the way of a good story, my friend."

Asher grinned with a spark of amusement in his eyes. "There's a similar old Jewish saying: 'A good story can warm the heart better than the truth.'"

As the men shared a chuckle, Natalie reappeared, wheeling in a gleaming silver tray laden with plates of seared Chilean sea bass, accompanied by a medley of roasted vegetables and a delicate lemon butter sauce. The aroma was tantalizing, and Asher's mouth watered in anticipation.

Natalie delicately placed the completed plate in front of Asher.

"I trust you like fish?" Winston inquired, a hint of anticipation in his voice.

Asher's eyes lit up at the sight of the dish. Fish, especially sea bass, was among his favorite meals. "Yes, very much so," he answered eagerly.

Winston's smile broadened as he raised his glass in a toast. "Bon appétit," he exclaimed, his words resonating with excitement. "To new beginnings and exciting adventures—the kind legends are made of."

As they clinked glasses, Asher noticed the change in wine, a glorious white that perfectly complemented the flaky fish. He couldn't help but wonder about the spectacular wine cellar that must be somewhere in the house.

As they savored the exquisite meal, Winston subtly guided the conversation. "You know, Asher," he remarked casually between bites, "time has a curious way of shaping our destinies. One moment can alter the course of history forever."

Asher nodded thoughtfully, intrigued by Winston's cryptic words. "Yes, it's fascinating how the smallest actions can have the greatest impact," he agreed as he sipped wine.

Winston smiled, his eyes gleaming with hidden knowledge. "Indeed," he said with a mysterious tone. "But what if I told you that time itself was not as immutable as we once believed?"

Asher looked puzzled. "What do you mean?" he asked as he placed his fork on his plate.

Winston hesitated for a moment before carefully considering his words. "Imagine a world where the past and the future are not fixed points in time but rather fluid possibilities waiting to be explored," he mused as he took a bite of fish.

Asher suddenly began to wonder if Winston was some type of mad scientist. He sure sounded like one.

Realizing Asher was a more pragmatic man, Winston shifted the conversation back to Asher. "Ah yes, the ever-so-simple mysteries of time," he said smoothly. "But I'm curious to hear more about your archaeological expeditions. Which one was your favorite?"

Asher paused, reflecting on the various digs he had participated in over the years. "One of the most memorable experiences I had was about ten years ago when I had the opportunity to work on an excavation in the Valley of the Kings in Egypt," he began. "We were investigating some lesser-known tombs in the area, hoping to uncover artifacts that would shed light on the lives of the nobles buried there."

As he spoke, Asher's eyes lit up with excitement as he recalled the thrill of uncovering ancient treasures. "We didn't find anything as spectacular as the treasures of Tutankhamun, of course," he continued, "but the sheer history and mystery surrounding the site made it an unforgettable experience."

Winston nodded thoughtfully. "Interesting," he remarked. "I've been to the Valley of the Kings myself, although it was many years ago." He paused as if lost in thought before adding, "It's a place that holds many secrets, wouldn't you agree?"

Asher raised an eyebrow, intrigued by Winston's comment. "Yes, absolutely," he replied. "There's still so much we don't know about the ancient Egyptians and their burial practices."

As they savored the meal, Natalie periodically checked on their progress. Her demeanor was professional and efficient. She cleared away the empty plates and appeared oblivious to the conversation unfolding between Asher and Winston.

Despite her businesslike demeanor, Asher was intrigued by Natalie's presence. Something about her hinted at a depth of knowledge and experience beyond her role as a mere assistant and nurse. But try as he might, Asher couldn't quite put his finger on what made her so fascinating.

After they finished their meal, Winston gestured toward the hallway. "Shall we continue our conversation downstairs?" he suggested, his tone casual yet tinged with a hint of mystery.

Asher nodded, intrigued by what Winston might have to show him in the basement. "Of course," he replied, following Winston as they made their way down the hallway. For once, Asher felt like he was one step ahead of Winston. He was about to be taken to the wine cellar.

As they approached a sturdy-looking door at the end of the hallway, Asher grew in anticipation about what lay beyond. Winston reached out and pressed a button on the wall, causing the door to slide slowly open, revealing a small elevator.

Winston politely motioned for Asher to enter first. Asher stepped inside, and Winston followed, effortlessly wheeling his chair into the compact space.

As the elevator descended, Asher felt anticipation build within him. He couldn't shake the feeling that he was about to discover something truly remarkable.

When the elevator finally stopped and the doors slid open, Asher found himself standing in a well-lit basement. But instead of the wine cellar he had expected, he was greeted by an array of high-tech equipment and machinery.

The Laboratory

As Asher surveyed the room, he realized it was not a wine cellar but a laboratory. Strange machinery was scattered throughout and connected by a jumble of wires. Computer mainframes and multiple monitors were interconnected, suggesting some type of highly sophisticated system. A growing sense of unease crept over him as he tried to make sense of it all.

Winston approached the control panel and typed a few keys that brought the computer screen to life. The screen illuminated with a soft glow as Winston leaned closer and placed his eye before a scanner, which began performing a retina scan to verify his identity. A series of intricate patterns danced across the display. After a moment, the screen flashed green, and the computer mainframe sprang to life. With practiced ease, Winston began inputting commands. Asher's confusion only deepened as he tried to make sense of what he was seeing.

Then, to Asher's astonishment, he heard Winston's voice, slightly muffled by the machinery's hum. "This is my time machine," Winston declared, his tone matter-of-fact yet tinged with a hint of excitement.

Asher blinked, certain that he must have misheard. *A time machine?* It sounded like something out of a science fiction novel, not something that could exist in the real world.

"Time machine?" he echoed, his tone laced with disbelief.

For a long moment, silence hung between them, and Asher's mind scrambled for an explanation. This had to be a joke. A setup. Another tall tell or wild story.

Then, suddenly, Asher laughed. "Don't let the truth get in the way of a good story, right?" he said, wagging a finger at Winston, amused by the absurdity of it all.

But Winston simply smiled, entirely at ease. "No, I'm completely serious. And I'm about to prove it to you," he said, his voice carrying an unsettling confidence.

Prove it? Asher thought, *prove it how?*

A chill ran down his spine as reality set in. He was in a strange basement with a man he hardly knew—one he had already likened to a mad scientist. And now, Winston was talking exactly like one. His eyes darted to the door, instinctively mapping an escape route in case Winston's next move proved as unpredictable as his words.

Sensing Asher's unease, Winston's expression softened. He nodded understandingly.

"I fully understand your concern and skepticism, Asher. You may leave if you want," Winston said as he motioned towards the door.

Asher stood frozen—part of him wanted to flee, yet another part couldn't. Like a moth drawn to a flame, his curiosity anchored him in place. If this was some sort of joke, Winston had gone to extreme measures to pull it off. The sheer amount of electronics and equipment hinted at something more sincere.

Feeling Asher's internal battle, Winston continued, "Please, give me a chance to fully explain."

Asher exhaled, shaking his head. "I must admit, what you're suggesting is implausible, to say the least. But I'll give you a chance to prove yourself," he said, crossing his arms with a skeptical smile.

"Very well, I accept your challenge," Winston replied, his face completely serious.

Asher tried to appear calm, but his mind raced with a million questions, doubts, and uncertainties, all swirling around like a storm. With a mixture of fear, doubt, and curiosity, Asher prepared himself for the conversation ahead, unsure of what he would discover.

Winston gestured towards the array of machinery before them, his eyes alight like those of a proud father. "You see, Asher," he began, "this time machine is the culmination of years of research, experimentation, and innovation."

He paused and gathered his thoughts. "It all started with a simple idea – an idea that time, like any other dimension, is not fixed, but rather fluid, capable of being manipulated and traversed."

Asher listened intently, his doubts momentarily overshadowed by a growing sense of fascination. "But how is that possible?" he interjected.

Winston smiled, his eyes crinkling at the corners. "Ah, that's the question, isn't it?" he replied. "You see, I began by studying the principles of quantum mechanics, exploring the intricacies of space-time and the nature of reality itself."

He gestured towards the screen before them. "Using advanced algorithms and cutting-edge technology, I developed a system that could manipulate the very fabric of time itself."

Asher's mind reeled at the implications of Winston's words. *Could it be possible? Could time travel truly exist?* "But how does it work?" he pressed, his voice barely above a whisper.

Winston chuckled softly as if relishing the opportunity to share his knowledge. "The key lies in synchronizing the machine with the temporal fluctuations of the universe," he explained. "By harnessing the energy of these fluctuations, we create a temporal vortex—a gateway through the corridors of time. But the real question isn't how it works, but rather that it *does* work."

His eyes gleamed with a mixture of scientific curiosity and a hint of mischief.

Asher's eyes widened in astonishment. "So, you're saying that this machine can actually transport someone through time?" he asked with a tinged with awe.

Winston nodded with pride. "Indeed," he replied. "But it's not without its risks. Time travel is a delicate and dangerous endeavor, fraught with unforeseen consequences."

Asher struggled to comprehend Winston's words. It was as if he had stumbled into a place of make-believe, where the boundaries of reality and fantasy blurred. One thing was clearly apparent: the old man was either mad or a genius. Asher didn't know which one was true, but he reasoned he was about to find out. Besides, the thought of time travel was exhilarating, to say the least.

Winston, noticing Asher's thoughtful expression, leaned forward in his wheelchair. "Like I said, I understand your skepticism, Asher," he began, his voice steady and resolute. "If I were you, I wouldn't believe it either. But I assure you, this is no mere flight of fancy. What you're seeing is real—*very real.*"

As Winston spoke, Asher couldn't help but feel a glimmer of doubt creeping into his mind. The idea of time travel seemed too fantastic, too far-fetched to be taken seriously. And yet, there was something in Winston's demeanor, a steadfast conviction that resonated with Asher on a deeper level.

"But why reveal this to me now?" Asher asked, his voice betraying a hint of uncertainty. "Why entrust me with such a monumental secret?"

Winston regarded Asher with a knowing look, his gaze piercing and intense. "Because, Asher," he replied with sincerity, "I believe that you possess the intellect, the passion, and the integrity to understand the significance of what lies before you. And more importantly, I believe that you have the courage to embark on this journey with me."

Asher felt conflicting emotions coursing through him—fear and excitement, doubt and curiosity. The prospect of delving into the mysteries of time itself was both exhilarating and daunting, a leap into the unknown that held the promise of untold wonders and unimaginable dangers.

Without another word, Winston began typing on a computer keyboard, and shortly after, a portal appeared on the far side of the room. "Let's stop all the conjecture and get to the proof. And there's all the proof you will need," Winston said, gesturing for Asher to step into it.

Asher stood still, his arms crossed tightly. "Where does it go?" he asked, his voice laced with hesitation.

"To a safe place," Winston answered. "You'll be able to come back whenever you're ready.

Asher took a deep breath as his pulse quickened. He stepped back, shaking his head slightly as questions surged through him. *Somewhere safe? What does that even mean? Is this real? Is Winston out of his mind? Am I?*

He stared into the strange blur of the portal, mesmerized yet deeply unnerved by its dangers and mystery.

"This... this isn't what I signed up for," Asher muttered, rubbing the back of his neck. "This is insane. I need more than just your word that it's safe. What if something goes wrong? What if I can't come back?"

"You've spent your life chasing answers," Winston said, his voice measured, almost fatherly. "You've uncovered truths buried beneath centuries of dirt and dust. But this—this is the ultimate excavation, Asher. To begin this journey, you must boldly step forward. No more maps. No more theories. Just action."

Asher hesitated, torn between fear and temptation. He had always prided himself on being adventurous and willing to take risks others wouldn't dare. But this was different. It wasn't about boldness—it was about wisdom.

The portal loomed before him, a doorway to either a dream or a nightmare. The allure of its power and the promise of adventure beckoned him. The fantasy of every man, woman, and child stood right in front of him.

"I know you have more questions than answers, but this is the moment where you have to decide to trust," Winston stated calmly. "Or not. If this feels wrong, we can stop now, and you can walk away."

"What happens if I don't go?" Asher asked as he exhaled slowly.

"Then nothing," Winston replied simply. "You return to your life as it is. But the regret? That stays. Some choices come only once."

The reassurance followed by Winston's challenge only deepened Asher's internal struggle. This wasn't like choosing a new dig site or writing a paper. This was something he couldn't fully understand or control. "And you're sure it's safe?" he pressed.

Winston nodded, "Perfectly. But the choice is still yours."

Asher took a step closer to the portal. Every instinct screamed at him to turn back, but another part of him whispered that his destiny lay on the other side. "This is crazy," he muttered under his breath.

"Perhaps," Winston said. "But isn't that what makes it worth doing?"

Asher hesitated at the edge of the portal and cast a final glance at Winston, who nodded in silent encouragement.

"I hope I don't regret this later," Asher said as he forced a small, nervous smile.

Asher steeled himself and stepped into the portal. The sensation was strange—like stepping through a curtain of water, though he remained completely dry. A shiver ran down his spine as the world around him blurred and shifted.

And then, in the blink of an eye, he was gone.

As he emerged on the other side, Asher stood in front of the bookcase in the study they had just left earlier, but something was undeniably different. The room was decorated in a manner that felt both familiar and foreign, with many of the artifacts and paintings that had adorned the walls now conspicuously absent.

The absence of the roaring fire in the fireplace and the significantly brighter ambiance of the room caught Asher off guard, too. It wasn't the chandelier providing the additional light but rather the natural sunlight streaming through the French doors and windows.

Confused, Asher made his way over to the doors, a surge of bewilderment coursing through him as he took in the sight before him. Gone was the blanket of snow that had covered the ground, replaced instead by lush green grass and the warmth of the sun's rays.

In the distance, he could see the shimmering surface of a pond, its tranquil waters reflecting the brilliant blue of the sky above. Seated at the table on the balcony he had seen earlier was someone with their back towards him.

Opening the door, Asher cautiously stepped onto the balcony, greeted by the unexpected warmth of what felt like a pleasant summer morning. The temperature hovered somewhere in the mid-70s—at least fifty degrees warmer than when he had arrived. As he stood, taking it all in, the figure seated at the table slowly turned, revealing a striking resemblance to Winston. A mixture of confusion and disbelief clouded Asher's mind as he hesitantly approached the table, uncertain of what to make of the surreal scene unfolding before him.

Winston's broad grin only added to Asher's bewilderment as he gestured for Asher to join him at the table. "I see you've arrived, welcome," he said. "Surprising, isn't it? Please, take a seat," Winston said as he motioned towards a chair.

Still grappling with the strangeness of it all, Asher moved cautiously toward the table, his eyes darting around the balcony as if searching for some hidden explanation. Each step felt heavier than the last, but he lowered himself into the chair despite his unease.

"This is a glimpse into the past, a different time," Winston explained. "The time machine isn't just a device; it's a doorway to history."

Asher's mind raced with disbelief, struggling to comprehend the implications of Winston's words. This had to be some elaborate trick, he reasoned, a figment of his imagination brought on by exhaustion or too much alcohol. Or maybe he had been drugged. There had to be some other explanation for what he was perceiving.

Before he could fully collect his thoughts, a surge of panic coursed through Asher. Pushing himself up from the chair with unsteady legs, he hurried back inside, reentering the study. He made a beeline for the door leading out of the study, gripped the handle, and twisted it – but it didn't budge. The door was locked.

He yanked on the handle one more time, his breath coming in short, shallow bursts. "Come on, come on," he muttered through gritted teeth. His pulse pounded in his ears as he continued twisting and pulling. It didn't move.

He turned to see Winston, who had wheeled himself into the study and was blocking the other exit from the room. To Asher, it felt like Winston was a predator watching its prey, waiting for it to wear itself out. His hand lingered on the doorknob, giving it another twist, but it didn't budge. "Dammit," he muttered under his breath.

Speaking almost to himself, Winston reminisced, "I remember my first time too. My reaction was somewhat different, though. I had been working on time travel for years and couldn't believe it really worked."

Asher totally ignored Winston's words. He was too busy trying to process it all. Was this some kind of game? Some twisted psychological trap? "This is insane," he whispered to himself, backing away from the door. "Completely insane."

"Please, try to relax," Winston said gently, raising his hands in a placating gesture. "I understand that what you just experienced was... disorienting."

Asher's patience wore thin. He raised his voice, his tone sharp with frustration. "Look, old man, I don't know what this is, but you can drop the act. I'm leaving this room one way or another."

"True," Winston replied with a knowing smirk. "But I'm afraid you can't leave any way other than how you entered. It's for your safety, of course." His words were calm, but they hung heavy in the air.

Asher's eyes darted toward the balcony door. His gaze lingered there for a moment, calculating. The old man couldn't stop him from leaving that way. He could shove Winston's wheelchair aside if it came to it. But something about Winston's unwavering calm made him hesitate. What else was he hiding?

He glanced at the portal again; its glow seemed more intense than before. "I'm not sure what's happening here, but I'm not going back through that," Asher declared with a firm voice.

"Do you know why you're here, Asher?" Winston's voice was calm and measured, like a parent explaining the world to a child. "You came here for answers. You came here to prove to them all that you were right. The treasure. The truth. Your legacy. You came here for it all, didn't you?" He leaned forward, his eyes locked on Asher's like two points of gravity pulling him in. "That's why you have to walk back through the portal. It's all waiting for you on the other side."

Something about the way Winston spoke the words reminded him of his father. How he often tried to manipulate Asher. But another part of him knew Winston's words were true. He wanted to validate his book and himself as a knowledgeable archeologist. As much as he hated to admit it, Winston was right.

Winston continued gently, in a trusting tone, "Please, walk back through the portal, and I'll explain it all to you."

After what felt like an eternity, Asher's resolve crumbled. His fists, once tightly clenched at his sides, slowly relaxed. His eyes locked onto the portal, unblinking, as his breathing steadied into a slow, deliberate rhythm. His heart still pounded like a distant drum, but his mind had gone quiet—eerily quiet. It was the stillness that follows a violent storm—the unsettling calm when the winds die and the world holds its breath, waiting for what comes next.

With a soft but firm voice, Winston extended a hand toward the portal. "Please."

"To hell with it," he muttered, his voice barely more than a whisper.

With a final breath, he took the second biggest risk of his life and stepped back through the portal.

The Explanation

Emerging from the portal, Asher stepped back into the laboratory, his senses still reeling from the disorienting journey through time. The events of the past moments seemed surreal, like fragments of a dream that refused to fade with waking.

Winston watched Asher closely, concerned about how he might react to his trip through time. Asher immediately sat on the floor just outside the portal, trying to process his thoughts.

After a moment, Winston broke the silence. "Well, Asher, how was your trip?" he inquired.

Asher continued processing the event before saying, "It was..." Slowly, reality sat in. "But you know, because you were there, waiting for me."

Winston nodded knowingly. "Yes, and now I'm *here* with you," he remarked, a faint smile playing at the corners of his lips.

Asher rose to his feet, crossed the room, and sank into a nearby chair. His mind continued to reel from the weight of his recent journey through time.

"Asher, I know you have many questions," Winston remarked, watching Asher struggle to gather his composure. "Let's retire to my study, and I'll answer all the questions I know you have."

With that invitation, Winston turned off the machine and began to wheel himself back towards the elevator. However, Asher remained seated, lost in his own contemplation. Winston paused at the doorway, noticing Asher's hesitation. He rolled back to Asher's side and spoke with calm reassurance, "What you're experiencing is totally normal. I asked you to trust me, and you did. Now, I ask you to trust me again."

With those words, Winston turned and headed back toward the elevator, leaving Asher to wrestle with his own uncertainties and decide on his next course of action.

'I'll be in the study when you're ready,' Winston declared over his shoulder, his voice reassuring as he continued toward the elevator.

Alone in the lab, Asher's mind was full of questions and disbelief. He still believed it was some kind of trick, a secret door or clever illusion. However, Asher was aware that they had descended at least one story when using the elevator. The distance he covered in mere steps between the laboratory and the study defied any physical possibilities he could comprehend.

Ah, an identical room; that explains it, Asher thought. *The old man has created an identical room of the study and built it next to the lab. That had to be it.*

It occurred to him that the old man was quite the magician. But the weather, how could he change the weather? He had clearly stepped outside and witnessed the drastic change himself. And more shocking still—it had been daytime, not night! As much as he hated to admit it, this was no magician's trick; what he had experienced was real. He had time-traveled, but how?

After about ten minutes, Asher regained his composure and made his way to the study where Winston awaited him. "So, Asher, let me explain what happened," Winston began confidently. "You traveled back six months in time."

Asher's mind raced as he tried to process Winston's words. *Six months?* That explained the change in the weather. Evidently, this event had been orchestrated for months, perhaps even longer.

“So you have the ability to go to any past event you want?” Asher asked curiously.

"For the most part, yes, but it's not just that simple," Winston replied, sensing Asher's desire to fully understand. He also knew that too much information too soon would only confuse him more.

“I know what you're thinking," Winston continued, trying to reassure Asher. "Despite the fear and confusion you felt earlier, you know what you experienced was real.”

Asher nodded slowly. "I do," he admitted.

Winston's gaze became serious, and his voice filled with caution. “There are countless dangers associated with time travel,” Winston warned. "Time travel isn't just a journey through history; it's a venture into the unknown, fraught with dangers that most people can't even begin to comprehend."

Asher listened intently as he tried to understand. "What kind of dangers?" he inquired with a mix of curiosity and apprehension.

Winston shifted in his chair, his eyes reflecting a lifetime of knowledge and experience. "First and foremost, there's the risk of altering the course of history," he explained. "Every action we take in the past has the potential to ripple through time, reshaping the fabric of reality in ways we can't predict."

Asher nodded slowly, the enormity of the concept sinking in. “The Butterfly Effect," he said, both a question and a statement.

Winston nodded solemnly. "It's actually a phenomenon known as the 'Temporal Paradox,'" he explained. "If we inadvertently alter the past in a way that prevents our own birth, we erase our very existence."

"Yes, I can see that. So why even take the risk?" Asher asked almost to himself as his mind raced with the danger that Winston had presented.

"Exactly—risk versus reward. That truly is the question, is it not?" Winston asked, probing Asher for his reaction.

"But surely there must be safeguards in place to prevent such disasters?" Asher curiously asked.

Winston's expression grew somber, his eyes reflecting the weight of their conversation. "Unfortunately, time travel is filled with uncertainty," he replied in a grave tone. "While we can take precautions to minimize the risks, the truth is that we're treading into uncharted territory with every journey we undertake. Think for a moment of the ramifications if you had chosen not to step back through that portal."

Asher pondered the possibilities. *Would there have been two of him? No, he had left the future for the past. But how would that even work? Would the past six months of his life simply vanish? And if so, how could that possibly be explained?* The thoughts and possibilities were overwhelming.

After a moment's consideration, Winston spoke, his tone laced with quiet caution. "But with all those dangers comes power," he said, his words deliberate. "The power to uncover artifacts of immense value—like the lost treasure of Herod the Great."

Asher leaned back slightly as he pieced it together. "So that's what this is all about," he said, his voice laced with a mix of intrigue and skepticism. "Using it to solve the mystery of the treasure?"

Winston nodded solemnly. "Yes, we will answer all those questions you pose in your book, but we will do more than just that. We will prove to everyone you were right," he said with confidence. "Of course, it's a delicate matter—one that requires the utmost discretion."

As Winston spoke, Asher's mind raced—not just with excitement, but with uncertainty. The idea of proving his theories right, of validating his life's work, was intoxicating. But the strangeness of it all still clung to him. *Time travel? Lost treasure?* It sounded like the plot of a novel, not the foundation of serious research.

He hesitated, his fingers tapping against his leg. "This is... a lot to take in," he admitted, still trying to reconcile logic with the reality in front of him. "If what you're saying is true—if this really is possible—then this changes everything."

Winston nodded again, his expression understanding. "You're right; it is a lot to process. And I don't expect a decision now—only that you'll give my offer genuine consideration." His tone was calm and reassuring.

Asher exhaled slowly, the tension in his shoulders easing just a little. "I won't lie—this is hard to wrap my head around," he said, his voice steadier now. "But if there's a chance to uncover something groundbreaking... I'm, at the very least, interested."

Winston's lips curved into a knowing smile. "Thank you. That's all I ask," he replied with a hint of satisfaction.

Asher momentarily hesitated, his brow furrowing in thought. "I'm confused about what's in it for *you*?" he asked, searching Winston's expression for any hint of ulterior motive.

"For me, the prospect of unraveling such a captivating mystery alongside someone as passionate and knowledgeable as yourself is reward enough," Winston replied with a reassuring and convincing tone.

He paused for a moment, his weariness evident in the slight tremor of his hands and in his voice. "There's much to discuss," Winston continued, his words trailing off slightly, "but it will have to wait until tomorrow. Let's get some rest before we continue."

Asher could see that Winston was quickly tiring; it was evident he had reached the limits of his energy for the day. Besides, it must be close to midnight by now, and Asher himself had been going for almost 24 hours. It had been a long day of travel—both conventional and unconventional.

Without a word, Winston reached up and pressed the device around his neck that he used to summon Natalie. In a matter of moments later, Natalie appeared, stepping into the room as if she had been waiting just out of sight.

"She'll take care of everything," Winston said, his voice quieter now. "Get some rest, Asher. I will see you at breakfast."

After studying Winston's condition for a moment, Natalie quickly placed his oxygen mask over his face and gently said, "Deep breaths."

Winston inhaled deeply as the oxygen worked its way through his system, easing the tension in his weary frame.

"You must not go so long without your oxygen. It puts too much stress on your system," she said firmly.

"Of course, you're right. I just got caught up in the great conversation," he said between breaths, smiling at Asher.

As before, Asher found himself captivated by Natalie's beauty. She was effortlessly stunning, a perfect ten on the beauty scale. Despite her attempts to adopt an American accent, Asher detected traces of her European origins, most likely Eastern European. As he found himself intently staring at her, Natalie turned towards him, catching his gaze. Flustered, Asher spoke to break the silence, "Is he okay?"

"Yes, but he needs rest," Natalie calmly replied as she began to wheel Winston out of the study. "Stay here; I will return shortly and show you to your room," she continued, her voice gentle yet firm.

Left alone in the study, Asher once again found himself drawn to the artifacts scattered throughout the room. His expertise as an archeologist made him particularly interested in the Peking Man. The term "Peking Man" referred to a collection of fossilized remains discovered in the early 20th century near Beijing, China. Archeologists believe they belonged to Homo erectus, an ancient human ancestor that lived approximately 750,000 years ago.

The Peking Man fossils consisted of skull caps, teeth, and other skeletal fragments, all of which were lost during World War II. Fortunately, plaster casts had been made and preserved for study. Yet, the artifact before Asher appeared different somehow. Its texture felt more organic, as if it were composed of genuine bone rather than mere plaster.

Asher leaned in closer, scrutinizing every detail with a newfound intensity. His trained eye picked up on subtle imperfections in the bone surfaces and intricate patterns of wear on the teeth. Glancing around the room in search of a magnifying glass to aid in his evaluation, Asher came up empty-handed. Undeterred, he refocused his attention on the sculpture before him, determined to uncover the truth.

As his fingers brushed against the surface of the skull, Asher's heart quickened with a mix of excitement and apprehension. *Could it be possible he was holding the genuine article, lost to the annals of history for decades? And had Winston used his time machine to acquire the actual Peking Man?* The thought sent a shiver down Asher's spine as he continued his close examination, his mind racing with the implications of such a revelation.

Suddenly, he heard a voice from the doorway, breaking the silence of the room and snapping him back to reality.

"I'll show you to your room now," Natalie said, her voice calm and composed as she stood in the doorway, gesturing for Asher to join her.

As he approached, she began to walk ahead, leading the way with graceful strides. "This way, please," she said, her tone gentle yet authoritative, guiding him towards the staircase.

She led him up the stairs to the second floor. As he followed, he watched how she walked with grace. Perhaps she had experience as a model. Her dress was hemmed just below the knee, highlighting the definition of her calves. Although not excessively muscular, they were more defined than typical for a model. She wore strapped clogs, though he had hoped for stilettos. Swiftly ascending the stairs, she directed him down a hallway with numerous doors. Halting at the second door on the right, she opened it, stepped back, and gestured for him to enter.

The room was quite spacious, featuring a ten-foot ceiling and a four-poster bed with nightstands on either side. A large chair occupied one corner, and an elegant chandelier hung from the center of the ceiling. Large windows adorned one wall, their heavy drapes drawn back to reveal a view of the moonlit night reflecting off the snow. The wooden floor was adorned with a Persian rug. Various pieces of artwork, including paintings on the walls, added character to the room. Asher noticed his bag resting at the foot of the bed.

"I think you'll find your accommodations adequate," Natalie remarked.

Adequate, Asher thought. *Was that a serious comment?*

"In case you get thirsty in the night," Natalie said, gesturing toward the nightstand beside the bed, where a small pitcher of water and a glass sat neatly next to the telephone. "And should you need anything, just pick up the phone—it will ring directly to my room."

Well, of course it does," Asher thought sarcastically.

"Breakfast will be served at 8:00 in the dining room on the first floor where you ate earlier this evening," Natalie continued with her instructions.

With a polite "Goodnight," Natalie turned and walked away, leaving Asher to ponder her role in the household.

Shutting the door behind her, he couldn't shake the nagging question of who handled the interior decorations. Surely not Natalie; she seemed more like the personal assistant type. Natalie, as he had noticed, also served as Winston's butler and personal nurse. Did she handle cooking, cleaning, and decorating too? The absence of additional staff members puzzled him. A residence of this magnitude would typically require a team of workers to maintain. He surmised that they must all be off duty for the day.

As Asher settled into the plush comfort of the bed, exhaustion weighed heavily upon him, yet sleep remained elusive. His mind continued to churn through the details of the past twenty-four hours, trying to rationalize what he had experienced.

Feeling strangely disoriented, Asher struggled to pinpoint the source of his unease. It wasn't just fatigue from the long day of travel—this was something deeper, something intangible, beyond explanation. Perhaps it was the nature of time travel itself. Each time he stepped through the portal, a strange sensation followed—brief, fleeting.

Maybe it was the sheer enormity of what lay ahead. The possibilities. The unknown.

As he placed his head on the pillow, one thought refused to fade—how much had the experience already changed him?

Breakfast

As Asher descended the staircase, the enticing aroma of cooking drifted through the air. Having enjoyed a restful sleep, he felt rejuvenated and curious about the day's potential surprises. Upon entering the dining room, he discovered Winston already seated at the table, enjoying his meal. Winston appeared refreshed and greeted Asher with a smile, "Ah, I trust you slept well."

"Yes, quite well. You look rested, too," Asher replied as he took a seat next to Winston.

Pointing to a prepared plate, Winston said, "Natalie took care of your breakfast. I hope it's to your liking." The plate featured scrambled eggs, corned beef hash on toast, and a bowl of assorted fruits. Jam, butter, and a glass of orange juice completed the setup in front of his plate.

"No complaints here, thank you," Asher responded with a grateful smile as he began to dig in.

Jokingly, he added, "Is there anything Natalie doesn't do?"

Winston chuckled, a twinkle in his eye, and replied, "She is indeed remarkable, and no, I couldn't do without her."

As if on cue, Natalie entered the room. "Is there anything else you require?" she asked, her demeanor professional and efficient.

"No, this is fine. My compliments to the chef," Asher said with a smile, attempting to establish some type of rapport with her.

"The driver will be here at 1:00 to return you to the airport," Natalie stated matter-of-factly, her focus on the logistics of their schedule.

Realizing that any attempt to move their relationship to anything other than business was futile, Asher replied, "Okay, thank you," maintaining a polite but professional tone.

With a nod, Natalie turned and left the room, leaving the two men alone to continue their conversation.

As Asher and Winston ate breakfast, Asher's curiosity grew about the Peking Man. After a few moments of internal debate, he decided to press Winston about it.

“Winston, last night I had a chance to examine your Peking Man,” Asher began cautiously, “it appeared to me that it was actually bone. Is it a replica?”

Winston's demeanor shifted slightly, his expression guarded. "Why do you ask?" he responded evasively.

Asher's brow furrowed as he sensed Winston's reluctance to answer directly. "I'm just curious," he replied. "It looks incredibly authentic."

Winston hesitated, his gaze flickering away momentarily before he replied, "It's a replica, but you're right; it's a good one. Many people have been fooled by it through the years."

Asher's intuition told him that Winston wasn't being honest with him. “Remember yesterday when you talked about trust?” he pressed. “Trust is a two-way street, Winston. For me to trust you, you have to be honest with me."

Winston studied Asher's face closely for a moment before saying, "You are correct; trust is indeed a two-way street. And your instincts are correct as well. Yes, it is the original."

Asher nodded, his suspicions confirmed. “How did you acquire it?”

Winston hesitated once more, choosing his words carefully. “It's one of my favorite memories,” he said, a smile sweeping across his face. “And, like all my travel adventures, one I've never told before.”

As Winston paused and reflected on the memory, Asher waited in anticipation of the story to come.

“It was one of the first things I acquired with my machine. I knew it was lost, so it was a perfect prize to capture. Looking back on it now, I took way too many risks. But the short of it is, I saw what actually happened to it, and I pulled a little sleight of hand, you might say,” Winston continued with a chuckle.

As Winston recounted the story of acquiring the original Peking Man, Asher couldn't help but sense the pride in his voice. The daring feat held a special place in Winston's heart, a testament to his ingenuity and resourcefulness.

Despite the risks involved, Winston had successfully retrieved a priceless artifact lost to history, an achievement that spoke volumes about his capabilities as a time traveler. Asher couldn't help but admire the audacity and skill required to pull off such a heist, even if it came with its own set of moral dilemmas.

"The sad part is I can never show it to anyone nor sell it. It's a treasured and priceless possession that has no monetary value—at least to me," Winston said with a bittersweet laugh.

As Winston finished his story, Asher sat in stunned silence, his mind reeling from the revelation. Winston's actions had profound implications, and Asher couldn't help but feel a mixture of awe and unease at the power of the time machine.

Glancing at his watch, Winston remarked, "We'll have time for more stories later. Right now, we have less than five hours to complete our mission. Eat up." He gestured towards Asher's plate, emphasizing the importance of quickly finishing their meal.

"Mission? What mission?" Asher asked, his curiosity piqued by the cryptic statement.

"We're going to take a little trip—just the two of us," Winston casually explained as he finished his breakfast. "Meet me in the lab when you're done," he added before hastily rolling out of the room, leaving Asher to finish his meal in contemplation.

Asher felt a surge of apprehension about using the time machine again so soon. He hesitated, replaying Winston's words in his mind and wondering.

A trip? A trip to where?

Risk vs. Reward

As Asher entered the lab, he found Winston already engrossed in the computer connected to the time machine. The machine itself lay silent. Winston glanced up, a hint of excitement in his eyes.

"I trust you're ready," he announced.

Asher hesitated before responding, his voice tinged with nervousness. "Honestly, Winston, I'm feeling a bit apprehensive about this whole time travel thing," he admitted.

"I understand, but rest assured, I'll take every precaution to ensure a safe journey." Winston's tone was both comforting and firm, offering reassurance while acknowledging Asher's concerns. "That's also why I'll be going with you today–to show you firsthand that it's completely safe. I'm not asking you to do anything I haven't done myself."

He paused, then leaned forward slightly. "But safety is only part of the equation. It's one thing to hear and think about the power of the machine, but it's totally different to experience it firsthand. That's what I want to show you today. It's something that you will find nowhere else."

Asher studied Winston closely. His words were reassuring. If it were safe for someone in Winston's condition, it had to be safe for anyone.

Winston leaned forward slightly. "Asher, the only way to answer all those questions you have is to take the risk. I believe that after today, you'll feel differently. But, as I said before, the choice is yours." He sat back in his chair, waiting for Asher's response.

Asher thought for a moment before responding. "I had a strange sensation each time I went through the portal. Can you explain that?"

Winston nodded, his confidence unwavering. "Yes, it's completely normal. It's simply part of the process." He paused before adding, "The real dangers come from your actions while you're in the past."

Winston's expression turned serious. "And that's exactly why we need to go over something important–the rules of time travel."

Asher nodded in understanding, realizing the gravity of the situation. "Of course," he agreed, eager to learn more.

"First and foremost," Winston began, his tone sincere, "as we discussed yesterday, the greatest danger of time travel is the potential to alter history."

"But isn't that inevitable?" Asher interjected, voicing his concern.

Winston nodded in acknowledgment. "Yes, to some extent. However, our goal is to minimize our impact on the timeline. We must tread lightly, making only subtle changes to avoid disrupting the natural course of events."

Asher nodded, absorbing Winston's words.

"And attempting to correct past wrongs in our lives is strictly prohibited," Winston stated firmly. "It is unquestionably the greatest temptation—one that must be resisted at all costs."

Asher nodded solemnly. "Makes sense," he replied, though his mind briefly wandered to the things he would change if given the chance.

Winston continued, his tone grave with experience. "The complexity of each trip is daunting and brings its own set of challenges. You must dress the part, speak the part, and know the area and culture. While it's vital to speak the native language, accents are a clear giveaway to one's origin."

Asher nodded, reminiscing about his college days as a tour guide in Jerusalem. He had developed a knack for identifying people's origins based on their accents. However, he also realized the stark contrast between modern conveniences and the realities of the past. In ancient times, there would be no cell phones to call for help, no internet to book a hotel, and certainly no GPS to navigate unfamiliar terrain.

"Placement of the portal is critical too," Winston went on. "Placing yourself in the wrong place at the wrong time could have dire consequences. I once stepped out of a portal to find myself standing within twenty feet of a pride of lions."

Asher raised an eyebrow, intrigued by Winston's story, but the old man merely pressed on, leaving the details of his escape to the imagination.

"The good news is, you already have the skills needed to blend into first-century Jerusalem," Winston stated matter-of-factly.

Asher nodded in agreement. It felt as though his entire life had been preparing him for this. "So, you want to go there today?" he asked, a note of apprehension in his voice.

Winston shook his head. "No, we're not ready for that yet. But before we decide our destination, I need your agreement to go," he stated, waiting for Asher's response.

Asher exhaled slowly. He wasn't fully convinced but knew he couldn't turn back now.

"Okay, I'll do this," he agreed, though uncertainty still lingered.

Winston's face lit up. "Good. Now, let's decide where to go today. I suggest we start with something in the 20th century. That should eliminate some of the challenges of traveling to the first century.

Asher nodded in agreement, understanding the importance of familiarity with the chosen event and region.

"Let's pick an event in an area that you are familiar with," Winston added. Given Asher's extensive time in Israel, they both agreed that selecting an event from that region would be the wisest choice.

They also concurred that the event should predate Asher's birth, eliminating any potential interference with his own timeline. However, they deemed anything before the 1950s too risky due to the volatile nature of historical conflicts. This decision narrowed their options to a window of approximately 30 years.

Asher suggested several archaeological finds, such as the Dead Sea Scrolls and the Statue of Hadrian, but they both agreed that involvement in these discoveries would carry too many risks.

Instead, Winston proposed a more personal event, one that carried its own set of dangers. "I suggest we attend a wedding, but not just any wedding, the wedding of your parents," Winston said with a broad smile.

Winston's suggestion caught Asher off guard. His mind raced with a whirlwind of emotions. He had heard the story of his parents' wedding countless times, a cherished event often shared at family gatherings.

His parents, devoutly raised in the Reformed Jewish tradition, had tied the knot in a wedding hall in their hometown. Growing up in the same close-knit community, attending the same synagogue, and their parents sharing a close friendship, their union had been a natural progression. Though they often joked about their marriage being arranged, the truth was that their love had blossomed organically, and they considered each other "bashert" – the Hebrew term for soulmates.

As Winston's proposal sank in, Asher couldn't help but wonder if attending his parents' wedding would violate the rules of time travel. After all, this was his own family's history they were delving into.

Winston acknowledged the dangers and emphasized the need for Asher to strictly adhere to their established guidelines to minimize potential complications.

"What about the risk of encountering my family?" Asher asked, his voice tinged with uncertainty. "Attending my parents' wedding feels like meddling with my own past."

Winston nodded in understanding. "It's a valid concern. But as long as we maintain our distance and only observe, we should be fine."

Asher nodded in agreement, fully understanding the necessity of maintaining a low profile during their trip.

"Now, give me the date, time, and location," Winston prompted, his fingers poised over the keyboard.

Asher didn't hesitate, reciting the details from memory. "Sunday, May 12, 1985, at 6:00 PM. I don't know the address, but it was at a quaint outdoor venue nestled in the heart of Jerusalem's bustling Old City, near the Western Wall," he replied promptly.

Winston's fingers pecked at the keyboard, summoning a digital map onto the computer screen. "Let's narrow down the location," he said, his tone focused. "Can you give me other details about where the wedding took place?"

Asher leaned closer to the screen, studying the intricate network of streets and buildings. "It was in the Old City," he replied, pointing to a bustling area on the map. "Near the Jewish Quarter, near this area here."

Winston adjusted the map accordingly, zooming in on the designated area. "Recognize anything here?" he suggested, indicating a cluster of public venues.

Asher scrutinized the screen, looking for something familiar. After a moment, he nodded. "Yes, that's it. That's the building," he confirmed with excitement.

"Perfect," Winston declared, finalizing their choice on the map. "Let me look for a safe portal location." Winston continued pecking away at the keyboard.

It was obviously a complicated process because it took about 20 minutes before he was satisfied. Asher didn't pay much attention to the actual details, but he did hear Winston mumbling about various technicalities.

As they finalized their plans, Winston gave Asher a lab coat. "Here, wear this," he instructed, his tone decisive. It'll cover your modern clothing, making you look like my caretaker, blending in with our cover story."

Asher nodded, slipping into the coat and adjusting it for a better fit. "Thanks," he said, appreciating Winston's attention to detail.

Asher hadn't paid much attention to Winston's attire, but he had chosen a simple plaid long-sleeve shirt. Across his lap, he had laid a beige blanket. Asher realized that Winston had come prepared for the era of their travel.

"Okay, time to activate the machine," Winston declared, his voice steady with determination. The machine whirled into action. As the familiar hum filled the air, the portal began to materialize in the same location as before, its shimmering surface beckoning them into the past.

As the machine's hum grew louder, Asher felt a surge of excitement mixed with a flutter of nervousness in his stomach. This wasn't just another archaeological dig; this was a journey back in time. He watched in awe as the portal stabilized, its edges shimmering with a light that seemed both eerie and inviting. He tried to calm his racing heart, focusing on what lay ahead, yet the magnitude of what they were about to do made it hard to remain composed.

Winston interrupted Asher's contemplation, stating, "Okay, everything is ready. Remember, we're only staying for 30 minutes or less. We're to have no contact with anyone. Do you understand?"

Asher nodded in agreement.

“Very well, let’s get started,” Winston said as he rolled his wheelchair towards the portal.

Asher stepped behind the wheelchair, his fingers tightening around the handles. His pulse quickened, a silent war waging between doubt and curiosity.

For a brief moment, he hesitated.

Then, with a deep breath and newfound resolve, he pushed them through.

Wedding Crashers

Winston had placed the Jerusalem portal in an isolated area behind a building where it should go unnoticed. As Asher wheeled Winston around towards the front of the building, he could recognize the surroundings, even though they lacked some of the improvements of the 21st century. From outside, they could hear voices.

As they entered the doors, David and Leah stood beneath the wedding canopy called the chuppah. Leah circled David seven times, symbolizing the creation of a new family unit. The rabbi recited the traditional blessings over the wine, and David placed a simple gold ring on Leah's finger, sealing their vows.

As the ceremony reached its climax, David was handed a glass wrapped in a cloth. He took a deep breath, looked at Leah with a smile, and brought his foot down firmly, shattering the glass with a sharp crack. The crowd erupted in cheers, their voices ringing out in unison: *Mazel Tov!*—a joyous exclamation meaning *Congratulations!*

With the ceremonial breaking of the glass complete, the celebration officially began. The band struck up the familiar melody of *Hava Nagila*, a Hebrew song meaning *Let Us Rejoice*. Soon, the entire hall was clapping and singing along, their voices rising in joyful harmony. David and Leah were lifted into the air on chairs, laughter and clapping filling the room as they grasped hands, their joy radiating throughout the hall.

His father, dressed in a finely tailored black suit with a crisp white shirt, looked every bit the proud groom. His mother, glowing with happiness, wore a modest yet elegant gown. Her auburn hair was swept up into delicate curls. A linen shawl embroidered with intricate floral patterns was draped over her shoulders.

Asher recognized it instantly. It was one of her most cherished keepsakes, passed down from his grandmother, who had received it from her own mother before her. It was a family heirloom, treasured across generations. He had seen his mother wear it only on the most special occasions, and now, watching her clutch it around herself as she laughed with his father, the sight stirred something deep inside him.

He had never given it much thought before. It was just a piece of fabric. But now, he understood. It wasn't just about warmth or elegance—it was about history, legacy, and love.

It felt surreal to witness them at this young age, both in their twenties. The desire to rush in and join the festivities suddenly overwhelmed Asher. While a part of him felt this was precisely where he belonged, another part deemed it utterly wrong.

As Asher scanned the crowd, he recognized almost every face, familiar from the many shared memories and past encounters. But it was the sight of his paternal grandfather that caused his heart to leap with excitement. He was full of life and exuberantly dancing and singing with abandon. This was the man he had cherished, the one who had filled his childhood with love and laughter.

It was lung cancer that had taken his grandfather's life fifteen years ago. The aggressive nature of the cancer led to his death within six months of its discovery. Earlier detection would have significantly increased his chance of survival. Witnessing his grandfather's deterioration had been difficult, and Asher harbored a profound resentment towards the illness that had caused so much suffering.

Watching his grandfather, a part of him yearned to intervene—to pull him aside and warn him of the grim future that awaited.

Yet, he knew how bizarre and unsettling such a warning would seem, especially at such a joyous event. The very notion of explaining how he knew of his grandfather's future illness and diagnosis held him back. The complexity and potential consequences of such an intervention weighed heavily on Asher, leaving him torn between his desire to save his grandfather and the ethical and practical dilemma it presented.

As these thoughts tumbled in his mind, he began to feel the benefits outweighed the risks. Saving his grandfather would not only spare the man he so deeply admired but could also fundamentally alter the course of his family's life. His parents might never have felt the profound grief that led them to convert to Christianity, a move that drastically shifted their family dynamics and deepened the rift between them. Additionally, their Christian views would not have influenced Rita, which contributed to their divorce. All these things orbited around this man and his health. Asher felt an increasing urge to act, driven by the possibility of changing their lives for the better.

Obviously, this would be a big violation of *the rules of travel.* Considering he was not even allowed to interact with anyone, especially those associated with the wedding, it seemed impossible. Of course, Winston's presence further complicated matters.

Even though he wasn't religious, Asher did have a set of moral beliefs he tried to follow. And while he didn't trust others, he did hold to a strong set of beliefs about treating others fairly and doing good, akin to the Hippocratic Oath's principle of "primum non nocere" or "first, do no harm."

While the world may be evil and unfair, he would not bow to such levels. It was all part of his complex personality, one that was still evolving. The moral dilemma he faced now centered around the desire to save his grandfather—an act that seemed inherently good. This was a man he loved and cherished. Asher questioned what harm it would cause. The true power and purpose of time travel began to reveal itself to him, emphasizing the necessity of rectifying certain wrongs.

As Asher stood on the sidelines, watching his parents dance amidst the joyous celebration of their wedding day, a wave of regret washed over him. Seeing them so young, so full of hope for the future, felt surreal.

The sight of them, vibrant and carefree, was a painful reminder of what had been lost over the years—the closeness, the laughter, the moments that once defined their family. As they twirled and swayed, Asher couldn't help but wonder—how had they drifted so far apart?

Watching the traditional Jewish wedding unfold before him, he found himself swept away by the richness of his cultural heritage and the depth of tradition that permeated every aspect of the ceremony. Each ritual, from the breaking of the glass to the circling of the bride, spoke volumes about the sacred bond between two individuals and the enduring strength of their faith. All of these were a poignant reminder of the pain he had caused his own family by straying from his roots.

The contrast between the joyous celebration before him and the shattered remnants of his failed marriage to Rita was undeniable. For the first time, Asher understood the hurt and disappointment his parents must have felt when he chose to marry outside of the faith traditions they still cherished. And despite their conversion to Christianity, these traditions remained a part of their lives, their heritage. He realized how his decision had deeply wounded them, fracturing the bonds of trust and understanding that had once united them. As he grappled with the weight of his choices, Asher vowed to make amends, to repair the damage he had caused, and to honor the traditions and values that, while modified, remained a significant part of his family's identity.

Amidst the whirlwind of emotions, Asher's thoughts turned back to saving his grandfather. Beholding his grandfather in his youth only strengthened his resolve to alter the course of history and prevent the tragedy that had befallen him in later years. Asher's mind raced, formulating a plan of action, steeling himself for the challenges that lay ahead.

Since the focus was entirely on the bride and groom, the two uninvited guest remained unnoticed. Recognizing that this unique situation might never recur, Asher felt he had to seize the moment. Yet, even as uncertainty gripped him, his body moved on its own—propelled by a force he couldn't explain, as if something beyond his control was pulling him forward.

As a surge of boldness welled up within him, he stepped away from the wheelchair, moving toward his grandfather. Just as he was about to pass Winston, he felt someone firmly grab his wrist. Noticing it was Winston, he was surprised by his strength. "No," Winston said. "I know what you're thinking. We must go now." Asher attempted to pull his arm away, but Winston held on tightly. "Now," Winston said firmly.

Asher faced a new dilemma. He could break free from Winston and continue on his quest, or he could submit.

"You can't save him," Winston calmly added.

What?! How did he know? Asher sensed that somehow the old man knew of his plan, but how?

"You must trust me," he continued.

Once again, Winston was asking for his trust. *But was he truly trustworthy?* Asher wondered.

Though it seemed like an eternity, it was only moments before Asher made a decision. He realized that causing a scene would be inappropriate. Reluctantly, he wheeled Winston out of the building and back towards the portal. Passing through, he returned them to the laboratory.

The tension between them was palpable. Asher sensed he was about to be lectured about his violation of *the rules of travel*, but the old man was gasping and struggling to catch his breath. It was apparent that the trip had taken a toll on him. The most Winston could muster to say was, "Natalie. Take me to Natalie."

Asher didn't hesitate, wheeling Winston out of the laboratory and toward the elevator. As soon as they entered, Winston reached up and pressed the device around his neck to summon her.

Noticing Winston's worsening condition, Asher quickly grabbed the oxygen mask from the side of his wheelchair and handed it to him. Winston's fingers trembled slightly as he secured it over his nose and mouth, inhaling deeply.

By the time the elevator doors slid open, Natalie was already in the hallway, moving toward them with urgency, her medical bag in hand. She instantly took over, quickly assessing Winston before pulling a syringe from the bag and administering an injection into his upper arm.

The shot had an immediate effect, steadying his breathing and easing the tension in his weary frame.

"No more conversations for him today. He must rest. I will get your things, and you can prepare to leave," she said to Asher in the form of an order.

He knew he had dodged a bullet. He wasn't the confrontational type and was glad to miss out on what was surely a lecture by Winston. Natalie wheeled Winston out of the room, leaving Asher alone with his thoughts.

He was also much more emotional than he had expected. Seeing his healthy grandfather brought him mixed emotions of joy and grief. Witnessing the joy of his parents reminded him of his dream as a child, a dream he had somehow totally forgotten. Asher recalled his childhood certainty that one day he would have a marriage like his parents'—strong, enduring, and built on an unshakable bond. They genuinely loved and cared for each other, and for him. As an only child, he was cherished and doted on by both his parents. Back then, he had dreamed of having the same life when he grew up.

When had that changed? And how? The emotions that welled up shocked him. Part of him felt as if he had abandoned himself. Grief for his failed marriage surfaced in a way he had never experienced before—raw, undeniable. An inexplicable desire to repair it took hold.

And the solution was simple—the time machine.

Yes, the time machine could fix all this, but should it? Could turning back time really mend what had already broken?

Of course, doing so would be a direct violation of Winston's established rules. The fact that there were rules at all seemed absurd anyway. Why shouldn't the machine be used to repair the wrongs of life and even the world?

Natalie reappeared with Asher's travel bag. "Your driver has arrived," she said. "Winston will contact you after you have returned home."

Without comment, Asher took his bag and headed for the front door. Winston had promised to show Asher the power of the machine.

Mission accomplished.

Reflecting

During the flight home, Asher found it difficult to sleep as he continually replayed the events of the last 48 hours. At times, he found himself questioning the reality of his experiences, doubting the vivid memories etched into his mind. Yet, the sensations of what he had seen, smelled, and touched were undeniable.

As the plane descended into the Jerusalem airport, Asher's mind wrestled with the weight of his newfound knowledge and the responsibility it carried. Winston's obsession with lost treasure echoed in his thoughts, but Asher's priorities were different. And already, a mental list had begun to take shape.

At the top of that list was his grandfather—the chance to spare him from pain and suffering, to save his life before cancer could take its toll. But Asher couldn't ignore the fractures in his own life. Repairing his broken relationship with his parents was next—something he wanted, yet knew would not come easily.

And then there was Rita. Moving on from their marriage felt necessary, yet painfully difficult. Despite the heartache and all the ways they had failed each other, part of him still clung to the love they once shared.

But even as these thoughts weighed on him, he knew it wasn't that simple. He didn't fully understand all the risks, but he was certain that altering history and rewriting the past carried dangers—ones that might outweigh the benefits.

As Asher stepped off the plane and onto the familiar ground of his hometown, a new clarity emerged. He realized he didn't need the complexity of the time machine to fix his relationship with his parents. The central issue of their conflict was religion—a central pillar of his parents 'lives but a point of deep conflict for Asher. Accepting a faith he didn't believe in felt impossible, a betrayal of his own convictions. Yet, knowing the pain and disappointment he had caused them, he couldn't help but wonder: *Was there a way to meet them halfway? Some common ground that could bridge the divide?*

Driving back to his apartment, he rehearsed the conversation he would have with his mom. He envisioned his words, the apologies he would offer, and his heartfelt desire for reconciliation.

Asher was exhausted as his car rolled to a stop in the driveway. Weary from the long flight and the emotional toll of the past few days, he stepped out of the car and made his way toward his apartment.

Once inside, he barely managed to kick off his shoes before collapsing onto his bed. Despite his exhaustion, a sense of anticipation stirred within him. Though daunting, the conversation with his parents was no longer something to dread—it was a step he was eager to take.

For the first time in years, the past no longer felt like a weight to carry—it was a bridge he could finally cross.

Return to Familiar

The persistent ringing of Asher's phone woke him from a deep sleep. He fumbled for the device with tired eyes, squinting at the bright screen in the dimly lit room. The time displayed read 3:00 PM, a stark reminder of how long he had slept. Rubbing the sleep from his eyes, he answered the call, his voice still heavy with sleep.

"Hello?" he mumbled.

"Hi, Asher. It's Mom," said the familiar voice on the other end of the line. "I was just checking to see if you made it home safely. I hadn't heard from you, and I was getting worried."

Asher was relieved to hear his mother's voice. "I'm sorry, Mom," he replied, his voice tinged with remorse. "I made it home fine. The flight was smooth, just a bit exhausting. I didn't mean to worry you."

There was a sigh of relief on the other end of the line. "Thank goodness," his mother breathed. "I'm just glad to hear you're okay. Did you have a good trip?"

Asher hesitated for a moment, contemplating how to broach the topic that weighed heavily on his mind. "Yeah, it was... eventful," he admitted cryptically. "But listen, Mom, I was actually planning on calling today to see if it's okay if I come over and visit."

His mother's voice held a mix of excitement and hesitation. "Of course, Asher," she replied. "I would love that!" He didn't miss that she didn't say "we."

"Great, uh, how does Friday evening work?" Asher asked.

There was a moment of silence on the other end of the line before his mother spoke again. "Of course, Asher," she said gently. "I'll fix us a nice dinner."

"Thanks, Mom," Asher replied gratefully. "I'll see you then."

"Ok," his mother replied before they bid each other goodbye.

As Asher ended the call, he was surprised at how smoothly it had gone. Even though there was some hesitation and awkwardness, his mother seemed open and welcoming. Now, he hoped the visit itself would be as easy.

With that call behind him, Asher felt a weight lift off his shoulders. The first steps toward reconciling with his parents had been taken, and it had gone better than expected. But now he found his thoughts returning to the time machine.

The lure of altering the past still pulled at him, stronger now that he had a taste of what it could do. He could envision himself as a modern-day hero, capable of righting the wrongs of history and preventing untold tragedies. Saving his grandfather and fixing mistakes in his life were all within reach. Yet, the more he thought about it, the more he questioned if it was truly the right path. The complexity of time travel, the potential consequences of even the slightest change weighed heavily on his mind. Could he really risk tampering with the past? Or was the real challenge learning to face his future without trying to rewrite it?

As Asher mulled over his next move, he knew he had to tread carefully. His personal desires were pressing, but the responsibility that came with the time machine was greater. He resolved to balance his own goals with a larger sense of duty, knowing that whatever he chose, the stakes were high—for both himself and humanity.

With a sense of determination, Asher continued his mental list of the events he deemed worthy of intervention. The possibilities were endless, from preventing wars and natural disasters to rectifying personal regrets and reconciling fractured relationships.

As Asher pondered the weighty responsibility now bestowed upon him by the time machine, one name suddenly loomed large in his mind: *Hitler*. The mere mention of the infamous dictator sent a shiver down his spine, a stark reminder of the atrocities committed during one of the darkest chapters of human history.

Asher knew he had to prevent Hitler's evil; not doing so would be evil in itself. Asher could save millions of lives—millions of his people's lives! It was the right thing to do even if, as Winston had warned, it cost him his own life.

Growing up, Asher had been deeply affected by horror stories of the Holocaust. For his family, it wasn't just history—it was personal. Relatives who had survived the horror shared their experiences, and those memories stayed with him, shaping his perspective on the world. Now, with the time machine at his disposal, he couldn't help but wonder if he should try to change the past and what the consequences of such a decision might be.

The thought of saving millions of lives filled Asher with a profound sense of purpose. Even though it meant personal risk, he knew that intervening to stop such unimaginable suffering was the right thing to do.

Yet, amidst the urgency of preventing historical tragedies, Asher couldn't ignore the implications of altering history on a personal level. The realization dawned on him that changing the course of events would have unforeseen consequences, potentially altering his very own existence. As he grappled with this revelation, he questioned the significance of repairing his marriage if he no longer existed in the altered timeline.

The complexity of Asher's decisions pressed on him as he navigated the moral challenges of time travel. The stakes grew with every thought, and the weight of his choices became more apparent. Still, his sense of duty and desire to correct history's wrongs drove him forward. He was resolved to face the challenges ahead, knowing they would impact both his personal life and the world at large.

Over the next several days, Asher heard nothing from Winston. Fears that the old man's health might have deteriorated and left Asher powerless to make the changes he so desperately desired crept into his mind. Asher knew he couldn't wait any longer, so he decided to reach out and check on Winston's condition.

Determined, Asher prepared himself for the conversation, though he knew that Winston would never go along with his plans. Still, he carefully crafted his arguments and rehearsed his words, hoping to sway the old man's perspective. But deep down, couldn't shake the feeling that they were headed toward an impasse.

In the midst of his thoughts, a realization overcame him. He had been so focused on his own goals that he missed Winston's reason for their partnership—the treasure. It all made sense now: Winston only cared about the gold. Winston was driven by greed, not any higher purpose. If Winston truly had noble intentions, wouldn't he have acted on them by now?

Asher felt a surge of anger and betrayal rising within him. Asher believed in the possibility of making a positive impact on the world, but Winston was simply a thief driven by greed and selfish desires. The thought gnawed at Asher's conscience, casting doubt on their entire partnership. *How many other people had he used through the years? Now what? Does he tell the old man he's on to him, or just let the whole thing go?*

While he was processing it all, he was startled by a knock on his door. He wasn't expecting company.

Opening the door, he froze. Winston sat in his wheelchair, his sharp eyes locked on Asher, while Natalie stood behind him, hands firmly on the chair's handles.

"I hope we haven't come at a bad time," Winston said as he glared at Asher.

Asher felt like he was in a dream; *how could this be?* Winston was once again a step ahead of him.

Breaking the silence, Winston continued, "May we come in?"

Still struggling to speak, Asher stepped back and motioned them in.

"Actually, it will be just me," Winston added smoothly. "Natalie has some errands to run." With that, Natalie gave a polite nod, excused herself, and closed the door behind her.

Winston wheeled himself into Asher's living room. "I know you were expecting a call," Winston said with a smirk, "but I thought a visit in person would be better."

Asher hesitated. "Yes, to be honest, I was getting concerned. Last I saw you, you were..." He trailed off.

Picking up the thought, Winston nodded. "Yes, it was not my best day. And that's exactly why I came instead of calling—I wanted you to see for yourself that I'm doing much better." He straightened in his wheelchair, almost as if presenting himself for inspection.

Asher, unsure how to respond, forced himself to nod, hoping it looked like relief.

Sensing the tension, Winston attempted to lighten the moment with a broad smile. "Of course, it would have been nice if you had checked on me."

"I, uh... actually, I was just thinking of calling you today," Asher muttered.

Winston chuckled, his tone laced with amusement. "Yes, I bet you were." He leaned forward slightly. "Well, enough about me. I imagine you have many questions."

Grateful for the shift in conversation, Asher admitted, "Yes, I do."

"Of course, and that's exactly why I am here," Winston said, looking directly into Asher's eyes. "Let me answer the big question first. You are the first and only person with whom I showed, much less shared, my time machine." And yes, I selected you to get to the treasure. And yes, you may consider me a thief. But, in my defense, I only steal amounts that won't be noticed or harm others. For example, if we were to find Herod's treasure, we would only take a small portion. A valuable portion, but small."

Shocked that he knew the exact questions on his mind, Asher asked the only thing that came to mind, "So you are a modern-day Robin Hood?"

Winston chuckled and replied, "Yes, you might say that. But, like I said, I've never harmed anyone. Actually, I do just the opposite. I have given millions to charities, all anonymously, of course. I think it's fair to say that I do much more good than evil. I also understand the dilemma that you are struggling with the most. The grandiose idea that you must save the world or even yourself. Yes, I had those thoughts at first, too. But I quickly learned that history is not to be altered."

Winston settled into his chair, his demeanor heavy with the weight of memories. "Let me share a story with you. When I was a teen, my grandmother lost her wedding ring. It slipped off her finger while she was swimming in the lake near our home. We searched hard to recover it, but our search was futile. She was devastated, as you can imagine."

He paused, reflecting on the event. "Of course, it was hard for me to watch. She literally cried for weeks. It was a family heirloom. Adding to her grief, my grandfather had unexpectedly died several years earlier. For her, it was like losing him all over again."

Additionally, this was to be the ring I would give to my future wife. It was actually an easy decision. I'd go back and make sure she didn't wear it in the water. It would remove a lot of pain from my grandmother's life and restore the heirloom to my family."

Asher leaned in, captivated by Winston's story. "What happened?" he curiously inquired.

"There's a little more to the story," Winston continued with a hint of sadness. "I met Elizabeth just before I created the machine. We dated for a couple of years and then became engaged. The ring would one day be on her finger if I prevented the it from becoming lost," Winston continued with a tone of sorrow. "But in doing so, I inadvertently altered the course of my own life." He paused, the memory still vivid in his mind. "Yes, I prevented the loss of the ring, but when I returned to the present, Elizabeth was gone."

Asher's eyes widened in disbelief. "Gone? What do you mean?" he pressed, eager to understand.

Winston's expression darkened with sorrow. "She was married to someone else," he explained, his voice barely above a whisper. "And she didn't know me. It was as if I had never existed in her life."

Winston's words hung heavy in the air, the story weighing on his soul. "I learned a harsh lesson that day," he continued, his voice tinged with regret. If you interfere in your past, you're likely to experience something similar, most likely worse."

Asher listened intently, his mind grappling with the implications of Winston's story. The idea of altering the past only to suffer unforeseen consequences struck a chord within him. "That's... quite a lesson," he murmured, his voice reflecting a mixture of awe and apprehension. "It's incredible how one small change can have such far-reaching effects. Thank you for sharing that with me, Winston. It's given me much to think about."

As Asher grappled with the implications of Winston's story, a profound realization dawned upon him. The story revealed more about Winston than seen at first glance. He told the story in a compassionate way, but compassion wasn't his goal in the story—it was the ring, the treasure. If Winston truly wanted to comfort his grandmother, wouldn't preventing the death of her husband have been a more compassionate gesture?

Asher thought back to the story of the Peking Man. That story, too, pointed to a heartless thief and not a protector of priceless artifacts. Instead of saving it from becoming lost, Winston's intervention ensured that very outcome. By his own admission, it had no value to him. Was this just Winston's personality, or was it just another power of the machine? Asher couldn't help but feel the lure to control one's destiny, but would that result in changing your personality as well? Was this a byproduct of the time machine—that all the lines blurred until there was no truth, only desires?

The thought of prioritizing material gain over the sanctity of relationships and the well-being of others left a bitter taste in his mouth. *No*, Asher resolved silently; he didn't want to become someone who valued treasure more than the bonds of family and love. The notion of emulating Winston's actions filled him with a sense of moral conflict and inner turmoil. If Asher were to be involved with Winston and the machine, it could only be for good.

The warnings of Winston's cautionary tale had brought their conversation to a grinding halt. Just as the silence threatened to become oppressive, Winston's voice broke through. "So, I've come with a proposal," he began, his tone carrying a hint of urgency.

Asher turned his attention back to Winston, his curiosity piqued.

"Help me find and retrieve the treasure. Not only will I share the gold with you, but I'll also grant you the opportunity to save humanity."

Asher didn't miss Winston's sincere yet sarcastic remark. After a moment of reflection, Asher spoke up, his voice measured. "And how do I know I can trust you?" he questioned, his gaze steady.

Winston met his eyes without hesitation. "You don't," he admitted frankly. "But do you really have any other options? Can you live with the guilt of not taking the chance?"

Asher felt a sinking sensation in his chest as he absorbed Winston's words. He realized that he truly was a pawn in Winston's chess game. "Besides," Winston continued, his voice conveying a hint of persuasion, "at the very least, you can validate your book. That is worth the price of admission by itself."

Asher found himself caught in a whirlwind of conflicting thoughts and emotions. The prospect of proving his book correct while delving into the mysteries of the past was undeniably enticing. However, despite his lack of passion for teaching, he couldn't ignore the fact that he had made a commitment—to his students and his role at the university.

"Are you talking about doing this now?" Asher asked, his voice betraying his hesitation. "I have obligations at the university. My students rely on me, and I can't just abandon them. You'd be asking me to just up and quit my job on a hunch that we might find some gold? Besides, how would I pay my bills if I quit my job?"

"Those are all good points and things I've considered too," Winston said. "You could approach the university about taking a sabbatical or a hiatus and promise to return in the fall. Since I would expect our endeavor to last no more than a few weeks, you might be able to get a fellow professor to cover for you."

As always, Asher marveled at how meticulously Winston had considered every aspect of his plan.

"And regarding finances, I'm prepared to transfer $100,000 to your bank account today," Winston offered. "You may retain the money regardless of the outcome of our expedition."

Asher blinked, momentarily caught off guard. *One hundred thousand dollars for a few weeks' work?* That was nearly equal to his current year's salary.

Winston continued, "If you need time to think about it, I understand. I'm staying in town for a couple of days. Do you think you can make a decision by then?"

Asher took a moment to ponder Winston's offer, considering the weight of the decision before him. Finally, he replied, "Thank you, Winston. I appreciate your understanding. I'll do my best to come to a decision within the next couple of days."

Winston nodded. "Of course, Asher. This is a significant decision, and I want you to feel completely comfortable with it. I'll be staying nearby if you have any further questions or need to discuss anything further."

Winston retrieved his cell phone from his pocket and sent a text message. Promptly, Natalie appeared at the door, and Asher watched in silence as they left without another word. Collapsing into a nearby chair, he struggled to process the events unfolding around him. It was surreal to even consider accepting Winston's offer, yet the allure of the opportunity was undeniable.

The amount of quick and easy money was tempting. But honestly, it was the chance to delve into the mysteries of the gold that genuinely captivated him. Years of research and speculation could finally culminate in unraveling the mysteries that had consumed his thoughts for years.

Deep down, Asher knew that his decision had already been made. There was simply no way he could pass up this once-in-a-lifetime opportunity. As he grappled with the weight of his choice, a resounding thought echoed in his mind: *only God knew what would happen next*.

The God that he didn't believe existed.

Preparations

Asher's footsteps echoed through the halls of the university as he braced himself for the conversation ahead. He had rehearsed his request countless times but still didn't feel fully prepared. Approaching Dean Shimon Levinsky's office, he paused to take a deep breath. The dean was known for his strong leadership and dedication to the academic community. Additionally, he had always been a strong supporter of Asher's work. But this request was unusual, and Asher knew it wouldn't be easy.

Knocking softly on the open door, Asher peered inside and asked, "Dean Levinsky, do you have a moment?"

The dean looked up from his paperwork with a hint of surprise. "Ah, Asher. Please, come in. What can I do for you?"

Taking a seat, Asher cleared his throat, trying to find the right words. "Sir, I have a personal matter that I need to attend to, and I'll need to take a short break from my teaching duties."

"Asher, is everything okay? Is it some kind of health issue?" the dean asked with a puzzled yet concerned look.

"No, no, it's more of a career opportunity. Although I can't provide specifics, it's genuinely a unique opportunity. And it will just be for a few weeks," Asher answered.

The dean's eyebrows knit together in concern. "I see. It's hard to imagine your timing being worse. We're in the middle of the semester, Asher. Your courses are critical, and your students depend on you."

Asher had expected this would be a point the dean would mention. "I understand the timing isn't ideal, Dean Levinsky. And I wouldn't ask if it weren't absolutely necessary. This... opportunity, it's something I can't pass up. It has the potential to greatly contribute to my research and bring a new dimension to my teachings."

Dean Levinsky leaned back in his chair, folding his hands across his chest. "Asher, you're one of our most promising minds. Your expertise and contributions to the field of archaeology have always stood out. But you're asking me to disrupt the academic process for something *you* consider a unique opportunity. Can you give me more details? Perhaps there's another way to handle this." The earnestness in the dean's voice was both a reassurance and a challenge.

Asher hesitated, knowing he couldn't divulge the true nature of his quest. "It involves fieldwork essential to my ongoing research. I've made arrangements to ensure my classes will be covered during my absence. I've spoken with Professor Katz, and she's agreed to take over my lectures temporarily, with your permission, of course."

Dean Levinsky sighed, the weight of decision-making evident in his posture. "Asher, you're putting me in a difficult position. Professor Katz is capable, yes, but your sudden departure... it sets a precedent I'm not comfortable with."

"I understand, sir, and I wouldn't ask if there were any other way. I promise to make this up to the university and my students. I'm fully prepared for any repercussions you feel are appropriate," Asher stated, his determination clear.

The dean leaned forward in his chair and asked casually, "Does your request have anything to do with Winston Saunders?"

Asher was caught off guard, and his complexion went flush. He was unsure how to respond, but his demeanor answered the question.

"Yes, I suspected as much," the dean stated confidently, sitting upright in his chair. "He has reached out to me multiple times over the past year or so. He's asked me about all of the professors in the archaeology department, especially you. He's even hinted at making a significant donation to the university, although he hasn't followed through yet. Quite an intriguing individual, to say the least."

The dean began to tap his fingers lightly on his desk as he took a long pause. Finally, the dean spoke, his voice laden with reluctant acceptance. "Alright, Asher. I'll grant your request for a short break. But on two conditions: your absence does not exceed three weeks, and you provide a detailed report of your findings and how they'll enrich your teaching and contribute to the university."

A wave of relief washed over Asher. "Thank you. You have my word. I won't let you or the students down."

Dean Levinsky nodded, a mixture of trust and apprehension in his eyes. "I'm counting on that, Asher. Best of luck with your fieldwork. Make sure it's worth our while."

Standing up, Asher extended his hand across the desk. "It will be, sir. Thank you for understanding."

As Asher turned to leave the office, the dean interjected, "Oh, Asher, one last thing. Be careful, like I said, this Winston fellow... Well, I'm not fully sure what to think of him."

Asher nodded in acknowledgment. The dean's words didn't reveal anything new but reinforced what Asher already felt—Winston was still essentially an enigma to him. Stepping out of the office, he found himself once again perplexed by Winston's uncanny ability to stay ahead of the gam,e, orchestrating his plans with precision.

Asher glanced at his watch, noting the time with a mix of relief and apprehension. Now, he faced a more personal challenge: reconciling with his parents. He realized he had just enough time to go home, change, and prepare for the visit.

On his way home, Asher stopped by a local florist, a quaint little shop nestled between a cafe and a bookstore on one of Jerusalem's bustling streets. The fragrance of fresh blooms filled the air as he stepped inside. He wandered through the aisles until he found what he was looking for: a bouquet of lush, vibrant irises, his mother's favorite flowers. He remembered how the garden back at their family home used to come alive with their blooms each spring and how his mother gently tended to them.

With the bouquet securely in hand, Asher's thoughts turned to a more personal gift for his father. After some consideration, he decided on a map of 1st Century Jerusalem that he had painstakingly worked on for years and frequently used in his classes at the university. This was not merely a map but a labor of love, reflecting his years of researching the ancient city and its history. Asher also felt the map was a connection between his profession and their family heritage, and he hoped his father would as well. He rolled the map and put it in a cardboard tube, thinking his father, who liked woodworking, would enjoy framing it.

As he drove to his parents' house, Asher rehearsed his words. The aroma of the flowers gave his car a pleasant smell and calmed his nerves. He hoped these gifts would express what he struggled to say out loud: his regret, his desire to reconnect, and his determination to repair their relationship.

When Asher arrived at his childhood home, the evening had started to fall, casting shadows that framed the front door. Every step towards the house felt significant, like he was moving towards a future he hoped to mend.

Asher paused at the front door, taking a moment to gather himself before knocking gently. The door soon opened, revealing his mother. With her welcoming brown eyes and silver-streaked auburn hair, Asher was instantly comforted.

"Asher!" She greeted him with an unexpectedly intense and warm hug, reminding him of their deep bond and how much he had missed her.

“Hey, Mom," Asher managed to say, his voice a mixture of relief and apprehension.

“Come in,” she continued. “Your dad is waiting in the living room.”

As Asher walked through the house, he was greeted by a familiar smell that immediately transported him back in time. It was a comforting blend of scents—the earthy aroma of old wood that spoke of the house's age, mixed with inviting smells of cooking spices and freshly baked bread. These were the smells of his childhood, a reminder of the pride his mother took in her excellent culinary skills.

Asher's father sat in his favorite chair in the living room, a space within the house that seemed reserved for him. In his early 60s, David maintained a fit and solid physique, his dark hair full and brown eyes sharp. As he sat there, absorbed in a book, his furrowed brow gave him a look of deep concentration.

As Asher entered the room, he spoke first, "Dad."

"Hello, Asher," he said, placing his book aside and standing up. Asher extended his hand for a handshake, immediately feeling the firmness of his father's grip, a reminder of his strength. Despite being two inches shorter than Asher, David's broader and more robust frame was evident, as was the tension in the air.

"What's that you're reading?" Asher inquired, hoping to lighten the atmosphere.

David glanced at the book and then back at Asher, saying, "A colleague recommended it. It's about the Second Temple's construction. It's quite fascinating."

As Asher picked up the book, he recognized it. "Ah, I'm familiar with it. It is indeed intriguing, but I believe some of the author's claims are debatable."

His father's brow furrowed slightly, a sign of his disapproval or perhaps disappointment at Asher's critique. Instantly, Asher realized that he shouldn't have made a critical remark. Leah quickly intervened in the conversation, her maternal instincts kicking in as she sought to diffuse the situation.

"Asher, I fixed your favorite meal," she said, gently taking him by the arm. "Chicken schnitzel with lemon wedges, couscous salad on the side, and for dessert, homemade apple strudel. I even remembered to add the extra cinnamon you love so much." Her words were successful, and he gently placed the book back beside his father's chair.

"That sounds wonderful, Mom. Thank you," he expressed, grateful for her intervention. His gaze drifted across the room, landing on photographs scattered across various surfaces, each capturing moments with his parents throughout his life. As their only child, he had been the center of their pride and joy in those earlier uncomplicated days.

Asher suddenly remembered the gifts he had brought for his parents. "Actually, I brought something for you," he said, a tinge of excitement in his voice. "Just give me a moment. I left them in the car."

With a quick, apologetic smile, Asher excused himself to retrieve the gifts. As he walked towards his car, he realized he would need to be more careful with his words when he returned inside if this evening was to go as he hoped.

Returning, Asher carried the concealed gifts with renewed confidence. "Got something for you both," he announced, his voice striving for a casual ease to lighten the mood.

First, he presented Leah with the bouquet of irises, which he knew would bring a smile to her face. "For you, Mom. I remember how much you love these," Asher said as he tenderly offered the flowers.

"Oh, Asher, they're gorgeous! Thank you, sweetheart," Leah responded, her eyes reflecting the joy brought by the simple yet thoughtful gift. She then excused herself, saying, "Let me just put these in water," leaving Asher alone with his father.

Asher turned his attention to David, who appeared to be in deep thought. He extended the tube towards him. "This is for you, Dad," Asher announced with a respectful nod.

As he lowered his reading glasses from his forehead to his face, David took the tube, withdrew the map, and slowly unrolled it. Asher could immediately see that his father was intrigued.

Seizing the opportunity, Asher explained, "I thought you might like this. It's what I believe to be an accurate depiction of the ancient city, a project I've been perfecting for years through both fieldwork and the study of ancient texts. I use it in my university class but haven't published it yet. This is one of the few copies in existence," he shared, aiming to leave a lasting impression on his father.

David examined the map, a visible shift in his demeanor as he traced the detailed streets of a Jerusalem long past. "This is indeed remarkable, Asher," he admitted.

"It complements the book you're reading, doesn't it? We both have this passion for history, something I definitely learned from you," Asher mentioned, reflecting on his childhood visits to museums and historical sites, led by his father's interest in history.

In that moment, with Leah tending to the irises elsewhere, the room seemed to shrink around Asher and David. The map served as a focal point, a shared interest that momentarily eclipsed the disagreements that had punctuated their past interactions.

As they continued discussing the intricacies of the map, Leah returned to the room. "The table is all set. Let's eat," she announced, effectively drawing David and Asher's attention away from the map and towards the dining area, where the irises stood proudly in the center of a beautifully set table.

As they took their seats, the atmosphere was one of peace, the kind that often comes from a shared meal. "Looks wonderful, Mom," Asher offered, genuinely appreciative of the effort to make the evening feel special.

As they settled into the meal, Leah took the lead in the conversation, gracefully steering it toward neutral grounds. She began by sharing updates about her garden, noting how the early blooms were starting to appear despite the chill that still lingered in the air. "It's always so rewarding to see the garden come to life in spring," she commented with enthusiasm.

Leah then shifted the topic to her volunteer work at the church, specifically focusing on the preparations for the upcoming holy week. "I've been helping Pastor Cohen prepare for Easter. It's quite a task but so fulfilling. We're trying to make it special, especially for the families who need extra support this year," she explained.

To complement the meal, Leah had chosen a Cabernet Sauvignon with a rich, ruby color and a layered aroma that hinted at ripe blackberries, cherries, and a touch of oak and spices. The wine, she explained, was a recommendation from a boutique downtown, praised for its exceptional quality from a small vineyard. "I thought it'd be perfect for tonight," Leah said, pouring a glass for Asher. "I hope you like it."

Asher took a sip, immediately impressed by the wine's complexity and the way it enhanced the flavors of the meal. "This is really good, Mom," he said earnestly.

The conversation, aided by the wine, Leah's tales from the garden, and the church, provided a much-needed break from the underlying issues. Asher found himself easing into the warmth of family and the familiar, even if just for the evening.

As they neared the end of their meal, David, seizing a quieter moment, began to share about his latest project in the workshop. "I'm working on a new birdhouse crafted from cedar," he mentioned, his eyes lighting up with enthusiasm. "It's actually designed for the doves in our yard. I've even considered installing a camera inside to watch the eggs hatch and the little ones grow."

Asher, intrigued, leaned in. "A camera, really? That sounds like quite the setup," he commented, impressed by his father's innovative approach to a traditional hobby.

"Yes, I figured it'd be a nice way to observe without disturbing them. It's peaceful, watching nature at work," David added a hint of pride in his voice for merging his love of woodworking with his appreciation for nature.

The conversation shifted as Leah stood to bring out dessert. She presented a homemade apple strudel that filled the room with the aroma of warm apples and cinnamon. She added a scoop of vanilla ice cream to each plate, offering a perfect balance to the warm pastry. "I hope you saved room for dessert," she said with a smile, placing the plates on the table.

The first bite was a mix of warm, spiced apples and flaky pastry, cooled by the melting vanilla ice cream. Asher couldn't help but savor the familiar flavors, a testament to Leah's culinary skills. "This is amazing, Mom. It's been too long since I've had your apple strudel," he said with a mixture of nostalgia and satisfaction.

Leah returned to her seat, pleased with the reception. "It's my pleasure. There's nothing like a homemade dessert to round off a meal," she responded, watching her family enjoy the fruits of her labor.

As the last bites were savored, the cozy dining room hummed with a comfortable silence, marking the end of a heartwarming meal. Leah, always the gracious hostess, glanced around the table at her contented family and suggested, "Why don't we move to the living room? It's a bit more comfortable for us to continue our chat."

David nodded in agreement, placing his napkin on the table. "Sounds good. I could use a more comfortable seat," he replied as he pushed back his chair.

Asher, feeling a mixture of fullness and familial warmth, rose to his feet. "Let me help clear the table," he offered, but Leah waved him off with a smile.

"No, no, you're our guest tonight. Go on ahead, I'll take care of this," Leah insisted.

With a grateful nod, he and his father headed towards the living room, with Leah following shortly afterward.

The living room welcomed them with its familiar comfort, the soft lighting inviting them to relax and unwind. David found his spot in his usual chair while Leah and Asher settled onto the sofa.

"So, you haven't told us about your trip to Boston," Leah said with genuine interest.

Asher's enthusiasm was evident as he replied, "Boston was insightful. I met with some interesting people, and it got me thinking about my next steps."

Asher's comment instantly caught David's attention. "Thinking? Asher, you're not considering leaving your job, are you? You have a well-paying position at the university. You know we pulled a lot of strings to get you that job."

Asher knew that "we" actually meant "me." David believed his long-standing friendship with Dean Levinsky had been the key factor in securing Asher's position at the university. But Asher saw it differently—while he couldn't deny that his father's connection had helped, he was certain that his own qualifications and hard work had played a role in earning him the job, too. This unspoken divide between them only deepened Asher's frustration, reinforcing his sense that David never fully respected his achievements.

Asher prepared for the skepticism and responded calmly. "Actually, Dad, that's part of what I wanted to discuss tonight. I've decided to take a temporary leave from the university. There's a project I need to pursue, something significant."

David's disapproval was palpable. "Leaving a good job to chase after a whim? Asher, we've seen how these *opportunities* turn out."

Maintaining his composure, Asher chose not to escalate the disagreement. "I understand your concerns, Dad, but this isn't a decision I've made lightly. It's different this time."

"And how exactly is it different?" David pressed, not ready to let the matter drop.

"It's hard to explain without getting into all the specifics," Asher continued, attempting to avoid confrontation. "But trust me, there's real potential here."

Recognizing the limitations of discussing a topic with only veiled comments, Asher decided it was time to shift the conversation. "There's actually something else I wanted to talk about tonight," he gently said as he began steering the topic toward their relationship.

"I uh...," Asher began with a voice laced with a mix of nostalgia and regret. "There's something I've been thinking about a lot lately... something that's really important to me."

Sensing the seriousness of his tone, his mother gave him an encouraging nod. His father sat up straight, bracing for what was coming next.

"It's about family... about us," Asher continued, searching for the right words that could convey his feelings. "I've been reflecting on what it means to be part of this family, on the traditions and values that have shaped us."

He paused, the image of his parents' wedding vivid in his mind—the joy, the dancing, the undeniable bond of community and love that he had miraculously observed. It was an event he had "witnessed" in a way they could never understand, and the weight of this secret knowledge pressed him forward.

"I've realized," Asher said, choosing his words with care, "how important these connections are... how much they've given me a sense of belonging and identity. I was, uh, visualizing how joyful your wedding day must have been."

A smile crept across Leah's face as she recalled the event, her eyes sparkling with the memory. Meanwhile, David shifted in his chair and looked reflective, also reminiscing about the same cherished moment, the shared joy, and the vows that had bound them together through the years.

Asher sighed. He wanted to tell the entire truth, but he knew it was impossible. "Seeing how our family came together... I mean, imagining it has had a profound effect on me." He corrected himself quickly, struggling for the strength to say his next words. He wanted to be honest and open, but vulnerability was never his comfort zone.

"It made me think about my own choices—about my walking away from my family," Asher continued, hoping those words would open a door—maybe even invite a little grace.

They all sat in silence for what seemed like an eternity before David spoke. "Asher, we all make choices in life. Some we're proud of, and some we wish we could take back or do differently."

He paused, then added with a sharper edge, "I won't pretend your choices weren't painful."

To Asher, David's words weren't filled with grace, but with the familiar tone of judgment—a tone he knew too well. He lowered his eyes, trying to take the comment in a different way, trying not to react. But the pain of years of conflict was like smoldering coals—never extinguished, needing only the breath of their words to reignite.

And in that moment, David's words were enough.

Asher wanted to let it go. He wanted peace. But his anger fanned the flames—old wounds flaring to life, causing the heat to rise in the room.

Leah shifted uncomfortably beside him, sensing the tension rising in the room. "David, Asher, please," she said softly, her voice trembling, trying to break the tension before it fully caught flame. But the moment had already turned, and the years of pent-up frustration and pain quickly surfaced

Asher looked up slowly, his voice quiet, controlled—but with an unmistakable edge. "I know they were painful, Dad. Painful for *all* of us. But I'm not the only one at fault."

He met his father's gaze fully now. "We all share in the blame."

David scoffed, leaning forward. "Really? Because the way I see it, you're the one who walked away."

Asher clenched his jaw. "Walked away from what? Judaism? Because it seems to me you did, too."

David's eyes darkened as he straightened in his chair. "I— we— left it for what we found to be the truth. We didn't abandon God. We just fully found Him."

Matching his father's tone, Asher replied, "And your father? What would he say about this 'truth'?"

David, his frustration peaking, interrupted, "Don't you dare bring him into this!"

Leah rose to her feet, her voice firm despite the tears starting to form. "David, Asher, that's enough. This is not what I had hoped for tonight."

Seeing the pain on his mother's face, Asher exhaled sharply and softened. "Me either, Mom. I'm truly sorry. I should go."

Asher was overwhelmed by a sense of defeat. The gap between him and his father seemed insurmountable, their heated words only widening the rift. Amidst the storm of their disagreement, Leah found herself ensnared, her tears a silent testament to the heartache caused by the conflict between her husband and son.

Leaving the living room and approaching the front door, Asher hesitated, caught between the desire to flee and the pull of reconciliation.

In the heavy silence, Asher's words were barely audible, a defense born of desperation, "It's not all my fault."

Leah, moving to the doorway, gently grasped Asher's arm. With a voice softened by love and hope, she appealed, "Give your dad some grace, Asher. This transition has been difficult for him. Many of his friends have abandoned him, but we're pursuing what we feel to be true. We've both spent countless hours soul-searching and seeking the Lord. We want no more than the same for you."

Her words, simple yet profound, lingered with Asher as he paused in the doorway. They reminded him that a foundation of love remained beneath the surface of disagreement and disappointment.

"Okay, Mom. I'll try," Asher responded, his words more a whisper of hope than a declaration. Asher left, crossing the threshold into the night.

Leah remained in the doorway, watching her son disappear into the darkness, her heart heavy with worry. David sat motionless in his chair, pondering what had just happened. The gap between him and his son was not what he desired, yet it was their reality. He thought deeply, questioning how much responsibility he bore for their strained relationship.

As Asher drove away, he reflected on how he had come seeking reconciliation and peace. Instead, he left with judgment and condemnation. It stung that those who knew him best held him in contempt, while a stranger saw value in him.

He hoped the odyssey he was about to begin would offer the time and distance he needed to sort through the pain, the anger, and the truth.

For him, tomorrow—and his call to Winston—couldn't come soon enough.

The Training

Asher rose early and well rested. With his resignation finalized and the difficult conversation with his parents behind him, Asher felt a mix of apprehension and excitement as he dialed Winston's number. His decision was made, and there was no turning back now.

Winston picked up almost immediately, his voice laced with eagerness. "Asher, I've been expecting your call."

"I'm on board, Winston," Asher announced without hesitation. "I've made all the arrangements on my end. We can proceed as you proposed."

Winston responded quickly, his voice rich with satisfaction. "Excellent. I knew you were the right choice for this. By the way, I've taken the liberty of renting an apartment nearby for us to use as our base. We will start your preparation immediately. I trust this won't be a problem?"

Winston's forwardness surprised Asher. "Immediately? You were obviously expecting me to accept your offer."

"In our line of work, time is of the essence, and yes, I was confident in your commitment," Winston replied smoothly. "Also, I've arranged for the $100,000 to be transferred to your account. You should see it by the end of the day."

Asher's mind raced at the thought of Winston's preemptive actions. It underscored the gravity of their venture and Winston's confidence in him. "Okay, Winston. What's the next step?"

"We begin your training and preparation today. Grab you something for breakfast, and then head this way. I'll have Natalie prepare us lunch and send you the address. I look forward to seeing you shortly, Asher."

Once again, Asher was surprised by Winston's quick actions. Winston had obviously been preparing for this day for months, just as he had when they first met.

It took Asher about twenty minutes to reach his destination. When he arrived, he found himself standing in front of a far more grandiose structure than he had anticipated. This was no ordinary apartment but a villa. Though it was smaller than Winston's residence in Boston, the building's expansive layout was impressive, covering over 5,000 square feet.

Natalie was there to greet him at the door, her presence as reassuring as it was familiar. "Asher," she said in her typical firm voice. "This way, please."

She led him through the foyer toward a room where Winston was waiting. She stopped at the entrance and indicated that Asher should proceed alone. Stepping into the room, she closed the door behind him. The closing of the door caught Winston's attention, who was at a table studying a map. "Ah, Asher, welcome! Come in, come in," he said with a blend of excitement as he wheeled toward Asher.

Asher was speechless. The room that lay before him was amazing, featuring tables covered with maps and documents crucial for their journey. Two large dry-erase boards, filled with notes and diagrams, dominated one end of the room, outlining their mission's intricacies.

His attention then shifted to the retina scanner, a piece of equipment he recognized from his visit to Winston's laboratory in Boston. However, a much smaller laptop was linked to the scanner instead of the desktop he remembered from the lab. Asher found the change puzzling and looked around for the rest of the time machine's hardware, expecting to see the familiar configuration.

"Winston, I see the setup here," Asher observed, motioning towards the laptop and scanner. "But aren't there some components missing?" he asked with a curious tone.

Winston smiled, his voice a mixture of satisfaction and excitement. "That laptop is our command center. It's linked to the time machine, allowing us to control it remotely. The retina scanner ensures only I can access it, so the machine itself doesn't need to be physically present."

Asher, absorbing the explanation, nodded.

"We have considerable challenges ahead, Asher," Winston started, pointing to a map of ancient Jerusalem sprawled across one of the tables. It was Asher's map, the same one he had given his dad. Seeing the map took Asher totally by surprise. "That's my map. It's not publicly available. How did you get it?" Asher inquired, examining the map more closely.

"Oh, Dean Levinsky was kind enough to provide it," Winston responded with a tone of satisfaction.

Asher's mind raced as he stared at the map, a mixture of astonishment and unease swirling within him. The fact that Winston had managed to obtain his map made Asher wonder about the depth of Winston's connections and influence. How did Winston convince Dean Levinsky to part with something so personal and unreleased? And why hadn't the dean mentioned it to him? It was a clear demonstration of Winston's persuasive power and reach, which was both impressive and slightly disconcerting.

Either ignoring or oblivious to Asher's reaction, Winston continued as he laid out the plan. "This map, your map, will prove invaluable in our quest. How well do you have it memorized?"

Asher, still reeling from the shock of seeing his own work in Winston's hands, tried to focus on the question. "I know it like the back of my hand," Asher replied, regaining his composure. "I've spent years researching, updating, and teaching with it. Every alley, every turn—I've got it memorized."

"That's good to hear," Winston nodded with a hint of approval. "You surely couldn't walk around with the map in your hand. It'll all have to be up here," he added, tapping his temple lightly.

Pointing toward a folded map on a side table, Winston asked, "Can you pass that?"

Asher quickly picked up the map, recognizing it as a current map of Jerusalem, and handed it to Winston. Winston then unfolded the map and placed it on the table next to Asher's.

As they compared the two maps, Asher couldn't help but notice the stark differences. His map showcased the city as it would have appeared in the ancient past, with narrow streets and ancient structures. In contrast, the contemporary map depicted the bustling modern city, with wide roads and towering buildings. Asher realized that, despite the passage of centuries, the essence of the city remained unchanged.

Securing a hidden location for the portal was essential, as its discovery could have disastrous consequences.

Winston, while studying the map, voiced his concern. "I can cloak the portal to make it harder to find, but it's not immune to accidental discovery. It needs to be well hidden," he explained, his voice weighted with the gravity of their situation.

Asher frowned, glancing between the maps. "Why not just place the entry portal here in this room and set the exit portal at a different location? That's what you did at your home."

Winston shook his head. "It's possible, but it makes the portals more unstable and unpredictable—far more dangerous. Placing them in separate locations increases the risk of distortions and anomalies."

Asher absorbed the answer, nodding slowly. It made sense, but it also confirmed that time travel was far from a perfected science.

"Then why not position them outside the city, somewhere remote? Wouldn't that ensure they remain undetected?"Asher proposed.

"That would mean longer travel times for you around the city and to the temple, given you're on foot throughout this mission," Winston replied.

As Asher meticulously examined the map, a sudden insight struck him. "I think I know the ideal location," he announced with conviction, capturing Winston's interest. He pointed to a location on the modern-day map. "There is an archaeological site near Ophel Hill I'm familiar with. It's not being excavated at the moment due to funding issues, so there's barely anyone there. Plus, it's directly south of the temple."

Winston, leaning over to examine the map closer, asked, "And its condition during the 1st century?"

"It housed a chamber, a small space. Its original purpose is unclear, but it seems suitable for our use, especially if we place the portal against its back wall," Asher explained, his research backing his proposal.

Seeing the logic in Asher's selection, Winston agreed. "Yes, that should work perfectly. I'll run some tests later to verify that it is indeed safe and viable."

Winston abruptly wheeled back, fixing an intense gaze on Asher.

"What's the matter?" Asher couldn't help but ask, puzzled by the sudden attention.

"My apologies, I didn't mean to stare," Winston quickly clarified, his gaze softening. "I was just thinking about your attire." Winston opened a nearby desk drawer and pulled out a worn woven linen tunic. He tossed it to Asher, followed by a much smaller folded strip of fabric.

"This should be your size. The smaller piece is a perizoma—an undergarment. Standard for the time."

Asher held both pieces, looking around hesitantly. "And where should I change into this?"

"Right here will suffice. There's no need for modesty," Winston replied with a reassuring nod.

Asher, albeit hesitantly, stripped and donned the undergarment and tunic. It seemed to him that this garment was mostly a one-size-fits-all as it draped over his torso and hung just above his knees. As he adjusted it to his body, the coarse fabric scratched against his skin, carrying with it a faint scent of body odor.

"Where did you get this?" Asher asked.

"A journey from the past, you could say. It's seen its fair share of adventures," Winston replied with a hint of nostalgia in his voice. "It's interesting to think how this simple tunic fits so many eras."

"It certainly has the aroma of history," Asher commented, not entirely sure how to feel about wearing something so... authentic.

Winston chuckled lightly, "The fragrances of the first century will be quite the departure from what you're used to today. The concepts of daily showers and deodorants were not part of their regular routine. And you will have to avoid doing the same. No colognes, deodorants, or scented shampoos. All these types of things will make you stand out."

Winston passed Asher a rugged leather belt and a small pouch, gesturing for him to put them on. "That pouch will serve as your wallet. I've provided you with a small amount of currency of the day—Asses and Denarii. You'll need it for meals and such," Winston said.

Asher untied the pouch and let the coins spill into his palm, his trained eye quickly assessing them. The Denarii, worn but still clear, bore the likeness of Emperor Tiberius. The Asses, heavier and coarser, had the distinct reddish hue of aged bronze.

"Sixteen Asses to a Denarius, correct?" Asher asked, examining the coins.

Winston nodded approvingly. "That's right. A Denarius equals a day's wages. But be cautious with the merchants—some are less than honest, especially if they sense you're a stranger."

"I'd expect nothing less," Asher replied as he wrapped the belt around his waist, securing the pouch to hang comfortably at his side.

"What shoe size do you wear?" Winston asked as he searched through a drawer.

"Eleven," Asher responded.

"Try these on; they should fit," Winston suggested, handing over a pair of scuffed leather sandals.

Finding a chair, Asher sat down to try them on. "They're a tad snug, but they'll do," he commented after finding that the sandals fit closely but not uncomfortably.

Now fully dressed in attire befitting the ancient era he was about to step into, Asher indeed looked ready to merge seamlessly with the past.

Winston sat back in his wheelchair and considered the final touches to Asher's clothing. "Your hair presents a bit of a challenge," Winston noted, his tone mixing concern with contemplation. "If you avoid combing it, the natural wave will help some."

With a thoughtful stroke of his hair, Asher acknowledged the dilemma. "Should we give it a rugged cut?" he pondered aloud, uncertain of how they might convincingly alter his look.

Winston, however, was already thinking ahead. He retrieved a textured, woven shawl from a nearby storage space. "This will be your solution," he announced, presenting the shawl to Asher. "When worn properly, it will hide your hair and align with the period's customary attire."

Accepting the shawl, Asher examined its fabric and draped it around his shoulders and head in a manner that obscured his hair, letting it fall in a way that framed his face. The shawl not only concealed his hair but also complemented the natural ruggedness of his beard, which he had allowed to grow, albeit unintentionally, enhancing his overall authenticity.

"That's much better," Winston observed with a nod of approval. "You now have the appearance of a traveler from afar and not that of a time traveler."

Now fully adorned in his historical garb, Asher was not just dressed but genuinely ready for the past. The ensemble wasn't just a costume but a necessary component of his mission.

"Wear these as much as possible between now and the time you begin your trip. Just make sure no one else sees you in them. We don't want any unwanted attention," Winston advised with a hint of humor in his voice. "Also, I'll provide you with an additional set of the attire, just in case you need them. You never know when a garment will get ripped or a sandal strap break. Just keep them at your apartment."

Asher nodded, acknowledging once again how Winston was prepared for any happenstance.

"Completing your appearance leads us to our next issue—your origin," Winston continued. "You'll need a plausible place of origin to explain your presence in Jerusalem. Do you have any ideas?" he asked, encouraging Asher to draw upon his own knowledge and experiences.

Asher leaned over a map of Jerusalem and its surrounding areas, his gaze sweeping across the ancient landscapes. After a moment of thoughtful deliberation, his finger came to rest on a specific location. "How about Capernaum?" he suggested with a hint of familiarity in his tone.

Winston looked intrigued. "Capernaum? That's an interesting choice. Why there?"

"I did an archaeological dig several years back," Asher explained. "I'm familiar with the area's history and layout, which could be useful if I need to provide detailed backstory or navigate related questions."

Winston nodded, showing his appreciation for the strategic choice. "Asher from Capernaum, I like it."

Asher walked to the board, picked up the marker, and proudly wrote, "Asher from Capernaum." He was genuinely beginning to feel like part of a team with Winston and experienced a newfound sense of camaraderie and purpose. Contributing to the planning, he felt valued and integral to their mission. This collaborative effort boosted his confidence and deepened his trust in Winston.

Winston transitioned to the next critical aspect of their preparation as he continued through his mental checklist. "Now, we need to tackle the issue of language," he announced. "They can be tricky. I understand you speak several. Which ones are you comfortable with?"

Asher responded with a hint of pride in his linguistic capabilities, "I'm quite proficient in Hebrew and have a reasonable grasp of Aramaic and Koine Greek. I believe those will be the primary languages I'll encounter."

Winston nodded. "You are correct, and Aramaic will be the most common tongue. However, given that it's the Passover season, Jerusalem will be a bustling hub of diverse cultures and languages, a veritable melting pot. This diversity will work in your favor, as your foreign accent and mannerisms will blend in more smoothly with the throngs of pilgrims and visitors in the city," he explained. "Understanding the language is one thing, but blending in means mastering the local dialects and idioms. You'll need to sound as authentic as possible."

Asher absorbed Winston's advice with a nod. "I was thinking about that on my drive over this morning. Any tips on how to avoid drawing unnecessary attention with my speech?"

"Listen more than you speak," Winston advised. "Observe how locals interact, the flow of their conversation, their body language. And when you do speak, do so with confidence."

"That makes sense," Asher acknowledged, realizing the importance of the task. "And what about cultural norms? I don't want to offend someone or do something wrong that draws attention accidentally."

"Actually, I think your upbringing will serve you well here," Winston said with reassurance. "I'm sure your childhood years were filled with learning Jewish laws and customs. Things that pertain to dietary laws, the Sabbath, and ritual purity—especially during Passover."

This comment caught Asher somewhat off guard. He had expected his training and experience as an archeologist to be of great value, but never his teachings in Judaism. After a moment of internal reflection, Asher asked, "Is there anything else I should be wary of?"

"Just keep your wits about you. The city will be crowded, and tensions can run high during such a significant festival. Stick to your purpose and avoid getting entangled in local disputes or political discussions. And remember, our main goal is to find the gold. This is going to be harder than you think. You're about to enter an entirely new world. There will be more temptations than you can imagine, especially since you have spent a lifetime studying this place and era."

"Understood. I'll tread carefully," Asher promised with a determined look in his eyes.

Winston methodically ticked off the next item on his mental checklist and steered the conversation toward the practical aspects of their mission. "Now, let's pivot to strategizing our search locations. What are your thoughts?"

Asher leaned in, his research-laden hours now finding a voice. "My initial thought was Herod's Palace, considering its historical prominence. However, I hit a dead-end there. No evidence suggests it ever harbored the treasure.

Besides, if the Romans had stumbled upon it during their takeover, history would have recorded it," Asher said, his brow furrowed in thought. "That's because they never found it," he stated with quiet conviction. "And I believe I know why."

Winston's eyes sharpened with intrigue.

Asher hesitated for a moment, then decided to share something he had never put in his book, something he had always suspected but had never dared to voice publicly. Lowering his voice as if revealing a long-guarded secret, Asher whispered, "I believe the temple wasn't just the religious center of Jerusalem—it was the city's ultimate vault. The safest place to secure something of immense value. Herod's treasure was never lost; it was hidden, deliberately concealed within the temple itself."

Winston sat back, momentarily speechless. The revelation wasn't just plausible—it was brilliant.

"Now that... that is fascinating," he admitted, clearly impressed. "If you're right, this would be one of the greatest discoveries in history."

But then, a flicker of doubt crossed Winston's face. He shook his head slightly. "But wouldn't it have been easily seen by all the people visiting the temple? After all, it was one of the most frequented places in Jerusalem—there's no way something of that magnitude could stay hidden in plain sight."

Asher smiled knowingly. "Not if it was in the one place no one could go."

Winston's brows lifted as realization dawned. He inhaled sharply and exhaled a quiet, almost reverent whisper. "Of course... the Holy of Holies. But do you realize what you're implying here? That the Holy of Holies wasn't a sacred place where the Lord Almighty dwelled, but instead a treasure vault?"

Asher laughed, "Please don't tell me you're unfamiliar with the wickedness of the Jewish kings—and even some of the High Priests—throughout history.

The room fell silent as the weight of the revelation settled between them.

Winston's eyes widened. "But only the High Priest could enter there, and only once a year. Trespassers faced death by the hands of God Himself," he reminded Asher with concern in his voice.

Asher was unconcerned about religious beliefs and replied, "I'm not worried about ancient superstitions. If there's a chance to find the treasure, it's a risk I'm willing to take."

Winston shook his head slightly. "Maybe so, but it's still a heavily guarded place, Asher. You can't just stroll into the temple unnoticed."

A smirk crossed Asher's lips. "You can if you go at night."

Winston narrowed his eyes. "You're saying security was weaker after dark?

Asher nodded. "I've spent years researching the activities of the temple, and it's my belief that security at night was severely lacking. Guards were minimal, mostly stationed at important locations like the Antonia Fortress and outer gates."

Winston raised an eyebrow. "The Antonia Fortress?"

Asher nodded. "The Roman garrison built right next to the temple. It housed soldiers who kept an eye on temple activities, especially during festivals when tensions ran high. Besides, fear ruled over them. The very idea of defiling the temple or breaking the law was enough to keep people in line—for most people, no guards were needed."

Winston exhaled, considering the implications. "How would you enter? Aren't the gates closed at night?" he inquired.

"Most likely," Asher confirmed. "Historical records suggest the gates were closed at nightfall to maintain the sanctity of the temple and for security reasons. I think our best plan is for me to enter the temple during the day and conceal myself somehow until the gates are closed, giving me free access to perform a thorough search."

Winston considered this, stroking his chin thoughtfully. "How will you manage to stay hidden until morning when the gates reopen? It's crucial you're not discovered."

Asher's eyes darted around as he considered the question, "I guess that's just how these things work, right? I'll have to figure it out on the fly."

A smile crept across Winston's face as he thought back to his numerous trips. "Yes, that's precisely how it works. And the lack of light?" Winston asked, concerned about the difficulties of navigating and searching in darkness.

"The temple's design works in our favor here," Asher explained. "Much of it is open to the sky, so the moonlight will be helpful. Additionally, I'll use the torches stored in the temple. Between the two, I should be able to see well enough to move around."

Winston nodded, reassured by Asher's meticulous planning. "What about the temple guards? Will they perform patrols that pose a risk?"

Asher's confidence stayed strong. "Most guards are stationed along the outer walls and gate entrances, focusing on external threats. Inside, the high walls of the Inner Court should shield me from their sight."

Winston's face became very serious. He then sat back in his wheelchair and said, "I think we have a plan, my friend."

Asher nodded in agreement as a look of excitement filled his face. "Yes, I believe we do. But I do have a question for you. How am I supposed to transport 50 tons of gold back without drawing attention?"

A hint of a smile played at the corners of Winston's mouth. "Ah, Asher, we're not embarking on a heist to move mountains of gold," he began, his voice laced with a reassuring calm. "We're not taking all 50 tons. Just a single ton of gold would be valued at well over 50 million dollars. I expect the treasure will have numerous precious gems as well. I think our haul will be in the neighborhood of 100 million."

Asher had never really considered the treasure's true value; to him, it was more about solving the mystery than its monetary value. Yet now, he could see himself living comfortably with half of the loot.

Asher agreed with a nod, responding, "Yes, that does sound more feasible."

"Additionally, when you find the treasure, we will move the portal to its location," Winston continued, "making it a quick and short haul."

Once again, Asher was struck by how Winston was prepared for every event and always ready with an answer. This gave Asher confidence in the potential success of the mission and Winston's concern for his safety. "So, what's next?" Asher inquired.

Before Winston could answer, the sudden ring of his phone interrupted the conversation. It was Natalie announcing that lunch was ready. Winston had requested sandwiches to ensure their preparations remained uninterrupted.

Following Winston's directions, Asher retrieved their lunch, understanding that this room was off-limits to Natalie. In the kitchen, she had prepared a simple yet thoughtful meal of bite-sized sandwiches, chips, and canned sodas. Bringing the meal back, Asher returned to find Winston deep in thought. As they ate, Winston continued preparing Asher for his trip by outlining various dangers he might encounter.

As they shared the meal, the atmosphere became a blend of earnest discussion and insightful exchange. Winston utilized his vast experiences to underscore potential pitfalls Asher might encounter during his journey. These weren't just tales of adventure; they were lessons in the dangers Asher might face and how to navigate them. Winston talked about close calls with historical conflicts, the importance of fitting into past societies, and the critical need for quick, adaptive thinking.

In addition, he stressed the unpredictability of time travel. Plans could go awry with unexpected historical twists or overlooked details. Winston recounted instances where his deep historical knowledge and fast decision-making had saved him, giving Asher a clear picture of the challenges and risks involved.

As their time together continued, Asher couldn't help but notice the signs of exhaustion beginning to creep up on Winston's face; the day's efforts were clearly wearing him down, with shadows under his eyes and a certain slowness in his movements hinting at his exhaustion.

Acknowledging his fatigue, Winston suggested a break. "I think it's a good idea for you to spend some time mentally preparing, followed by a good night's rest," he remarked, his voice betraying a hint of exhaustion. "Be back here tomorrow at 2:00 PM. We'll finalize some last-minute details."

As Asher rose to leave, Winston called out, "One more thing, Asher. Come here." He motioned for Asher to follow him to a small, secluded area of the room, where an assortment of items lay carefully arranged on a table. Among them was a simple, unassuming bar of soap.

"This," Winston said, picking up the soap and handing it to Asher, "is not just any soap. It's Castile soap made purely from olive oil. It's as close as we can get to what they might have used."

Asher, intrigued, turned the soap over in his hands; its simplicity belied its significance.

"Is this to help with scents?" he asked.

Winston sat up straight. "Exactly," he paused for emphasis, "it will help remove any modern scents from your body—scents that we discussed earlier."

Asher understandingly nodded, "So, use this tonight before I come back tomorrow?"

"No," Winston replied. "Bathe with it in the morning; sleeping in your bed would most likely put the unwanted scents back on your body. And like I said, don't use any of your usual products—no deodorants, no colognes, nothing. Just this soap. Remember, you'll have to do this before every trip."

"Got it. Bathe in history, so to speak," Asher quipped.

Winston's smile briefly broadened. "Indeed. I'll call you in the morning, around 8:00. Rest up and get ready. The journey you're about to embark on will be intense. Every detail counts."

Until this moment, the whole adventure had seemed like an outlandish fantasy. But now, Asher could vividly envision this fantasy transforming into a tangible reality.

On the Brink

Asher found it hard to sleep with all the excitement. He woke at 6:00 AM and began his day with a strong cup of coffee. The thrill of the upcoming journey made him realize how routine his life had become. This was a chance for something new, a second chance that he was fully ready to take. He was expecting a call from Winston around 8:00, so he spent the early morning going over every detail, practicing his Aramaic, and familiarizing himself with the layout of ancient city.

In the midst of his morning routine, Asher recalled Winston's specific guidance: to use the Castile soap he had been given for his shower. This plain, fragrance-free soap was a departure from the scented products he typically used. Following his shower, Asher noticed that it was time for Winston to call.

Right at 8:00 AM, his phone rang. "Hello," Asher picked up.

"Good morning, Asher. Did you manage to get some rest?" Winston's voice came through.

"Sort of," Asher replied. "I'm just eager to start."

"That's what I'm calling about. I've checked the portal location you suggested. It's secure and all set. I'll activate it after our meeting this afternoon. It'll stay open until you're back safely," Winston explained.

"Got it," Asher said. "Anything else?"

"Have a light but filling lunch. It's best for these trips. Also, come by at noon for a final check. Natalie can prepare lunch for you if that's helpful."

"No, I'll eat something here. See you at noon," Asher said, ending the call.

Just as he hung up the phone, it began to ring again, "What did you forget?" Asher asked with a laugh.

"Asher?" It was the voice of his mom, Leah.

"Oh, sorry, mom. I thought you were someone else," he said, realizing it was his mother.

“Did I catch you at a bad time? Can you talk for a minute?” Leah asked tenderly.

“I have to leave soon, but I have a minute,” Asher answered.

“Good. I wanted to talk about the other night," Leah began, her voice carrying the weight of unresolved issues between Asher and his father. "Your dad... well, we don't have to solve everything right now, but..."

"I know, Mom. And I appreciate it," Asher cut in, keen on keeping the conversation from delving too deep into the raw emotions still fresh from his recent visit. His mother's intent to smooth things over was clear, yet Asher wasn't ready to dive back into the complexities of his relationship with his father.

"So, what's on your schedule today?" Leah's attempt to shift the conversation to lighter topics was evident, a mother's way of maintaining some connection, however small.

"Actually, I've got quite a bit on my plate. It's that project I mentioned the other night," Asher replied, deliberately vague. The less he said about the true nature of his day, the better. His earlier conversations about the opportunity had been wrapped in half-truths and evasions, a pattern he found necessary to continue now.

"Yes, I remember. Can you tell me more about it?" Leah pressed curiously.

"It's just this thing I'm helping with. I’ll be working on it for the next several weeks or so," Asher said, skirting around specifics.

“Will you be traveling, or is it a local project,” his mom asked.

“It’s a little of both,” Asher said, finding it comical that the statement was entirely true and a lie at the same time.

Leah's concern came over the phone: “Do you think you and I could have lunch together one day this week? I mean, if you’re in town.”

"I don't know, Mom. I'm not sure what my daily schedule will be," Asher assured her, eager to steer the conversation to its end. "I'll contact you when I know more."

Leah remained silent, and Asher could tell she was upset.

"Mom, I love you and Dad. Please know that I'm still committed to working things out. This project is going to consume a large amount of my time," Asher continued. "Like I said, I'll call when I know more."

They said their goodbyes and ended the call. Their conversation brought Asher's emotions back to the surface, and he began to doubt his decision not to meet with her. But he also knew that some time apart would give them both a chance to reflect on the best way to proceed.

Asher attempted to shift his focus to the day's preparations. He launched an app on his tablet, a tool specifically developed by a colleague for archaeologists working in foreign lands. The app, designed to facilitate language learning for fieldwork, had been invaluable to Asher on multiple occasions. He had first used it during a dig in the ancient city of Dura-Europos, where locals who spoke Aramaic helped with the dig. The app proved vital in communicating with the community and understanding historical inscriptions.

Reflecting on the app's familiar interface brought Asher back to the early days of his and Rita's expeditions. In the early days of their marriage, before the advent of the sophisticated app, Asher and Rita's language practice sessions were rooted in a more traditional approach. Surrounded by piles of language guides, ancient texts, and a collection of CDs painstakingly gathered from various libraries and online resources, they would transform their living room into a makeshift classroom. Due to his upbringing, Asher was more versed in speaking numerous languages, so he would lead the sessions.

These moments were deeply collaborative, and intimate, and a memory cherished by Asher. Rita, ever eager to learn, would enthusiastically pour over the texts with Asher. These times were filled with laughter and lighthearted competition, each mispronunciation a cause for amusement rather than frustration. They were the moments when their bond had grown the most.

As technology evolved, so did their method of study. When the app was developed, it transformed their learning process and made it more efficient. However, the transition to using the app also marked a shift in their relationship. The intimate, collaborative nature of their study sessions gave way to a more solitary learning experience. Asher attempted to push those memories to the back of his mind, trying to focus on the task at hand.

The app functioned through a series of interactive exercises, including listening to native pronunciations and repeating them. It would analyze his attempts, offering corrections and tips to improve his accent and fluency. As he navigated through the phrases, a particular sentence popped up: "The road to Rome is difficult to travel." This mundane phrase halted his practice mid-breath. The phrase tugged at a memory, something familiar yet distant. He had heard something similar before, not in the context of geography or history, but in a more personal discussion.

Nostalgia and sorrow washed over him as the phrase connection dawned on him. Rita had once used the concept of the "Roman Road" as a metaphorical path to explain the basics of Christianity to him, utilizing a series of verses from the Book of Romans to outline the path to salvation. This method, while meaningful to her, had irked Asher. The "Roman Road" felt like an oversimplification of complex beliefs to him.

The memory was a sharp reminder of why he found himself where he was today—about to finalize his divorce. The papers, already signed by Rita, lay on the table, symbolic closure to a chapter of his life filled with both love and conflict. All they required now was his signature. Compelled to put the past behind him, Asher signed, placed it in the envelope, and headed out to mail it to his attorney, a task he approached with a heavy heart.

On his way, he stopped at his favorite deli. It was also one that he and Rita used to frequent. Sitting alone among the familiar sights and sounds, Asher couldn't shake off the feeling of loneliness that enveloped him. It was clear he longed for companionship, but this time, he hoped to find someone who shared his cultural background—Jewish, yet not overly religious. His experiences with Rita had taught him the importance of shared values, but he also sought a balance that could accommodate his views on faith and spirituality.

After eating, Asher headed toward Winston's house. This moment felt like the definitive closing of one chapter in his life, yet emotionally, Asher felt as though a piece of his heart lingered in the pages just turned.

Through the Portal

Asher arrived at Winston's house, parked his car, and retrieved the carefully packed garments. As he made his way to the entrance, each step was filled with anticipation and hesitation.

Just as he reached the top step, the door swung open before he could knock. To his surprise, it was Winston—not Natalie—waiting to greet him. He was in his wheelchair as usual, but surprisingly, he was rejuvenated and alert. The difference in his appearance was striking; Winston looked healthier and more animated than in any of their previous meetings. Asher pondered the cause of such a transformation.

Noticing Asher's glance, Winston seemed to anticipate the unasked questions. "Natalie's out running errands," he explained, addressing the absence of the usual welcome. "Today, it's crucial we have no distractions."

The two made their way to the preparation room they had used the day before. The familiar space, with its maps and notes, felt even more significant now. Asher quickly changed into the ancient garments for Winston's inspection.

Winston circled Asher, inspecting him with a meticulous gaze that missed no detail. Finally, he rolled back, satisfaction etched across his face. "You look the part, Asher. Remember, the primary goals of this trip are to get comfortable with the city and observe the temple gates. Also, avoid unnecessary interactions as much as possible."

"Relax. I understand, and I'm prepared," Asher said confidently, trying to convey this to Winston.

"Ok, contact me immediately upon your return. It's imperative I know you've made it back safely and what you've discovered so we can plan for the next trip," Winston replied as a man sending his son on his first date.

As they prepared to part ways, Winston imparted a final piece of advice, a powerful reminder of the dangers and responsibilities ahead. "Be vigilant, Asher. The past is not a place for the reckless. Every action, every word, can ripple through time."

"You have my word. I understand the dangers," Asher said with confidence.

It was now time for Winston's final instructions, "Park your car near the Ophel Hill dig, where it should be safe. Leave your modern clothes and cell phone in the trunk. Hide your key under the front bumper. I'll activate the portal ten minutes after you leave here. It will remain active until you return. When you're safely back, drive to your apartment and call me. Tomorrow morning, you will come over for a complete debrief. Got it?"

"Yep, got it," Asher replied.

With that, Winston began the process of starting the time machine as Asher left the room.

Asher found a parking spot within 100 yards of where Winston had placed the portal. Before he headed to the portal, he stowed his personal effects and hid the key to his car. Because it was cloaked, he would have never found the portal if he hadn't known its exact location.

As he entered the portal, a familiar sensation enveloped him. It was as if every cell in his body vibrated, adjusting to the shift between worlds. Winston had described the sensation as the body's response to the temporal shift, a necessary discomfort that marked the passage through time.

Asher stepped out of the portal to find himself in the small room that they had selected to help conceal its location. The careful planning behind the portal's placement was immediately apparent; the room provided a discrete transition from one era to another, ensuring Asher could arrive and leave unseen. This brief solitude allowed him a moment to gather his thoughts and emotions after the jarring experience of time travel.

As Asher stepped outside the room, he found himself in a place that was similar but very different. The immediate difference was the air. As Winston had mentioned, it carried a distinct aroma—fresh yet laden with a scent Asher couldn't immediately place. It took a moment for his senses to adjust before it dawned on him. It was the distinctive smell of animals, a combination of the earthy and the pungent, that filled the atmosphere. This was not just the background scent of rural life but the everyday reality of ancient Jerusalem. The freshness of the air, mixed with this omnipresent aroma, was a stark reminder of the authenticity of his surroundings. Asher recalled experiencing similar smells on his various archaeological trips to rural areas, but never this strong.

Stepping onto the stairs leading to the temple, Asher was immediately struck by the vibrant cityscape of Jerusalem, a city he had come to know through countless hours of research and excavation. Yet what lay before him was vastly different from the Jerusalem of the 21st century. Instead, he was met with the ancient city in all its historical splendor. The most striking sight was the temple, its breathtaking beauty and grandeur dominating the landscape. The temple towered over the city. Seeing it in its beautiful and untarnished state was a dream come true for an archaeologist. The outer walls of the temple enclosed about 35 acres, a sprawling expanse that hummed with the activity of people and animals. Some of these animals, Asher realized, were likely destined for sacrificial purposes, a common practice of the time.

The entire area was alive with a variety of sounds and a flurry of activity, painting a vivid picture of daily life in ancient Jerusalem. The emotional impact of standing in the midst of a city he had only known through artifacts and texts was overwhelming. Asher found himself momentarily stunned, the reality of his surroundings catching him off guard.

Here was Jerusalem, a place he considered home, yet it was a version of the city entirely alien to him. This ancient Jerusalem showcased the temple in its full magnificence—the very temple he believed held the hidden treasure. Despite being 2,000 years before his time, Asher felt a sense of connection.

For several hours, Asher wandered the ancient streets of Jerusalem, immersing himself in the city's sights, sounds, smells, and even tastes. As he navigated the bustling marketplace, a particular stall caught his eye, its display of dried figs promising a taste of the local produce.

Asher approached the merchant. "How much for a handful of these figs?" he inquired, his interest evident.

The merchant, assessing Asher's interest, responded with a practiced ease, "Two asses for a good handful, sir. They're the finest we have, dried under the Judean sun."

Asher retrieved the two coins from his pouch and placed them in the merchant's outstretched hand. The merchant accepted the coins with a nod and, in return, gave Asher a generous portion of the dried figs.

Asher selected a fig and took a bite. The flavor, bursting forth with an intense sweetness akin to honey, immediately captured his senses. The fig's texture was ideal, offering a satisfying blend of chewiness and tenderness.

While savoring the taste, Asher noticed the merchant observing him, clearly interested in his reaction to the fruit.

"Well, what do you think?" the merchant inquired, his tone laced with a touch of pride. "Does it meet your expectations?"

Asher, still processing the flavor, enthusiastically replied, "Incredible. I've never tasted anything quite like it." His words conveyed genuine appreciation, yet his accent betrayed him as an outsider.

The merchant's curiosity peaked, and he noted the accent. "You're not local, are you? Where do you come from?" he asked, his tone friendly but inquisitive.

Asher, briefly unsettled by the direct question, quickly recalled the background story he had concocted. "Well, I've lived in many places, but most recently, Capernaum," he calmly said, hoping the vague response would satisfy his curiosity.

"Ah, Capernaum, by the Sea of Galilee. I know it well," the merchant replied, accepting Asher's answer.

Despite the merchant's casual demeanor, Asher felt a stirring of caution. Conversations like these, innocent though they might seem, were precisely what he needed to navigate carefully. Recognizing the risk of drawing too much attention, he concluded the interaction.

"The figs are exceptional; thank you," Asher smiled before withdrawing from the stall.

"Shalom," the merchant called with a hint of suspicion.

With a polite nod, Asher turned and blended back into the crowd. Winston had warned him to avoid interacting with people, and Asher better understood now. Each encounter held the potential for danger.

Asher recognized it was time to transition from the role of an awestruck tourist to that of a focused man on a mission. As he wove through the bustling streets of Jerusalem, he made mental notes of the city's dynamics. The streets were crowded with people, not just Jerusalem citizens but also numerous visitors for Passover.

Another group stood out—Roman soldiers whose presence was impossible to miss. Asher could feel the hatred between the Roman soldiers and the Jewish populace. There was little to no interaction between the two groups, at least no friendly interactions.

As Asher continued to roam the streets, he noticed the long shadows of the buildings signaling the setting of the sun. He found himself about a 15-minute walk from the temple, and that's where he needed to be. Asher hastened his walk in that direction.

As he neared the temple, his gaze fell on a segment of the Western Wall, though its profound importance didn't immediately register. Gradually, the realization struck him with the force of a physical blow. This was no ordinary part of the wall; this area would come to be known as the Wailing Wall, the enduring fragment of the temple.

Drawn irresistibly towards it, Asher reached out to touch the wall, believing he was in the same spot his father had once brought him to as a child. That visit was woven with a complex array of emotions and teachings. With deep reverence, his father had placed his hand against the cool stones. His eyes closed as tears traced paths down his cheeks, his lips moving in silent prayer. In that moment, he was connected with the divine, a bond facilitated by the ancient, worn stones under his palm. In a voice filled with emotion, his father had whispered to Asher, "These stones offer a direct line to Elohim. As we touch them, we bridge the gap across generations, connecting with the very essence of our faith. And one day, Elohim will rebuild these walls."

The moment of recognition brought with it a flood of memories. While that trip was a cherished memory, it brought a mixture of emotions. His father had been eager to pass on the significance of the place, a connection to their faith and history. Yet, as he grew older, Asher grappled with the beliefs and convictions his father cherished and rejected them.

Lost in a whirlwind of memories and conflicting emotions from his past visit to the Wall with his father, Asher was suddenly jolted back to the present by the sound of a shofar. Asher was well-acquainted with the distinctive sound of the ram's horn. It had been a constant presence in his life, primarily due to his father's tradition of blowing it during various religious events.

Its deep, reverberating blast cut through his thoughts, a clear signal that the temple was preparing to close for the evening. This sound marked the moment he had been waiting for. Asher's internal struggle with his faith momentarily faded into the background as he realized the significance of what was happening. Now would be the moment that the temple doors would be closed. Asher observed the last of the worshippers leaving the temple as the shofar continued to blow. Recognizing this as his chance, he strategically positioned himself to gain a clear view of the nearest doors. He needed to observe this critical juncture: *would these doors close with the setting sun as he speculated?*

As if on cue, the temple's massive doors began to close slowly. The sight of the large doors swinging shut offered a silent yet clear confirmation of his theory. With this critical observation, Asher knew it was time to leave. The mission for today was accomplished, and now, the priority was to return to the portal safely.

As the sun continued to set, another notable distinction between the two centuries emerged—darkness. Unlike the well-lit streets and buildings of the 21st century, only a few scattered torches and lanterns provided light for the streets. Fortunately, just days from being full, the moon provided some beneficial light in the absence of street or building lights.

Asher was concerned about the temple's proximity to the portal. While the distance wasn't considerable, he understood the night's inherent dangers. Winston had repeatedly warned Asher about the prevalence of thieves, and the dangers of robbers resonated in his mind.

Roman soldiers appear to be more abundant and alert. Asher couldn't determine whether it was due to the darkness or if there was a disturbance in the city. They intermittently halted and interrogated individuals, and Asher, witnessing their brutality firsthand, swiftly concluded they couldn't be trusted, nor did they extend trust to anyone else.

In his nervousness, he inadvertently increased his pace, a mistake that drew the attention of the Roman soldiers. Though he heard one call out to him, he pretended not to hear, prompting an even louder shout and a subsequent pursuit. Panic gripped him. *Was he going to be arrested on his very first trip?*

He sprinted through the darkened streets, the soldiers in hot pursuit. Desperation led him down a street that, to his dismay, turned out to be a dead end. Uncertain if the soldiers had seen him take the turn, he felt trapped.

Aware that capture could mean the end of his mission—or worse—Asher spotted his only chance of escape: an unassuming doorway. With the soldiers' shouts growing louder, he pushed the door open and slipped into the room, quickly pulling it shut behind him.

He was met with an unexpected sight: a woman standing calmly in the single-room dwelling. Surprisingly, she neither screamed nor tried to escape his sudden intrusion.

The outside commotion intensified as they stood in a tense silence, assessing each other. The clatter of armored footsteps echoed down the narrow street, and Asher could hear the soldiers barking orders as they moved from door to door.

Heavy fists pounded against the wooden doors of nearby homes. A gruff voice commanded, “Open up! We’re searching for a fugitive!”

The knocks moved progressively closer. Asher’s pulse quickened. If they searched every house, it was only a matter of moments before they reached this door.

He glanced at the woman, his eyes pleading for cooperation. *Would she turn him in—or help him hide?*

Suddenly, a sharp, forceful pounding rattled the door he had just slipped through.

"Open up!" one soldier barked authoritatively, his voice sharp and impatient.

The woman glanced towards the door, then back at Asher, a silent communication passing between them. She moved closer to the door but did not open it immediately.

The woman turned to Asher with urgent, whispered instructions. "Lie down on the bed, pretend you're napping," she said, her tone both commanding and calm. “I’ll get rid of them.”

Understanding the moment's gravity, Asher moved swiftly to the bed, lying down and trying to steady his breath so that he appeared asleep. The woman watched him for a brief second, ensuring he looked convincing before she approached the door.

"Who's there? This is a private home!" Her steady voice betrayed none of the tension that filled the room.

“We’re in search of a fugitive. Open the door, or we will kick it in!" the soldier commanded, more insistently this time.

Asher tried to remain calm, aware that much depended on the woman's next actions. The woman remained surprisingly composed, and Asher wondered if she would attempt to protect him.

With resolve and confidence, she slowly opened the door to see two Roman soldiers. "Are you here alone?" the taller of the two asked.

"No, I am here with my brother; he is tired after a long day traveling to the city for Passover," she declared confidently.

The soldier turned his attention to Asher. "You, sit up. What is your name?" the soldier ordered.

Asher slowly sat up, attempting to look as if they had awoken him. "Asher," he answered, trying to avoid talking too much.

"Are you a Jew?" The soldier asked with disgust.

"Yes," Asher replied, again to say as few words as possible.

The soldiers look Asher over with disdain. "A thief is working in this neighborhood," the soldier said as he sized Asher up. After a brief but tense moment, he continued, "But you don't seem to fit his description."

Asher let out an internal sigh of relief, grateful that his ruse worked.

"I suggest you stay indoors," the soldier warned before they stepped out the door and disappeared back into the dark.

Once the soldiers' footsteps faded, Asher turned to the woman, his expression etched with gratitude and confusion. "Thank you, but why did you protect me?" he asked, genuinely puzzled.

The woman locked eyes with him, her gaze steady and resolute. "Like any Jew, I have no love for the Roman pigs," she said, her voice laced with a mix of defiance and weariness. "We don't trust them. As a Jew, you don't know this?" she asked as if confused.

Her words resonated with Asher, underscoring the deep-seated hatred between the Jewish people and their Roman occupiers. This animosity felt all too familiar to him, reflecting the ongoing conflicts he had witnessed between the people of Israel and groups like Hamas and Hezbollah. He was deeply saddened as he realized that even after two thousand years, Jerusalem had yet to experience true peace.

"Yes, of course, I understand. It's just... you took a big risk, and I am grateful," Asher sincerely expressed.

"You are welcome, but now you must go. You cannot remain here," she said with indifference.

Asher hesitated, wanting to wait just long enough for the soldiers to leave the immediate area. Cautiously, Asher looked down the darkened street and saw no evidence of the soldiers. With a quick goodbye, he slipped out into the night and down the street. Quickly, he started to mentally map a path back to the portal. His heart raced as he navigated the streets and alleyways, being mindful to avoid detection.

Finally, the familiar silhouette of the room containing the portal emerged from the shadows. Relief washed over him as he stepped through the portal, greeted by the now-familiar warm sensation it provided. The feeling was comforting because it meant he was home, but it also zapped the last of his strength. He collapsed on the ground as he took a few steps away from the portal. His head was spinning, and his heart was pounding. The stress of the day had fully caught up with him. After finally steadying himself enough to make it to his car, Asher's drive back to his apartment was marked by silence, his thoughts still racing from the day's intense preparations and his harrowing experience reaching the portal.

Upon arriving at his apartment, Asher's sole intention was to briefly rest before fulfilling his promise to call Winston. He barely made it to his bed, convincing himself that a few minutes of lying down would help him gather the energy needed for the phone call. However, the weight of the day proved too much for his drained body and mind. What was meant to be a short rest turned into deep sleep.

Trip Aftermath

Asher was awakened by a vibrating sound. Trying to adjust his eyes to the sunlight beginning to fill his bedroom, he glanced at the clock and felt a surge of panic. Twelve hours. He'd slept for twelve hours straight, missing not only the crucial call to Winston to confirm his safe return but also the time for their scheduled trip debriefing. Asher discovered the source of the vibration was his phone. He had put it on silent when he placed it in his car's trunk.

He hurriedly answered the phone, bracing himself for Winston's inevitable displeasure.

"Hello?" Asher's tone was hoarse, laden with sleep and apprehension.

Winston's voice, tinged with both concern and frustration, filled the line. "Asher, are you okay? You were supposed to call after returning last night. And we had a debrief scheduled for this morning. I've been trying to contact you for hours! What happened?"

Asher swallowed hard. "I'm so sorry, Winston. I... I just lay down for a moment and unexpectedly fell asleep. The trip was much more of a drain on me than I had expected." His apology was sincere and laden with the realization of his misstep.

Winston exhaled sharply, his tone shifting from frustration to controlled concern. "The computer logged your return yesterday evening, but when you failed to call, I became concerned."

There was a brief pause before Winston continued, his tone softening slightly, "I'm pleased you're okay, Asher, but we can't afford these types of oversights. Get here as soon as you can. We have a lot to cover."

Asher sat up, rubbing his temples. "I understand, Winston. I should have called. It won't happen again."

Winston was silent for a moment before replying, "Good. Because keeping track of your movements isn't just about protocol—it's about your safety."

"Understood. I'm on my way," Asher assured him, the gravity of his oversight propelling him into swift action.

He dressed hastily, grabbed two bananas and an orange from his kitchen counter, and ate the food during the drive to Winston's. Asher debated telling Winston about the close call the night before. But Asher knew it would only lead to more stress in their already tense relationship.

Upon arrival, Asher recounted his experiences, deliberately omitting his near capture. However, he did share the exciting news about the temple doors closing at dark. "The doors closed exactly as we theorized. It was incredible to see," Asher said, hoping to regain Winston's trust.

Winston's reaction was more enthusiastic than Asher anticipated. "This is excellent. Good work!" Winston exclaimed, momentarily setting aside any lingering frustrations from earlier.

The conversation quickly shifted to the next steps. "Now, you'll need to explore the temple during the day. Understand its layout and routines. It's essential for planning your search at night," Winston directed, laying out a clear path forward for Asher.

It was then that Winston shared news of his impending absence. "I'll be out of town for the next two days, so I will need you to check in by text daily—once before you leave and once when you return. The portal will remain active for you to use as necessary," he explained, a decision underscoring his trust in Asher's capabilities.

The Winston sitting before Asher now bore little resemblance to the man he had seen just the day before. The rapid decline in his health was startlingly evident, casting a shadow of concern over their meeting. Winston's vitality had vanished, replaced by a frailty that seemed to have happened overnight.

Mid-conversation, Winston was seized by a coughing spell unlike anything Asher had witnessed before. When it passed, Asher noticed the alarming sight of blood on Winston's handkerchief. The sight was shocking and worrisome.

Winston knew he needed immediate medical attention. His hand trembled as he reached for the device around his neck, but his fingers fumbled, struggling to press the button.

Without hesitation, Asher stepped in, pressing the device for him.

Knowing Natalie couldn't enter the room, he quickly moved behind Winston's wheelchair and rolled him toward the door. By the time they entered the hallway, Natalie was already approaching, moving quickly toward them.

"What happened?" she asked, her voice laced with professional concern as she assessed Winston's body.

Winston, struggling to regain his breath, managed a weak smile. "Just a little coughing spell, nothing to worry about," he tried to reassure her, but the blood-stained handkerchief in his hand told a different story.

Natalie's reaction was immediate. "Stay with him; I'll be right back," she announced, hurrying away to fetch her medical supplies.

Seizing the brief moment of privacy, Winston leaned towards Asher, his voice a raspy whisper. "Remember, Asher, the gold... we must find it. That's our mission," he stressed, the importance of their quest outweighing his physical condition.

Before Asher could respond, Natalie returned, medical bag in hand. She swiftly began examining Winston, her nursing skills evident as she checked his vitals, her brow furrowing in concentration. "You need to rest, Winston," she said firmly, preparing a syringe.

"What's that for?" Asher asked, watching as she administered the shot.

"It's to help him sleep and recover," Natalie explained while focusing on Winston. As the medication took effect, his body slumped over, and his eyes fluttered shut as consciousness slipped away.

Natalie quickly supported and straightened Winston's body. Turning to Asher, she instructed, "He needs sleep, and it's best if you leave now." Her command was not a request.

Asher nodded, understanding the gravity of the situation. He glanced at Winston, now in a peaceful slumber. The mission's weight seemed heavier in the room's silence, but Winston's parting words echoed in his mind. Winston had made a clear directive, and Asher knew he had to obey it. With a final look at Winston, Asher quietly exited and began the drive back to his apartment.

Asher also realized that if anything happened to Winston, the knowledge of how to operate the time machine would be lost. It was a delicate balance between meeting Winston's priorities and pursuing his goals. While Winston was fixated on the gold, Asher saw a greater purpose beyond mere wealth. Completing this mission was just a stepping stone towards a more significant endeavor—one that held paramount importance to him.

The realization that these future explorations were in jeopardy weighed heavily on him. Winston was the linchpin of their operation, the only one with the knowledge and expertise to navigate the complexities of the time machine. Without Winston, the machine was nothing more than an intricate piece of technology.

Asher pulled into his complex and quickly entered his apartment. Once inside, the urgency of the situation spurred Asher into action. There was no time for rest; the stakes were too high, and the clock was ticking on their mission and Winston's health. With Winston's condition precarious, each moment felt critical.

In his bedroom, Asher quickly changed back into his ancient attire. He looked around his apartment and saw several items that he knew would greatly help but were strictly prohibited. A flashlight and a digital camera would make his mission much easier, but both could have dire consequences.

He also considered the convenience of more basic items like sunglasses or a cap. Though seemingly trivial, these were essentials in the modern world, offering comfort and protection that he now had to forego. The absence of such simple items underscored the vast differences between his everyday life and the historical world he navigated.

Before leaving, Asher took one last look around his apartment, silently acknowledging the uncertainty of what lay ahead. Then, with a deep breath, he left the secure confines of home, locking the door behind him. The drive back to the portal's location was swift, as traffic was unusually light.

Upon reaching the designated area near the Ophel Hill dig, Asher parked his car and stowed his items as before. The vicinity was still largely unoccupied, making his approach to the portal swift and unobstructed. As he passed through the portal again, the now-familiar sensation of entering it was accompanied by the unmistakable rumble of hunger. Asher recognized this not as a quirk of the portal but the result of skipping lunch, a decision he regretted as he contemplated his next move.

Eating before exploring the temple was essential, yet retracing his steps through the portal for a meal was impractical and risky. Of course, eating here was risky too, especially considering his previous dining experience. After a brief moment of consideration, Asher resolved to find food in the ancient city. This time, however, he would be more cautious.

Return to Russia

Winston wrestled with doubts about the progress of his medical treatments. On certain days, he noticed marginal improvements. Yet, more often, he found himself feeling decidedly worse. During their consultations, Dr. Vinogradov reminded him that such ups and downs were an expected part of the treatment. The reality was that Winston had no other options. If these treatments failed, he was doomed. And the high cost of the treatments was becoming a more significant issue.

Previously, Winston had never worried about money, especially after the creation of the time machine. This invention had not only been a scientific breakthrough but also a financial boon, securing his independence. However, his current health predicament had changed all of that. Time travel was all but impossible for him to do, especially alone. He was totally dependent on the success of Dr. Vinogradov's treatments; he was now equally dependent on Asher's success.

Winston and Natalie settled into the familiar confines of the same hotel they had stayed in during their previous visit. Winston hated being out in public. The curious stares and puzzled looks from strangers constantly reminded him of his predicament. To them, he appeared to be in his eighties, a stark contrast to his actual age of fifty-two. He thought about how ironic it was that the invention that had brought him immense wealth was now draining his resources.

As he was contemplating these things, there was a knock on the door. Winston glanced at Natalie, signaling her to answer the door. Dr. Vinogradov entered, carrying a medical bag that, to Winston, symbolized the cure to his ailment.

"Good afternoon, Winston. How you feel since we last met?" Dr. Vinogradov asked, his tone professional yet lacking warmth.

"It's been a mix. Some days, I feel an improvement; other days, it's as if I've taken two steps back," Winston replied, trying to mask his frustration. "The shots have given me the strength I need to conduct important meetings, but they don't seem to last long. I can feel myself fading by the end of the day."

Natalie, quietly observing, watched as the doctor unpacked his medical bag and retrieved his stethoscope.

After a brief examination, which seemed more a formality than a thorough check-up, Dr. Vinogradov nodded, seemingly satisfied. "Is normal, these fluctuations. Treatment very strong, effects can vary." Then, turning to Natalie, he handed her a syringe. “Please, you do injection.”

Natalie quickly followed the doctor's orders. Winston felt the now-familiar warmth as the medicine entered his system, a sensation eerily similar to that experienced with each passage through the time machine portal. However, this time, the accompanying dizziness was overwhelming, sending him into unconsciousness. The last thing Winston remembered was Natalie's quick actions to support him before everything went black.

Waking up groggy, Winston was unsure how long he had been out. As he tried to gather himself, he found Natalie and Dr. Vinogradov engaged in a deep conversation in what sounded like Russian. Winston felt he was surely mistaken because, to his knowledge, Natalie didn’t speak Russian. Confused and disoriented, he managed to groan out her name, drawing her attention immediately.

Rushing to his side, Natalie began tending to him, her care efficient and gentle. It took several moments for Winston to fully emerge from the fog of unconsciousness.

Upon noticing Winston's awakening, Dr. Vinogradov attempted to reassure him. “This is normal reaction. With future treatments, you should expect this," he explained, his voice void of concern.

But it was the doctor's next revelation that truly unsettled Winston. "Because of war between Russia-Ukraine, price for treatments now will be $200,000 each time," Dr. Vinogradov announced, his tone matter-of-fact. "Is very dangerous now to get these drugs, adding to cost."

Winston was seething with anger, yet his physical state left him no room to argue. What choice did he have but to continue? His options were severely limited, a fact painfully clear to both him and Dr.

Vinogradov. Discovering that the cost of the injections had doubled, plunging him deeper into financial strain, only intensified his frustration. To realize he was entirely at the whim of Dr. Vinogradov's doubled pricing amid his dwindling health and shrinking financial reserves was incredibly difficult to accept.

Observing Winston's visible anger, the doctor carefully chose his words, "I know this is significant change, but treatment must continue for quality," he added, closing his medical bag with a deliberate click. Without awaiting a reply, he left, pausing only momentarily at the door to look back. "In 30 days, I expect to see you. Should you have any questions, do not hesitate to contact me."

With that, Dr. Vinogradov exited the room, leaving behind Winston and Natalie in a heavy silence. The door clicked shut—a soft sound that seemed to echo the finality of the moment.

Winston spent the next twelve hours recovering before he was strong enough to fly back to Jerusalem. The flight home was very restless for Winston. He had so many things on his mind. First and foremost was his health and the increasing cost of the treatments. Additionally, Asher had once again failed to check in as required. Had something gone wrong? Had he run into trouble—or worse, decided to abandon the mission altogether? Or was this just Asher being Asher? Winston had to return to Jerusalem and take control of the quest for the gold!

By the time the plane touched down, Winston was exhausted. It was a struggle for Natalie to get him home and in bed. Winston was quickly off to sleep, where he dreamed of being young and strong again.

Second Trip

Asher's growling stomach continued to remind him of his forgetting to eat before beginning today's mission. Determined to resolve his dilemma before his tour of the temple, he headed towards the market, a place teeming with life and the aroma of fresh produce and baked goods. The market was near where he had narrowly escaped arrest the previous night, a memory that made him tread cautiously.

Asher navigated through the lively market, searching for something to eat. As he scanned the stalls for a quick bite, his gaze landed on a woman whose presence felt oddly familiar. Dressed in a flowing beige tunic that grazed her ankles, complemented by simple sandals, she exuded a natural elegance.

Her rich olive skin, deep brown eyes, and cascading brown hair—only partially covered by the off-white headscarf typically worn by Jewish women—made her stand out. The sight evoked memories of his mother, who often wore a similar covering. The woman's presence halted Asher in his tracks; her striking beauty was impossible to ignore.

Suddenly, he realized it was her, the woman who had helped him. In the dim light of her home, under the shadow of danger, Asher hadn't fully appreciated her allure. Now, in the clarity of daylight and away from the stress of Roman soldiers, her true beauty was unmistakable.

She was unaware of his presence as she examined some fruits at a nearby stall.

Unable to resist the urge to repay her kindness, Asher approached a nearby merchant. "Who is that woman?" he inquired discreetly, nodding towards her.

The merchant looked up from his task at hand and studied her for a moment. "Miriam," the merchant replied with a cautious tone. Offering no further details, his focus quickly returned to his goods.

Taking a deep breath, Asher approached her, his heart racing with a mixture of gratitude and something deeper he couldn't fully name.

"Excuse me, Miriam?" he called out, hoping his presence wouldn't startle her.

She turned, her expression one of surprise. "Yes? Do I know you?"

"It's me, from last night," Asher began, realizing how absurd that must sound in the broad daylight of the market. "I... I wanted to formally introduce myself. My name is Asher. And I want to thank you again for your kindness."

Looking around to see if anyone was watching her, she gently replied, "As I said before, you are welcome." She turned her attention to the merchant. "Yes, I will take those," she said, referring to the olives for sale.

In an attempt to show his genuine appreciation, Asher replied, "Allow me to pay for your items as a small token of my gratitude."

With her head slightly lowered, she again glanced around the marketplace. "No, that would not be appropriate," she snapped back before calming herself.

Miriam's initial resistance was evident in her posture, but Asher's persistence, coupled with the sincerity in his eyes, slowly broke down her defenses.

"Please, it's the least I can do," Asher pressed on, handing a few coins to the merchant before Miriam could protest further.

As the merchant took the coins from Asher, he placed the olives in her woven basket, which already contained some bread and fish. "Please, allow me," Asher said as he reached to try to carry her basket.

"That will not be necessary," she replied as she pulled away. "Thank you for your generosity, and enjoy the rest of your day."

Asher watched as she walked away. Mindful of not imposing too much, Asher focused on quelling his growing hunger. Wandering through the bustling market, his attention was captured by a vendor selling an enticing array of pastries. Selecting one filled with spiced lamb, he was pleasantly surprised by its rich taste, far surpassing his initial expectations.

Despite understanding the potential risks, Asher felt an undeniable pull to learn more about Miriam from the merchant who had first mentioned her by name.

"Could you perhaps tell me a bit more about her?" Asher ventured cautiously, attempting not to come across as prying.

"You like the pretty ones, huh?" The merchant jests before becoming more serious and warns Asher, "Don't let her beauty get you in trouble. I suggest you stay clear of that one."

Driven by a blend of intrigue and concern, Asher gently asked, "May I ask why?"

"There are many eyes on her," whispered the merchant, a warning tone in his voice.

Concerned, Asher inquired softly, "Is she in any sort of trouble?"

"Trouble?" mused the merchant. "Depends on how you define trouble."

Asher was confused and didn't want to be too pushy for information. To his delight, the merchant continued. "Lots of rumor. Some say she is a harlot, others that she's a Roman collaborator. I don't know about any of that; I mind my own business. As should you," he said with a mischievous look.

"So, she's not married," Asher asked.

"She's betrothed, or at least she was. That's how I hear it," the merchant said in hushed tones.

"Was? Do you know what happened?" Asher persisted, curiosity getting the better of him.

The merchant gave a solemn nod. "Hard to say, but it was to a man named Amos. I've never personally liked him. He's rude and thinks too highly of himself if you ask me," he disclosed. "Their engagement ended amidst allegations of her infidelity. I never saw any evidence of that, but either way, now she's overshadowed by his accusations."

"Why would he lie?" Asher inquired with a sense of urgency in his voice.

The merchant gave Asher a significant look, signaling the end of their discussion. "I've said enough. Amos is a powerful man with friends in high places. I have no desire to entangle myself in such affairs. I suggest you do the same."

Realizing that he had taken the conversation as far as he could safely go, Asher thanked the merchant and began to head towards the temple. He couldn't help but feel compassion for Miriam. He realized that women in the first century were often mistreated. The simple thought of Miriam enduring such hardship filled Asher with profound sadness. He wondered if he could be of some type of help to her.

Asher's thoughts were interrupted as he rounded a corner to witness Roman soldiers emerging from a modest house. Roughly, they drug a man between them. The man's resistance was futile against their iron grip as they threw him onto the dusty street with a disdain that spoke volumes of their authority.

"Reveal your accomplices," one soldier demanded, his voice edged with steel, his stance imposing against the backdrop of the city's stone buildings. "Fail to comply, and you'll face Roman judgment!"

The man locked eyes with his accuser, a spark of defiance flickering within. "My only desire is freedom," he declared, a statement as much a testament to his resolve.

"Freedom?" another soldier scoffed, advancing with a sneer. "Such freedom is insurrection in the eyes of the Emperor. Produce your collaborators or die in solitude."

The situation escalated quickly when the man, in a desperate bid for defiance, unsheathed a sica—a blade that seemed almost primitive compared to Roman weaponry. The skirmish that ensued was swift and merciless, ending with the man subdued and even more vulnerable on the ground.

Hovering over their captive, the soldiers issued their ultimatum. "Name your co-conspirators, or prepare to embrace the crux," one threatened, the term 'crux' hanging in the air—a dire reminder of the brutal punishment reserved for rebels and enemies of the state. This wooden apparatus, synonymous with agony and humiliation, was Rome's stark message to those who dared defy its authority.

From the home they'd raided, a woman—presumably his spouse—emerged, desperation displayed across her face. "He's innocent!" she pleaded, rushing towards them in a futile attempt to intervene. "Please, have mercy, I beg you!"

Her appeal was met with harsh rebuff, a soldier striking her to the ground with a disdainful backhand. The act of violence drew a collective gasp from the assembled onlookers; their murmured discontent rose into vocal condemnation. "Cowards!" someone in the crowd shouted, and another, "Roman dogs!"

Watching the soldiers drag the man away, leaving behind a scene of despair and a murmuring crowd, Asher's thoughts deepened. This was the Holy Land, a place central to faiths and stories of divine promises and profound teachings. Yet, the reality seemed to be a far cry from anything that was holy. The scene he'd witnessed was a somber reminder of the millennia of conflict and spilled blood that had plagued the land.

As Asher continued his sojourn down the streets, the temple came into full view. Its imposing structure and activity drew him closer, the stark reminder of his earlier encounter.

The closer he got, the more the air buzzed with the sounds of merchants calling out prices, pilgrims murmuring prayers, and the rhythmic shuffling of sandals against the stone pavement. The towering outer walls loomed ahead, marking the threshold between the bustling city and the sacred grounds within.

Asher quickly ascended the broad steps leading toward the entrance. As he passed through the massive gates, the sheer scale of the temple complex became even more overwhelming.

Asher's entry into the Court of the Gentiles was an immersion into a world where spirituality intertwined with commerce. The vast courtyard, accessible to both Jews and Gentiles, hummed with the activity of faithful worshippers and devious merchants alike. Amid this scene, Asher's attention was drawn to the significant offerings being made. It dawned on him that these very activities could be the source of Herod's fabled treasure—a reservoir of wealth amassed away from Roman taxation.

Curiosity piqued, Asher went to one of the many money-changing stations, where a line of Gentiles waited to exchange their Roman coins for the shekels required for temple offerings.

Approaching a money changer, Asher engaged him in conversation. "You seem to do quick business here," Asher remarked, gesturing to the coins passing hands.

The money changer, his eyes shrewd beneath a furrowed brow, nodded. "The temple requires offerings in shekels. We provide a... necessary service," he explained, the hint of a smile.

"And the exchange rate? Is it fair for everyone?" Asher pressed, already suspecting the truth.

"There's a small fee, of course," the changer admitted, not meeting Asher's gaze. "For the convenience, you understand."

Asher nodded, his suspicions confirmed. The 'small fee' was likely anything but—a surcharge on devotion that lined the pockets of those clever enough to exploit the faithful's needs. Asher had experienced this unfair exchange on trips to third-world countries. He would arrive at a foreign airport carrying Israeli currency and need to exchange it for the local currency. The money changers at the airport would exchange the money and charge a fee by not giving the actual exchange rate.

As he observed the transactions, Asher considered the broader implications of what he witnessed. For all its sanctity, the temple operated behind a veil of greed and exploitation. Sacrificial animals were sold at inflated prices, a markup justified in the name of religious purity but reeking of corruption.

Listening to a family haggling over a lamb, Asher heard the frustration firsthand. "This is nearly twice what I'd pay outside these walls," the patriarch lamented as he reluctantly counted out his shekels.

"It is the price for ensuring your offering is acceptable to Elohim," the seller retorted, his indifference to the family's plight all too obvious.

Such exchanges solidified Asher's growing disillusionment. The financial schemes, the inflated costs for sacrificial animals, and the advantageous currency exchange all painted a picture of a religious experience exploited by money. These practices helped justify Asher's thoughts on religion and God.

As he continued exploring and observing within the bustling Court of the Gentiles, Asher realized hours had slipped by. While open to all, the area provided him with valuable insights into the complex interplay of faith and commerce that characterized the temple's outermost courtyard. Yet, he knew this was just the surface of the temple's vast and intricate layout.

His gaze turned toward the inner sections of the temple, areas where only Jews were permitted—places like the Women's Court, Court of the Israelites, and Court of the Priests, each holding its significance and mysteries. Asher understood that to truly grasp the scope of the temple and better estimate where the treasure might be hidden, he would need to venture into these sacred confines.

However, evening was approaching, and he knew he had limited time before nightfall. There was still something he needed to do before leaving, something that couldn't wait. With a final sweep of the courtyard, committing to memory the layout and noting potential points of interest for his return, Asher stepped out of the temple.

As he made his way through the streets, his thoughts lingered on the woman with the captivating brown eyes. He simply couldn't get her out of his mind. An emotion stirred within him—something profound and exhilarating, yet familiar in its intensity. It had been years since he had felt anything like this, leaving him both excited and bewildered.

The whirlwind of feelings he found himself in brought back memories of meeting Rita. Their initial meeting had been filled with barriers, deemed off-limits, too. Just as he had been irresistibly drawn to Rita despite the obstacles, he felt a similar pull towards Miriam.

Asher knew the customs of the 1st century offered no straightforward path for what he was contemplating. Marriages were mostly arranged, courtship was practically nonexistent, and the idea of openly pursuing a woman felt almost absurd. There was no simple way to justify seeing Miriam again—at least, not one that wouldn't raise questions.

Maybe he should just check on her and ensure she hadn't faced trouble after hiding him. No, that seemed too transparent. He considered other excuses, but none felt natural. He needed something tangible, something that provided a legitimate reason to visit her.

Then, it struck him. A gift. A small token of gratitude would make perfect sense—harmless, appropriate, and, most importantly, justifiable.

With renewed focus, Asher wandered through the market, scanning the stalls for something that felt right.

His gaze settled on a fabric stall, where finely woven linens swayed in the breeze. Among them was a pale linen shawl with delicate embroidery along its edges. It reminded him of his mother's—the one she had worn at her wedding.

He knew instantly. It was the perfect gift.

He ran his fingers over the fabric, feeling its softness. Miriam had risked everything for him. She had no wealth or status, yet she had given him the only thing that mattered—her courage.

A shawl like this... it wasn't just something useful. It was a way to acknowledge what she had done.

"A fine choice," the merchant said, stepping forward. "This one is strong, light—good for a woman who works hard."

"How much?" Asher asked.

The merchant named the price, and Asher didn't haggle. He handed over the money and watched as the man carefully folded the fabric.

Asher gently tucked it into his tunic. Now, it was time to see Miriam.

Before long, Asher found himself before a door—the very door behind which she lived. He hesitated.

Maybe this was a mistake.

The weight of the moment pressed upon him; this choice could redefine his entire mission. To walk away would be the logical, sensible action—preserving his focus and maintaining his discretion.

Yet, the impulse to knock—to see her once more—tugged at him.

His mind became a battleground of reason and desire, and he struggled to reconcile his mission with the pull of his heart.

Almost without realizing it, his hand lifted, forming a tight fist.

It hovered there, poised to knock.

The Doorway

Before Asher could knock, the door swung open. Miriam stood there, startled. To Asher, it appeared she was about to leave. A brief moment of awkward silence ensued as they scrambled for words.

Miriam broke the silence first, a hint of curiosity in her voice, "Is there something...?"

Asher felt the urgency to say something—anything. "It's me, Asher, and I was just nearby and wanted to..." He stumbled over his words, only to be met by her unyielding gaze.

"I know the truth of why you're here," Miriam stated, her voice taking a more serious note.

Asher froze. How could she know? Had his mission been compromised?

"Amos sent you," she declared suddenly.

"What, who?" Asher responded, taken aback before the memory of Amos came rushing back. "No, no, he didn't. I don't even know him," he blurted out, immediately realizing how unconvincing he sounded.

Miriam's expression turned skeptical, and she began to close the door.

Panicking, Asher quickly added, "Wait, listen, I know who Amos is, but I don't know him personally. Someone at the market mentioned him...and you."

He paused, then shifted his tone, trying to regain his footing.

"May I just come in for a moment?" he pleaded. "I have something I'd like to give you. A small token of thanks."

Miriam hesitated. "No gift is necessary."

As she started closing the door again, Asher gently said, "Please. It's just a simple gesture."

There was a pause, a moment of hesitation, before she stepped aside, allowing him entry.

Her home was modest, a single room with a dirt floor. A simple stove sat in one corner, next to a small table with two stools and a bed.

She gestured towards one of the stools, inviting him to sit.

Asher entered and sat at the table. "Like I said, I wanted to express my gratitude once more. I mean, you basically saved my life," his tone filled with genuine appreciation.

"That's probably a bit much," Miriam humbly replied.

Slowly, he retrieved the shawl and handed it to her.

Miriam glanced at it, then back at him. Slowly, she took it, her fingers brushing against the cloth. Unfolding it carefully, she let out a quiet gasp as the pale linen shawl slipped through her hands, its delicate embroidery catching the dim light.

"Asher, I..." She shook her head as if struggling to find the right words. "This is beautiful."

He nodded, pleased by her reaction. "I saw it and thought of you."

She ran her fingertips over the fabric, tracing its patterns. It was soft and finely woven—far too fine for someone like her.

"I can't accept this," she whispered.

"You can," he said gently. "And you will."

Her gaze lifted to his, searching, questioning.

"I don't have much to give," he admitted with a slight quiver in his voice. "But this—this is something I could do."

Miriam looked down at the shawl again, weighing his words. Finally, after a long moment, she said, "Thank you."

Asher hesitated, then spoke again, softer this time. "Go ahead, try it on."

Miriam blinked, glancing up at him. "Now?"

He nodded. "Yes, I want to see if it suits you."

She hesitated for a moment. Then, slowly, she lifted the fabric, draping it over her shoulders. The linen fell smoothly, resting against her frame as though it had always belonged there.

Asher stepped back, his eyes lingering on how effortlessly the shawl seemed to complement her. "It looks..." he started, then stopped before finishing. "Perfect."

Miriam pulled the ends of the shawl closer around her as though absorbing its warmth. "It's lovely," she said softly, meeting his gaze.

"Good," he said, his voice quiet but firm. "Then it was the right choice."

A silence settled between them, not awkward but weighted with something unspoken. Trying to avoid the awkwardness, Asher swiftly shifted the conversation. "The market seemed unusually crowded today. Is it always like this around the Passover season?" he inquired, seeking safer ground.

"The Passover brings people from all corners to Jerusalem. It's why the market's so lively," Miriam explained, her voice softening.

This mention of Passover led Miriam to probe a bit further. "Your accent... it's different. Where are you from?" she probed gently.

"I'm from Capernaum," he said, trying to sound casual.

"And what's your trade?" Miriam's interest seemed to deepen.

Caught off guard by the question, Asher scrambled for a believable occupation. "I, uh, I'm a fisherman," he said, hoping the city's well-known location on the Sea of Galilee would lend credibility to his claim.

Miriam's gaze shifted to his hands, and she scrutinized them with a discerning eye. The smoothness of his skin and the absence of calluses that should have marked the hands of a seasoned fisherman did not escape her notice. She looked up from his hands with suspicion, yet she said nothing about her doubts.

Her next question was more probing. "So, what brings you here, to Jerusalem?" she asked, maintaining a conversational tone but with a hint of inquiry.

Asher found himself fabricating on the spot. "For the Passover. It's a spiritual journey," he explained, attempting to sound convincing.

Her eyes narrowed slightly, and the corner of her mouth twitched as if suppressing her next words. Asher was confident she didn't buy his hastily spun tale but chose not to challenge him outright. She was obviously astute and accustomed perhaps to the various travelers and tales that passed through Jerusalem, especially during such a bustling time as the Passover.

Instead, she shifted the conversation. "Are you hungry?" she asked gracefully.

"Yes, I am, thank you," Asher replied, relieved for the change in topic and the reprieve from his tangled web of lies.

Miriam then turned to a simmering pot on the stove, its contents sending a warm, inviting aroma through the small space. She revealed a hearty bean soup, stirring it gently before serving.

"Smells delicious; what is it?" Asher asked, drawn in by the comforting smell.

"It's something my mother used to make," Miriam shared as she filled a bowl for him, "a bean soup recipe passed down in our family."

The taste was simple but pleasing to the palate. "This is wonderful," Asher said.

The soup was a simple blend of beans, onions, and a hint of garlic. While not as spicy as Asher was accustomed to, the flavor was thoroughly enjoyable.

Alongside the soup, Miriam served freshly baked bread, still warm from the oven, its crust golden and slightly crisp.

As they ate, the barriers between them seemed to melt away. Miriam complemented the meal with a glass of wine. It was a white wine with a pleasant aroma and a complex flavor, and he instantly recognized it as a Galilean Wine. They were some of his favorites, although he usually preferred red. A smile came across his face as it occurred to him that if he took the cup back through the portal, he would be drinking a 2,000-year-old wine, but sitting here, it was probably less than a year or two in age.

As dinner came to an end, the comfort of their shared meal gave way to a growing sense of awkwardness. The confined space of Miriam's single-room home seemed even smaller now, with nowhere for Asher to casually retreat. The room offered only the basic stools, lacking both arms and a back, far from the inviting sofas of modern living rooms.

Then, there was the bed, a mere wooden frame supporting a thin mat and a solitary blanket, a stark contrast to the plush mattresses he was accustomed to. Asher's mind wandered, pondering the reality of everyday life in such frugal conditions. His introspective silence didn't go unnoticed. "Is something the matter?" Miriam's voice cut through his thoughts, concern evident in her tone.

Realizing his contemplation had become too apparent, Asher quickly sought to restore his claim. "Just a lot on my mind," he said with a measured tone, aiming to keep the atmosphere light. Aware that he had stayed longer than intended, he rose from his seat, signaling that it was time for him to leave.

Asher felt a tug of gratitude once more. "I guess I should say thank you one more time," he remarked, chuckling at his predictability.

Miriam laughed, a light, easy sound that filled the small room. "You really do like to thank people, don't you?" she teased, her eyes sparkling with amusement.

"I guess it's a habit of mine," Asher admitted, sharing in the laughter. The brief exchange lightened the mood, casting aside any lingering awkwardness. "I would like to see you again," he added, the words sincere and hopeful.

"I'd like that too," Miriam replied, her smile warm and welcoming.

Standing at the doorway, Asher paused, considering how to properly close out their time together. The customs of the time were unclear to him, especially regarding farewells after such an intimate evening. After a brief internal debate, he decided against a kiss, opting instead for a respectful nod. "Goodnight, Miriam," he said softly.

"Goodnight, Asher of Capernaum," she teased with a hint of flirtation.

As Asher quickly stepped out the doorway and into the night, the immediate darkness enveloped him, starkly contrasting the lit warmth of Miriam's home. For a moment, he stood still, allowing his eyes to adjust to the absence of light and his mind to the events of the evening.

Walking back towards the portal, he realized he had made another foolish mistake. It was late, and darkness shrouded the city. Again, he would face the dangers that come with darkness in Jerusalem. He quickened his pace as he walked through the back streets, driven by the urgency to reach the safety of the portal as fast as possible.

The ambush was swift and unexpected. Before he could react, Asher was thrown to the ground—grit in his mouth, a knee in his back, and the cold edge of a blade at his throat.

"What's your life worth?" a voice hissed into the night.

"I have some money. It's yours," Asher managed to say, his voice shaking.

The reply was cold and mocking. "I don't wait for offerings. I take what I want." The attacker rifled through Asher's belongings, finding the small pouch of coins. "This? This is hardly worth the effort. Seems you'll die over a pittance tonight," the attacker sneered, the knife edging closer.

"Wait! I can get more," Asher pleaded, desperation creeping into his voice.

The assailant paused, a moment of silence hanging between them. "Where?" he demanded.

With his life on the line, Asher realized that he better come up with something good. "You'll need to give me some time," Asher stammered, scrambling for a convincing lie.

"Stop lying Jew! I'm not falling for your tricks. Either produce the money or die. Now!" the thief shouted.

"I don't have it on me..." Asher attempted to explain, only to be cut off.

"Then die," came the words from the thief as he pressed down with his knee and up with the knife.

"Wait, hear me out. Killing me gains you nothing. You have nothing to lose by letting me live. Please, just give me a chance," Asher begged in desperation.

The thief weighed his options and realized that Asher was right. Keeping him alive potentially could earn him more money, while killing him would eliminate that chance.

"Okay Jew, but it better be good," the thief grudgingly replied.

Asher, seizing the moment of reprieve, launched into his hastily concocted story. "I've got a plan... to rob the temple."

The thief laughed scornfully at the audacity of the idea. "Rob the temple? That's foolish."

"Yes, and that is why it will work. They would never expect to be robbed. I was there today watching and observing. They are so greedy that they are careless," Asher argued, realizing that his plan was working because the tension on the knife had lessened.

"So you plan on robbing them in broad daylight? You are indeed a foolish Jew. No such plan could ever work," the thief snarled.

"Oh, but it will. It already did. That is exactly where I got the coins in the pouch," Asher bluffed. The lie was a gamble, but it was the best he could do.

"Take the sash from around my waist and securely tie my hands, and I'll give you more details," Asher said calmly.

The request caught the thief off guard as he had never had a victim ask to be tied up. Yet, after a brief pause, curiosity or perhaps greed got the better of him. “Alright, but try anything, and that's the end of you,” he warned with a sharp tone.

Once his hands were securely tied behind him, the thief cautiously allowed Asher to stand. Towering over his assailant by a good six inches, Asher assessed the situation. All things being equal, Asher figured he could easily take the thief, but all things weren’t equal, not with his hands tied behind his back and the thief holding a weapon.

But Asher had something else on his side—his intellect. He understood that in this encounter, brains could triumph over brawn. With his physical movements limited, Asher knew he'd have to rely on his wits to navigate his way out of this perilous situation.

Over the next several minutes, Asher detailed a plan to rob the money changers at the temple. Of course, he was making it up as he went, and he had to be careful that the thief didn't realize that. The comment that sealed the deal was the amount of the loot. If successful, the heist would be far larger than anything the thief had ever stolen before. The best part of the plan was the thief wouldn’t have to do anything other than cause a distraction. The distraction would allow Asher to make the score.

Asher was quite proud of his plan and thought it might actually work if implemented. Of course, Asher had no intentions of going through with it. He just needed to get to the temple, where Jews and Gentiles were quickly separated. He would be out of harm's way before the thief knew what happened. The only bad part of the plan was being tied up all night. There was no way the thief would release him.

What happened next was the most shocking event of the night. “Okay, I’ll meet you at the temple in the morning,” the thief said as he began to untie Asher.

What? Was it really going to be this simple? Was he just going to let me walk away? Asher thought.

And just as if he were reading his thoughts, “Oh, and just so you know, I followed you here. You know, from her house,” said the thief.

What?! No! Asher's mind was spinning.

The thief continued, "Yeah, you don't show up in the morning, and she's dead. What? You didn't think I was going to watch you all night, did you Jew?"

This twist made Asher wonder if he had underestimated the thief's intelligence. Just as the thief had entered his life from the darkness, he exited back into it.

Asher's mind was spinning. *Did all that just really happen? Should I go and warn her?* As he was pondering these questions, he heard an ominous sound—something between a low growl and verbal utterances coming from the darkness. Was it some kind of wild animal? The sound terrified Asher more than the encounter he had with the thief. Realizing he was still in great danger, he quickly returned to the portal and stepped back into the 21st century.

The Plan

As the sun began to rise, Asher had spent the night tossing and turning, his mind racing with thoughts of the predicament he found himself in. Frustration bubbled up within him. How had he managed to get into this mess? He had envisioned himself as a daring adventurer, a modern-day crusader, but now he felt more like a misguided schemer, misled by his delusions. And at the heart of his troubles, once again, was a woman.

The idea of abandoning the whole scheme crossed his mind more than once. The entire affair seemed ludicrous. How had he ever been convinced this was a good idea? Winston, with his grandiose plans, now appeared as nothing more than a deluded old man and Asher, his unwitting accomplice. Walking away seemed like the most sensible option, except for one crucial factor: Miriam. Not going back would surely lead to her death.

So, it seemed the best plan wasn't even an option. Maybe a better plan would be to turn the thief in to the authorities. His arrest would end the entire issue. It was such a simple plan that it had to be the best plan.

But how would he explain himself? What if they started questioning him? Questions he couldn't easily answer. And what authorities? The Romans? They don't trust Jews. No, it would be foolish to get them involved.

Of course, he could go to the Jewish leaders. They had great authority. Unfortunately, it was only over the Jewish people. The thief was a Gentile. Asher pondered whether robbing the temple might extend their authority to punish a non-Jew. That plan had too many unknowns, and the thief would surely implicate Asher. Getting on the Jewish leaders' radar on any level was not a good idea either.

One option came to his mind that he quickly dismissed: murder. Killing the thief would be the easiest solution. Asher realized he might be many things, but a murderer was not one of them.

After evaluating all the options, there was only one obvious answer. He'd have to proceed with the plan to rob the temple and look for the opportunity he needed. Intellect was the resolution to the problem, and using his brain was where he was most comfortable.

Above everything, Asher knew he couldn't let Miriam suffer any consequences from his actions. The responsibility for the chaos that had unfolded was his alone, and it was up to him to resolve it. The path ahead was fraught with risk, but he was determined to protect Miriam at all costs, even if it meant walking straight into danger himself.

Asher wished he had someone to confide in and assure him that he had thoroughly examined all the options and was making the right choice. Of course, he could never tell Winston. He would be outraged. Plus, the old man would probably vote for the murder plan.

Miriam wasn't an option either. He was unsure of how she might react. He would surely have to warn her of the danger, but only when he felt the time was right.

And that was it. To whom else could he say, "Hey, I went back in time to the first century, and this guy robbed and threatened to kill me. I saved myself by convincing him that I had a plan to rob the temple." Yeah, do that, and he'd find himself in the funny farm.

In a moment of reflection, his thoughts drifted to the one person who had once filled that role perfectly—his father. His father had dedicated countless hours to educating Asher about Jewish customs and the essence of their faith. A man of profound faith and devotion, he had introduced Asher to praying to Adonai—the name for God, meaning Lord or Master. Those times had built a deep bond between them, a bond that was now broken. In his current predicament, Asher recognized that his father was precisely the mentor he longed for, yet, regrettably, turning to him was not an option either.

Suddenly, a vivid memory surfaced—his father's voice from childhood: *Son, when you feel there is no one else, there is always the Lord. He is there to listen and lead.*

Was that what he should do now? Pray to Adonai, just as he had been taught in his youth?

The unexpected yearning stirred something deep within him, unlocking a flood of emotions and reviving memories of a faith he once held dear but had since abandoned. Despite his skepticism, a part of him longed to embrace that faith once more—yet he couldn't shake the feeling that such a desire was foolish.

As Asher wrestled with his thoughts, he glanced at the clock. The realization hit him like a wave—it was time to head to the temple to face the thief and execute their risky plan. His heart pounded as he braced himself for what was to come. He quickly changed into his first-century clothes, readying himself for the inevitable meeting at the temple.

Turning The Tables

Asher arrived at the temple around 9:00 AM. Even at this early hour, numerous people were present. In addition to the morning sacrifice, a group attended the daily Torah reading and prayed. Asher remembered listening to such readings as a boy.

Today's reading was from Exodus Chapter 20, one he was required to memorize. Subconsciously, he found himself mouthing the words in unison with the reader until the recitation of the eighth commandment, "You shall not steal," caused his heart to seize. The irony of hearing these words on this particular day, of all days, was not lost on him. For a moment, he wondered if the universe was mocking him.

The coincidence set his thoughts spiraling. Could this be a manipulation by Winston? But that seemed far-fetched. The timing was uncanny; besides, Winston's focus had always been singularly on the treasure, not on orchestrating such elaborate moral dilemmas.

The thought that perhaps a divine hand was at play crossed his mind. It was the kind of explanation his ex-wife would have readily offered after she converted to Christianity, attributing everything to God's plan and guidance. Asher caught himself before he wandered too far down that path. To him, this was all serendipity, nothing more, nothing less.

Asher's thoughts were interrupted when someone called his name. "Good morning, Asher." The voice belonged to the thief—but the fact that he knew Asher's name sent a jolt of surprise through him. *How did he know it?*

His confusion must have been evident because the thief quickly added, "Don't look so surprised. I make it my business to know who I'm dealing with. And yes, I've been keeping an eye on you since you arrived. You'd do well to remember that asking questions gets people's attention. And, well, you never know who you're really talking to, do you?"

The realization that the thief had been observing him, learning his movements and name, made Asher reassess the situation. The depth of the thief's reconnaissance was unsettling.

The thief pressed on, eager to get started. "Okay, let's put this plan into action."

Asher began to outline the plan, “See the man sitting at the table where the sacrificial animals are sold?” he asked, catching the thief's attention. “He has a large bag under the table where he keeps the gold and coins. Go to the area where they are selling the animals for sacrifice and create a distraction.”

"How exactly should I do that?" the thief inquired, puzzled by the instruction.

"Start a quarrel over the prices of the animals. Make it loud. Then, begin to release them," Asher suggested. "The more chaos you create, the better our chances. While they are distracted, I'll grab the money bag."

"And once you have the money, what's next?" the thief probed further, trying to understand the full scope of Asher's plan.

“I'll meet you back where we met last night. I'll give you the money, and my debt to you will be paid,” Asher explained, outlining the conclusion of their arrangement.

“Okay, but you better not try anything foolish; I have friends, you know!” the thief threatened with a dark tone.

“No tricks, let's just get this done. I have other important matters that need my attention,” Asher reassured him, hoping to expedite the process.

With a nod of understanding, the thief turned and made his way toward the tables. However, as he disappeared into the crowd, an unexpected uproar erupted from the direction of the money changers' tables. Shouts filled the air, but to Asher's surprise, the source of the disturbance wasn't the thief. Another individual was already causing a scene, arguing vehemently with the money changers, unintentionally setting Asher's plan into motion without any involvement from the thief.

As the commotion escalated, the scene descended into chaos. Tables were upended, their contents—a mixture of coins from various regions—clattering to the stone floor of the temple courtyard. Amidst the pandemonium, people and animals scattered in all directions, seeking refuge from the sudden turmoil.

The man at the center of the uproar pursued the money changers with righteous indignation. His voice boomed across the courtyard as he proclaimed, "It is written, 'My house shall be called a house of prayer,' but you have made it a den of robbers."

Asher watched, dumbstruck, as the unfolding scene mirrored the very disruption he had once planned to orchestrate. Who was this figure taking such bold action against the temple's practices? Could he be one of the accomplices the thief had mentioned? The possibility stirred a whirlwind of speculation in Asher's mind. But the man's fervor—his raw, unflinching conviction—seemed to speak of a motive far removed from theft or conspiracy.

As people were scattering, Asher noticed the money bag lying on the floor near the overturned table. All eyes were transfixed on this man shouting and chasing people out of the temple. Asher knew it was now or never as he made a dash for the bag. The plan was working, just in a different way than he had conceived it.

In a swift movement, Asher scooped up the bag of coins, concealing it beneath his tunic to avoid drawing any attention to himself. Without looking back, he made his way through the scattering crowd, blending in with the throng of bewildered onlookers as he escaped from the temple. The plan had worked!

Asher hurried to the agreed-upon meeting place, his heart pounding with the thrill and exertion of their unconventional success. The thief was already there, pacing back and forth—a clear display of agitation and confusion.

The moment Asher arrived, the air between them crackled with mutual suspicion. "Was that your doing? Did you bring others into this?" the thief demanded, his eyes narrowing in accusation.

Asher, equally baffled and defensive, shot back, "Me? I thought that was your doing. Who was that man?"

The thief shook his head, his voice full of suspicion. "I have no idea who that was. I was going to start the commotion when the whole place erupted. That was your attempt at a double-cross, wasn't it, Jew?"

"What? No! I thought you brought in one of your friends you referred to," Asher retorted, the absurdity of the situation not lost on him. "Besides, why would I come *here* if I planned to double-cross you."

"I'm not sure, but I do know it was a mistake," the thief hissed as he drew his knife.

This time, however, Asher was prepared, as he had also brought a knife. He clearly broke the rule of time travel because the knife was from the 21st century. It was a large knife with an 8" blade. But it wasn't really from the 21st century because Asher found it during an archaeological dig in Jerusalem. He had estimated the knife came from the latter part of the 1st century. It was a prized possession that he didn't want to lose, but this was a dire situation.

His life truly was on the line. The size and appearance of the knife definitely caught the thief's attention. Desperate, Asher said, "Look, I don't exactly know what just happened, but I know I held up my end of the deal. And all the money is yours."

Asher tossed the bag to the thief, who caught it and began to weigh his options. A knife fight with the much larger Asher would likely end badly. And besides, Asher's words rang true.

After a tense moment, a slow smile crept across his face, revealing his crooked, yellow teeth. "Okay, Jew," he said coolly. "And who knows—maybe we'll work together again."

Fat chance, thought Asher, who instead said, "Yeah, maybe." With their business arrangement complete, the thief turned and left. Asher felt a temporary feeling of relief.

Asher rushed to Miriam's home to ensure that she was safe. She opened the door and appeared glad to see him, but quickly noticed the look on his face. He quickly hugged her and said, "Thank goodness you're okay."

Over the next hour, he told her of his encounter with the thief and all that happened. Together, they went over all the possibilities of who could be behind all that played out. Maybe Amos had orchestrated the entire encounter. He indeed hated Miriam enough to do it, and if he had seen Asher at Miriam's house, it all made sense.

Maybe the man he had talked to at the market was the mastermind. Asher's skepticism was in full force. He even began to wonder about Miriam. Was she using her looks to play him? It wouldn't be the first time that had happened. Asher had learned the hard way not to trust others, and this encounter reinforced his belief in self-reliance.

Miriam asked more questions about the man at the temple. As Asher gave greater details, she believed she knew who he was or at least had heard of him. Miriam said, "There's this man I've heard about lately. He's been causing trouble with the religious leaders and making outrageous claims. Some even say he's a prophet and performs miracles. He goes by the name Jesus, Jesus of Nazareth."

Asher knew the name Jesus was a common name used in 1st century Jerusalem, but Jesus of Nazareth would refer specifically to the Jesus of the Bible—the one that claimed to be the Son of God. Asher had always considered Jesus more of a fictional character than a real person. Could he have just encountered the man he thought didn't exist? Then it occurred to him that even if Jesus were real, it didn't mean he was the Son of God. And it didn't matter; Asher had to return to his mission—the gold.

Or was it the woman?

Conflictions

Miriam asked Asher to eat lunch with her, but he refused. He needed to spend some time alone to regain his focus. She was understanding and asked if he would return later, and he promised to try. Asher started towards the temple but soon found himself wandering the streets of Jerusalem in deep contemplation.

His mind was heavy as he wandered, still trying to sort through the tangle of thoughts and emotions that had taken hold of him. Consumed by questions without easy answers, he drifted through the streets as the noise of the city faded into the background. It wasn't until the sound of distant murmurs and the hum of a gathering crowd pulled him from his thoughts that he realized where his steps had led him—beyond the city gates and directly to a harrowing sight.

Two men, crucified, their bodies suspended in agony, bore the brutal testimony of Roman justice. Roman soldiers stood guard, preventing any attempts at mercy or comfort from the gathered crowd of family and onlookers.

Asher stood frozen. He had studied crucifixion during his doctoral work—had read scholarly accounts and historical texts that described it as the most cruel and humiliating form of execution known to man. Victims were left hanging for hours, sometimes days, exposed to the elements and the jeers of passersby. Death didn't come quickly—it crept in slowly through exhaustion and suffocation. With each breath, the condemned had to push up against the nails driven through their feet just to lift their body enough to inhale. Eventually, their strength would fail, and they would hang limp, unable to draw another breath. It was beyond brutal, stripping the condemned of all dignity.

No academic description could ever fully capture the raw horror of what stood before him.

The victims were a stark representation of physical suffering—their skin marred by the scourge of whips and their bodies nailed to wooden crosses. Asher noticed the crude nails piercing their hands and feet, the visible signs of dehydration and blood loss speaking to the slow, torturous nature of their deaths.

The area around the crosses was marked by the remnants of previous executions—dark stains on the ground, pieces of discarded rope, and the ominous presence of abandoned crosses adding a permanent shadow to the location. This place was chosen for its visibility, situated along a busy road into the city, ensuring that the message of deterrence reached as many as possible.

The Roman soldiers shared jests among themselves, their laughter sharply out of place against the backdrop of human anguish they guarded. Their dark and cruel amusement seemed to stem not just from the authority they wielded but from a morbid satisfaction in the pain they inflicted and oversaw. They occasionally directed their mockery not just at the men hanging in torment on the crosses, but also at those who had gathered to watch. This behavior underlined a grim reality: these soldiers, while executioners by duty, had honed their skills in the art of psychological torment.

Family members stood at a distance, their cries of sorrow blending with the groans of the dying. Asher watched as one woman—likely the man's wife—was forcibly restrained as she attempted to approach with water, her pleas for mercy cruelly denied. In a display of callousness, a soldier sauntered over and snatched the vessel from her hands. With a mocking smirk, he drank the contents himself, greedily gulping down the water meant to ease a dying man's thirst. Wiping his mouth with the back of his hand, he smashed the empty container at her feet and sneered, "Thank you for the refreshment. Please—bring more." His words dripped with ridicule.

Above the heads of the condemned, placards bore the written accusations—stark reminders of the crimes for which they paid the ultimate price. Ravens circled overhead, drawn by the scent of death, their black forms casting shadows over the scene, waiting for their turn at the bodies.

The entire sight was overwhelming. The sounds of suffering filled Asher's ears, and the smell of blood, sweat, and impending death depicted the price of defiance to the Romans.

Despite his resolve, Asher found himself unable to look away; his gaze fixated on the horror being inflicted. The sight of a young boy, tears streaking his dirt-covered face as he looked on helplessly at what Asher assumed to be his father, sent a chill down Asher's spine. He recognized that crucifixion wasn't just about criminal punishment. It was also about public humiliation.

The reality of what it meant to challenge Rome—the physical torment, the psychological warfare waged against the victims and their families, and the ultimate desolation of death on a cross—was laid bare before him. Crucifixion, a deterrent designed to instill fear, had found its mark in Asher. Doubts about his mission and the potential cost of being discovered suddenly became all too real.

As Asher rushed away from the harrowing scenes of the crucifixions, a wave of nausea suddenly washed over him. The sights and sounds of suffering, combined with the oppressive heat of the Jerusalem sun, became too much for his senses to bear. His stomach churned violently. Stumbling to his knees on the side of the road, Asher doubled over, his body convulsing as he retched, trying to expel the horror he had witnessed.

Gathering his strength, Asher pushed himself up and hurried back through the city gates and away from the nightmarish sight behind him. Uncertainty clouded his thoughts about what lay ahead. His immediate concern was whether he'd been exposed at the temple. The ill-conceived plan with the thief—had it compromised his anonymity? The stakes were clear: discovery could mean capture or, worse, face the same fate as those he had just seen. With a heavy heart and a mind swirling with what-ifs, doubts about the entire mission began to creep back into his head again.

Asher's resolve crumbled as he faced the overwhelming reality of the dangers of staying. The potential costs, now starkly apparent, were far greater than he could justify. Admitting defeat wasn't in his nature, yet logic dictated a retreat. The first and hardest step in his withdrawal would be to inform Miriam. It was a conversation he dreaded, yet he owed her for the bond they had formed.

Before long, he once again found himself standing outside her door. All the emotions that he had standing there a day earlier quickly returned. This time, he was bold enough to knock. Or was it stupid enough? She opened the door and immediately embraced him. It somewhat took him by surprise.

"I was so scared I'd never see you again," she proclaimed as she fell into his arms.

"I just needed to do some thinking," he said, the comfort of her embrace making the goodbye he was preparing all the more difficult.

"Come in, stay with me. I'll fix us a meal," Mariam said warmly, gesturing towards the table.

"I really can't stay," Asher said, the words a battle—his heart pleading with him to remain, his mind insisting he couldn't. "I just came by to tell you I'm returning to my home."

Immediately, Miriam began to cry. "It's him, isn't it? He ran you away," she said through her tears.

"No, no, it's not that at all. It's just... I just have to return. It's difficult to explain," Asher said earnestly, trying to comfort her.

She rushed back to his arms and said, "Stay with me. It's too late to leave now. It wouldn't be safe. Something could happen again, like yesterday." Asher was hesitant but agreed to stay at least for the meal.

Miriam carefully prepared the table, laying out a small loaf of bread and a bowl filled with ripe olives and dried figs. She carefully sliced the bread with a knife, the crust breaking with a soft crackle under her gentle pressure. She spread the figs evenly across each piece, their warm, sweet aroma filling the air. As she diced the olives, their scent mingled with the figs.

As Asher watched, she picked up a piece of the prepared bread. Holding it up to his lips, she offered him a bite, which he eagerly accepted. Her touch enhanced the simplicity of the moment; each bite was an act of intimacy. The flavors of the olives and figs combined in a delightful harmony, but her attention stirred strong emotions in Asher.

He found himself captivated by her touch and sexuality. With each bite, Miriam moved closer to Asher. The atmosphere was charged with an unspoken connection. This simple meal was quickly becoming something much deeper. Asher found himself tangled in a web of emotions. Was this connection with Miriam genuine or mere infatuation?

He remembered the intense early days with Rita, filled with undying affection and closeness, only to recall how it eventually waned, leaving a mix of disappointment and sorrow. Now, facing the potential of a new relationship, Asher wondered if he was ready to risk heartache again.

With all these thoughts racing through his head, they sat quietly as she gently and passionately fed him. Like the walls of Jericho, the walls around his heart began to crash down. He was vulnerable, and at that moment, he realized that it was love he had always wanted. Miriam arose from the table and motioned for him to join her on the bed. As he sat down beside her, she embraced him and said, "Stay with me."

Staying the night with her was easy and natural. He fell asleep in her arms but awoke early. She was still sleeping, and he lay beside her, staring at her beauty. She was helping him forget about the pain of his previous relationship, one that he thought he would never recover from.

As Asher lay beside Miriam, another battle churned within him, the battle between the instinct to flee back to the familiarity of the 21st century and the comfort he found in her presence. Only a day before, he had been consumed by thoughts of returning as quickly as possible, driven by the fear of the unknown. Yet, now, wrapped in the warmth of Miriam's embrace, those fears seemed distant and less pressing.

He found himself wrestling with the idea of abandoning the mission, of walking away from everything he'd left behind. Could he truly forsake his own time for a life in the past—for comfort, for love... for the possibility of peace?

The contrast between his life in the future and the raw simplicity—and unexpected intensity—of the connection he felt here was striking. In his own time, life felt tangled and exhausting. Teaching brought no fulfillment; it was a routine of repetition, empty lectures, and ungrateful students.

His relationship with his parents was a constant source of tension—strained by unmet expectations, old wounds, and words spoken in anger that still hung in the air. And Rita—what began with passion had ended with heartbreak, leaving him with a deep reluctance to trust again.

But here, everything felt different. There were no lectures to give, no expectations to meet, no lingering failures. With Miriam, things were easy—her presence was calm, accepting, and honest. And beyond the personal, there was something else: here, in this time, he would be without question the smartest man on the planet. His knowledge, his education, his perspective—they would all set him apart. Life could be simple, and success almost effortless.

Did he owe it to Winston to return and tell him of his decision? That would be risky because Winston could deactivate the portal before Asher could return to Miriam. And if he didn't return, would Winston come looking for him? Surely not. The old man was in no condition for the stress of time travel. Besides, Winston would probably just think Asher had been arrested or killed.

As all these thoughts ran through his head, a wave of nausea overtook him. Though he couldn't fully explain it, Asher had no doubt the side effects were tied to time travel—and they were getting worse. At first, it had been little more than strange tingling sensations, but now they had intensified into moments of blurry or double vision, aching joints and muscles, and nausea. In the beginning, the discomfort mostly faded within a few hours, but now the recovery stretched longer with each trip.

And then, with a flash of clarity, a darker question surfaced: *What if the damage was permanent?*

The Encounter

As he lay in Miriam's arms, thoughts rushing through his head, a loud banging rattled the door. Had the Roman soldiers returned? The noise awakened Miriam from her sleep.

The door burst open before either of them could get out of bed. Several men rushed into the room. These were not Roman soldiers—their attire made that clear. They wore layered robes of dark, fine wool, their garments well-maintained and draped with intention. Their beards were neatly trimmed, their hair clean and orderly, and their eyes sharp with purpose. They carried no swords, but several gripped polished staffs or rods—symbols of authority but just as capable of violence.

Asher jumped to his feet to protect Miriam but was quickly overpowered by the men. One of them hit him in the back of the head with a rod, and he collapsed on the ground. Dazed, he barely registered the scuffle around him.

One of the men yanked a robe and the linen shawl Asher had given Miriam from a nearby chair and threw them at her.

She scrambled to clothe herself before they dragged her out the door.

Asher was stunned that they hadn't killed him and confused about why they had taken her. Dizzy and bewildered, he staggered to his feet. *What was this all about? Was she some type of criminal?* He knew the Jews had a trial system and military presence to enforce it, all under the watchful eyes of the Romans, of course. But these men's appearance revealed they weren't soldiers.

Miriam's heart pounded with fear as she was forcefully brought through Jerusalem's streets, her fate uncertain, her dignity stripped away by the hands that gripped her. Ahead, she could see a courtyard and more men awaiting her arrival.

Asher, driven by a deep impulse to protect Miriam, inconspicuously followed the mob that had taken her. He now found himself blending in with the crowd. In the heart of the courtyard, he spotted a figure who stood out amidst the chaos—a man marked by an unmistakable calmness. This was the same individual who, in a fit of outrage, had previously disrupted the temple's market by overturning tables and driving out the merchants—the man known as Jesus.

In direct contrast to Jesus's calmness, the mob of men that had taken Miriam thrust her at the feet of Jesus. From their clothing, Asher determined they were Jewish religious leaders. As they circled Jesus and Miriam, their intentions were clear, their hands gripping stones tightly, ready to exact the punishment they deemed just.

"Teacher," they called out, ensuring their voices reached every corner of the gathered crowd, "this woman was caught in the very act of adultery. According to the Law of Moses, we are commanded to stone women like her. What is your judgment on this matter?"

The sight of the stones in their hands sent a jolt through Asher, a jarring shock that rooted him in place. It was just like the crucifixion—something he had read about, studied, even lectured on but never imagined witnessing firsthand. Stoning belonged to history books, not reality.

Yet here it was. Real. Raw. Brutal. And this time, personal.

The jagged edges, the rough weight of each stone in their grasp, the righteous fury in their eyes—it was all too much. This wasn't a reenactment. There was no historical distance to protect him from the horror of what was about to happen.

Then, an even deeper horror hit him. He was doing nothing!

The urge to intervene burned in his chest—to rush forward, to shield her from the first blow. But he didn't move, his instinct for self-preservation outweighing his courage.

He remained hidden, paralyzed by fear. Fear of stepping into a world where death was routine. Fear of becoming the next victim.

He was more afraid for himself than for the woman he loved. And now, Asher couldn't help but wonder—*what kind of man was he?*

In contrast, Jesus's face was calm but protective. As Jesus heard the questions being hurled at Him, he stooped down and wrote in the dust, confusing those watching. Impatient, they pressed him again. "What do you say, teacher?"

Calmly, Jesus rose to his feet and looked them in the eyes. "Let him without sin throw the first stone," He proclaimed.

Each man began to look to each other for the proper response. Asher was astonished at what he saw next. One by one, the stones fell, not hurled in judgment but dropped in acknowledgment of personal failings. The accusers departed, leaving Miriam alone with Jesus.

Gently, Jesus stooped back down to Miriam, who trembled in fear and had tears freely flowing down her cheeks.

"Woman, where are they? Has no one condemned you?" Jesus asked with compassion.

In astonishment, Miriam looked around to see that all the men had vanished.

"No one, sir," Miriam replied as she returned her gaze to the ground in shame.

Jesus then did something that took her by surprise. With a tender gesture, he lifted her chin, guiding her gaze to meet his.

"Then neither do I condemn you," he said firmly, yet with a kindness that enveloped her like a warm embrace. "Now go, and sin no more."

In that moment, something broke open inside Miriam—a dam of guilt, fear, and shame she hadn't even realized she carried. His words weren't just mercy; they were truth. Not the harsh accusations the men had hurled at her, but something deeper. As she knelt in the dirt, Jesus's voice stirred something long buried—teachings from childhood about righteousness. But it wasn't just memory. Something was moving inside her, something not entirely her own. The conviction rising within her revealed just how far she had drifted.

She thought of Amos—how much anger and bitterness had shaped her choices. She had used his abuse to justify her own behavior, convincing herself she had every right to live as she pleased. But now, she saw it clearly. She was wrong. She was lost. And somehow, Jesus knew. He saw it all—and still didn't condemn her.

After a moment, Jesus left her alone in her contemplation and slowly walked away. A small crowd followed him.

Miriam remained—alone, sitting, sobbing.

Asher hesitated before approaching, then silently sat beside her. Something was different. He could feel it, see it in her face—but what, exactly, had changed?

Asher's respect for Jesus grew. He recognized a courage and conviction he wished he'd had. He thought of reaching out to Jesus to express his gratitude. Yet, he knew Miriam needed him now, and her sobs were a clear call to be there for her.

"Let me walk you home," he suggested gently, hoping to offer comfort.

"No," she said, her words slicing through him. "What we were doing... What I was doing. It was wrong. I realize it now. What we have is sinful."

Asher's immediate reaction was disbelief, followed swiftly by anger.

"Sinful? How can caring for someone, wanting to be with them, be wrong?" His voice rose, tinged with a mix of confusion and indignation.

Miriam shook her head, tears welling up again. "Look, I understand. I'm as confused as you are, but what I experienced, what I saw.... what He said, it changed something in me."

Her words shook him to his core. He had already lost her, and he didn't even know it yet.

"Are you saying that just like that, we're done?" Asher's voice rose with rage.

"Please, Asher. His presence, the things He said... He saved me; I was about to be stoned!" Miriam cried, her conviction unwavering despite the tears.

"Oh, Miriam..." Asher's voice faltered, the weight of her words hitting him like a blow. "I know what almost happened—I saw it. But I..." He hesitated, guilt gnawing at him. "I realize I should have done something."

He searched her tear-streaked face—for reassurance, for understanding, for something to hold on to.

Trying to compose herself, Miriam slowly rose to her feet. "This, all of this, it's made me see my life differently. You have to give me time, time to process all of this."

Her plea did little to quell Asher's growing resentment.

"How can one moment—one person—undo everything?" he demanded.

The question left a bitter taste in his mouth. It echoed another argument, in another time, with another woman.

Rita.

Rita's transformation had also been instantaneous, a sudden shift that had changed the course of their marriage. She had described it as being reborn, a moment of profound clarity and change. He remembered the sparkle in her eye when she shared it with him. He also recalled the anger that simultaneously exploded within him. From that time forward, their relationship was never the same, and now he sensed it was happening here, too.

Miriam rose slowly, her decision made. "I need to be alone," she said softly, her voice steady despite the tears. "Please, Asher... try to understand."

As she walked away, Asher grappled with a mix of emotions. The parallels between Miriam's words and Rita's were too striking to ignore. He had lost Rita to a transformation he couldn't understand, and now it seemed he was losing Miriam to a similar fate. She had asked him never to leave hours earlier, and now she didn't want to talk to him. No, he wouldn't take this sitting down. Without question, this Jesus character had saved her from stoning, but that didn't make him God.

Just moments earlier, he was grateful for Jesus's intercession, but now, Asher was filled with anger toward the same man and swore to get revenge. With his wife, Asher had no way of confronting Jesus about the damage he did to his marriage, but this was different. He needed to develop a plan—a plan that would prove to Miriam that this Jesus character was a fake. The real question was how. Then it dawned on him.

He had used the Bible numerous times in his historical studies. While, in his opinion, it contained primarily fictional stories, historians often confirmed its historical accuracy. He was sure the same would apply to Jesus. While he had read parts of the New Testament, his focus had never been specifically on Jesus. He felt sure that the Bible would be a good resource in helping him expose Jesus as a fraud, and he knew the perfect place to get one: his apartment.

Rita had given him a Bible once—the one with his name engraved on the cover. He'd never opened it, not even once. But he would now. He would use the very book that helped destroy his marriage to prove Jesus was a fraud—and, in doing so, save his new relationship.

To Asher, it was a brilliant plan. He made a beeline for the portal.

After all, he was the smartest man on the planet. And now, he would prove it.

Accountability

Asher entered his apartment and headed straight for the Bible. But before he could reach it, someone grabbed him from behind. In a blur, a gag was forced into his mouth, a hood yanked over his head, and his arms wrenched behind him. A low, stern voice growled near his ear, "Don't resist."

Though he couldn't see his assailants, the multitude of hands that manhandled him suggested there were at least two. The aggressiveness of their grip revealed their size and strength. In a desperate bid for freedom, Asher's mind raced to his knife—a potential equalizer. But as he grasped its handle, it was swiftly knocked away, rendering any thought of resistance futile.

Would it all end this way? Murdered by strangers? And why? Asher wanted to ask the men questions, but the gag prevented that. And the men weren't talking either. Whoever they were, they were professionals.

Next, the men rolled him up in what felt like a rug, picked him up, and carried him out of his apartment. He could tell he was being placed in some type of vehicle, most likely a van. The men started the vehicle and began driving. Asher tried his best to keep up with all the stops and turns, but just breathing was a task. After what seemed like an eternity, the vehicle stopped, and the men took Asher out of the vehicle and carried him inside a house or building.

Once inside, they unrolled the rug, leaving him sitting on the floor as they unbound his hands and yanked off the hood and gag. It took a minute for his eyes to adjust to the light, but when they did, he recognized where he was and who the man was before him.

Winston sat staring at Asher. This was the house that Winston had rented. As Asher looked around, he didn't see Natalie, and it was evident that the old man's health had declined since he had last seen him. He was pale, and his face was pained. Slowly, Winston took a deep pull from his oxygen mask before lowering it. "Please have a seat," Winston said, motioning towards a chair.

Asher's first impulse was to run, but the two men stood slightly behind him on each side, and he knew attempting to escape would be useless.

"Please," Winston softly requested.

Reluctantly, Asher consented.

"Our agreement was for you to report daily; I haven't heard from you in days. I was getting concerned that maybe you were hurt or had changed your mind," Winston said while rolling his wheelchair closer to Asher.

"Are you crazy? You just kidnapped me! And you're worried about my safety?" Asher shouted as he rose to his feet. "It's become obvious that my welfare is of little concern to you!"

With this, the two men stepped closer to Asher, pressing him back into the chair. Winston held up a hand to stop them. "No, it's okay. In fact, the two of you can wait outside. I'll let you know when I need you."

With those instructions, the two men picked up the rug, rope, and hood and exited the house. "I understand the difficulty, and obviously, I did not communicate properly. My apologies. Now, please update me on your progress," Winston said with a forgiving tone.

Asher wondered if he should tell him the truth. Definitely not the whole truth. "Over the last 48 hours, I've been robbed, beaten, betrayed, and, now, kidnapped. I don't remember any of that being part of our original discussion," Asher snapped.

"I don't know about the others, but you were not kidnapped; you may leave at any time you wish," Winston said, gesturing towards the door.

Seated across from Winston, Asher weighed his options, aware that departing could mean another unsettling run-in with those two goons. The room's tension momentarily eased as Winston, with a calm demeanor, prompted, "Now, please continue with your update."

"I have encountered some difficulties. It has been challenging for me to establish trustworthy relationships, and I apologize for not reporting as we agreed. It has all been a bit overwhelming," Asher explained, hoping to satisfy the old man.

Winston responded with understanding, "That's not surprising. But remember, forming bonds wasn't our goal. It is to search for the gold." He paused before shifting the topic, "So, have you located it yet? The gold?"

"No, but for me to thoroughly search the temple, it will require me to spend the entire night in it. I plan to do that on my next trip," Asher said, hoping this would satisfy the old man.

Winston's tone shifted towards concern, "I don't think you're taking this seriously enough," he remarked, then softened, "It appears that you've spent little time actually looking for the gold."

Asher could fully feel the weight of Winston's accusation. "You're expecting results too quickly," he insisted.

Winston leaned slightly forward and asked, "How old do you think I am?"

Caught off guard, Asher questioned, "How is that relevant to our discussion?"

"Just indulge me with a guess," insisted Winston, a hint of playfulness in his voice.

Observing Winston's deeply lined face, the sagging skin under his eyes, and sparse gray hair, Asher estimated, "About 80?"

Winston laughed lightly, "That's very generous of you. Actually, I'm 52, merely 14 years your senior."

Asher was more than skeptical. The claim seemed far-fetched. "What? You're only 52?" he questioned, unable to reconcile Winston's appearance with his claim.

"Yes, and you see, my life depends on you finding the gold," Winston stated sternly.

Asher didn't see the connection.

Winston continued, "And I look so old, and my health is so bad because of the time machine. I won't bore you with all the scientific jargon, but using the time machine changes your DNA. I have been searching for a cure for years, and I believe I have found one. Unfortunately, the cost of the cure is extremely expensive and I need the gold to pay for it."

Asher was untouched, but the old man let it sit momentarily. As in previous discussions, it appeared the old man could read Asher's thoughts.

"Yes, unfortunately, your life depends on it too. Untreated, the trips you have taken will kill you. Since you have taken many fewer trips than me, it will take years, ten maybe more, but believe me, you will die. I'm sure you have noticed some side effects by now. They will only get worse. Look there on your arm. The small sore. That's how they begin, and then they progress until they look like mine," Winston said as he pulled up his sleeve, revealing his arms filled with oozing sores.

Asher noticed the sore on his arm a day earlier but didn't think much of it. He figured it was a result of being accosted by the thief. But now he knew that Winston was right.

"But I asked you if it was safe," Asher exploded. "You assured me it was!"

"No," Winston said evenly. "You told me you experienced strange sensations when you went through the portal. I told you that was completely normal. That was no lie."

Asher's anger boiled over. "Then what? You're a murderer? And I'm just another pawn in your sick game?"

"Think of me what you wish. I had no other choice. I chose you because you were perfect for the job. You speak the necessary languages, have the right educational and work background, and have the right personality. I spent years trying to put the right puzzle pieces together with the right loot and prospect. You should feel honored," Winston said with arrogance.

"I don't think you know how sick you really are," Asher responded in disgust.

Winston didn't miss Asher's accusation and chuckled. "Like I said, I had no other choice. And now, neither do you. Just know that the gold cures us both. So, yes, you must find the gold, and the sooner the better. While you will have years before you are completely consumed, I don't. And my demise means the end of the time machine and, thus, you too," Winston plainly stated.

Unsure of trusting the old man, Asher said, "Then tell me the cure so I can believe you."

"That is the only card I still hold, and unfortunately, if you don't find the gold, it will die with me. Besides, even if I told you, the cost is beyond your resources as it is currently beyond mine. But the gold changes all that," Winston stated as his voice trailed off.

Asher realized Winston was more twisted and devious than he had ever imagined. He hated him. He hated everything about him. He felt used because he *was* being used. And maybe the thing he hated most was how Winston remained in control.

"I already know you didn't return last night. The only thing I don't know is—where did you stay?" Winston pressed.

Asher looked surprised by the question and wondered how he knew this.

"Asher, you know that the computer logs each portal use. I know exactly when you leave and when you return. So, again, where did you spend the night?" he pressed.

Asher hesitated before responding, "I let time get away from me, and it was late. I didn't want to risk getting to the portal, so I stayed with someone, a friend."

"It wouldn't be a female friend, would it?" Winston probed further.

“That’s none of your business,” Asher defensively and firmly stated.

“Everything you do is my business. Besides, don’t think I didn’t have a few relationships through the years of time traveling. I quickly learned that they only make things more difficult. You’ll learn the same thing,” Winston explained with a hint of reminiscence.

“I suggest you take the rest of the day to recuperate. Tomorrow's another day. Don't hesitate to ask if you need anything before your next venture. There's a taxi arranged for your return. You're free to leave,” he added, his tone softening slightly.

“What, your goons aren’t going to take me back?” Asher asked sarcastically.

Winston smiled and replied, “Actually, they left when they went outside. But they do know where you live,” Winston said as a subtle warning.

Asher turned and left. When he got outside, he noticed that the men and their vehicle were gone, but he did see a cab sitting out front. As he started towards the cab, Natalie exited the back and started walking towards the house. As she approached him, she smiled.

He responded by walking past her and saying, “Your boss is a sociopath.”

Revenge

Thankfully, the rest of Asher's day unfolded quietly within the confines of his apartment, where he found himself engrossed in the Bible that Rita had given him. Supplementing his reading with online research, he delved into the New Testament, specifically the Gospels of Matthew, Mark, Luke, and John. These texts, he understood, chronicled the life and teachings of Jesus.

Not long into his study, Asher stumbled upon the narrative of Jesus driving the merchants and money changers from the temple—a scene depicted in all the Gospels. He was shocked at how accurately the story aligned with what he observed. The realization of standing in the very moment recorded in scripture was both surreal and unsettling.

Further reading led him to the story of the woman caught in adultery and the realization that Miriam was the woman. Knowing that he was the unnamed man in the story gave him chills. Again, the accuracy of the story was astounding.

Despite his persistent disbelief in Jesus as the Messiah, Asher couldn't deny the historical accuracy of the Bible. That's when it all clicked. Of course! It had been right in front of him the whole time—this wasn't just a historical document; it was Jesus's actual itinerary. He would use the Bible as a roadmap to know exactly where Jesus would be, what he would be doing, and when it would happen. With this information, it would be easy to expose Jesus as the fraud he believed him to be. It felt satisfying to rely on his intellect to craft such a brilliant strategy.

Asher flipped to the events leading up to Passover. There, he read the story of Jesus raising a man from the dead. The dead man's name was Lazarus; according to the scriptures, he lived in Bethany. Asher knew the location of this small town, which was a short distance from the portal.

Quickly, Asher's plan came together. He would locate Lazarus and prove the story was a complete fabrication, thus revealing Jesus as a fraud. Asher beamed at the simplicity. Obviously, this 1st-century son of a carpenter was no match for Asher's education and intellect.

However, this quest introduced a complex challenge: How could he juggle his mission to unearth the treasure with his newfound objective of exposing Jesus? Winston anticipated daily updates, and both of their lives hinged on discovering the gold. Striking the right balance would be crucial.

Even with Asher's eventful day, it was only early afternoon, leaving Asher with enough time for another quick journey through the portal. As he arrived at his hidden location, he felt a profound hesitation about entering. The object that once seemed full of promise—capable of bringing change, even restoring life—was now the very thing stealing his. He wondered if he would even get a chance to save his grandfather or alter the heinous acts perpetrated by Hitler, or would he simply die a pawn in Winston's pursuit of money?

He found himself challenging everything he thought he knew.

Winston—"the old man"—wasn't old at all, just trapped in a body that lied about his age. His marriage, which once felt like happiness, had disintegrated into dejection. And his career, full of ambition and promise, had collapsed into irrelevance.

And now?

He was searching for treasure with a murderous thief, pursuing the love of a woman he barely knew, and trying to discredit a man who claimed to be God.

Undoubtedly, it was the best trifecta of all time!

Yes, everything in his life up to this point summed up to a big fat zero. But then again, what were his choices? Step into the portal and closer to death? Or not, which would *ensure* his death and complete his failure as a man? One thing he was sure about, he was never a quitter. He also knew a light was at the end of this tunnel, and he hoped it wasn't a train speeding his way.

With that thought, Asher went back through the portal, felt the tingle of death run through his body, and stepped into the 1st century.

Quickly, he headed east towards Bethany. It was only about a 30-minute walk, and it didn't take long to find Lazarus's home because he was well-known in the area.

As Asher approached the home, he could hear the sounds of wailing and weeping. There was a sizable group of people there trying to comfort Lazarus 'sisters, Mary and Martha. It was evident that they were all mourning the death of Lazarus. Asher's timing was perfect, except for one crucial detail—Jesus wasn't there. Recalling from his readings, Jesus waited four days before visiting Lazarus, which greatly upset Mary. Asking around the crowd, he learned that Lazarus had been dead for only three days, meaning Jesus wouldn't arrive until tomorrow.

Initially, Asher was frustrated by the delay, but then he realized it was to his advantage. The extra day would give him time to conduct reconnaissance at the temple. He could also use it to persuade Miriam to accompany him to Lazarus' home, where he intended to debunk Jesus.

Asher headed back toward the temple. His first obstacle there would be to see if he was recognized. Something was different about the temple—it was the money changers. They were no longer in the temple as before but now outside the gates. As he walked by them, no one gave him a second look.

He entered the temple gate, but again, no one paid him any attention. Moving around the temple was easy in some parts and challenging in others. The difficulty increased when he moved closer to the Women's Courtyard. Each corner of this courtyard contained a chamber; in the northeast was the Chamber of Wood, in the southeast the Chamber of Nazarites, in the southwest the Chamber of Oils, and the Chamber of Lepers in the northwest.

Each of them was well over 10,000 square feet in area. Passing through the Women's Courtyard, he encountered the Court of Israel. Here, things became much more difficult. Sacrificial requirements were necessary to enter this area, which posed a problem for him. However, passing through this area was necessary to get to the Holy of Holies, the location he suspected of holding the treasure. But entry was all but impossible. According to the Torah, only the high priest was allowed to enter and only once a year on the day of Atonement (Yom Kippur). The penalty for improperly entering was death. Death by man and, according to the Torah, it also incurred the wrath of God Himself. Of course, being an atheist, Asher wasn't concerned about the latter.

His first task was to find a suitable hiding place until after dark. He didn't take long finding the ideal location—the Chamber of Lepers. Due to the fear associated with leprosy, most people avoided this area. The chamber even contained an enclosed ritual bath area that Asher planned to use as his hiding place.

Next, he would need a light source. Since a roof did not cover the vast majority of the temple, the now full moon would provide enough light to move about safely but not enough for a thorough search. Casually, he made his way towards the Chamber of Oils. Glancing around the room, he saw the items he would need—oil and torches. The Chamber of Oils was a storage area for the olive oil used to fuel the menorah. It also housed meal and wine offerings. Additionally, the chamber contained numerous torches utilized for various festivals.

The final step was lighting the torch. The temple would also provide that solution. The altar in the Court of Israel held smoldering ashes that would supply the flame.

It was getting late, and the temple gates would soon close. But everything was in place. Asher turned toward the portal, knowing what tomorrow would bring.

It was the day everything could fall apart... or into its rightful place.

Checking In

Upon returning to his apartment, Asher immediately called Winston. The call was met with mixed reactions; Winston expressed satisfaction over the check-in yet voiced frustration over the slow progress of their mission. Asher braced himself for a familiar reprimand, but unexpectedly, Winston's voice trailed off into silence, followed by distressing sounds of gasping and struggling for air. Despite Asher's urgent calls, Winston remained unresponsive.

Panic set in as Asher realized the gravity of the situation. Driven by concern for Winston's well-being, Asher dashed to his car and navigated the nighttime roads toward the residence. Thanks to light traffic, Asher arrived at Winston's residence in less than 15 minutes. Without hesitation, he pounded on the door, a sense of dread mounting with each knock. The door swung open after what felt like an eternity, revealing Natalie.

The moment he saw her, Asher urgently demanded, "Is Winston all right?"

"Yes, he is fine," Natalie assured him with a composed voice. "I've put him to bed. Why are you here?"

Ignoring her, Asher moved to step inside, stating firmly, "I need to see him."

Natalie reached out, caught his arm, and firmly stated, "Now is not a good time, Asher."

Asher jerked his arm free from her grasp and headed down the main hallway. He wasn't sure which room was Winston's bedroom, but there weren't many choices. The door to the first room was open and appeared to be Natalie's bedroom. In the second, he opened the door and found Winston. He was lying in bed looking almost lifeless; his breaths were faint, and his complexion gray.

"He should be in a hospital," Asher insisted, turning to Natalie, who had followed him into the room.

"He will be okay; this is normal for his condition," Natalie calmly replied.

"Normal? You call this normal?! He looks like he's barely alive!" Asher said, his frustration evident in his raised voice.

"Please, there is nothing we can do. He's under a doctor's care, and these are his instructions," Natalie insisted, maintaining her calm.

"Doctor, what doctor?" Asher demanded more details, skeptical of Natalie's reassurances.

All the commotion in the room caused Winston to begin to stir. "Asher, is that you?" Winston whispered.

Asher moved quickly to the side of the bed, grasping Winston's hand. "Yes, I'm here," Asher gently assured him.

Through a weak and breaking breath, Winston asserted, "The gold... did you find it..."

"I'm on it, Winston. I'll head back tomorrow and," Asher began, but before he could elaborate, Winston's eyes closed once more, and his shallow breathing evened out as he drifted back into unconsciousness.

Grabbing Asher again by the arm, Natalie firmly said, "Sleep, he needs sleep. Please, let him rest."

Realizing there was little he could do, Asher left the room and headed back to his car.

So, this is it, Asher thought. *Winston is dying. And if I don't find the gold, I'll die too.*

The drive back to the house was slow, not because of traffic but because his mind was racked with thoughts. Every scenario played out in his head, none offering an easy path forward. Time was running out. Winston might live long enough to share the cure—if Asher found the gold quickly. But a deeper question gnawed at him: *Did he have time to chase both truths?*

Abandoning his quest to expose Jesus would free up valuable time. If he dropped it, he could focus entirely on the treasure. That was the logical choice. The rational choice.

And yet... it wasn't that simple.

Walking away meant more than just conceding to Jesus—it meant abandoning Miriam. Could he really just let her go?

Then, another thought. Maybe he didn't have to choose.

The timeline of the coming days offered a chance for both—Lazarus' resurrection was a daytime event. The temple infiltration would happen at night. If he was willing to stretch himself thin, it was doable.

As he pulled into his apartment complex, the weight of tomorrow's significance hit him fully. He had no choice. He would do both.

Expose Jesus. Find the gold. Save Winston. Win the girl.

It was reckless.

It was dangerous.

But mostly, it was exhilarating.

Unexpected News

Asher awoke as the morning sun streamed through his bedroom window. Eager to start, he leaped out of bed and began his trip preparations. As he adored his 1st-century attire, a sudden, heavy knock at the door startled him. He opened it to find his father standing there, David's expression etched with worry and urgency.

"Asher, I've been trying to call you since midnight. Why haven't you called me back?" David asked in desperation.

The question made Asher remember that he had put his phone on silent and hadn't checked it this morning. In the chaos of the last 24 hours, it hadn't even crossed his mind.

"Sorry, Dad. I've been really busy with work," Asher apologized. "Is there something wrong?"

"It's your mom; she's had a stroke. She's in the hospital. We need to leave now," David pressed, his eyes searching Asher's for any sign of understanding and urgency.

The news blindsided Asher, leaving him scrambling to grasp the reality his father presented. "A stroke? When did this happen?" he managed to ask.

His father, clearly exhausted from the last hours with his wife and heavy with worry, answered Asher, "It was yesterday, right before bed."

"What have the doctors said about her condition and recovery?" Asher asked, hoping for some good news.

David's face was a mix of concern and hope as he responded. "They've told us the next 24 hours will be critical. The medical team is doing all they can. We should be there for her," he said, emphasizing the situation's urgency.

This information set Asher's mind racing. He desperately wanted to go to his mother's bedside, but another thought struck him with equal force—his impending quest for the gold and his plans in Bethany. The timing couldn't be worse, and Asher felt he was being torn in two. The meeting in Bethany, the search for the gold, and now his mother's critical condition—each demanded his attention, yet he could only be in one place at a time.

Asher quickly estimated that the journey to Bethany to uncover the truth about Lazarus could take up until the afternoon. However, this would still afford him enough time to return and visit his mother before heading back to the temple just before dusk. The schedule would be tight, but it appeared manageable.

"Okay," Asher finally said, the decision heavy in his heart. "I have a commitment I need to handle first, but I'll make it back this afternoon. I promise."

His father's response was immediate and pointed. "A commitment? At a time like this, when your mother's life is in the balance?" His voice was laced with disbelief and frustration. "And what's with these clothes? What kind of commitment requires you to dress in this crazy costume?"

His father's puzzled and accusing look hit Asher harder than he thought it would. Still committed to a plan, he stood by his decision, hoping his father would somehow understand.

"I'm sorry, Dad. Please, just trust me on this. I'll explain everything later. Right now, I have to do this," Asher insisted, the words feeling inadequate even as they left his mouth.

The argument between Asher and his father escalated rapidly, with accusations and misunderstandings flying between them.

"You continue to tear this family apart! How can you abandon your mother at a time like this?" David thundered with disappointment and anger.

Asher felt trapped and misunderstood and met his father's question with equal intensity. "I know you don't get it, Dad. You never have. My work, my life—it's never been important to you. But I must do this. It matters," he argued.

Their heated exchange climaxed in a moment of profound despair for Asher's father. In an act steeped in ancient tradition, a gesture of mourning and profound sorrow, he tore his clothes. The fabric rent with a sharp sound, a symbol of the deep grief and betrayal he felt.

"If you can't be there for your family now, you're no son of mine," David declared, the words heavy with the weight of final judgment.

With those devastating words, Asher's father stormed out, leaving behind a silence that was as piercing as the argument had been loud. The door slammed with a finality that seemed to echo the severing of their bond. Asher was left standing alone in the aftermath of their argument. The path ahead had never seemed so daunting, nor had Asher ever felt so conflicted.

For a moment, Asher's resolve wavered. The pain of his father's condemnation and the thought of his mother lying in a hospital bed, possibly in her final hours, tugged at him, urging him to reconsider, rush to the hospital, and be by her side. The idea of changing course, abandoning his plan to ensure he didn't miss these crucial moments with his mother, was tempting.

Yet, Asher recognized the hard truth of the situation. At the hospital, he would be just another anxious family member waiting for news, feeling helpless and unable to contribute to his mother's recovery. The doctors and nurses were doing all they could; his presence, while emotionally significant, wouldn't change the course of her medical care.

On the other hand, his life was in danger if he didn't find the gold. Unlike his mother, whose illness was beyond his control, he had the power to alter his fate. The stark difference in his ability to influence the outcomes in these two critical situations became the deciding factor.

With a heavy heart, Asher made his choice. He would go forward with his plans, a decision that felt like a betrayal to his family yet was dictated by the unique circumstances he found himself in.

Turning to leave, Asher collected himself, set his jaw, and walked out of the room and toward the portal.

Confrontation Day

Asher stepped through the portal without hesitation. It would be a long day, but he was up for the challenge. His first mission was to persuade Miriam to join him in Bethany. Arriving at her residence, he knocked but received no reply. With a sense of urgency, he nudged the door open and entered. Inside, the emptiness was striking. The usually simmering stove was cold, and many of Miriam's belongings were absent, suggesting a hasty departure. Confused and concerned, Asher exited her home and hurried to the marketplace, hoping to find her there. He began inquiring about her, but no one had seen her since yesterday.

Miriam's absence struck a chord of concern, yet he clung to a shred of hope. He reasoned that disproving Jesus in Bethany could still sway Miriam's beliefs when he found her. This setback in his plans was troubling but not insurmountable. Knowing the choice he had to make, Asher directed his focus toward Bethany.

As he approached the town and then the house of Lazarus, he realized that he had arrived in time because all the mourners were still present. Asher tried to remain unnoticed and not raise any suspicions about why he was truly there.

For his plan to work, he would need to locate the tomb of Lazarus. He knew it would be nearby, but would he be able to find it? And if he did, what would he find inside? Some guy playing dead and wrapped up like a mummy? Fortunately for Asher, he quickly found the graveyard as it was less than half a mile from Lazarus 'house.

Numerous tombs were scattered about, but only one showed recent activity. Asher was familiar with tombs and their use because of his years in archaeological digs. He knew that the tomb would likely contain the bodies of several family members. The custom was to place the body in the tomb and then return years later to place the bones in a box called an ossuary.

Although he couldn't be positive, Asher would have to gamble that this was the correct tomb. The next hurdle would be moving the stone to look inside. Moving the stone could draw attention, but thankfully, there were no people in the immediate vicinity. As he approached the tomb, he was hit by its dreadful stench. The stone in front of the tomb was far from airtight, and whatever awaited him on the other side smelled of decay and death.

But perhaps that was a deliberate part of the deception—a deceased animal strategically placed in the tomb to mimic the scent of a lifeless body. He hadn't come this far to stop now, and the difficulty of moving the stone was an obstacle he needed to overcome. Heaving against the stone, he finally managed to roll it aside just enough to slip in.

The dim light from the entrance faintly illuminated the interior, revealing a shape wrapped in linen on a slab to his left. The outline, distinctly human in form, suggested the peaceful position of arms and legs. This was the origin of the unpleasant odor that permeated the air. Carefully, Asher extended his hand to gently touch the linen-wrapped form. It felt rigid, confirming its state as a body devoid of life. The fabric was taut over the form beneath, cold to the touch, and, most of all, lifelessness.

As he surveyed the rest of the tomb, he observed numerous ossuaries but no additional bodies. It became apparent to him that this was not the correct tomb, for it contained a corpse. Exiting, Asher struggled to push the stone back into its original position, sealing the entrance once more. He needed to find the correct tomb, and he needed to find it fast.

The area showed no apparent signs of other recent burials. This raised a troubling question—had he come to the wrong place entirely? As much as Asher didn't want to draw attention to himself, he would have to ask someone for the tomb's location.

Asher headed back toward the mourners, and as he approached, he noticed a large group heading toward the house. As they grew closer, he could see the man leading the group was the one who called himself Jesus. Many other people followed behind the main group.

The atmosphere shifted as Jesus approached, the mourners' anticipation becoming an electrified buzz of excitement. He passed within mere feet of Asher, offering no sign of recognition, entirely focused on the task ahead. The men trailing closely behind him were undoubtedly his disciples. Each of them had solemn looks on their faces.

After the disciples had passed, Miriam unexpectedly captured Asher's attention among the followers. At first, he wasn't sure—it was just a glimpse of someone in the moving crowd. Then, his eyes landed on the linen shawl draped over her shoulders, the one he had given her.

Despite the solemnness of the moment, there was an undeniable change in her demeanor, a peacefulness that seemed to radiate from within. Spotting her, Asher couldn't help but call out, "Miriam!" She didn't hear him, prompting Asher to raise his voice, "Miriam, Miriam, over here!" His persistence paid off as she turned, her gaze finding him in the crowd. With mutual recognition, they began moving towards one another.

"What are you doing here?" Miriam's question caught Asher off guard.

"Me? I was wondering the same thing about you," Asher replied, confusion and curiosity mixing in his voice.

Miriam's expression transformed, radiating an even more pronounced glow as she shared her revelation, "I have found Him—the Messiah!"

Messiah? The word echoed in Asher's mind, leaving him staggered by her statement. No, this couldn't be happening. He struggled to process her words, the implications swirling chaotically in his mind.

His bewildered look momentarily caught Miriam off guard. A smile returned to her face as she gently took his hands. "Come with me. Let me introduce you to him. You can see for yourself," she urged.

The irony was more than he could stand. Asher had come to Bethany to disprove Jesus's divinity to Miriam, yet here she was, inviting him to greet the very man he sought to expose. "No!" Asher exclaimed, pulling his hands away from hers.

As tears streamed down her cheeks, Miriam pleaded, "Oh, Asher, please don't miss this moment."

Firmly, Asher responded, "Trust me, I won't." With that, he turned and walked away.

She stood for a moment, watching him before rejoining her group.

Asher's attention was wholly focused on Jesus, sensing that a crucial moment was imminent. Jesus was deep in conversation with a woman, and Asher was too distant to catch their exchange. Based on the woman's demeanor and how others deferred to her, Asher surmised she was one of Lazarus 'sisters. After a moment, Jesus and the woman started walking away from the crowd, leading everyone assembled to follow them.

As they made their way, it became clear to Asher that they were heading toward the graveyard—the very place he had just left. The crowd swelled around him, making maintaining a clear line of sight difficult. Caught off guard by the unfolding events, Asher realized his initial plan was quickly unraveling. The prospect of debunking Jesus's miracle now seemed out of reach. How could he possibly disprove the resurrection of a man if he couldn't even get close enough to witness the event firsthand?

Amidst the throng of onlookers, Asher caught a glimpse of Jesus positioned before a tomb—remarkably, the very one Asher had investigated earlier. Observing intently, he watched several individuals roll aside the stone that sealed its entrance. Jesus then lifted His hands skyward, seemingly in prayer, before bringing them down and calling out with authority, "Lazarus, come out!"

Asher scoffed internally, convinced of the scene's impending failure. The notion that the lifeless body he had just confirmed as dead could somehow heed the call and emerge from the tomb seemed beyond belief. In his mind, this moment would, without doubt, expose the falsehood of the entire narrative surrounding Jesus. Of one thing, he was sure, that dead body was not about to come walking out of that tomb.

Asher strained to get a clear view of the tomb, initially hearing only gasps from the crowd. Soon, those gasps evolved into a murmur, escalating into shouts of joy. The crowd began to part, revealing a figure shrouded in linen, emerging from the tomb's shadow, each step tentative yet determined. Asher pressed forward to get a better look. He was now within feet of whoever this was.

Some people began to remove the burial garments as they called out the name Lazarus. What was more astonishing was the smell. The stench of death had been replaced with the fragrance of sweet perfume. The crowd erupted in praises, shouting *Hallelujah* and *Praise God.* Asher stood amidst the jubilant crowd, his convictions shaken by the undeniable reality before his eyes.

Lazarus, accompanied by Jesus and his sisters and followed by jubilant family and friends, proceeded towards their home, the air filled with an infectious celebration. The sorrow that had hung heavily around them had transformed into an overwhelming joy, turning tears of mourning into shouts of elation. The vibrant crowd began to disperse, each person seemingly eager to spread the word of the miraculous event.

Amidst the dispersing crowd, Asher grappled with the spectacle he had just witnessed. How, he wondered, had Jesus managed such a feat? In Asher's mind, the only explanation was that he had misjudged the situation earlier. It occurred to him that Jesus was not just a charismatic leader but a skilled illusionist, orchestrating his tricks with meticulous planning.

Suddenly, Asher felt a tug on his sleeve. It was Miriam, and she gushed, “Did you see it? Did you see?” Asher could only stare, knowing she didn’t want to hear what he had to say. “Come, let me take you to Him, please,” she begged.

Asher gently stepped back, his voice soft but firm, "No, I have something I must do." Turning away, he began his solitary walk back toward Jerusalem, leaving Miriam and the miraculous scene behind.

The long journey back was filled with soul-searching. Doubts mingled with wonder as he replayed the bizarre events, each detail gnawing at the edges of his certainty. The closer he got to the portal, the more tangled his thoughts became, none offering the clarity he desperately sought. And one question refused to let go.

Was it possible that what he had witnessed was real?

Hospital Trip

Racing against time, Asher hurried back to the portal, the urgency of his mother's condition fueling his every step. The transition through the portal, especially with all his recent trips, drained him physically. Running on adrenaline, Asher pressed on.

Once he returned to his apartment, there was no time to waste. Asher quickly changed into something more appropriate for a hospital visit. As he drove to the hospital, concern for his mother's health and the difficulties of his relationship with his father swirled within him. But as he parked and went inside the hospital, his focus narrowed to one thing only—his mother.

Upon reaching her room, he found his father sitting beside Leah's bed and her sister, Hannah, standing close by. Hannah greeted him with a warm hug. Realizing that father and son needed time alone, she placed a gentle hand on Asher's arm. "I'll give you both some privacy," she said softly before slipping out of the room.

The sight of his mother lying unconscious was jarring. An array of medical equipment surrounded Leah. Wires connected her to machines that monitored her vital signs, each beep echoing ominously in the sterile room. Sitting beside the bed, his father held his mother's hand tenderly but somberly. The unresolved tension with his father loomed in the air, yet the immediate, shared worry for his mother provided a fragile bridge for communication.

Asher broke the silence that filled the room, his voice barely more than a whisper. "Has there been any change?" he asked, dreading the potential answers.

His father's response was silence.

Understanding the need to mend fences, especially now, Asher ventured further. "Dad," he started as he struggled to find the right words, "I'm sorry about earlier. Seeing Mom like this... it's hard. And I realize I've only made things harder between us."

His father's continued silence was heavy, broken only by the quiet rhythm of the monitors. "Dad, I was just trying to do what you taught me—fulfill my commitments," he added in a way that he hoped would appeal to their shared values.

Finally, his father spoke, his voice a blend of weariness and disappointment. "I taught you to prioritize commitment to God and your family, Asher. You seem to have forgotten both."

The accusation stung, but Asher chose not to escalate the conversation. "Mom wouldn't want us to be at odds, not now," he countered softly.

His father's reply was sharp and edged with frustration. "Don't you see? This fighting—it's the cause of the problem," David said, pointing toward the bed to emphasize his point.

Asher's resolve softened; this was not the time for pride or stubbornness. "I agree, Dad. We need to stop. We should be here for her, together," he insisted, moving slightly closer, signaling his willingness to set aside their conflict.

The room became silent once more, a quiet acknowledgment of the tentative ceasefire. It was only then that his father finally addressed Asher's initial question. "The doctors...they're saying we can only wait now. It's in God's hands," he admitted, resignation lacing his words.

For the first time, David's eyes left his wife and gazed upon Asher's disheveled state. "Asher, what's going on? You look awful son. What's happened to you?" he inquired, noting Asher's appearance and odor.

Asher, caught off-guard by the question, fumbled for an excuse. "Oh, it's just work stuff. You know how it is," he said, attempting to deflect and steer away from his recent, unbelievable experiences.

"Your skin, are you having some type of allergic reaction?" David asked, noticing several small spots on the back of his hands and a larger one on his arm.

Glancing at his wounds, Asher tried to downplay it. "Yeah, I'm not sure what happened, but I must have come into contact with something," he chuckled nervously. "I'm going to make an appointment with my dermatologist and see what he says."

His father sensed Asher was hiding something and continued asking questions. "And the clothes I saw you in? Is it part of your work, too?" he probed further, his skepticism evident in his tone.

Scrambling for a believable explanation, Asher replied, "Yeah, we were doing a historical reenactment for work. Had to get into character," he lied, hoping to satisfy his father's curiosity.

His father regarded him skeptically. Still, he seemed to accept the explanation for the moment, perhaps recognizing that his immediate concern for his wife outweighed his need for further answers.

"I see," he replied, letting the matter rest as they returned to the silent figure on the bed.

For the next hour, they sat in silence, and the only conversation came when the nurse checked on his mother.

Sensing his father's unwavering dedication to staying by his mother's side and the quiet exhaustion etched into his face, Asher extended an olive branch. "Dad, why don't you take a break? Get some coffee, clear your head... I'll stay with Mom for a while." His voice was steady, his intent clear.

His father's refusal was immediate, a gentle but firm shake of the head. "No, I left to find you, but I'm not leaving again. Not even for a moment. This is where I belong," he said, his voice low but resolute, the depth of his commitment clear in his eyes.

Asher understood all too well; the silent vigil was his father's way of coping, of being there for his wife in the only way he could. Yet, Asher also recognized that his place wasn't at her bedside—not because he cared less, but because he was powerless to help. He and his father still had much work to do in their relationship, but that wouldn't happen here.

Realizing that he would rather be alone with his bride, David offered Asher a way to leave. "I know sitting here isn't easy for you, especially with all your commitments. You tend to your affairs; I'll update you if things change," his father said, giving Asher an easy way out.

Asher hesitated. Commitments. The word hit him hard. What commitment could be greater than being here with his mother? What kind of son walked away when she might be dying? Yet the urgency of his other pressing obligation—his own health—pulled at him just as fiercely.

One thing was certain—he couldn't do both. No matter how hard he tried to balance everything, something had to take priority. And in this moment, he wasn't sure if he was making the right choice. But a choice had to be made.

With a slow exhale, Asher made his choice. Yet, instead of relief, all he felt was defeat. "Alright, Dad. Call me if there's any change or if you need anything at all. I'll come back in the morning," he said, his voice thick with unspoken emotion.

David didn't answer. His hands were folded, his head bowed. He was praying. Praying for the miracle Leah needed.

Once, Asher would have joined him.

Now, he just walked away—followed by his guilt.

Confusion

Returning to his apartment to prepare for his trip back to the temple, Asher went through his usual preparation steps. As much as he wanted to focus on searching the temple, his mind continually returned to the events he had witnessed in Bethany.

Feeling light-headed and unsteady, he questioned whether it was the lingering effects of the time machine or simply the consequence of not having eaten all day. Hoping it was the latter, he quickly prepared a sandwich and ate. Yet even after finishing his meal, a jittery restlessness remained, his hands unsteady and his thoughts racing. Wanting to calm himself, he poured a glass of wine, thinking it might help him relax. But as he took a few sips, a strange sensation crept over him—his head felt heavy, and a wave of dizziness, almost like vertigo, set in.

He sat down on his sofa and attempted to collect himself. After a few minutes, the symptoms faded somewhat, at least enough for him to focus on the task at hand. Again, his mind returned to Lazarus walking out of that tomb. He grappled with the profound nature of what he had witnessed. Every fiber of his being insisted that what he saw was a dead man brought back to life, but his rational mind resisted accepting that explanation.

If it was a trick or illusion, as he initially believed, catching Jesus in a lie seemed impossible. His maneuvers were too well-conceived and executed. There had to be another way to expose the truth. Lying on the table before him was his Bible. Asher quickly turned to the Gospel of John and the story of Lazarus. Reading the story, he found every detail precisely as he had witnessed. Moving forward in the book, he realized that Jesus was just days from being crucified.

He spent about an hour cross-referencing the events of the days before Jesus's death in the Gospel of John with those in the Gospels of Matthew, Mark, and Luke. Each told of the arrest, trial, crucifixion, and death of Jesus. After that, the grand finale: rising from the dead after three days. That was it! The resurrection, if true, set Jesus apart from all other prophets—an unparalleled historical event. How had he not considered this earlier? If Jesus indeed emerged from the grave, he was the Messiah. However, if, as Asher believed, he remained in the tomb, then he was nothing more than a mortal man.

The first prerequisite for validating the truth of the gospel accounts was Jesus's death. Asher had witnessed the men hanging on crosses, understanding that death on the cross was an inevitable outcome. He decided to attend Jesus's crucifixion and verify it to ensure certainty. He would then focus on confirming the resurrection, which he believed should be relatively straightforward. Empowered by this new plan, Asher felt renewed purpose, and the path ahead seemed more apparent.

As evening approached, he went through the portal and directly to the temple. His arrival was perfect. It was a mere hour before they would begin emptying the temple and closing the gates. Amidst the bustling crowds in the Court of the Gentiles, he found a secluded spot among the outer colonnades where he could be alone, preparing his mind and body for the challenges ahead.

There was a new calmness to this temple area since Jesus had overturned the tables. He could hear scripture reading and see people praying and worshiping God. Once again, he thought back to his childhood and remembered the first prayer he learned—the Shema. "Hear, O Israel: Adonai is our God, Adonai in One! Blessed is God's name; His glorious kingdom is forever and ever! And you shall love Adonai, your God, with all your heart, with all your soul, and with all your might."

Unexplained emotions surged within him, prompting the same question to echo in his mind: Why had he forsaken his childhood faith? Suddenly, he found this question difficult to answer. Part of the response was tied to his intellect. He considered himself too intelligent to believe in a god. As a scientist, religion seemed anything but scientific. But whatever it was that was stirring in him couldn't be explained by science. It was as if his soul was searching for something. *What soul?!* His brain screamed.

As he paced back and forth, lost in these thoughts, he suddenly felt a tap on his shoulder. Startled, he turned to find the gentile thief with whom he had conspired to rob the money changers. "Hello, my friend.

I figured I would find you here. Planning your next theft?" the thief sarcastically asked. Seeing the fear in Asher's eyes, the thief tried to put him at ease.

"Relax, you have nothing to fear from me. As I said, we're friends. Let me formally introduce myself; my name is Julian."

Asher remained speechless.

"I understand your hesitation; after all, I did have a knife to your throat just days ago," Julian said with a laugh. "Of course, that's the past, and now we're friends. Yes?" he probed.

Unsure of where this was going, Asher responded with the only possible answer, "Yes, of course."

A big smile spread across Julian's face. "Good, good. Besides, we work well together. And I have *friends, friends* that can be very helpful," Julian said, emphasizing friends.

Asher's brow furrowed. *There it was again—that "friends" comment.* The first time Julian said it, Asher brushed it off, unsure if there was a hidden meaning. Now, hearing it again, he couldn't ignore the weight behind it. *Was Julian trying to send a message? Or was he testing Asher's reaction?* Either way, Asher knew better than to press for answers—at least not yet.

Julian continued, "So tell me, what's next? I ... *we* want to help."

The last thing Asher needed was his help. Once again, he searched his mind to find something to satisfy this guy. "I... I don't, I don't know," Asher stumbled with the words.

"But you seem so deep in thought. Surely, a clever man like you has some kind of plan. Besides, once a thief, always a thief. Right, my friend?" Julian asked with that sarcastic smile.

A thief, yeah, that's exactly what I've become. Nothing more than a common thief, Asher thought.

Julian continued, "One thing is for sure: we make a good team. Maybe if we put our heads together, huh?"

Asher had to think fast before this went any further. He just needed to avoid this guy for a few days, and the whole thing would be over. "Yes, that's a good point. Let's meet here tomorrow at about this same time. I'm going into the Inner Courts to check on some things," Asher said, knowing that the gentile couldn't follow him there.

"Ahh, plenty of riches in there, I'm sure. Yes, I'll meet you here tomorrow," Julian replied.

His response seemed strange to Asher. Could he know about the gold Asher was hunting? He seemed to know everything else about Asher, but surely not that, too. Asher tried to clear his head of these thoughts as he turned and walked away.

"Tomorrow, see you tomorrow, my friend," Julian called out as Asher left.

Asher made his way into the Women's Court. He could see the twelve steps leading to the Inner Courts as he looked to the west end of this court. It was now or never. The crowd was thinning out, and it would soon be time to implement his plan.

Asher hid himself in the corner of the room that contained the ritual bath. As he expected, the guards did not thoroughly search the area, and before long, he began to hear the closing of the temple gates. For safety, Asher waited another 30 minutes before moving about the temple. Although it was night, the moonlight provided enough light to find his way around safely.

Swiftly, he navigated to the Chamber of Oils, snatched a torch, and drenched it in oil, ensuring it was ready to ignite once he reached the altar. Clutching it tightly, he turned toward the stairs leading to the inner courts.

But as he began ascending the stairs, a sudden wave of severe dizziness overcame him. His vision blurred, the world tilting beneath his feet. He barely made it to the fourth step before his body betrayed him, forcing him to collapse onto the stairs. His breath came in short, desperate gasps. His heart pounded violently—too fast, too hard. He clutched his chest, panic surging through his veins. *Was this a heart attack?*

After a brief rest, he fought to gather his strength. Gritting his teeth, he forced himself upward, step by agonizing step. But as he reached the sixth step, the dizziness intensified. His legs gave out. He fell—hard—his knees slamming into the stone. A sharp jolt of pain shot through him as his body collapsed backward, tumbling down to the fifth step in a helpless sprawl.

And then—he heard it.

"Asher... what are you looking for?"

The voice was no louder than a whisper, yet it was profound—searching, steady, and impossible to ignore.

His eyes snapped open. That hadn't been a thought. Someone had spoken. Someone who knew his name.

He struggled to sit up, every muscle aching, and scanned the dark edges of the temple. Only a few people in this time even knew who he was. *Miriam? No—the voice had been too masculine. Julian? The tone didn't match.*

There was a weight to the voice—an authority laced with compassion. And though it was soft, it had landed deep inside him like thunder.

"Asher..."

He felt he should answer. But to who?

The voice had felt close, so close—as if the source were just beside him, close enough to touch. And yet, as far as he could tell, he was completely alone. He turned his face upward. Nothing. Only the vast, silent night—and the full moon above, casting its silver light across the ancient stones.

He was so lightheaded he wondered if he was hallucinating. That had to be it. Just another side effect. A trick of exhaustion and time travel.

But the voice still echoed in him.

A chilling realization overtook him—he was about to lose consciousness. With one last desperate glance at the sky, he saw the full moon above him—a silent witness to his downfall.

Darkness closed in.

Then—nothing.

Discovered

As daylight began to gently enter the temple, Asher slowly regained consciousness. Disoriented and groggy, he struggled to piece together the events that led him to this spot. A sudden realization struck him as he attempted to stand—he was not alone. The imposing figures of the temple priest and his attendants loomed over him, their expressions a mix of curiosity and suspicion.

"This is sacred ground on which you trespass with such disregard. What is your purpose here?" the temple priest asked with an air of authority.

Filled with fear and desperation, Asher attempted to rise to his feet and swiftly escape. However, his legs betrayed him, causing him to stagger down the steps. A sudden blast of a trumpet from one of the attendants served as an alarm, alerting the temple guards. In a matter of moments, a dozen guards pursued Asher through the temple. Despite his efforts to evade capture, the temple guards closed in rapidly. Employing a swift and coordinated strategy, they intercepted him, cornering him against the wall in the Court of the Gentiles.

Violently thrown to the ground, Asher found himself pinned on his back. Shortly after that, the temple priest arrived, questioning him sternly, "Who are you, and what are you doing here?"

This was not a situation he had anticipated, and Asher once again needed a quick answer—and it had better be a good one. "Rabbi, I'm a traveler and visitor to your city. I have leprosy and have come to ask Adonai to heal me," Asher declared, hoping to evoke both pity and fear.

Apprehensive of the potential contagion, the temple guards promptly released him and stepped back. After studying Asher momentarily, the Rabbi said skeptically, "I see no such signs on you."

Rising to his feet, Asher raised his sleeve to reveal the worsening sore on his arm. Seizing the opportunity, he continued his fabricated story, "I entered the temple yesterday and went into the Chamber of Lepers to take a ritual bath. Afterward, I sat in the corner of the chamber, exhausted from my long journey. There, I fell asleep. When I awoke,

I was alone and scared. I spent the night praying to Adonai to heal me of my sickness. I fell asleep on the steps where you found me. Please search me. You will find I have stolen nothing. And examine the temple, I have done no damage. Rabbi, please have mercy on me," Asher pleaded with a tone of desperation, hoping his words would further convince the temple priest and guards of his innocence.

Now came the moment of truth: would the priest believe Asher's elaborate lie? What was only a short moment seemed like a lifetime as the priest pondered the tale before finally speaking, "Have you secured offerings?"

Asher possessed only a vague understanding of the offerings and sacrifices required for lepers. Clearly, he lacked these items, but he hoped this would be his path to freedom. "No, Rabbi, I haven't," Asher replied.

Seemingly eager to be done with Asher, the priest instructed, "Go and purchase the necessary items. Then return with them to commence the purification process properly."

Asher suppressed his overwhelming excitement, itching to exclaim, "It worked!" Instead, he replied, "Thank you, Rabbi, and may God's greatest blessings be upon you."

Asher quickly turned and headed towards the nearest temple exit. After only a few short steps, the priest's call stopped Asher in his tracks. His heart raced with anxiety as the priest approached and unexpectedly took hold of Asher's arm to examine the sore. Asher wondered if the priest would notice that it wasn't actually leprosy. To Asher's relief, the priest summoned one of his attendants, who quickly provided a strip of cloth to bind Asher's wound.

The priest's unexpected compassion caught Asher off guard. Just moments ago, he had feared the worst from this man, but now he found himself receiving aid. Next, the priest reached into his robe, retrieving a small pouch. "Take this," the priest said, his tone less stern than before. Asher, puzzled, accepted the pouch. Inside, he found a few coins. The priest explained, "Use it to purchase the necessary offerings. Shalom."

With a nod of acknowledgment, Asher thanked the priest and made a swift departure. As he walked away from the temple, a crushing realization washed over him—the quest for the gold was over. Returning to the temple was no longer a viable option, and the dream of the sought-after fortune wasn't just slipping away—it was gone.

The grand plan he and Winston had meticulously crafted failed. In truth, he was lucky not to have been arrested.

Asher's only option was to return to Winston and develop a new plan for a different treasure. But he knew this, too, was not an option. Winston would be furious, and Asher doubted that Winston's health could survive a new plan.

With his mission in ashes and his hopes shattered, nothing was left but to walk away.

The Recovery

As the early morning sun peeked through the blinds of the hospital room, casting long shadows across the floor, David sat quietly by Leah's bedside, holding her hand. He had been there every day, whispering to her about their memories and the plans they still had to fulfill, hoping she could hear him. Beside him, Hannah sat knitting quietly, her presence a constant comfort during the long hospital days. During one of these moments, as David was reminiscing about their first coast trip, he noticed a slight flutter beneath her eyelids.

"Leah?" he whispered, his voice a mixture of hope and anxiety.

Her eyelids trembled again, and then, slowly, her eyes opened. Disoriented at first, she blinked against the soft light, her gaze wandering until it met David's.

David pressed the call button frantically. "She's awake! She's looking at me! Praise Adonai!" he exclaimed as soon as a nurse appeared at the door.

Quickly assessing Leah, the nurse nodded and hurried to retrieve the doctor. Moments later, the doctor entered, his expression cautiously optimistic.

Leah blinked, struggling to form words. Her voice, barely more than a whisper, trembled as she asked, "Where... am I?"

"Leah, you've had a stroke. We placed you in a medically induced coma to give your brain a chance to recover. It's remarkable to see you awake so soon," the doctor said in a warm yet professional tone.

David squeezed her hand, his eyes never leaving her face. "Did you hear that, love? You're going to be all right," he said, his voice thick with emotion.

Leah tried to speak, her voice barely a whisper. "David?"

"I'm right here," David assured her, leaning closer. "You had us all worried there for a while. But you're strong. Leah, oh, Leah, the Lord has healed you," he whispered, kissing her hand gently.

Leah managed a weak smile. Her mind was still foggy, but she was aware of her husband's presence. "Asher, where's Asher?" she asked with a trembling voice.

David's face clouded over. He turned slightly to Hannah, who had set aside her knitting and was watching the scene unfold with concern.

David quickly picked up his phone and called Asher, only to get his voicemail. Remembering that reaching Asher had been difficult before, he made a decision. A decision that would require him to leave Leah's side—but one he felt was necessary. Asher needed to know what was happening, and waiting for a return call wasn't an option.

Thinking on his feet, David looked at Hannah and asked, "Hannah, could you stay with her for a bit? I need to try and find Asher. He needs to know about all this."

Hannah nodded understandingly, moving closer to Leah's side. "Of course, David. Find Asher. I'll be here with Leah. We'll be just fine," she assured him warmly.

"I'll be back as soon as I can," he said softly. "Hannah will stay with you, love." He paused, his voice steady despite the emotion behind it.

"And I'll bring our son back with me—I promise."

Quest for Answers

David was relieved that Leah was recovering but still anxious about Asher. Quickly he left the hospital, his resolve to find his son deepening with each step. The drive to Asher's apartment was quick, as the roads were nearly empty in the early morning. Unlike before, Asher's car was not there.

Knowing his son wasn't home, David contemplated his next move: the university. Surely, someone there might know something useful. He would begin with his old friend Dean Levinsky.

It was a short drive to the university, and David headed straight for the dean's office, unsure if Levinsky would be in this early–but he had to try. If anyone on campus could help him find Asher, it would be the dean. As he stepped into the university's grand old building, his footsteps echoing through the quiet hallways, David was relieved to find Levinsky already in his office.

Levinsky warmly welcomed David inside, gesturing toward a chair. His office, lined with books and memorabilia of academic achievements, reflected a lifetime dedicated to scholarship.

"David, this is a pleasant surprise," Dean Levinsky greeted him, his expression concerned at the sight of David's anxious demeanor. "What brings you here so early?"

David wasted no time; his words rushed with urgency. "It's Leah, she's had a stroke."

Before David could explain further, the dean interrupted. "A stroke? David, is she okay?" he asked with concern.

"Yes, yes, she's fine. She's had a marvelous recovery, praise Adonai," David responded. "But she's asking for Asher. I've been trying to reach him, but he's not responding. I was hoping you might know where he is."

The dean's eyebrows raised in surprise. "That's wonderful news about Leah, but I'm sorry, I haven't seen Asher recently. Are you aware he has taken a short break from his teaching?" the dean asked.

“Yes, he told us that, but I’ve had a hard time locating him lately, and I'm not sure what he’s actually doing,” David stated with concern.

Seeing this, the dean quickly replied, "I think I might know who can help you with your search. Winston Saunders. I understand that he and Asher were involved in some extensive research together. Just a word to the wise. I have never personally met him, but I have found Winston quite the character, if you know what I mean."

David’s interest was piqued at the mention of a name he didn’t recognize. "Do you have any idea how I can reach him?"

"I don’t have his contact, but you might find something in Asher’s office. You have my permission to look there. Maybe you’ll find something there that would be helpful," Dean Levinsky suggested. Come with me, and I’ll unlock his door.”

Grateful, David nodded, and the two men quickly made their way to Asher’s office, unlocking the door to a room cluttered with maps, books, and various archaeological tools.

“Help yourself; just close the door when you leave. I’ll lock it later,” the dean said as he excused himself. He paused briefly, his expression softening. “Oh, and David, please give Leah my best. I hope she recovers quickly. Keep me posted on her condition, and let me know if there’s anything else I can do to help find Asher.”

David nodded in sincere appreciation and turned his attention to searching the office. He started by looking through Asher’s desk, flipping through notebooks and papers. Amidst a pile of field notes and research articles, David found a notepad with several numbers scribbled on it. His eyes caught a number labeled clearly with 'Winston Saunders' with a Boston, MA address and phone number.

Relief washed over David as he quickly dialed the international number.

After several rings, the call was redirected to a generic voicemail. Recalling the dean's somewhat cautious remarks about Winston, David chose not to leave a message. He figured it was prudent to gather more information before revealing his intentions.

David, confident he was close on Asher's trail, felt a surge of renewed hope. With a fresh strategy, he exited the office, closing the door behind him. His next destination was Asher's apartment. Years ago, Asher entrusted his parents with a key for when he was away, which they kept safe at home.

After collecting the key, David headed to the apartment. Upon entering, he quickly noticed signs of Asher's absence as the rooms lay in disarray.

In Asher's closet, he found clothes and sandals similar to the ones Asher had worn when David visited just a few days ago.

A Bible was open on the living room table as if he had been reading it. As David looked at the Bible, he could see the pages outlined the story of the trial of Jesus from the Gospel of John. Through his conversion to Christianity, David was well aware of the stories concerning Jesus.

David discovered a notepad on the kitchen counter with an address in Jerusalem scribbled on it. Recognizing it as a residential area, he speculated it had some connection to Winston.

David thought it worth the risk to drive to the address and see if it connected to Winston somehow. As he arrived, he was taken aback by the home's impressive architecture, which hinted at the residence of someone quite influential. He rang the bell, his heart thumping slightly faster, anticipating what he might uncover.

The door opened, revealing a woman who appeared to be in her thirties. "May I help you?" she asked politely but cautiously.

"I'm looking for Winston Saunders," David stated directly, trying to gauge her reaction.

"And you are?" she inquired, her expression unreadable.

"David," he replied, his mind racing. Her question confirmed his suspicion that this was indeed Winston's residence.

“Is Mr. Saunders expecting you?” she posed with suspicion.

“No, but I think he knows my son, Asher, Asher Meyer,” David answered confidently.

The woman nodded slightly, “I see, please wait here. I'll see if Mr. Saunders is available."

After a brief wait that felt longer to David, the woman returned. "Mr. Saunders will see you now. Please, come in," she ushered him through a richly decorated hallway to a sunroom where an elderly man awaited, his presence imposing yet frail.

"David, I presume?" the man spoke, his voice firm but carrying a strength that belied his frailty. "I'm Winston Saunders. Natalie, thank you, you may leave us."

As Natalie exited, David took the opportunity to observe Winston. Despite his courteous greeting, his eyes spoke of deception. David knew this meeting could lead him to Asher, and he was determined to find out how Winston fit into the puzzle.

David’s mind was a whirlwind of questions. "Mr. Saunders, do you know where I might find my son, Asher?"

Winston's gaze was steady, his voice even. "David, I must tell you, I do not know Asher’s current whereabouts."

David frowned, sensing evasion in Winston’s calm demeanor. "Mr. Saunders, it's critical that I find him. His mother is currently hospitalized, and I’ve been unable to reach him. Any information you could provide would be immensely helpful."

Winston sighed, a trace of frustration crossing his features. "David, I’m sorry to hear about your wife’s health, but unfortunately, there’s nothing I can tell you. But rest assured that I will convey your message should I encounter him.”

"But you do know him," David pressed, his voice rising slightly in desperation and suspicion. "And I think you know more than you're letting on. I understand the two of you are involved in some type of project."

Winston shifted uncomfortably in his wheelchair. "David, our relationship was purely academic. I may have discussed some historical theories with Asher, but – "

"Mr. Saunders, please," David interrupted, his tone insistent. "He wouldn't have just vanished without reason. If you know anything..."

Winston's face suddenly contorted in pain as he clutched at his chest, his breathing becoming labored. With trembling fingers, he fumbled for the device around his neck and pressed it. Desperately, he reached for his oxygen mask, but his grip faltered. He gasped, struggling to speak.

"Mr. Saunders!" David exclaimed, rising to his feet in alarm. Seeing the severity of Winston's distress, he rushed to his side. His eyes flicked toward the door just as Natalie appeared, moving swiftly with her medical bag already in hand.

Using her medical expertise, she instantly assessed the situation. She moved swiftly to Winston's side, her hands expertly checking his vitals. Seeing his struggle, she grabbed the oxygen mask and gently placed it over his face. "Winston, can you hear me? Just breathe slowly, I'm here." She then administered medication from a prepared syringe.

As Winston's breathing gradually stabilized, Natalie glanced up at David, her eyes firm. "He needs to rest now. I'm sorry, but you'll have to leave."

David hesitated, torn between concern and his need for answers. As Natalie wheeled Winston away, David knew he couldn't leave—not yet.

"Please see yourself out," Natalie called over her shoulder as she disappeared with Winston down the hallway.

Once they were out of sight, David's resolve hardened. He needed answers and had a hunch they lay somewhere within these walls. After a quick search of the surrounding rooms, he found one that caught his attention and seemed out of place amid the grandeur—a large room with several tables strewn with maps and various historical texts. It was a space that breathed a different air, one of meticulous planning and deep study. There were several whiteboards with various notes and confusing information written on them. David's eyes were drawn to a particular map spread out on the table—it appeared identical to one Asher had given him, a map of 1st Century Jerusalem. Beside it, there was a modern-day map.

David realized he was standing in what must have been a planning room for Asher—a place where strategies and perhaps more were formulated. His son had been here, working closely with Winston on something secretive, something important. The reality of his discovery set in, deepening the mystery of his son's disappearance and fueling his determination to find him.

His pulse quickened as he leaned closer to examine the older map. There were notes in the margins, scribbles that looked remarkably like Asher's handwriting. David recognized the temple because it was the centerpiece of the map. Directly south of the temple was a circle drawn with the words "Portal Location" written by it. Comparing it to the modern map, the same circle existed at Ophel Hill. David knew this place; he had visited it numerous times.

But what kind of portal could this be, and what did it mean? Was it an information portal where they were sharing data with other researchers? While that was certainly a possibility, it didn't fit the two maps. Looking around the room, he saw the only computer equipment was a simple laptop. Slowly, a strange and inconceivable thought entered his mind. *Could it be some kind of time travel portal?*

As far-fetched as it seemed, it was the only explanation that fit David's current facts. It explained why Asher wouldn't discuss his work and odd clothes. This wild idea also aligned with the details David observed in the room, including the two maps and all the jargon jotted on the boards. But where was the machine itself?

David looked back at the modern map and again saw the words Ophel Hill, immediately realizing that he would find the answers he sought there.

Ophel Hill

David rushed from the house directly to his vehicle and quickly made the short trip to Ophel Hill. Arriving, he saw Asher's car parked nearby. The vehicle was locked, and there was no sign of Asher. On a hunch, he checked for the keys under the wheel well—bingo! David quickly unlocked the door and looked throughout the car; nothing was unusual. Turning his attention to the trunk, a chill ran down his spine before he opened it. *What would he find here?* Some of the possibilities were too difficult for him to think about.

His hand trembled as he inserted the key and lifted the trunk lid. A wave of relief washed over him when he saw that it did not contain his worst fear—his son's body. The things that were there only deepened the mystery. His personal effects, including his cell phone, were all neatly arranged. He picked up the phone and saw the numerous missed calls he had placed to Asher. Of course, it all made sense. He could not take these items to the 1st century, so he left them there.

David was convinced that he had solved the mystery, and now it was time to find the portal itself. He half-joked about finding a convenient sign marked 'Portal This Way, 'but he knew the reality would be far more subtle and concealed.

He searched the area for the next half hour until he came upon a small ancient building. Instantly, he knew this location would fit the requirements for the portal, as it existed in both eras.

As he stepped into the modest room, he scanned every inch of the walls, uncertain what he was looking for, yet trusting he would recognize it when he saw it. His gaze eventually settled on the back corner, where the stonework appeared slightly altered. Also, a set of footprints led directly toward it. *This must be it,* he thought with growing certainty.

Approaching the suspicious wall, he pressed his hand against it and met no resistance. His entire right hand simply disappeared as if it didn't exist. The sight frightened him so that he quickly jerked his hand back, which now was filled with a tingling sensation.

David's breath caught—he had found the portal and would find Asher on the other side. While part of him yearned to step through, he understood the practical realities of such an action. His modern clothing would make him stand out immediately and place him in great danger.

He briefly toyed with stripping off his contemporary attire, hoping to find suitable garments on the other side. Still, the risk of arriving entirely out of place—and without any clothes—was too great. Then, a solution dawned on him: the clothes in Asher's closet. Those weren't just random outfits but an extra set of clothes. Or maybe he left them behind for a rescue such as this.

David quickly returned to his car and proceeded back to Asher's apartment. As he contemplated the day's events, it almost felt as if Asher had intentionally left the clues for him to find and bring him home.

Betrayed

As Asher returned toward the portal, he turned a corner in the street and ran directly into Julian, who four Roman soldiers were questioning. “Him,” Julian shouted, “That's the man that gave me the money!” Stunned, Asher stopped in his tracks.

"You, come here!" one of the soldiers barked.

The portal was less than five hundred yards away and Asher's only option for escape. He quickly reversed his tracks and rushed down a narrow alleyway. Two of the soldiers immediately pursued him. Their heavy armament slowed them down, giving Asher the advantage. He was faster, and confidence surged through him—he could make it. The portal was only seconds away.

Once safely through, he vowed never to return to this god-forsaken place. Asher turned the last corner and saw the portal location in the distance. The faint sound of a whistle pierced the air—presumably, the soldiers signaling for reinforcements. No matter; he was now less than one hundred yards from home.

Suddenly, two soldiers emerged from around a corner near the portal, closing in on Asher. With his escape route cut off, Asher swiftly turned another corner, attempting to outmaneuver them. The soldiers' shouts grew louder, blending with the piercing whistles that echoed through the air. As Asher circled the block, the portal came into view again, and the path seemed clear this time. Determined to reach safety, Asher summoned the last of his strength.

As it drew closer, a man stepped out of the building, hiding the portal. The sight stopped Asher in his tracks. Someone had discovered it—but who? The shape and form of the man looked very familiar, but that couldn't possibly be.

As he stood there, with a mere twenty-five yards to go, he felt an abrupt, searing pain in his right hamstring. Crumbling to the ground, he sensed warm blood flowing from the wound. In moments, Roman soldiers surrounded him. One soldier approached Asher, planting his sandaled foot on Asher's thigh and extracting his javelin, intensifying the agony. The soldiers reveled in their capture, sharing laughs and cheers. Without warning, a soldier delivered a vicious kick to Asher's stomach, leaving him struggling to breathe.

Gasping for air, Asher struggled to crawl the short distance to the portal.

"Where are you going, Jew?" one soldier taunted.

Before Asher could react, another soldier abruptly swung the handle end of his javelin into the back of his head, blinding pain exploding through his skull and dragging him toward unconsciousness.

As his vision blurred, his gaze fell on the building that housed the portal and the man standing there.

He had one final thought before complete darkness overtook him:

Why does this man look like my father?

A Plea for Mercy

David instantly knew that he had found Asher, but why was he being taken away by Roman soldiers and to where? David kept his distance as he trailed the group. Moving swiftly through the bustling streets of ancient Jerusalem, pushing through traders, travelers, and townspeople, they eventually arrived at what appeared to be a jail.

David could feel his heart pounding in his chest. Watching the guards and officials move in and out of the building, he searched their faces for hints of mercy. Drawing a deep breath, he approached a guard at the entrance. His command of Aramaic was rudimentary at best. "Please, I need to see the man brought in today," David stammered.

The guard looked at him with a mix of suspicion and confusion. "Speak properly! What do you want?" the guard demanded.

David struggled to find the words. "Mercy, please. My son, I need to see my son," he managed to get out, hoping his desperation would translate even if his words did not.

The guard scoffed, dismissing him with a wave of his hand. "Go away, foreigner. Your words make no sense," he snapped, turning his back to David.

Realizing his attempts in Aramaic were useless, David turned to his rusty Latin, hoping it would resonate more with the Roman guards. Taking a steadying breath, he approached another soldier, hoping that a language more familiar to them would yield better results.

Summoning his courage, he spoke. "Domine mi, quaeso, filium meum videre permitte" (Sir, please allow me to see my son.) His Latin was not fluent, but he could see the guard understood.

The guard turned, slightly taken aback by the use of Latin from such an unlikely source. His brow narrowed as he processed David's words, his stance shifting from dismissive to mildly curious. "Quid ais? Quis es?" (What are you saying? Who are you?) the guard responded in Latin, his tone mixed with suspicion and interest.

David continued the conversation in Latin, "I am the father of the man taken today. I beg you, I seek justice."

The guard eyed David more carefully, considering his words. "It is not the custom to allow visitors. Leave now before you, too, are arrested. You can see him after his trial," he replied, with a coldness that David had never experienced.

David pushed on, his desperation evident in his voice. "As a father, I have the right to see him. Can you at least tell me of his charges? Sir, please have mercy, help me!"

The guard responded with indifference, "I understand it is theft. He will be tried and sentenced, likely crucified. Now, go; I have other matters of importance." With this, the guard simply turned and walked away.

Crucified! Surely, David reasoned, he had misunderstood. His head began to swim, and he stumbled to the ground. How could any of this be real? This was all just a horrible nightmare that would soon end.

But it wasn't a nightmare. It was history, raw and unforgiving. He had left the comfort of the 21st century and stepped into the brutality of the 1st—a world where justice was swift, cruel, and merciless.

David's heart shattered. Instinctively, he turned to the only refuge he had ever known—God. On his knees in the dust of ancient Jerusalem, he prayed. He pleaded for intervention, strength, and something beyond the crushing reality before him.

After what felt like an eternity, David rose to his feet. The city bustled around him, but he was utterly alone. Unless God intervened, the fate of his son was in the hands of those who ruled this ancient world.

He carefully weighed his options, knowing each choice had risks and uncertainties. Initially, he considered seeking local advocates or lawyers who might understand the complexities of Roman legal procedures. However, the language barrier and lack of resources made this option seem hopeless.

David also considered trying to appeal directly to Roman officials who might be sympathetic to his plight. Still, his encounters with the soldiers had left him skeptical of receiving any compassion from them.

David realized he needed a more strategic approach to assist his son. He thought of the Sanhedrin, aware of their significant role as a religious and judicial authority, but he was unsure where to locate them. Determined, he approached a group of locals bustling near a market stand. He was encouraged that they were speaking Hebrew, a language he was much more comfortable with.

"Excuse me," David began tentatively. I am looking for the meeting place of the Sanhedrin. Can you direct me?" He carefully enunciated each word, trying not to attract unneeded attention.

A kind-faced elderly man recognized the urgency in David's voice, nodded, and pointed towards the Temple Mount. "You will find them in the Chamber of Hewn Stone, within the Temple complex," he explained.

David thanked him with a nod and set off towards the Temple Mount, a site he overlooked while transfixed by Asher's arrest. Based on all the activities and conversations of the people along the road, it became clear that it was the week of the Passover. As he approached, the grandeur of the Temple slowly came into view.

For the first time, he took in the entire majesty of the Western Wall—not a remnant, not a ruin, but whole, unbroken, standing in its full glory. The very wall where he had spent countless hours in prayer, where he had often brought Asher as a child, was now before him in its original majesty.

Memories surged forward with each step. He recalled the sacred times he had pressed his hands against the worn stones of the modern-day ruins, whispering prayers between the cracks. He could still hear his voice as he once told Asher, "One day, Elohim will rebuild these very walls."

And now, it was as if He had.

The thought sent a shiver through David's body. It felt surreal—as if he had stepped into the fulfillment of that very promise. This wasn't just the wall as it had been; it was the wall as it would be, restored in all its splendor.

Reaching out, David placed his hand on the cool, ancient stones, feeling the rough texture beneath his fingertips. He was no longer a man praying at the ruins of the past—he was touching history before its fall.

His breath caught as he took it all in. The immensity of the moment was unlike anything he had ever experienced. He had stepped beyond time into an era where the Temple still stood, and its walls remained a testament to faith and endurance.

His knees weakened, and he slowly sank to the ground. Forgetting everything else, he simply remained there—overcome, silent, in awe.

Then, a stirring—not from the world around him, but within. A voice, silent yet undeniable. Firm. Steady. Clear.

"Arise, My child."

The command pressed into his spirit.

"Your son needs to be saved."

David's breath caught. He had heard from the Lord before, but never this strongly. The words were simple and clear. Asher needed him. He needed to fight for his son, free him, and do whatever it took to bring him home. The awe of the moment faded beneath the urgency of those words. David rose to his feet, determined to face the Sanhedrin with conviction and resolve the situation.

David's heart raced as he entered the imposing structure of the grand Temple complex. Temple guards directed him to a small office where requests to meet with thc Sanhedrin were managed. Inside the office, a clerk, a middle-aged man with a stern demeanor, looked up from his scrolls as David entered. "How may I assist you?" the clerk asked in Aramaic, his tone formal.

“Shalom, I need to speak with the Sanhedrin about my son, Asher. He has been wrongfully detained," David replied in Hebrew, hoping to express his urgent need clearly and for swift action.

The clerk raised an eyebrow, surprised by the switch in language. “Shalom. Do you have a previous engagement with the council?” he asked, slightly suspicious.

David, sensing the clerk's scrutiny, chose his words carefully. "Unfortunately not, sir, but I am a sojourner and a visitor to your city. I have an urgent issue for which I need assistance," he replied, hoping his honest and direct approach would allow him to plead his case.

The clerk paused, assessing David with a measured gaze. Finally, he broke the silence by asking, “What do you need?”

David's voice held a trace of urgency as he responded to the clerk's inquiry. "My son, who was traveling with me, has been falsely arrested by the Romans. As a Jew, I'm requesting any help you might provide," he explained.

The clerk's response was straightforward. "This thing, it is a matter for the Roman courts, not the Sanhedrin," he stated firmly.

David felt a sinking feeling as he realized his plea was not making an impact. With a growing sense of urgency, he pressed on, "Please, sir, I'm desperate. My son is in danger, and I fear what might happen if I don't do something soon."

The clerk eyed David with disdain. “You will need to arrange an appointment. The Sanhedrin cannot be approached without proper scheduling. Besides, the council is currently busy with an urgent matter. Come back next week."

Interrupting, David’s voice was laced with urgency: "Please, I implore you. There isn’t time. I must speak with them today. It’s critical—my son's life might be at stake."

The clerk paused, studying David’s face. "Wait here," he said before standing and disappearing into a back room.

David waited anxiously, pacing the small space.

When the clerk returned, he nodded reluctantly, "I will allow you to speak to a preparatory committee member. They can decide if your case is urgent enough for today's session."

David sighed in relief, "Thank you, truly, thank you."

He was led through a series of corridors to a smaller, less ornate chamber where a senior member of the Sanhedrin, an elder with a kind but serious face, listened to concerns and decided on their urgency. He was accompanied by a younger man who appeared to be some type of assistant.

David repeated his plea as he described Asher's character and their predicament. "My son, a good man, a scholar, finds himself trapped by a misunderstanding. He has no voice to defend himself, so I must be that voice."

The elder's expression slightly softened as he leaned forward. "What is your son's name?" he asked.

David quickly responded, "His name is Asher."

The younger man leaned over and whispered something into the elder's ear. Though David couldn't catch the words, he noted the sudden curiosity across the elder's face.

"We encountered a man named Asher in the temple this morning. Asher, Asher the Leper. He, like you, is a sojourner to our city. Is this who you are inquiring about?" the elder man asked as he recalled the familiar name.

David's heart sank at the mention of "Asher the Leper." He remembered Asher's recent visit to the hospital, during which he had questioned Asher about the sores on his arms and hands. Could his son indeed be a leper?

"He does have some unusual marks on his skin, but I assure you, they are not leprosy," David explained, his voice firm yet composed to dispel any misconceptions. "We share a home, and as you can see, I am not afflicted by any such condition. Possibly, that was a different man."

The elder man nodded, stroked his long beard, and calmly replied, "Possibly. Your concern for your son is clear, and your fear for his safety speaks deeply to us. It just so happens that we have another pressing matter with the governor this morning. We shall bring this matter before him as well. Please return this afternoon, and we will inform you of his decision."

"Sir, may I accompany you? I believe time is crucial in this matter," David desperately pleaded.

The elder man regarded him with a firm gaze before responding, "No, it would be highly inappropriate for you to join us." He paused momentarily, then added with a hint of compassion, "However, you may wait outside the governor's residence. This way, we can communicate Pilate's decision more swiftly."

Pilate. The name resonated strongly with David. The very man who had sentenced Jesus to death.

And now, Asher's life was in those same hands.

Judgment Day

Uncertain of how much time had passed, Asher slowly regained consciousness in a dimly lit jail cell. The air was thick with a pungent odor that Asher could only associate with the scent of death. As his eyes adjusted to the subdued light, he realized he wasn't alone in the cell. In a corner, Julian lay battered and bruised, a vivid testament to the Roman brutality he had endured. Julian's face was swollen, one eye sealed shut, and he clutched his ribs in a fetal position.

Asher, too, felt the throbbing pain at the back of his head, the persistent ache in his stomach, and a constant throbbing in his leg. Fortunately, the leg wound had stopped bleeding as someone had wrapped a makeshift bandage around it. Against a wall on the opposite side of the cell was another man. He had a wild look in his eyes, and he was chained to the wall. This man, too, wore the marks of Roman brutality.

"Julian, are you okay?" Asher asked with concern in his voice.

Julian, with difficulty, replied, "Don't talk to me, Jew. You set me up."

Asher was perplexed. "I don't know what you mean. You're the one that led the soldiers to me," Asher responded.

"I should have killed you when I had the chance," Julian mumbled, his bitterness evident.

Julian's anger and accusations confused Asher, but he knew that addressing the issue further was useless. Suddenly, Asher was startled by the other prisoner, who began grunting and jerking at his chains as he attempted to gain his release. Asher was grateful for the chains that kept him at a safe distance. His eerie sounds sent shivers down Asher's spine.

At times, the man's cries would morph into unearthly howls, reminiscent of a wild beast with occasional bouts of manic laughter. These sounds were familiar, but from where? Yes, the night the thief had attacked him, the sound in the darkness. This man must have been hiding there. All this only further puzzled Asher.

Asher's thoughts returned to the moment before he had lost consciousness and the figure he observed by the portal. Although the moment was still very foggy, he remembered thinking how much the man favored his father. But that was impossible. Who that man was and whether he had discovered the portal would remain unknown for now. The mysteries here never seemed to end.

Asher reeled from the bitter truth—his mission had failed. But as the weight of that failure settled over him, something else stirred beneath it: resolve. He would not give up. He would not surrender. Survival was now his mission, and somehow, he would find a way out of this godforsaken place.

Breaking his concentration, three guards entered the jail cell. Asher, Julian, and the third prisoner were bound in chains and escorted from the prison to a nearby makeshift courthouse. A sense of foreboding settled over him as they were brought before the judge. Asher had imagined being represented by some type of council, but it was just the three of them, the judge, and several soldiers—no advocates to be found.

Asher quickly thought that this might be his best opportunity for freedom. He would again draw on his quick wit to convince the judge of his innocence. Asher tried to imagine how the trial would progress and what charges would be brought against him. Hopefully, he would only be required to pay a fine or something similar. Asher was confident he would talk his way out of this and regain his freedom.

The judge, a stern-faced Roman official, regarded them with a cold detachment that sent shivers down Asher's spine. It quickly became apparent that this was no ordinary trial; it was a kangaroo court, a mere formality before their inevitable sentencing.

The judge read the charges, "The three of you have been charged with and found guilty of theft. The sentence is death."

"Wait, what?!" Asher cried out. Suddenly, Asher felt a sharp pain as a soldier brought a club violently across his back. Asher fell to his knees.

“Watch your mouth, Jew!” the guard spewed. The third man began to emit guttural sounds as his eyes darted wildly. Asher wondered if the man even spoke a written language.

Asher rose to his feet, trying to regain his composure and control of the situation. He knew he had to act quickly. Softly, Asher said, “Your honor, there seems to be some kind of mistake. I assure you, I am innocent.”

The judge, who had been writing out the decree, slowly turned toward Asher with a piercing gaze. Without a word, he tossed a small bag onto the table in front of him. The soft thud echoed in the tense silence.

“Do you recognize this?” the judge asked with a hint of sarcasm.

Asher’s eyes locked onto the bag—and his stomach dropped. He recognized it instantly: the very one he had stolen from the temple. There was no mistaking it.

But he said nothing.

The judge reclined in his chair. "Open it. Take a look inside."

With trembling hands, Asher opened the bag. Inside was a single coin. Asher took the coin and began to examine it. It was unlike any he had ever seen. The coin featured an intricate engraving of a palm tree.

At the base of the tree, Asher noticed the inscription: σὺνδεση. He recognized the Koine Greek script and understood its meaning—"connection" or "linking."

"This coin, the one you are holding, is exclusively possessed by the money changers in the temple," the judge explained, a wry smile on his lips. "Silly as it is, to them, it symbolizes strength, resilience, and a supposed connection to the divine," he added with a tinge of mockery.

Then his expression darkened. "But for you, it means death," the judge declared as he leaned forward to resume writing the decree.

Asher stood in stunned silence.

"Seems your idiotic friends tried to trade the bag and its contents for gold, not knowing about the unique coin contained inside," the judge remarked casually, his pen pausing momentarily as he glanced back up at Asher.

"While I've never seen you before, I am well acquainted with your two accomplices—Julian and Barabbas." The judge gestured toward them with contempt. "These two have been a thorn in our side for years. But it appears no longer."

He let his words settle before continuing, his tone laced with mockery. "You should have picked your friends more carefully."

The judge tapped his stylus against the table, then pointed once more at the two men. "Now, they are caught and have testified to your guilt as well. That's more than the court requires," he concluded, resuming his writing with a sense of finality.

With a defiant snarl, Barabbas spat at the judge and lunged forward, his chains clanging as he hurled his weight at the soldiers. Caught off guard by his ferocity, one guard stumbled, and Barabbas seized the opportunity. He drove his shoulder into the man's chest, knocking him backward. In a flash, he twisted around and yanked a gladius from the belt of the nearest soldier.

The gladius—a short Roman sword, razor-sharp and designed for quick, close combat—was in his hands before anyone could react. With a swift, brutal motion, he plunged the blade deep into the man's chest. The soldier gasped, eyes wide with shock, as blood poured from the wound, and he collapsed, lifeless, to the stone floor.

“Stop him!” the judge shouted, his voice filled with fury as additional soldiers rushed into the room.

The soldiers closed in, driving Barabbas back with clubs and spears, herding him like a wild animal into the corner. Barabbas fought savagely, but with his hands bound and outnumbered, he was eventually overwhelmed. Bloodied and panting, he was forced to his knees and then to the floor as the soldiers stood over him.

Asher stood frozen, horror washing over him. He had seen Barabbas ' violent outburst in the jail cell—but now, he saw the true evil of the man. This wasn't theft or rebellion. This was pure savagery.

The judge rose, drew his sword, and stepped slowly over to the fallen prisoner. With deliberate menace, he pressed the blade to the soft flesh beneath Barabbas 'chin.

"Enough," he growled. "You're no longer just a thief—you're a murderer. And it's clear this isn't your first."

With deliberate cruelty, he twisted the blade, drawing a thin trickle of blood down Barabbas 'neck. "I should kill you now... but that would spare you the agony of the crux," the judge sneered, his voice dripping with contempt.

With a dismissive gesture, he ordered Barabbas and his accomplices to be taken away.

Asher, Julian, and Barabbas were returned to their cell, aware that crucifixion was imminent, scheduled for before noon that same day. Thankfully, Barabbas was chained to the wall again, yanking and rattling his restraints as he uttered guttural sounds and howled. His actions were so disturbing that Asher couldn't think clearly. And now, more than ever, he needed to concentrate on his escape plan, and time was not on his side.

Yet, the odds seemed overwhelmingly against him. Even if he managed to open the cell door, walking was challenging due to the wound to his leg. Additionally, he lacked the funds to bribe the guards for assistance, and without a weapon—the knife long lost—his options were limited. The weight of his predicament bore down on him as Asher desperately sought any viable option.

Observing a soldier standing nearby, Asher noted the man's imposing physique. His large arms, chest, and head gave him a formidable appearance. The soldier's forehead boasted bushy eyebrows that extended over his eyes, contributing to an almost Neanderthal-like appearance. With a vacant expression, it appeared the lights were on, but nobody was home. Recognizing an opportunity, Asher thought this might be the man he could manipulate to his advantage.

Asher limped towards the cell door and called out to the guard, "Guard, guard." The soldier looked over but did not move. Undeterred, Asher called again, "Guard, please come here."

The guard reluctantly walked towards Asher's cell, stopping about five feet away. "What is it, Jew?" the guard growled.

Twice before, Asher had been able to use his intellect to work his way out of a bind; now, he would need to do it once more. Asher began, "I'm not supposed to be here; this is all a big mistake."

The guard started to turn away. "No, wait, please! I have something important to tell you," Asher continued, hoping to capture the guard's attention. The guard paid little heed and began walking away. "Money! I have money!" Asher cried out in desperation.

This caught the guard's interest, prompting him to stop. "Please, just hear me out," Asher begged, seizing the opportunity as the guard slowly returned to the cell, this time coming much closer.

"Yes, money. I have money. If you assist me in escaping from here, I'll share it with you," Asher continued.

The guard, intrigued, responded, "Where is this money? I'll go get it."

Thinking on his feet, Asher replied, "It's south of here, about a mile away. I'll take you there."

The guard, intrigued by the prospect of wealth, inquired, "You'll take me there?"

Capitalizing on the momentum, Asher turned on the charm, saying, "Yes, yes, I will. Just open the door. We can go now."

The guard retrieved a key from a chain attached to his belt, unlocked the door, and slowly walked into the cell. Taller than Asher by about three inches, the guard continued forward, forcing Asher to hobble backward.

Suddenly, the guard grasped Asher's tunic in both hands and thrust him against the back wall. Asher quickly crumpled to the floor, and just as quickly, the guard yanked him back to his feet. "Where, tell me where!" the guard demanded.

Before he could answer, the guard bashed his forehead against Asher's, opening up a large gash. With blood pouring down his face and on the verge of unconsciousness, Asher simply mumbled, "I don't know."

This only angered the guard more as he shouted, "Don't know? Tell me, Jew!"

From the other side of the cell, Barabbas grunted and laughed to encourage the guard.

Julian shouted, "Leave him alone! He's lying. He doesn't have any money. He's just trying to escape."

The guard dropped Asher to the floor and peered down at him. "I would kill you, but I don't want you to miss your upcoming appointment," the guard chuckled, "There's nothing I enjoy more than seeing Jews on the crux."

Outside the cell, voices echoed as soldiers roughly handled a prisoner, escorting him through the jail corridors. The guard swiftly departed from Asher's cell, securing the door behind him. Lying in pain on the floor, Asher observed the new prisoner being pushed and shoved down the corridor. He recognized the man; it was Jesus.

The soldiers didn't place Jesus in a cell but instead escorted him to a nearby courtyard. Asher couldn't see the courtyard, but he could hear the activities. From reading the gospels, Asher knew this was Jesus's flogging. Despite his deep-seated resentment toward Jesus, Asher couldn't help but feel a sense of compassion.

The brutality Asher had endured at the hands of the Romans paled in comparison to the merciless beating he now heard—each snap of the whip painting a vivid picture. Again and again, the sickening crack of the Cat-o'-Nine-Tails tore through the air, striking Jesus's body with relentless force.

And as if the flogging weren't enough, they mocked him with cruel laughter, jeering, "Hail, King of the Jews!"

The beating dragged on for nearly an hour. Yet through it all, Jesus never cried out for mercy.

Not even once.

As the brutal beating came to an end, Jesus was once more escorted past Asher's cell. The man he now saw vaguely resembled the one he had seen only a short time earlier. His back bore the gruesome marks of the scourging; his face was swollen and bloodied, and a cruel crown of thorns pressed into his brow. Jesus struggled to move forward as the Roman soldiers forced him onward.

Time, as Asher had once known it, no longer existed. Everything was seconds, and everything was an eternity.

Suddenly, the sound of keys rattling in the lock shattered the silence as two soldiers entered the cell and took Barabbas away, leaving Asher and Julian alone.

Bewildered yet resigned to his fate, Asher stumbled back and crumbled into the corner of his cell.

There, he wept bitterly.

A Father's Anguish

David paced quickly through the streets of Jerusalem. In the distance, he could see a crowd gathering near what he would soon learn to be the praetorium—the official residence of the Roman governor. Word quickly spread that Jesus had been arrested. As David continued to piece everything together, it became clear that this was no ordinary Passover. This was the Passover, where Jesus would be tried and crucified. A gnawing suspicion crept over him—could Asher somehow be involved in these events?

Interrupting his thoughts, David spotted the young man from the Sanhedrin's office walking in his direction. David rushed towards him and blurted out, "Is there any news?"

The man's somber expression answered the question. "I am sorry. The council was unable to help. Your son has been tried and found guilty," the young man said quietly.

"Guilty?! Guilty of what?" David demanded with disbelief.

Trying to remain calm, the young man replied, "Theft. It seems he was involved with some known criminals and stole money from the temple."

"Surely this is all some type of mistake," David said as his mind reeled with confusion and shock. "When can I see him? I must see him!"

The young man hesitated as a pained expression crossed his face. "Sir," he began gently, "there's something you need to know. Your son... he's been sentenced to be crucified. They're planning to carry out the execution today."

David's heart sank as the weight of the news crashed down on him. "Crucified?" he whispered, barely able to comprehend. "Today? No, there must be something that can be done! No, this is not possible." Tears flooded David's eyes and freely flowed down his face.

The young man nodded solemnly. "I'm so sorry," he said quietly. "There's nothing more we can do. The decision has been made, and the sentence will be carried out." He paused, clearly struggling with the gravity of the situation. "I wish I had better news," he added softly, then turned and walked away.

David was left standing alone in a place that felt so ugly and foreign.

Voices Raised

Pontius Pilate sat on his judgment seat in the courtyard of the praetorium. His face was stern as he surveyed the large crowd that had gathered for an annual Passover event—the "feast of the governor." Each year, the governor would graciously release a prisoner to appease the Jewish people. It was an event that Pilate disdained. Typically, the crowd would gather, and Pilate would simply present the prisoner to be released. However, this year, Pilate decided to take a different approach. He would offer the crowd a choice between two prisoners and let the people decide who would be set free.

Pilate had been frustrated with the Jewish leaders who had demanded he execute a man named Jesus. Pilate personally found no fault in Jesus, but the situation was increasingly becoming complicated. The leaders were exerting tremendous pressure on him, and he feared the people might riot or revolt. Additionally, he was concerned about reports of unrest reaching Rome and jeopardizing his position.

Even his wife had intervened and pleaded with him not to have anything to do with condemning Jesus. She had a dream—more like a nightmare—and she was fearful that Jesus was being convicted, although he was an innocent man. The entire ordeal was overwhelming for Pilate, but now he had a plan to alleviate the entire situation.

His plan was simple: present the people with a choice—the notorious criminal Barabbas or a man who seemed to be respected by them. Just days ago, great crowds had gathered, laying down cloaks and palm branches for him to ride over. The entire story of a man on a donkey struck Pilate as bizarre. If he were truly a king, wouldn't he be riding a majestic horse?

Strange as it all was, it demonstrated their respect and admiration for Jesus. Pilate was confident the choice would be simple and quick. Surely, the people would choose Jesus.

This decision would not only spare Jesus's life but also absolve Pilate of any blame—after all, it would be the people themselves, not him, who set Jesus free.

As the guards brought Jesus and Barabbas—both bound in chains—before the people, a murmur began to ripple through the crowd. Before them stood two men they knew well: the barbarian and notorious criminal Barabbas and the humble man they called Rabbi and teacher—Jesus. Jesus was barely recognizable—his face and body battered and bloody. Slowly and dramatically, Pilate rose from his seat and walked between the two men.

The crowd fell silent as he began to speak, "It is the custom at the feast of the governor to release one prisoner as chosen by the people. Today, I present you with two choices. Who do you want me to release? Barabbas or Jesus, who is called the Christ?"

Barabbas struggled against his chains and howled as the guard held him securely. Jesus simply stood in silence. The roar of the crowd grew. Some called for Barabbas, others Jesus. Seeing this, the chief priests and elders quickly began working the crowd and persuading them to pick Barabbas.

After a moment, Pilate raised his hand, demanding silence from the crowd. As a hush fell over them, he again asked, "Which of the two do you want me to release?"

With the chief priests and elders leading this time, the crowd began to shout Barabbas. Slowly, the crowd was whipped into a frenzy as they shouted in unison and repeatedly, "Barabbas!"

Their choice caught Pilate by surprise. It seemed his plan had failed. Part of him felt the Jewish leaders had manipulated him. Without question, the people had been manipulated—as he had witnessed the leaders influencing the people's choice. But now his hands were tied. His last chance to help Jesus would be to allow the people to choose the punishment.

As he looked at this man, Jesus, he felt the flogging he had received was punishment enough for his alleged crimes. Surely, the crowd would feel the same. Once again calling the crowd to silence, Pilate asked, "Then what shall I do with Jesus who is called Christ?"

In unison, the crowd cried out, "Crucify him!"

These events perplexed Pilate. He had found no fault in Jesus, yet the people who had previously worshiped him now called out for his life. "Why? What evil has he done?" Pilate asked.

But the crowd persisted, "Crucify him!"

Frustrated, Pilate realized that he was not making progress. In fact, the opposite was happening as the crowd was on the verge of rioting. Even though he held no animosity towards Jesus, he didn't care for Jesus enough to risk things escalating further. Resigned to the situation, Pilate walked to a nearby bowl, washed his hands, and declared, "I am innocent of this man's blood; his blood will be on your hands."

In response, all the people shouted, "His blood be on us and on our children!"

With this, Pilate released Barabbas and delivered Jesus to be crucified.

A Race Against Time

David's heart was pounding with fear and disbelief. The news that Asher was to be crucified struck him like a blow. It was incomprehensible. The thought that his son—his only child—was condemned to die in such a barbaric way was unbearable. He had to do something. He had to see Asher, speak to him, and try to stop this madness.

The streets of Jerusalem were bustling with people, but David moved through them as if in a trance. He pushed past the crowds, his mind fixed on a single goal: reaching the prison. He didn't care who got in his way or what waited for him there. All that mattered was Asher.

The prison loomed ahead, the same grim stone building he had visited earlier. As he approached the entrance, he could see the same guard he had talked with before.

"Guard!" David shakily called out as he rushed forward.

The guard looked up and recognized David instantly. A frown crossed his face as he grunted, "You again? I thought I told you to leave."

David swallowed hard. "Please, I beg you. I must see my son. I've come to appeal to you, to ask for mercy."

The guard's expression remained cold and without compassion. He shook his head. "Compassion has no place here. This is a prison, not a temple of mercy. Now go before you find yourself locked up alongside him."

David felt a surge of helplessness and rage. *How could they be so callous? How could they deny him this?* He looked around wildly, his mind racing. He had to find another way. He couldn't just walk away. Not now.

As he stood there, he noticed a man approaching from the side, wearing the robes of a Roman official. The man's expression was stern, but there was a hint of curiosity in his eyes. He stopped in front of David and looked him over.

"What's going on here?" the official asked the guard.

"This man," the guard said, gesturing at David, "claims he's the father of one of the prisoners. One of the thieves set for crucifixion. He wants to see him."

The official turned to David, his eyes narrowing. "You are the father of a condemned man? What's his name?"

David nodded, his throat tight. "Yes, yes. Asher. Sir, please let me see him. Just for a moment. I need to speak to him."

The official's eyes flickered with recognition at the name, and he scrutinized David for a long moment. Finally, he gave a curt nod. "Alright. You can have a few minutes, but no more. Come with me."

David felt a rush of relief, a glimmer of hope. He nodded gratefully and followed the official, who led him through the gate and into the prison. The air inside was cold and damp, and the stone walls were lined with heavy iron bars. The sound of chains rattling echoed through the corridors, mingling with the low murmurs of the prisoners.

They stopped in front of a cell near the back of the prison. David's heart lurched as he saw the figure inside. Asher was barely recognizable, sitting on the ground with his back against the wall. He was bruised and battered. On his forehead was a large gash that was still bleeding. His clothes were stained with blood. David wondered what Asher had done to deserve such a beating. As David stood at the cell door, Asher looked up. Even though his vision was blurry, he could clearly recognize the man—it was his father.

"Father?" Asher's voice was hoarse, barely a whisper.

David gripped the bars, his eyes filling with tears. "Asher... my son..."

Asher struggled to his feet and moved to the bars. "Father, what are you doing here? You shouldn't have come."

"I had to," David said, his voice trembling. "I had to see you. I had to try to help you. They... they told me what's going to happen. Asher, I can't let them do this."

Asher shook his head as a sad smile crept across his lips. "There's nothing you can do. It's too late. They've already made up their minds. You must go back. It's too dangerous for you to stay here."

"No," David said fiercely. "No, I won't leave, and I won't accept your fate. There has to be a way. I'll talk to the governor. I'll offer him money. I'll... I'll do whatever it takes. I won't let them kill you, Asher. I can't."

Asher's eyes softened. "Father... I know you want to help, but you must let this go. You have to let *me* go. There's nothing you can do. You have to accept that."

David shook his head, his heart breaking. "I can't... I can't lose you, Asher. Not like this. Please, there must be something..."

Asher reached through the bars, his fingers brushing David's hand. "You have to be strong, Father. You have to live. You have to take care of Mom."

Hearing those words, David's eyes lit up. "That's why I came to find you. Your mother has made a full recovery! Asher, the Lord has healed her."

A smile spread across Asher's face as he absorbed the news. *The Lord... could this same Lord save him too?* He wondered.

David gripped Asher's hand, tears streaming down his face. "I just don't understand any of this. Why are you here?"

Knowing it was too much to explain, Asher felt the full weight of the plan's stupidity. "Dad, I... I thought I was doing something good, but now I know it was foolishness."

The two men wept together, the iron bars between them no match for the decades of unspoken hurt collapsing in their embrace. It all seemed so petty now—so painfully, stupidly small.

"I love you, Asher," David said, his voice breaking. "I love you so much. I wish I could do it all over again—every word I said in anger, every time I chose silence instead of grace. I failed you... and I'm so sorry."

Asher's eyes brimmed with tears. He tightened his grip on his father's hand and silently cursed the iron bars between them—the cold steel that denied them the warm embrace they both longed for, but not the forgiveness. Not the love.

"No—it was me. Me and my foolish pride," he whispered. "And I love you too, Father. I always have. I just didn't know how to say it. I was stubborn and selfish, and I made choices that hurt you and Mom. Please... forgive me."

There was a long, quiet moment—just the two of them, breathing through the pain, holding on, finally speaking what had gone unsaid for far too long.

The sound of footsteps approached, and the official returned, looking impatient. "Time's up," he said, gesturing for David to step back. "Besides, it's time for your son's punishment."

David's grip tightened on Asher's hand, his heart shattering. "No... please, just a little longer..."

The guards moved forward, pulling David away from the bars. Asher stepped back, his eyes locked on his father's. "Goodbye, Father," he said quietly. "Be strong."

David struggled against the guards, his voice breaking. "Asher! Asher, no!"

But the guards dragged David away as Asher's figure faded from view. He didn't even notice the pain of being roughly tossed into the street as it paled in comparison to the pain of his broken heart and his crushed soul.

As he lay in the road, David's mind raced with thoughts of what he could do—how he could save his son. He had to find a way. He had to. Giving up was not an option. Not now. Not ever. He would free his son from this terrible fate.

He had to believe that—for Asher, for himself, and for the second chance he so desperately wanted with his son.

Golgotha

The appointed hour for Asher's crucifixion had arrived. The jail echoed with the clanking of chains and the heavy footsteps of Roman soldiers. Two guards, one of whom had previously assaulted Asher, approached the cell. The metallic jingle of keys announced the unlocking of the cell door. "Time to go, Jew! Golgotha awaits you!" the guard barked at Asher, his tone devoid of sympathy. "And you too," he added, addressing Julian.

Asher, weakened and battered, was roughly pulled to his feet. As he began to move forward, his gaze met Julian's. They both knew the fate that awaited them. Julian began to beg and cry for mercy. His pleas fell on deaf ears with the guards as they quickly dragged both of them from the cell.

In a desperate bid for freedom, Julian tried to escape, but a swift blow sent him crashing to the floor. He was no match for the strength of the soldiers, their hardened faces showing no trace of pity. The guards pulled him to his feet, forcing him to follow Asher through the corridor toward the courtyard.

David stood at the edge of the courtyard, his breath caught in his throat as he watched the guards haul Asher into the blinding sunlight. Painfully, his heart clenched as he saw his son being yanked forward. David held back as long as he could, but when the guard slammed the heavy patibulum—the wooden crossbeam—across Asher's shoulders, his desperation finally boiled over.

The coarse wood bit into Asher's skin, and David saw his son stagger under the weight, his knees buckling. Without thinking, David surged forward.

"No! Stop!" he cried, pushing through the crowd toward Asher. "That's my son! You can't do this!"

The soldiers barely turned to look at him. Asher's face twisted in pain as he struggled beneath the weight of the crossbeam—then collapsed.

David's heart shattered. He surged forward, arms outstretched, pleading through a voice cracked with agony.

“Please! Let him go!” he cried. “Take me instead! Please—not my son! Take me! Take me...”

He was nearly upon Asher when a soldier’s rough hand clamped down on his shoulder and shoved him backward. David stumbled, but his desperation overpowered his balance. He lunged again, reaching for the beam, reaching for any chance to take his son’s place.

But before he could touch it, a crushing blow struck the side of his head. Pain exploded through his skull, and the world pitched sideways. David collapsed, the ground rising up to meet him as his vision swam and blurred.

Above him, a soldier loomed, the butt of his spear still raised in warning.

The last thing David saw before the darkness claimed him was Asher—collapsed in the dirt, his face twisted in agony, pinned beneath the weight of the crossbeam as the soldiers shouted for him to rise and continue toward Golgotha.

The bodies of father and son lay only feet apart on this blood-soaked, dirt-covered, cursed Roman road.

The soldiers roughly jerked Asher back to his feet to continue his trek through the streets. The wooden patibulum lay heavy across his shoulders, every step sending a shockwave of pain through his battered body. His feet stumbled along the dusty path, each step slower than the last. His back burned from where the rough wood dug into his torn skin, and his vision blurred with sweat and exhaustion.

The soldiers offered no mercy. Asher tripped, his knees giving way under the crushing burden. One of the guards barked at him to rise, striking him across the back with the butt of his spear. Asher gasped, forcing himself up, but his body felt too weak to carry him much farther. He could taste blood in his mouth, and his thirst was unquenchable.

Ahead, Asher could see the path leading through the gates and out of the city. Beyond the walls, Golgotha—the place of the skull—with its barren hilltop loomed ahead. It was a place of death where the condemned went to meet their end.

Asher's breaths came in ragged gasps, his body shaking with the effort of carrying the beam. Every muscle screamed in protest, but the soldiers pressed him onward, their shouts sharp and unforgiving. They showed no sympathy, no hesitation as they forced him toward his final destination.

A crowd lined the street, and some followed behind. A sea of faces watched his every move, some with pity and others with malice. Whispers and shouts filled the air, but all Asher could hear was the thudding of his heartbeat and the gasp of his heavy breathing.

Asher's legs buckled again, but he managed to stay upright. His eyes, blurred by sweat and blood, saw he was only a few steps away. Death awaited him there, a brutal and certain end.

As they reached Golgotha, Asher's heart weighed heavily at the sight before him: Jesus, bloodied and battered, being lifted onto his cross. Asher strained to make out the inscription above Jesus's head, slowly deciphering the words: "Jesus, King of the Jews," written in Greek, Latin, and Hebrew. Their eyes met briefly, a silent understanding passing between them. Asher couldn't help but wonder if Jesus knew Asher's true identity. If Jesus truly were the Messiah, He would know all things.

Asher could see that he and Julian would be placed on either side of Jesus. Nausea gripped him as he realized the grim reality now upon him. The soldiers, well-versed in the brutal art of crucifixion, moved with practiced indifference.

They stripped him of his outer clothing, tearing the fabric away with mechanical efficiency and exposing him to the jeers of the crowd. Any dignity he had left was gone.

Then came the hammer and nails. They drove iron spikes through his hands and feet, fixing him to the splintered wood. Each strike echoed across the hilltop—a cruel, methodical rhythm of pain.

With the cross assembled, they raised it upright, and with a sickening thud, it dropped into the hole prepared for it. Asher's body jolted with the impact, and a cry tore from his throat as searing pain radiated through his limbs.

The onlookers—a mix of indifferent soldiers, curious spectators, and several followers of Jesus, mainly women—watched the spectacle unfold. The women were weeping bitterly. Looking at the women, Asher noticed that one of them was Miriam. At first, a fleeting sense of comfort embraced him at the sight of a familiar face, but swiftly, embarrassment overwhelmed him. He didn't want Miriam to see him in this pitiful state. The irony of the situation wasn't lost on him—Miriam, who had once wished to introduce him to Jesus, now witnessed his agonizing ordeal without realizing the connection. As he gazed at her, he realized she didn't recognize him due to the bloody, swollen, and battered condition of his face.

Over the next hour, numerous people came by to see Jesus hanging on the cross. Some wept, but many jeered and spewed insults at Him. They took joy in using Jesus's own words against him. "Where's your God now, Nazarene?" shouted a man, his voice filled with defiance. "Save yourself if you're so mighty!" Another laughed as he shouted, "Don't worry, he's going to destroy the temple and rebuild it in a mere three days!" Many in the crowd joined in the laughter.

But Asher's emotions were raw and difficult for him to understand clearly. Logic told him that Jesus's actions led Asher to this fate. *His trickery and lies brought this on me,* Asher told himself, trying to hold on to his anger. *And it brought this on himself.*

"Look at you," Asher muttered, his voice hoarse from dehydration. His lips were cracked and dry, and his throat felt like sandpaper. "The great miracle worker." His eyes darted toward Jesus, narrowing with cold disdain. "What's wrong, Nazarene? No clever parables? No last-minute illusions?"

Jesus turned His head slowly toward Asher—His eyes—oh, those eyes. Asher expected defiance, perhaps even defeat. But what he saw wasn't weakness. It wasn't resignation, either. It was something that unsettled him more than anything else.

Compassion, His eyes were filled with compassion and love.

Jesus did not verbally respond to Asher's insults.

Not a word.

No tricks. No veiled parables. Just silence.

And yet, somehow, that silence spoke louder than any words ever could.

Julian spent most of his time crying out in pain, begging for mercy from anyone who would listen. Julian even joined the crowd's mockery, taunting Jesus, "Fool! If you're the Messiah, save yourself and us!"

Asher looked on as the man in the middle didn't respond to Julian either. He only lifted his eyes toward the heavens and spoke in a gentle voice that seemed out of place on that hill of death.

"Father, forgive them, for they know not what they do."

It was maddening to Asher. *Forgive them? Forgive who?* His eyes darted to the soldiers and the jeering, snarling people who mocked Him and spat at Him. They didn't *deserve* forgiveness. They deserved anything *but* forgiveness.

Watching Jesus display unwavering resolve and compassion, even toward those who had condemned Him to this fate, unsettled Asher. Jesus's words of forgiveness echoed in his mind, challenging everything he had believed about Jesus.

But if Jesus was the Son of God, why was He here—on a cross, powerless?

Asher had always understood the Messiah's purpose to be one of deliverance—freedom from Gentile oppression. Instead, He was at *their* mercy, suffering beneath their rule. How could this serve that purpose?

Nothing about this made sense. Asher's mind was full of questions he felt would never be answered.

His thoughts drifted to a distant memory—the conversation with Rita in their apartment. He remembered the jolt of her comment like it was yesterday. *I've become a Christian, Asher*, Rita's voice echoed in his mind. Asher had called her a fool, just like Julian had called Jesus a fool moments ago. To Asher, the idea of transformation through faith felt foreign, even laughable. What he had hoped would be a passing fad for Rita instead was life-changing.

For the first time, Asher truly began to ponder Rita's words. The teachings of Jesus she had shared seemed to resonate in a different light now. Love, compassion, and a deeper understanding of life—ideals that had felt absurd back then were now displayed before him. Amid his agony, Asher found himself questioning the certainty he had clung to. The scientific explanations that once anchored him now seemed inconsequential compared to the reality of his situation. *There's more to life than we can explain with science,* Rita's words whispered through his mind. Was this, he wondered, the divine irony of his journey—a skeptic confronted with the inexplicable? As the world blurred around him, Asher found an unexpected comfort in the memory of that conversation. His certainty had shattered, leaving him with only one burning question: *Was it possible that she was right?*

As the pain surged through Asher's body, a fragment of the Gospel narrative flashed in his memory—the account of a thief receiving salvation alongside Jesus. Thus far, everything he had witnessed aligned perfectly with the biblical account.

From Jesus overturning the tables in the temple to Miriam's first encounter with Him to Lazarus being raised from the dead—every moment had led to this day, mirroring the sacred texts with chilling precision. Asher knew that everything else he had read would come to pass, too.

But a tormenting thought gripped him: Was that repentant thief him—or Julian?

His soul cried out for him to call upon Jesus, to plead for mercy and forgiveness, but his mind clung stubbornly to its contempt for Him. Suspended between heaven and hell, Asher was torn by the battle raging within him.

There was no escaping his destiny of death on this cross; he knew that now. No brilliant words, no quick actions, no cunning plans would allow him to escape. He would die here—on this cross, on this day.

All his dreams of saving the world were shattered.

He wouldn't save his people from the tyranny of Hitler.

He wouldn't save his marriage.

He wouldn't save his grandfather from cancer.

And he wouldn't save the day by finding the gold.

No, it was all gone.

Only one question remained:

Would he finally call upon Jesus—the very One he had resented—and be saved?

A Plea for Forgiveness

David woke to a sharp, throbbing pain in his head. His eyes fluttered open, and for a moment, everything was a blur—the sound of distant voices, the feel of cool hands dabbing a damp cloth smelling of herbs to his forehead. He blinked, trying to focus, the world gradually coming back into view.

As David became more aware of his surroundings, he saw a stranger beside him. The pain in David's skull pulsed as the cloth pressed against his wound, but it was nothing compared to the ache in his chest. The memories crashed back—Asher, the soldiers, the crossbeam.

His heart lurched.

"How long...?" David rasped, trying to sit up, but the stranger gently pushed him back down.

"Easy," the man said, his voice calm but firm. "You've been out for a couple of hours. You took a nasty blow."

David's panic flared. "Asher!" he gasped as he struggled against the man's grip. "My son... where is he? Where have they taken him?"

The stranger's expression grew somber. "They've already led him to Golgotha."

David's blood ran cold. "I must go there! I must save him!" he screamed with a trembling voice.

"There's nothing you can do," the man replied softly. "You need to rest."

But David couldn't rest. He couldn't wait any longer. Two hours... was it too late? He shoved the man's hands away and struggled to his feet, dizziness washing over him. His legs wobbled, and his head throbbed, but he forced himself to move, fueled by sheer desperation.

"I have to go," David muttered, stumbling forward. The stranger called after him, but David didn't hear. His mind was consumed by one thought—he had to find Asher.

He pushed through the streets, his vision blurring as he staggered onward. The city felt like a maze, its winding alleys pressing in on him, but David didn't stop. He passed through the gates of Jerusalem, the world outside opening before him as Golgotha loomed in the distance. The hill, so stark and unforgiving, seemed to grow larger with each step. His heart pounded in his chest as he forced his legs to carry him faster, each step feeling like an eternity.

As he neared the base of the hill, his breath caught in his throat. He could see the three crosses rising above the crowd, their wooden beams casting long shadows in the afternoon light. And there, on the center cross, was a man he didn't recognize but instantly knew by the writings over his head. It was Jesus! The Godman that had forever changed David's life.

David rushed to the foot of the cross, fell to his knees, and began to worship Jesus. David's mind went instantly to Hebrews 11:1: "Now faith is the assurance of things hoped for, the conviction of things not seen." At this moment, his assurance was no longer hoped for but fully seen. There, nailed to an old rugged cross, was *Yeshua*, the Lord that saves. The moment was surreal. Here hung his Lord and Savior, and next to him hung his son. Jesus had saved David's life, and now he prayed that He would do the same for Asher.

David cried out, "Jesus, son of the Most High, please have mercy on my son!" His plea seemed to be heard, but Jesus didn't respond to his request.

"Asher..." David's voice cracked as he gazed at his son—his only son—hanging before him, arms outstretched, nailed to the wood. His face was pale, drenched in sweat and blood.

David stumbled to the foot of Asher's cross, his hands trembling as he grasped the rough wood, as if holding onto it could somehow lift Asher up. His mind raced back to the very first time he had held Asher—so small, so full of life. He remembered how he had lifted Asher toward heaven, offering him to the Lord in praise and thanksgiving.

And now, he needed to lift him again to the only One who could save him. He had to lead his son to the saving grace of Jesus.

“Asher!” David called out, his voice trembling with desperation. “My son... please, listen to me! There’s a story in the Bible about a thief. But he asked for forgiveness... and Jesus promised him paradise.”

Asher looked toward his father, his face pale and drained. His lips were cracked, and his voice barely a whisper. “Father... why would it matter now? I’ve wasted my life... there’s no forgiveness for someone like me.”

David shook his head, tears streaming down his cheeks. "No, Asher, that’s exactly what grace is—receiving what we could never be worthy of. That’s why He came—to save people like you, like all of us. To have mercy and to give us grace."

His voice trembled as he continued. "That thief... at the very last moment, he believed. He asked, and Jesus forgave him."

David’s gaze locked onto his son’s, desperation thick in his voice. "He’s right here, next to you! Don’t you see, Asher? He can forgive you too!"

Asher closed his eyes, his face contorting in pain as it surged through his body. "Father... I don’t believe; I can’t. I’ve never believed in any of this. What’s the point now?" His voice wavered, filled with exhaustion and doubt. "You don’t know the things I’ve done."

David’s voice cracked with urgency. “None of that matters now, Asher. He’s here for this very moment. You don’t have to understand everything. You just need to simply trust.”

Asher’s life raced before him—his regrets, his failures.

He had always believed himself to be brilliant, capable, in control. But had he ever truly been any of those?

His ego had blinded him, convincing him that he could outthink, outmaneuver, outmatch anyone—even God. But now, for the first time, he saw it for what it was.

Foolishness.

And where had that foolishness led him?

To a broken marriage, ruined by arrogance and selfishness.

To a shattered relationship with his father, poisoned by anger and resentment.

To a life ruled by bitterness, distrust, and ambition—faults he had justified for far too long.

To this very cross, where all his plans ended.

And as he hung there, the truth struck him with finality—his life had been shaped by the *sin* of his folly.

Sin. There—he said it. He was sinful and needed forgiveness.

He had spent a lifetime denying God, rejecting grace, and clinging to his sin.

And as if his father could read his very thoughts, David simply said,

"Asher, behold—the Lamb of God, who takes away the sin of the world!"

It was as if scales had fallen from his eyes. A stirring deep in his soul—a faint hope. The kind he had never dared to believe. But now, it was so obvious, so undeniable.

Jesus truly was the Son of God.

He knew that as well as anyone. He had witnessed it firsthand.

With the little strength he had left, Asher attempted to speak. His voice was broken, barely audible, but it had a trembling sincerity.

"Jesus... remember me when You come into Your kingdom."

For a moment, the world seemed to be still. Then, through His agony, Jesus raised His head and turned to Asher. His eyes, filled with compassion, locked onto Asher's, and His voice, though weak, was full of gentle promise.

"Truly, I say to you, today you will be with Me in paradise."

David wept openly, collapsing to his knees as the weight of his relief overcame him. Even though his son was dying in front of him, he had never been more alive. "Thank you, Yeshua," he whispered, his voice breaking. "Thank you for saving my son."

Asher's body was wracked with pain, every breath a battle, but something had changed. A deep, unshakable peace settled over him like a quiet sunrise after a storm. The fear, bitterness, and endless chase for something more all melted away. The cross still held him, but it no longer felt like death. Somehow, he felt more alive than he ever had before.

He blinked slowly, his gaze lifting toward the sky, and for the first time in a long time, his mind felt clear. All the things he once fought for—the treasure, the acclaim, the power to rewrite the past, the chance to prove them all wrong—now seemed so small.

A memory surfaced, sharp and clear as if it had been waiting for this moment. He had come across the words once during his research, a quote from Jesus: “For what does it profit a man to gain the whole world and forfeit his soul?” He’d dismissed it then, thinking it was just another moral platitude meant for the weak and gullible. But now, with his soul laid bare, he saw it for what it was—a truth he'd spent his whole life running from.

Pride and arrogance had been his masters, and he had worn their chains as if they were his crown. And now, they had nailed him to this cross. Yet somehow, he felt it—the warmth of grace. Like a stone rolled away from a tomb, Asher felt the crushing weight on his chest lifted and replaced by the comfort of peace.

Not treasure. Not fame nor vindication, Asher realized. *But this, this is more valuable than gold.*

The words echoed in his heart, steady as a drumbeat. “I am forgiven,” he whispered, and for the first time, he believed it. His hands relaxed, fingers unfurling from the fists they’d been clenched in for far too long.

Asher’s body slumped further on the cross, his breaths coming slower and more difficult. David remained on his knees, his hands clutching the rough wood, whispering silent prayers. Heavy storm clouds began to fill the sky, and the crowd, sensing the growing tension in the air, spoke in hushed voices.

David lifted his face, looking up at his son. Asher's chest rose weakly, his face twisted in pain, but there was a strange appearance in his features. A peace, perhaps, or maybe just exhaustion—David couldn't tell. All he knew was that Asher's time was running out.

Around him, the voices of what appeared to be the Jewish leaders rang out. "He saved others; he cannot save himself. He is the King of Israel; let him come down now from the cross, and we will believe in him," they jeered.

But Jesus's serene face, despite His agony, whispered something, something David could barely hear. He strained to listen. "I thirst." A soldier immediately placed a sponge soaked in sour wine on a hyssop branch and held it to his mouth.

David's heart trembled at those words as he knew the end was near.

Then, Jesus cried out in a loud voice, "Eli, Eli, lema sabachthani?" which means, "My God, my God, why have you forsaken Me?"

The ground beneath David's knees began to tremble as the sky darkened unnaturally. The light dimmed, the air grew thick, and a suffocating stillness settled over everything. His soul quaked with the enormity of the moment. It was as if heaven and earth were mourning together, bearing witness to something cosmic, terrible, and eternal.

Jesus's head fell forward, and the following stillness was unlike anything David had ever known. "Father, into Your hands I commit My spirit," Jesus breathed, and with those final words, He died.

The earth shook violently, the ground splitting beneath them as if the world groaned with sorrow. David cried out, clutching the cross tighter as the crowd scattered in panic.

"Asher..." David whispered, his voice barely holding together.

Asher's head had fallen to the side. Occasionally, he would lift himself to breathe. Each breath was a struggle for life itself. David knew it would take hours for Asher to die, but he also knew the story that was about to play out before him.

Word spread quickly among the gathered crowd as the earth continued to tremble. The Sabbath was approaching – a holy day, especially for this particular day of Preparation—and it was against Jewish law to leave bodies hanging on the cross through the Sabbath. Many in the crowd began to murmur, anxious to leave before the day's sanctity was violated.

Not wanting to break their laws, Jewish leaders sent word to Pilate, asking that the legs of the condemned be broken so the bodies could be taken down quickly. This would prevent them from lingering on the cross into the Sabbath.

David's heart pounded as the soldiers approached. He knew what he was about to watch would be difficult, but he also knew he could do nothing to stop it. The soldiers advanced toward the men hanging on either side of Jesus first. With heavy mallets in hand, they struck Julian's legs, and the sickening crack of bones echoed through the air. The thief's body sagged further on the cross, and his breathing slowly began to falter.

Next, they turned to Asher. David's breath caught in his throat as the soldier approached his son, mallet in hand. Asher was weakened beyond comprehension and could barely lift his head. David screamed, rushing toward the soldiers desperately attempting to stop what was inevitable.

"No! Please!" David cried, his voice breaking. "My son, please don't hurt him anymore!"

But before he could reach them, a Roman soldier stepped in and seized him by the shoulders, forcing him back with brutal efficiency. David struggled, but the soldier held firm.

The executioner, unmoved by the pleas, raised the mallet high—and, with a sickening crack, brought it down on Asher's legs.

Asher's scream pierced the air, a raw, guttural sound of agony that tore through David's soul. His son's body convulsed in pain; his legs shattered beneath him. The ability to push up and relieve the pressure on his lungs was gone, and Asher's breathing became shallow and erratic.

David fell to his knees, clutching the dirt in helpless despair as he watched his son's final moments unfold before him. "Asher..." he whispered, his voice hoarse with grief. His heart pounded in his chest, his hands trembling as he reached out toward the cross.

Asher's chest rose one last time, and then he was still.

The world seemed to stop as David was overcome with grief. His son was gone.

Amid the darkness and shaking earth, David barely noticed the soldiers as they moved to the man on the center cross—Jesus. One soldier thrust his spear into Jesus's side to confirm His death. As the spear pierced His flesh, blood and water poured out, splashing onto the centurion's face and chest.

The centurion froze, staring at the blood dripping from his skin. His expression shifted as though something within him had been changed forever. He stepped back, trembling, as if in awe of what had just occurred.

Still hunched over in grief, David caught a glimpse of the centurion's reaction but was too consumed by his own sorrow to fully understand the moment's significance. He wept in the knowledge that his son was gone, but he rejoiced in the truth that he would see him again.

In tears, David made one last vow to his son. He would not leave Asher's body on the cross to suffer the same fate as others—to be discarded, forgotten. He would bring him down and bury him with dignity.

Gathering his strength, David stood on shaky legs, his heart shattered but resolved. He had to do one last thing for his son. Approaching the centurion, David swallowed his fear and bowed his head. "Please," he said, his voice spent from the strain of his emotions. "Please, let me take down my son's body. Grant me the right to bury him."

The centurion, hardened from countless executions, looked at David with a momentary glimmer of humanity in his eyes. The darkness in the sky, the quake of the earth—it had shaken even him. He studied David for a long moment before nodding slowly.

“The bodies of the dead are yours to claim. Take him and do what you will,” the centurion said, his voice low.

David’s breath caught in his throat as relief flooded him. He bowed his head in thanks. “Thank you,” he whispered.

David moved quickly to remove Asher from that evil cross. The darkness made the task even more difficult. Several people were holding torches as all three bodies were being removed. With the help of a few others, David carefully lowered Asher’s broken body from the cross. His hands shook as he untied the ropes and removed the nails that had held his son suspended in agony. Asher’s skin was beginning to cool, and his limbs were limp. David cradled him gently as though he could somehow protect Asher from the pain he had endured. His thoughts again went back to the first time he had held Asher on the day of his birth. Just as on that day, tears freely flowed down his face.

David held his son, his grief consuming him when a quiet presence approached. He had hardly noticed her before—one of the women who had stood at the foot of Jesus's cross.

She hesitated before stepping closer, her tear-streaked face filled with sorrow. "I heard you call him Asher," she said gently. "Is he Asher from Capernaum?"

David’s head snapped up at the name. Asher from Capernaum. He had seen it written on the board in Winston’s house but hadn’t understood its significance. Now, here was a stranger confirming it.

"Yes," he said cautiously. "You knew him?"

She nodded, her voice thick with emotion. "I didn’t recognize him at first... not battered like this. But yes, I knew him. My name is Miriam. We were...friends."

Slowly, she removed the shawl draped around her shoulders, the same one Asher had given her. "Here," she whispered, pressing it into David's hands. "For him."

David opened his mouth to thank her, but she was already stepping away. Within moments, she had disappeared into the darkness, leaving him alone with his son.

David's hands trembled as he wrapped his son in the linen fabric, fighting to keep his composure. Through his sobs, he whispered, "Rest now, my son. You are free." But even as the words left his lips, his mind raced. What would he do with Asher's body? He couldn't leave him here—this wasn't where Asher belonged. No, he had to bring him back to the 21st century, where Asher could be laid to rest properly. David couldn't leave Asher's body here to be desecrated by Roman hands or to rot away in a forgotten grave as a crucified thief.

But a realization quickly struck him. Returning Asher's body would create questions—questions David couldn't easily answer. The ache in his heart was unbearable, and the cruelty of it all screamed in his mind. But he knew one he had to do: take Asher home. Leah needed to see her son. For that reason alone, David had to take him back. He could explain everything to her. But even as the thought crossed his mind, doubt crept in. *Would she believe him? How could she?* He barely believed it himself. It all felt like a terrible nightmare. Yet, for Leah's sake, he had to try.

The darkness that had settled over the entire region created an eerie, almost suffocating atmosphere. The people of Jerusalem were not prepared for this—darkness in the middle of the day. Panic and confusion rippled through the city as fear gripped their hearts. David, however, knew what was happening. From the Gospel accounts, he knew this darkness would last three hours, shrouding everything in an unsettling gloom.

This would make it difficult for him to find the portal, his only way out of this time and place. But it also had an unexpected benefit: The cover of darkness would help him move more easily through the streets. He knew carrying a dead body through Jerusalem would draw unwanted attention, even in normal circumstances, and would undoubtedly violate Jewish law as the Sabbath was quickly approaching.

David began his journey towards the portal under the cloak of darkness. The city streets were almost empty. People huddled in their homes, clutching their lamps and oil-burning lanterns, too frightened to venture outside. Roman soldiers patrolled with torches in hand, their faces grim, but their vigilance lessened by the overwhelming fear that gripped them too.

David moved swiftly, keeping to the shadows where the torches could not reach. Every muscle in his body ached as he navigated the winding streets of Jerusalem, and Asher's body grew heavier with each passing moment. But he pressed on, knowing that time was slipping away. The veil of fear and confusion allowed David to carry Asher through the city undetected.

Finally, David reached the portal's secluded location. There was no time to linger, no time to think of what lay ahead. He had to get Asher's body through. Taking a deep breath, David stepped through. The sensation of the portal closing around him was disorienting, the world spinning and warping as time bent. His grip on Asher tightened, his only focus on keeping hold of his son's body as the landscape of ancient Jerusalem vanished around him.

And then, in an instant, it was over.

David stumbled out of the portal and into the present, the familiar surroundings of his own time rushing back with startling clarity. The city noise, the hum of electricity, the lights of the city—it was all there, unchanged.

David sank to his knees, trembling as he lowered Asher's body to the ground. He knew what had to be done. He had to leave Asher somewhere he could be found, somewhere the authorities could identify him. He knew there would be many unanswerable questions, but that was unavoidable. No one would ever believe what had happened, but they had to at least find Asher's body. Hopefully, the investigation would end in mystery.

With shaking hands, David carefully redressed Asher in the clothes left in his car. He placed Asher's wallet, complete with his ID, back into his pocket, ensuring someone would find it. Gently placing Asher in the parked car, David hoped the body of his only son would be discovered soon.

He would return home and call the police to report his son missing, which should expedite his discovery. "I love you, Asher," David whispered, his voice breaking.

Then, without looking back, he slipped away into the shadows of the modern world, his heart heavy with loss but knowing his son was finally home.

Questions Without Answers

Winston stirred, his breath shallow and labored. His body ached, and for a moment, he couldn't remember where he was. The familiar dim glow of his bedroom slowly came into focus—but something felt... off.

He tried to organize his thoughts. The last thing he remembered was David's visit—the sharp pain, the crushing weight on his chest. Then nothing. He must have blacked out. But for how long?

Natalie. He needed Natalie—but where was she?

Instinctively, he reached for the summoning device around his neck but couldn't find it. He searched again—nothing. His eyes darted across the bedspread and scanned the floor, but the device was nowhere in sight.

Fortunately, his wheelchair sat just within reach. But could he make it?

As he slowly sat up, a wave of dizziness crashed over him. The room began to tilt violently, the edges swimming in and out of focus. His arms felt like lead, useless and shaking as he strained to keep himself upright.

With a sharp exhale, he slid to the edge of the bed and pulled the chair close. His first attempt to get into the chair failed as he nearly collapsed to the floor. Gritting his teeth, he tried again. This time, he fell into the chair with a heavy thud, his body crumpling under its own weight.

Pain seized his chest—tight and relentless. Gasping, he fought for air, his breaths shallow and panicked. Oxygen. He needed oxygen. His trembling fingers scrabbled at the mask—once, twice—finally pressing it to his face.

He inhaled deeply. Nothing. Either the tank was empty, or someone had turned it off. The tank's location at the back of the chair made it impossible for him to reach.

Summoning the last of his strength, Winston turned the chair toward the hallway and wheeled himself out of the bedroom.

Navigating the hallway was agonizing. Every movement was a painful reminder of what his body had endured. When he finally reached the control room, he wasted no time, his fingers struggling to operate the laptop connected to the portal's system. He had to check the recent usage. He needed to determine Asher's location and if he had found the gold.

His eyes scanned the log. The first entry confirmed what he expected—Asher had entered the portal late the previous afternoon.

Then, his stomach twisted.

Asher hadn't returned. Instead, there was another activation—another trip to 1st-century Jerusalem. This one occurred the morning after Asher's.

Winston's breath hitched. The implication was clear.

Someone else had used the portal.

A chill ran through him. His breath came in shallow gasps, each one more labored than the last. Pain gripped his chest, sharp and unrelenting, as his trembling hand instinctively reached for the oxygen mask again. He pressed it to his face and inhaled—only to remember it wasn't working.

Darkness crept in at the edges of his vision, his body threatening to give out. But he forced himself to focus, clinging to the one thing he still had control over—his will to survive.

Who? Who had found it? Had the wrong hands discovered its existence?

His eyes darted further down the log, scanning the most recent data. Then, his blood ran cold.

Two people had returned at the same time.

A deep fear settled in his gut. Someone had followed Asher—and they had come back together.

The implications were terrifying. He had to act.

With the last of his strength, Winston reached for the controls. His fingers hovered for just a moment before pressing the command to shut down the portal.

He slumped back in his chair, exhaustion overtaking him.

Whatever had happened on the other side—whoever had come back—there would be no more surprises.

Unexpected Guests

Natalie, his supposed caretaker, sat patiently in the kitchen, her indifference a stark departure from her previous role. A sharp knock on the front door echoed through the room. Calmly, Natalie rose and opened the door to reveal three imposing figures. In Russian, she issued curt instructions. “Следуйте за мной.” (Follow me.)

Natalie led the trio to the room Winston and Asher had used to prepare for the mission. Their entry stirred Winston from his semi-conscious state. Struggling to focus through blurred vision, he weakly asked, "Natalie, who are these men?"

Natalie didn’t answer. Instead, she walked toward him, her expression unreadable.

His breath was shallow, his body heavy with exhaustion. "Natalie... my oxygen. Something is wrong with my oxygen," he rasped, reaching out weakly.

She remained silent. Instead, she leaned over him, placing her hands firmly on the armrests of his wheelchair.

As Natalie gazed directly into his eyes, Winston pleaded, “Quickly... please.”

She didn’t move. Her eyes—once familiar and caring—were vacant now, devoid of the warmth he’d come to trust.

Without a word, she reached into her pocket and pulled out a syringe.

Winston’s breath caught. “Natalie... what are you doing? Please—just turn on my oxygen first.”

She said nothing. With practiced precision, she uncapped the needle and plunged it into his arm.

The cold sting spread through him instantly. His body tensed, muscles locking in panic, then began to tremble uncontrollably.

Weakly, Winston mumbled, “Natalie, why?”

Immediately, his limbs grew heavier, and his vision blurred further. He tried to lift a hand to force out a protest, but his strength was failing. His head slumped slightly to the side as the world around him faded into a distant, muffled haze.

His last thought before losing consciousness was a desperate, hazy question—*Why isn't she helping me?*

Wordlessly, Natalie wheeled Winston into his bedroom. With ease, she lifted his frail body and placed him in the bed, adjusting his position as if he were nothing more than a fragile burden. Without a second glance, she pulled the blanket over him, ensuring he was tucked in—not with care, but with finality. Then, without hesitation, she turned and left, closing the door behind her.

In the other room, the three men moved with silent efficiency. One bagged up all the books and papers, another retrieved the laptop, while the third wiped the whiteboards clean, erasing every trace of their work. Once the items were secured in their vehicle, they reentered the house, where Natalie stood waiting.

She handed them a set of keys and a piece of paper and again spoke to the men in Russian. "These are the keys to the house in Boston. The security code is here," she said, pointing to the paper. You will find what we want in the basement. Disassemble it as we discussed. I will meet you in Moscow in a few days."

The men nodded in agreement and swiftly left the house, their movements as precise as their mission.

An Eye for an Eye

It had all begun a mere three years earlier when the SVR—the Russian Foreign Intelligence Service and successor to the disbanded KGB—breached Winston's research databases. Using their formidable cyber capabilities, they launched sophisticated attacks to secretly access his private files.

What they uncovered was both astonishing and uncertain—a machine that hinted at power beyond comprehension, yet its legitimacy remained in question. If real, it would be the greatest technological creation in history. A device that could rewrite the past, manipulate the present, and dictate the future. The sheer magnitude of its potential was staggering. The SVR couldn't afford to ignore it.

But they needed more than stolen data—they needed confirmation.

The SVR launched an extensive background investigation, but they uncovered very little—Winston was a man of secrecy with no close family or personal ties. However, one critical vulnerability stood out—his failing health.

Winston was suffering from a strange, unexplainable disease and had been quietly searching for a cure for years—private consultations, untraceable travel, payments routed through anonymous accounts. Winston was a desperate man. Desperation was the opening they needed. And to their good fortune, he had already begun searching for a full-time medical assistant.

They had just the person.

Natalia Ivanova, one of their most skilled undercover operatives. Fluent in multiple languages, trained in psychological manipulation, deep-cover espionage, and covert extraction techniques, she had successfully infiltrated high-profile targets before.

But this mission required more than espionage skills—it required medical credibility.

Natalia was skilled there, too. She had undergone training in emergency medicine and patient care, making her well-versed in caring for others. Under the carefully crafted alias "Natalie Evans," she was successfully planted in Winston's life.

Winston quickly bonded with "Natalie," and over time, she began to uncover key information. There was indeed some type of machine—though, to her knowledge, Winston used it rarely, if at all, likely due to his declining health.

Over time, Natalia systematically tightened her control over his estate, aided—ironically—by the global disruption triggered by COVID-19, a gift from the Russians 'Chinese allies. The pandemic proved a convenient smokescreen. With heightened concerns about Winston's fragile health, Natalia imposed strict isolation protocols. Under the guise of protecting him from infection, she quietly dismissed the housekeeper, the groundskeeper, and even his longtime personal chef. Health issues were cited, but in truth, it was all about control.

Security personnel were reduced to an as-needed basis, and the estate's driver was replaced with a car service—ensuring no one remained long enough to ask questions. She contracted outside vendors for tasks she couldn't manage herself, framing every change as practical cost-cutting rather than a calculated power play.

Winston never questioned it. To him, "Natalie's" adjustments were practical improvements—streamlining his estate with efficiency and care. In his eyes, she was not only a trusted caregiver but the indispensable overseer of his affairs.

Winston had no known source of income, leading the Russians to suspect that he was using the machine for financial gain. If they were correct, he would eventually have to use it—especially if the cure he sought was expensive.

This led the SVR to fabricate a medical breakthrough. They would use Dr. Sergey Vinogradov, a renowned Russian doctor and SVR agent, to dangle the carrot of a cure before Winston—but at a cost.

The treatment was an elaborate deception. Winston was injected with drugs that temporarily boosted his energy while secretly accelerating his decline.

The results were twofold. First, the drugs would weaken his mind and body, making him more susceptible to manipulation. And second, the escalating cost of treatment would force Winston to use the machine—revealing its true purpose.

Fortunately, the Russian-Ukrainian war made the escalating cost even more believable.

As Natalia monitored Winston, another name surfaced—Asher Meyer.

She discovered Winston planned to use Asher in some scheme to steal gold. To the SVR, the gold was of little concern. But if Winston and Asher used the machine, it would prove beyond doubt that it worked.

Either way, Natalia would be there to find out. Everything had fallen perfectly into place. Winston had no choice but to continue the treatments. As planned, the treatment's cost forced his hand, and now SVR had proven that the time machine existed.

Their plan had worked perfectly. They now possessed the time machine.

Only one step remained.

As Winston's feeble breaths echoed in the room, the air hung thick with the weight of finality.

Once his devoted caregiver, Natalia no longer pretended. The mask of compassion, warmth, and concern was gone. In its place was cold indifference. Her unwavering gaze reflected her total lack of empathy for this dying man.

His frail hand trembled as he reached for hers, desperate for some final gesture of comfort. He longed for her compassionate care—the care she had often provided. And yet, as his fingers brushed hers, he felt only ice.

No warmth. No reassurance.

A weak gasp escaped his lips as the truth sank in like a final blow.

In that moment, the truth settled in his dying mind.

She had never cared.

Never been his salvation.

Only his executioner.

Winston knew this was the end—not because of the disease he had feared, but because of the evil he had let through the door.

His chest rose and fell—once, twice—then stillness.

Her once-kind smile curled into something else entirely. A smirk. Dark. Knowing. Final.

She had played the part well. Now, there was no need to pretend.

His death wasn't a tragedy. It was a victory.

Her last task was to acquire the key that started the time machine. She retrieved a sterile scalpel from her nearby medical kit. Her steady and experienced hands approached Winston's face. In a delicate procedure, she removed Winston's right eye, the orb that held the unique retinal signature needed to activate the time machine.

Carefully, Natalia placed the eye in a prepared container, snugly nestled among its frigid surroundings. The sterile environment and the chilling temperature would act as guardians, preserving the eye's integrity until it was required to unlock the secrets of time.

Natalie retrieved her cell phone from her pocket, placed a call, and said, "Это завершено" (It is finished). The response was short and simple: "Хорошая работа, Наталья." (Well done, Natalia).

Eyewitness

The day after the crucifixion of Jesus, Pontius Pilate found his mind returning to the events. As noon approached that day, he had been reclining in his private chambers. The sheer curtain swayed gently in the breeze, letting slivers of sunlight dance across the floor. The moment's tranquility had been deceiving, as his furrowed brow betrayed the inner turmoil he had felt—the weight of the decision he had been forced to make that morning still hung over him. Despite the calm surroundings, his mind had been anything but at ease.

Looking back, Pilate deeply regretted the sentence of death he had pronounced on Jesus, a man in whom he had found no guilt. His wife's earlier warning about condemning Jesus echoed persistently in his mind, growing louder with each passing day. In hindsight, he questioned the wisdom of yielding to the relentless pressure from the Jewish religious leaders. The struggle with them had been ongoing, but this time, the weight of their influence sat heavily on his conscience. He couldn't escape the nagging feeling that he had been manipulated into an unjust decision.

On the day of the crucifixion, he had considered going to Golgotha himself to witness it personally. Yet he had known his presence would only stir more unrest among the crowd. Regardless, nothing could have prepared him for how the day would unravel—how the calm had collapsed into chaos. The day's gentle breeze had given way to a sudden gust, sending curtains whipping violently, as if nature itself had turned against him.

He vividly recalled the unsettling moment when the sunlight, which had peacefully filled the room, suddenly disappeared. In mere moments, darkness had consumed the room. It was as if night had abruptly fallen in the middle of the day. The memory of the shouts echoing through the palace, growing louder with each passing second, returned to him. The sense of turmoil and dread had gripped the entire city.

Pilate could still hear the haunting sound of his wife's voice in his mind. She had burst into his chambers in the sudden and eerie darkness, her voice trembling with panic, "What have you done? Death will surely fall upon us!"

He hadn't been able to see her in the pitch-black room, but he had sensed her presence. The memory of his guards rushing in to assist flickered in his mind. The feeble light of a torch had barely outlined Claudia's form in the doorway. Amidst the chaos, Pilate recalled how the guards had ushered her away to safety.

Pilate remained puzzled by the source of this inexplicable darkness. Though he had previously witnessed the gods veil the sun at various and unpredictable times, this occurrence felt different. Unlike the usual gradual dimming, this darkness had descended without warning, as if the sun had been extinguished.

Pilate, like his wife, still couldn't shake the gnawing thought that this unnatural darkness was somehow tied to the crucifixion of Jesus. Throughout that day, he had gathered varying reports from Golgotha, which was only made more difficult by its considerable distance from his palace and the persistent darkness. The initial messages had been perplexing, describing Jesus's actions as atypical and confounding. But as blackness fell over the city, he received reports that conveyed a city descending into panic and hysteria. The situation had quickly begun to spiral out of control.

Abruptly, Pilate's palace had been shaken by violent tremors. Screams echoed within its walls and surrounding areas as the earthquake rumbled for over a minute. The quake soon subsided, but the darkness lingered, bringing more chaos and disorder.

Now, on the day after the crucifixion, he had summoned Centurion Longinus, the man in charge of the crucifixion. Pilate wanted to hear Longinus's firsthand knowledge of the events. The soft clinking of the centurion's armor preceded his entrance into the room.

"Governor, you requested my presence?" Longinus asked, bowing to one knee.

Commencing the interrogation, Pilate began, "Yes, I've called you here to provide an account of the events at Golgotha. What did you witness?"

Longinus grappled with where to begin, unsure if he fully comprehended the magnitude of what he had seen. Slowly, he finally began, "Governor, it was the most unusual day. The crucifixion proceeded as normal, but the events took an unprecedented turn. The man on the middle cross, Jesus, displayed extraordinary composure. Despite his agony and people hurling insults at him, he spoke words of forgiveness. It was... unlike anything I've witnessed."

"Forgiveness?" Pilate asked in bewilderment.

"Yes, Governor, he asked his Father to forgive us," Longinus continued.

Puzzled, Pilate asked, "Was his father present at the crucifixion?"

Carefully, Longinus answered, "Not that I'm aware of, sir, but I believe he was referring to his Father in heaven. The God of the Jews."

Pilate was visibly shocked by this statement. *Could it be conceivable that the man he had condemned to death sought forgiveness on their behalf from his god?*" Forgiveness?" Pilate repeated, incredulous. "Forgiveness for whom?"

"I cannot ascertain the entirety of those included, but I know it encompassed me," Longinus responded, leaving Pilate perplexed by the revelation.

"Why do you say such a thing?" Pilate rebutted.

"Governor, I have not the words to explain it; I just know because I experienced it," Longinus said softly.

While Pilate pondered his words, Longinus continued his testimony, "The subsequent events were even more perplexing. The thieves on either side of him began to argue among themselves. One thief persistently hurled insults at Jesus, while the other... he had a change of heart and began to rebuke his companion. Then that thief acknowledged his own guilt and asked Jesus with a plea for remembrance," Longinus conveyed in a gentle voice.

Pilate was once again bewildered and asked, "Remembrance? Remembrance of what?"

Longinus continued, "His exact words to Jesus were, 'Remember me when you come into your kingdom. 'Then Jesus responded with, 'Truly I tell you, today you will be with me in paradise.'"

Pilate chuckled, "King of the Jews indeed." After a moment of silence, quizzically, Pilate asked, "And paradise, where is this paradise he is speaking of?"

A certainty instantly filled Longinus's voice as he responded, "I believe it to be the eternity that Jesus was known to often speak about."

Once again, Pilate began pacing the room as he pondered Longinus's comment.

Breaking the silence, Longinus continued, "As the darkness enveloped the land, there was an eerie stillness. I heard him speak again, this time crying out, 'My God, my God, why have you forsaken me?' It sent shivers down my spine, Governor."

The statement intrigued Pilate and stopped his pacing.

Longinus continued, "Then, there was a profound moment. Jesus, in his agony, uttered, 'It is finished.' Instantly, the ground shook beneath our feet. The darkness and the earthquake—they seemed like signs, signs beyond our comprehension."

Longinus hesitated, grappling with the enormity of what he was recounting. "As per our instruction to expedite the death of those being crucified, we began to break their legs. When we came to Jesus, it was obvious that he was already dead. To verify his death, I pierced his side with my spear," he continued with an emotion that betrayed him.

Pilate watched Longinus hesitate as tears filled his eyes. "As you know, Governor, I have struggled with my eyesight in recent years. But when I pierced Jesus's side, blood and water flowed out. It was...

it was unexpected. But something extraordinary happened to me at that moment. His blood flowed down upon my face and into my eyes. My eyes were, they were, suddenly restored. I can see clearly now, as I could as a child," Longinus said as excitement filled his voice.

The account by Longinus captivated and intrigued Pilate. "Restored sight? Blood and water? Longinus, is this your true testimony?" Pilate asked.

Longinus replied with a somber conviction, "Yes, Governor. I can't deny what I witnessed. It has changed me, and I suspect it has changed everything."

As he pondered the significance of the events, Pilate expressed gratitude to Longinus and dismissed him. He walked over to the window and gazed out at the city under his rule.

Through all that he had experienced and all that Longinus had conveyed, one question had taken root in his mind—a question that lingered still. He was certain it would follow him for the rest of his days. Perhaps even beyond.

He muttered it once again to himself.

"What is truth?"

Epilogue

People often ask the question, "If you could visit any person in history—alive or dead—who would it be?"

The quick answer that always comes to my heart is my mom. She passed away in 2006, before I ever wrote a single play or made a film. She was my biggest supporter, and everything I've created since—on stage, on screen, and now on the page—has been a quiet dedication to her. In many ways, I've spent my creative life trying to make her proud.

But when I sit with that question a little longer—when I look beyond this life into the eternal—my answer becomes clearer: Jesus Christ.

That, in turn, leads to a much deeper question: "If I could witness one moment from His life, which would it be? His birth? A miracle? The Crucifixion?"

And then it struck me. The moment I'd want to witness most is the one that changed everything: when He walked out of the tomb. It's the greatest moment in history—not just for what it meant in time, but what it means for eternity. That empty tomb validated every word He spoke, every prophecy fulfilled, every promise made.

In "More Valuable Than Gold", Asher never quite reaches that moment. But in his search, in his longing, in his questions—we see reflections of our own. We don't always get the full answer, the clear sign, or the finish line we hope for. Sometimes we're left, like Pilate, staring out a window, haunted by the question: What is truth?

That question is why I wrote this story.

This novel is fiction, but its foundation is built on something real. Something eternal.

Thank you for joining me on this journey.

Rodney

Author's Note

If you'd like to explore more of my work, please visit our website: R2Films.net

There, you can learn more about our films, watch trailers, and purchase DVDs.

Feel free to reach out—we'd love to hear from you. You can contact us anytime at: info@R2Films.net

About The Author

Rodney Ray is a writer, retired filmmaker, and full-time storyteller. He is the founder of R-Squared Productions and is best known for his award-winning films "Cowboy & Indiana, " "New Hope, " "Flag of My Father," and the veteran-focused documentary "We Call Them Heroes. "

While R-Squared Productions is widely recognized for its feature-length films and documentaries, Rodney's creative journey began in the theater.

He first stepped into the world of production in his early 40s, writing and directing Mystery Theaters with his wife, Jill, while they were leaders in the Singles Department at First Baptist Church in West Monroe, LA—locally known as First West. "We came up with the idea of doing a Mystery Theater. It was a big hit, and things just grew from there," he recalls.

From there, Rodney transitioned into filmmaking to reach a broader audience with the message of "Making Life-Changing Films." Every project was a close collaboration with Jill, whose creative partnership has remained central to his work.

In 2020, Rodney retired from filmmaking to focus fully on writing novels—bringing the same heart, purpose, and storytelling passion to the page that guided his work on screen.

A proud U.S. Navy veteran, Rodney is also a licensed Professional Land Surveyor and former owner of R-Squared Global, an engineering and surveying company he sold in 2019. A graduate of Louisiana Tech University, he now devotes his time to storytelling that encourages, challenges, and inspires—still working side by side with Jill, just as they always have.

Together, they have four children and ten grandchildren.

"More Valuable Than Gold" is Rodney's debut novel.

www.ingramcontent.com/pod-product-compliance
Lightning Source LLC
Chambersburg PA
CBHW051949240626
47153CB00005B/1692
* 9 7 9 8 9 9 8 8 1 6 3 1 4 *